Storm Unleashed

Storm Unleashed

Quantum Touch Book 4

Michael R. Stern

Published 2018 by Creativia
Cover art by Cover Mint

Dedication

For Linda,
A kind heart and an iron will

For all the people of the countries of the Middle East
May the peace we all wish for you become reality soon

Acknowledgements

The publication of a book is a team effort. I want to say thank you to those who have helped me present this latest effort to you, the reader.

First, my editor, Amy Davis of Riverfog Writer's Group, has molded this writer, and with tough love, forced me to take the next steps to becoming a competent storyteller. Believe me when I say that the many light-bulb moments I have experienced reflect lessons that have been beaten into me, and I hope are reflected in the story. Our collaboration in the four books of Quantum Touch thus far has been rewarding for me as a writer, and I hope the result will be enjoyable stories for the reader.

My designer, Jack Parry, and publication consultant, Elizabeth Parry, of Parry Design, are responsible for the fabulous cover and creative layout. They also have joined me on this quest through the first four books of this collection.

I would like to express my deepest thanks to George and Jill Hobson Kassis for sharing their knowledge and love of the countries of the Middle East. Our conversations have added to the perspective presented in the story.

The collective stories of Quantum Touch revolve around two teachers, Fritz and Ashley, and a high school. The teachers as characters are now a part of my life, but in reality, are based on two teachers from my school years, who left a lasting impression. Both have passed on now, but are remembered. Thank you, Russell Fritz, for introducing me to my own written words. Thank you, Gilbert Ashley, for making learning fun.

My final thank you is to you, the reader, those who have joined me on this journey. I hope you have enjoyed the tale, and that *Storm Unleashed* makes you happy you have returned for the next adventure.

Chapter 1

"**DARKNESS IS HARD TO DEFEAT.**" The gray-haired man stood by a bank of windows overlooking the black Pacific. A dimmed antique chandelier imprisoned the shadows and barricaded dawn's arrival. Polished, paneled walls reflected Tiffany lamplight. Floor-to-ceiling bookcases exuded first-edition mustiness. His minions, five silent figures sitting in a circle of plush chairs, weighed his remarks. "The others will be here soon," he said. "We need to find a successor for our dearly departed." His undisguised disgust darkened his pallid complexion. "His office has been searched and secured. They were thorough. No signs have been left."

"Do you have someone in mind?" asked the youngest of the group, a former corporate founder who took his money and ran.

"That's why we're here," the gray-haired man said as he crossed the room. "To choose a replacement." With his back to his guests, he watched through the bay window as four top-shelf cars approached on the long gravel drive. It was sunrise.

* * *

"MERRY CHRISTMAS, Mr. President."

"Merry Christmas, Fritz. I'm sure you have a busy day ahead, but I wanted to invite you here for New Year's Eve. You could stay a day and we could look around this place together."

When Fritz first stumbled through the portal that let him move around the world, time travel also ceased to be fiction. Since spring, when it began, his relationship with the commander-in-chief had intensified. Fritz had saved the president's life twice. As useful as it was, the portal also brought danger. They might be able to use it for good, but Fritz had almost been killed by men who had tried to destroy his passage to the past.

Fritz and Linda Russell sat in the family room, while TJ, their month-old baby, napped in his crib in the corner. The tree ornaments reflected the early morning light coming from the sunroom. "Thanks, Mr. President. I'll have to speak to Linda and call you back."

"Bring the baby. Jane and Ashley will be here too. We can celebrate having made it through this very strange year."

"Strange is an understatement, Mr. President."

Fritz and Linda's goal was simply to enjoy a quiet Christmas morning. A busy afternoon was in store, but coffee and a Christmas movie provided the perfect interlude. Fritz's parents were coming, and so were Ashley Gilbert and Jane Barclay. Putting dinner in the oven remained the sole, planned interruption to eating, drinking, and being merry. Until the phone rang.

"The president invited us for New Year's Eve," said Fritz. "He said to bring TJ."

"I wonder what he wants this time," Linda said. "It's strange that he would want to socialize with us."

"I've thought about that. But like he said, we treat him like a normal person. I think he likes that. We missed their Christmas affair. Do you want to go? Do you feel up to it?"

"Not really. I don't feel comfortable taking TJ. And I can't help but feel he wants you to use the portal again for something else. Though our staying away won't keep him from asking."

Since April, Fritz had used the portal to let special troops rescue the U.S. Ambassador to Eledoria and his family. To destroy

Naria's nuclear program. To save an Israeli community from an attack by the Eledorians. To end a conspiracy to assassinate the president.

"We don't need to RSVP yet. If he needs the portal, I'm sure he'll let me know."

Ashley and Jane showed up at two, early as usual. Ashley and Fritz were teachers at Riverboro High School and had been friends for years. Jane, Ashley's girlfriend, worked for the government as an advisor to the president. In official circles, she was known as Dr. Barclay. She also held the rank of major in the Army. Ashley blamed Jane for the ever-present smile on his face. When they arrived, Ashley volunteered to help Linda with Christmas dinner, and Jane joined Fritz in the family room with TJ.

"The president called this morning," Fritz said. "He wants us to come to the White House for New Year's."

"I know. We're going. It should be fun. Very few people are invited. Besides, he wants to talk to you."

"Linda thought that's why we were invited."

"It's not the only reason. I've been fine-tuning his plan for the Middle East summit, so he'll want to talk to you about that. He's also concerned about the chest-beating going on in North Korea again. It's certainly not dull." Fritz rubbed behind his left ear. "He invited us to insulate him from the politicians, I think," she continued. "He told me he feels closer to you than most of the people he sees every day."

"Jane, every time he wants to use the portal, it's for some world-saving event. And it's getting scarier each time. The portal isn't secret any more, and the bad guys know about it."

"I understand that. I've been trying to find out more about the people Koppler associated with. The problem is that he knew everybody. It's a Who's-Who list from around the world." James Koppler, a former advisor to the president, appeared to have been the center of a large group of conspirators. "We're still sifting through the stuff from his office. James and Mel Zack went back on Black Friday. They planted small cameras. By that Saturday, someone else had been there too, but they were masked. We're not the only interested party. Someone else is not taking chances."

"That worries me even more. Do you think he worked with some terrorist group or something?"

"Not terrorists. But I have a feeling that there's more to it than we've seen so far."

"One of your feelings? Now I know I have a reason to worry." Jane had had one of those feelings before the president had almost been killed at a summit conference in Geneva only eight weeks earlier. Fritz and Ashley had used the portal to save him.

They were interrupted by the doorbell. Fritz checked his watch. Too early for his parents. Jim Shaw, a former student and local police officer was standing at the door. "Hi, Mr. R. Merry Christmas."

"Come in. Are you working today?"

"Yeah. I switched with a guy with four kids."

"Hi, Jim," said Linda, coming from the kitchen. "Merry Christmas. Want to come for dinner?"

"Hi, Linda. Thanks, but I'm on duty. I just wanted to drop off a present for TJ."

"Thanks, that's very thoughtful. Can I get you a drink of something? Egg nog?"

"No, thanks. I have to go. But I'll be around if you need me."

Jim had taught Fritz to shoot, which had come in handy when the president was taken hostage in Geneva. When Koppler had tried to shoot the president, Fritz had killed Koppler instead.

"I have to get back to work," Jim said. "Hi, Mr. Gilbert, ma'am," he said as Ashley and Jane came to the door.

"Merry Christmas, Jim," they said together.

"Have a good day, Jim," said Fritz. "And thanks again."

Before Fritz closed the door, a black Suburban drove past. They all saw it and exchanged glances. Jane had jammed her phone to her ear before the door shut.

"Good morning, Mr. President. A black Suburban just drove by Fritz's house. Anything you know about?"

"Merry Christmas, Jane. I forgot to tell Fritz. Sorry. I asked the guys to keep an eye out and be visible, just in case."

"I'll tell him. Sorry to bother you. Merry Christmas."

Black Suburbans had played a significant role, good and bad, since Fritz had found the portal. The primary transport used by the Secret Service, they had also been used by the conspirators. One had tried to slam into Fritz when he climbed out of his car, and another had tried to ram him as he left school for the day. Each new one they spotted raised a red flag.

"It's time for some eggnog," said Ashley. "I'm buying."

"It's already in the refrigerator," Fritz said.

"I know that. But it doesn't have my personal touch, which of course I will provide. Free of charge."

Linda said, "You mean you're pouring it into glasses?"

"Absolutely. My personal touch."

JUST AFTER THREE, Fritz's parents arrived. Everyone opened presents, mostly for TJ, who had no idea what was going on but gurgled and squeaked. After a dessert pudding of fruits and nuts, a mix of spices, and some highly flammable brandy, they had just moved to the family room for coffee when breaking news disturbed the celebration.

"Here we go again," said Ashley. The report said North Korea had launched a missile that might have intercontinental range.

"If they're accurate," Jane said, "we might have a big problem. We know they're close to developing nukes. And now they probably have the delivery capability. I'll bet the president's already on the phone."

Linda's frown and furrowed brow reminded them all of the danger they faced. Fritz put his arm around her, pulled her close, and said, "I know."

Fritz's father, John, asked, "Do you think the president..."

Fritz interrupted. "I don't know. He's mentioned the North Koreans before. I hope he finds another way to fix this, Dad."

* * *

IN A ROOM FULL of suits, a man dressed in white slacks and a thin blue sweater glanced at his phone and said, "Turn on the TV. Something's up in Korea." The eight men and one woman gathered around a large screen enclosed in a custom-made mahogany cabinet. After watching, the host offered a toast. Standing by the crystal bowl of Christmas cheer, he said, "Gentlemen, and lady, to the Kim family. May their year be as bad as ours will be good."

* * *

"JANE," SAID THE PRESIDENT, "I think they picked today to disrupt the holiday. The football games will be interrupted. I've called the cabinet for 9 P.M. I need you here before then."

Chapter 2

"**MR. PRESIDENT,** we know where the nukes and the launching areas are," the secretary of defense said. "There's no indication they're trying to move the bombs, at least not yet."

The secretary of state said, "The parade is about to begin. The usual crowd is out, and the square is full. They're in high-level show-off mode, sir."

"What I have to decide is what to say and when," said the president. "The missile worked. But that's the first one that has, and we don't know its full range. It's not a threat at the moment, and I'm not going to push a national panic button."

"Mr. President, wait for a regular press conference and questions. Still, we should move some ships closer." The president held up his hand and looked around the table.

"John, have you spoken to the Chinese yet?" the president asked the secretary of state.

"Not yet, sir. I've called their ambassador, and I've called the foreign minister. I couldn't get through to either. I think they're still determining their response, particularly to us."

"Here's my thought," the president said. "In his next press briefing, Mac should say only that we're evaluating the situation. When we reach the Chinese and the Russians, then maybe I'll have a press conference next week. Tuesday or Wednesday."

"Mr. President, I think you should be visible on this. And it should be immediate," said the secretary of defense. "Show you're on top of the situation and will have more to say when we've gathered more information. Leave it at that. If you wait, the hawks will get to the media first."

"They're already at it, Charlie. The usual suspects interrupted their Christmas dinners to take shots at the president."

The meeting lasted until 10:30, with no final resolution. The president said he wanted to consider the options. Adjourning to his office, he went to talk to two people—the First Lady and Dr. Jane Barclay.

"Sorry to disturb Christmas, Jane."

"No problem, sir. I expected to hear from you."

The First Lady said, "The regulars are already piling on, hon. You'd think they had a direct feed to Fox."

The president thought he should make a TV appearance and let the public know that the administration wasn't worried and was making contact with leaders around the world. "Let the country enjoy the weekend. Mac needs to know what I want to do." The president looked through the window at the glowing top of the Washington Monument and the muted lights around the South Lawn. He dialed his press secretary. "Mac, arrange a statement for as quickly as possible. Tell the networks it will be five-minutes long. No questions."

"Mr. President, you need to call the leaders before you go on," Jane said. "We're going to need them with us for the summit. And the Joint Chiefs. You know how General Beech gets."

* * *

FRITZ AND LINDA were up before seven. Bacon wandered through the house and roused Fritz's parents. John settled in the family room with his coffee and turned on the TV.

"Fritz," his father called. "The president's talking about North Korea." Fritz turned off the flame under the bacon and went to watch the report. The president reassured the country that all diplomatic channels were open and that the situation was being monitored. He closed by wishing the country Happy Holidays and said he looked forward to the new year.

"I bet he does," said Linda, feeding TJ in the doorway. "Only one more year and he's done."

* * *

EARLY SATURDAY MORNING, phone traffic contained a conversation from California. "Do we have replacements yet for the ones we lost at the school?" He sipped his coffee. "Then see if we can fill the gap with Asians. We need them now. Get as many as you can. Time to rattle cages. We have to prove the president wrong."

* * *

ALTHOUGH SCHOOL would be closed until after the holidays, Fritz still had work to do. He needed questions for the history baseball tournament his ninth graders were planning. His seniors had outlined a play about a family's trek through the Twentieth Century. Ashley's tenth-grade creative writing students were writing the script. After breakfast, Fritz went back to his laptop to dig for questions.

Since the start of the school year, the teachers had embraced the marked changes from their students. Fritz had happily remarked that using the portal had caused his students to like school more. Far ahead of schedule, the students in all his classes worked harder than ever before, engrossed in the material.

In mid-afternoon, he put his work aside and joined his parents and Linda at the kitchen table. "Welcome back, stranger," said Linda. "We thought we'd lost you."

"Sorry. I discovered a new source for questions. These are harder, great for the final rounds. They'll mean low-scoring games. And faster ones."

"We were talking about how the president's going to handle this," said Linda.

Fritz changed the subject. "I'm surprised we haven't heard from Ash. I don't think he went with Jane."

His mother said, "He knows we're here. Maybe he wants you to be able to visit a little."

Linda said, "Well, visiting is what you should do. I need a shower."

"Mom, Dad, sorry. Linda's right. I got on a roll. When Ash is here, he helps me remember the questions we've already got."

"Too bad Ashley's picture of Robert E. Lee disappeared," said his mother. "Now that would be something to remember. I certainly will."

"I'm not sure you didn't hire a guy just to fool with us," his father teased.

Leaning forward, urgency in his widened eyes, Fritz said, "Dad, if you hadn't actually been through the portal, I wouldn't blame you for doubting the story. But you saw it for yourself."

With a wistful note in his voice, John said, "When you were a kid, you looked like you do now. I'm kidding, Fritz."

Visiting with his parents killed two birds. He had a chance to enjoy them and gave Linda a break. Until her phone rang.

"What's wrong? Where are you?" she asked.

"Hi, Lin. Merry Christmas to you, too."

"Ashley, you never call me. What's the matter?"

"Then let's get down to business. I have been instructed to call you, not Fritz, as ancient etiquette and social protocol demand."

"Oh, shut up. What are you up to?"

"I've spent my day working devilishly hard, and this is the thanks I get?"

She laughed. "I'm going to break your leg."

"And my reward is pain and suffering." Linda didn't respond. Melodrama was an Ashley specialty, so she waited. "Are you feeling guilty now?" he asked. "The purpose of my communication is an invitation, for you, your husband, child, and your guests for this evening's repast. You may arrive at my home at seven of the clock."

"Dinner. You are such a butthead. Why didn't you just say so?"

"Now my efforts bring scorn and ridicule."

"Have you been reading Shakespeare again?"

"Nope. Been cooking. And cleaning. And preparing. And being insulted."

"Ash, are you okay?"

"All I'm doing is inviting you guys for dinner. At seven. Why don't you just say yes already?"

"Yes. Is Jane back?"

"Not yet. But she will be."

"Can we bring anything?"

"No, thank you. However, dress is business casual. Jeans would be inappropriate."

"What are you up to?"

"Almost six foot three. See you at seven, then?"

Fritz stretched out on the sofa in the family room to watch the TV news. A reporter described the carrier task force preparing to depart for the western Pacific from San Diego. The scene switched to the White House press room, where the press secretary was briefing reporters on the latest information. Fritz sat up when Linda came in. His parents both looked up. She announced that dinner would be at Ashley's.

"What's he up to?" asked Fritz.

"I don't know. We're all invited, and he said business casual. No jeans. Seven o'clock."

Fritz said, "All my plans—up in smoke."

Chapter 3

FOR THE FIRST TIME in Fritz's memory, Ashley had decorated his two-story Cape Cod. Christmas lights were everywhere, and life-size statues of Old English carolers greeted them at the front steps.

As they emptied from Fritz's new car, the front door swung open and their grinning host stepped out. "Fritz, leave the baby's stuff in the car. Come on in." Jane waved as they came up the walkway.

"Like what you've done to the place," said Fritz.

"It seemed a bit lacking." Ashley swept his arm toward the neighbors' houses.

"Keeping up with the Joneses?"

"No, actually." He pointed to three houses. "Smith, O'Reilly, and Steinberg."

Linda said, "Don't start. Let's have a quiet dinner."

"Yes. Let's." Ashley held the door. "Please, do come in."

Linda handed TJ to Jane and took off her coat. She looked at Ashley and laughed. "You did it." Standing in the living room were James Williams, Mel Zack, the president and First Lady, and the vice president and his wife.

When it registered, Fritz shook his head. Even more shocked were his parents, who were introduced by the president to those they hadn't met. Ashley had told Jane to suggest an evening off and invite them for dinner. At the back of the room, Tony Almeida stood with a cup of eggnog.

"So may I offer anyone a libation?" Ashley asked.

"Jack and rocks for me," said Fritz. "In fact, I may have more than one." The president asked for sparkling water.

With drinks in hand, Ashley offered a holiday toast and announced, "Dinner is served." A complete baby corner, with a swing and a playpen, had been set up in the corner of the dining room.

"When did you get this stuff?" asked Linda.

With his smile broadening, he said, "Jane suggested it. She said we could have you here more often, although I can't imagine why."

"What's for dinner?" asked Fritz. "I'll decide later if I want to come back."

"This evening's entrée is the chef's specialty, Beef Wellington."

"You made it?" Fritz asked.

"I did. And it looks terrific. The president said this is a test, and if I pass, I have a job at the White House." Ashley had made broccolini, homemade French fries, and a large salad. The table was dressed with linen napkins. He had bought expensive china and glassware, as well as new silverware. The dining room had white twinkle lights on anything that didn't move.

"Fritz, you're awfully quiet," said the president.

"I'm not sure where I am. This can't be Ashley's house."

"I heard that," said Ashley from the kitchen. "It's your fault."

"How's it my fault?"

"You told me I was changing, so I just added a few details." Jane and Tony delivered bowls and serving pieces. With a large platter in his hands, Ashley followed, wearing a tall white chef's hat and carrying the main course.

"Where did you get that?" asked Fritz, trying not to laugh as he snapped a picture with his phone.

"A gift from the White House. Even autographed."

Fritz looked at the president, who held up his hands and shook his head. "I didn't sign it."

"I can get his autograph anytime," Ashley said. "The head chef signed it. Jane brought it back with her."

"Good thing you have big ears. It would be over your face otherwise."

"Please take your assigned seats, as indicated by the place-cards I have so carefully … placed.

The vice president said, "Mr. President, you were right. I think this is gonna be fun. We weren't sure you could match an embassy party, Ashley."

"But the chicken, excuse me, chicken-in-chief, didn't bring his sneakers," said Ashley.

When they finished the meal, Ashley wheeled in a cart with two ornate pitchers of coffee and decaf and a platter of cannoli for dessert. A selection of liqueurs stood on the bottom shelf.

"When did you get all this stuff?" Fritz asked.

"When I became civilized. On Wednesday. Jane and I went shopping after school."

"Now I know I'm in the wrong place. You went shopping, spent a bundle, and had your own state dinner. I can't wait to find out what's next."

Ashley nodded to Jane at the far end of the table. She lifted her left hand, and on her third finger, a diamond sparkled. The noise that greeted her woke TJ, who chirped. Linda started to get up, but the vice president motioned her to stay seated. "I'm closer. I'll get him."

Everyone found their way to the kitchen. Stacked plates in the sink, counters covered with all the glasses and silverware, and the cookware still on the stove, Jane and Ashley held hands, leaving the clean-up until later. "Did you see this coming?" Fritz whispered to Linda.

She nodded. "Maybe not yet. But uh-huh, and Christmas is such a good time for it. I'm surprised he didn't tell you."

"Me, too. I wonder when he decided." He called across the crowded kitchen. "Hey, goofball, when did you decide?" The room was suddenly silent, except for TJ.

"Actually, in September. But I had to wait."

"Why?" asked Fritz.

"I had just met her that day." Jane kissed his cheek.

The laughter almost drowned out the president's ringtone.

"HI, CHARLIE. What's happened?" The president listened as the secretary of defense reported. "Casualties?" The night became silent. He frowned at the response. "Okay, keep me advised." The president told them a destroyer, one of the ships headed for Korea, had blown up in San Diego. The explosion damaged two other ships. "They're still on fire." The president looked around. "Sorry, Ashley, but we have to leave. I need to find out what happened."

"Do you want to use the portal, Mr. President?" Fritz asked. "I have keys to the school."

"If you don't mind. We have the generator in the car. We should all go. Tony, you can come back when you want. I'll keep the plane here for now. Sorry about the inconvenience."

"No problem, sir."

Jane asked, "Do you want me to come with you?"

"No. I'll let you know when."

WHEN FRITZ AND TONY returned, Linda, Ashley, and Jane were cleaning up. Fritz's parents sat at the kitchen table, drinking coffee.

"He just doesn't get a break," said Fritz.

"After we got to school and Fritz opened the portal, the vice president saw the Oval Office and sounded like he was choking," said Tony. "The president laughed at him. He said, 'Pretty cool, huh?' I think the vice president was speechless for the first time in his life."

"Jane, what do you think this means?" asked Linda.

"Unless some kind of accident set off the explosion, it's an act of war or domestic terrorism. Let's check for any news," Jane said. Only one network had video, taken by a tourist who happened to be filming the harbor at night. They saw the initial explosion in the distance, followed by others when the ship's munitions detonated and hit the other ships.

Jane squinted, looking for what might have caused the explosion. "If they were set to go to sea, it would have been easy to miss seeing the explosives being set, especially underwater. They could have set them days ago." She pointed to the place where they first saw explosions. "It looks like the charges detonated where the most explosives are aboard. Someone knew the right spot."

"Will they be able to find out?" asked Martha Russell.

"Maybe. A lot more cameras than people know about are focused on that harbor." Jane pointed to the shops along the walkway as the news camera panned. "Quite a few analysts will be working overtime. They'll send divers in once the fires are out. I wonder who took the pictures?" Jane was asking, but mostly talking to herself. "Was it really a tourist?"

Chapter 4

FRITZ WAS making waffles when Ashley pushed the back door open and came in with Jane. "Ash, set the table in the dining room," said Fritz. Ashley took off his jacket, took Jane's coat, and dropped both on a chair.

"Hang them up," said a stern voice from the family room.

"Hi, Linda." He stuck his face around the corner. "Hi, TJ." The baby ignored him. Returning to the kitchen, he opened the drawer and asked, "Do you want this cheap stuff, or do you want me to go home for my brand-new, good stuff?"

"You can go home, but we'll still eat with ours," Fritz answered.

John and Martha were packed to go home right after breakfast. "Those look really good," said his father, watching Fritz add to the stack warming in the oven. Fritz wiped the griddle and poured more batter.

"When are you going back, Jane?" Linda asked.

"I don't know yet. The president said he would call. But probably by Wednesday. They should have a lot of info by then."

"If he hasn't been crucified by then," said Ashley. "The early shows all had guests claiming the president had failed again."

Jane said, "He's inured to most of that now. He's more concerned with things people don't see or hear." She stopped.

John asked, "What is it that you do, Jane? You seem to be involved in a lot. Different things, not like a regular job."

"I have a special position with the president. My jobs involve policy, programs, actions. Basically, I'm a planner, but that's just a part of it. That's my training and my experience. I'm just lucky that I met him when we were both starting out. I've never treated him as a politician, just as a person who has a great deal of responsibility. We've developed trust both ways."

"It doesn't hurt that she has me now," said Ashley. "She finally has a pretty face in her corral." Jane smiled.

WITH BREAKFAST OVER, everyone went to watch the rest of the talk shows. Live footage of the damage and scans of the area around the harbor appeared on the screen. Jane leaned close to the TV, not listening to the comments. Fritz asked her if she had seen something.

"Just looking at people and what's in the background. It's funny how often criminals return to see the damage."

"That's just weird," said Ashley. "You'd think they would want to disappear."

"Or see what they can report to someone later," Linda said.

Jane glanced sharply at Linda and took out her phone. "Mrs. Evans, is he free?"

Seconds later, "Mr. President, we've been watching the TV reports. I think we need to find the guy who took that first eyewitness film and check three days of surveillance, for Thursday through Saturday, from all the shops along the shore. We're looking for divers in wetsuits. We need to check when our guys did the last underwater sweep. It should have been on Thursday." In answer to his question, she said, "I'm not sure, but I think the eyewitness film might answer some other questions. Just a hunch. Linda just said something about reporting the result to someone else."

John said, "You just called the president, got connected, and you didn't even say who you were. That's impressive."

"Ms. Evans knows my voice. She's impressive. She gives him a second brain. I've never seen anyone better. Even on the non-policy stuff. If I had told her I was here, she'd have asked about TJ. She keeps the president up-to-date on the baby's doings."

* * *

WITH THE *LA TIMES* across his lap and a TV news channel for background noise, the man relaxed in his sunroom and looked out over the ocean. The breaking waves were calming, a rhythm he always enjoyed. His Christmas meeting had been productive, but not yet conclusive. The others would be back later with their opinions. He didn't care. He'd already decided, and they would do as he said. He snorted. The explosions had rattled the country, and he thought the president looked too complacent. His plan had begun well.

* * *

FRITZ USED his holiday break to plan for the entire second half of the school year. By mid-week, he had typed and printed most of the questions for the tournament, as well as a list of sources to hand out to the teachers who were coaching.

Jane worked at her office at the airport during the daytime as she prepared details for the upcoming summit. She and Ashley had come for dinner every night. "Tomorrow is New Year's Eve. We're going down in the morning," Ashley said. "Have you decided if you're coming?"

"We're not. I'll call the president later," said Fritz. "It's really too soon to travel with TJ. Besides, we haven't really had any down time in weeks."

Jane said, "He really wants you guys to come. He said he'll have a plane for us so you don't have to drive with the baby.

Or you could portal. Tony's also invited to dinner. You should come. We'll have fun."

"We're gonna pass. I'll call him later." As Linda set dinner on the table, everyone jumped when Jane's phone buzzed.

"I'm still at the Russell's. Ash and I are driving down tomorrow morning." She handed the phone to Fritz. For an instant, the only sound was gurgling from the swing.

The president told him a nuclear weapon had been stolen. It was not the first time. "Same short time frame as Pakistan, Mr. President?" Linda crossed her arms. "George isn't here, you know."

He grew somber as the president told him that time was even less than before, that it was in Russia, and that President Putin claimed he had no troops near enough to deal with it.

"Do you want him to know what we can do?"

"Who?" Linda whispered. Fritz held up his index finger and hurried to get a pad and pen.

The president wanted Fritz to get Putin and bring him back, along with some troops. Colonel Mitchell, whom Fritz had worked with before, was already on his way with soldiers.

"How soon, sir?" Fritz felt his entire body tense. "I really wasn't expecting this, and I need to call George."

FRITZ TOLD THEM what had happened. "What about Tony?" Linda asked. She had begun to chew her bottom lip.

"He's here, at the airport. We should write down what we'll need."

Jane said, "Colonel Mitchell has the lists we've made after each insertion. He created a checklist. He'll have everything."

Fritz said, "I need George."

"That's a first," said Ashley. "I'll call Al Kennedy."

"Good idea. And call Jim Shaw."

Linda said, "Why is this all happening now? It doesn't feel coincidental. It's like, I don't know, like a kid causing as much trouble as he can."

* * *

A STEADY WIND blew across the parking lot. Jim Shaw and Al Kennedy had already arrived. They emptied the car, and Fritz opened the school door. Al asked, "What do you need me to do, Fritz? Thanks for asking me to be here, by the way."

"Don't be too happy yet, Al. This is serious. A nuke has been stolen in Russia. We're going after it."

"Holy cow."

Jane, now Major Barclay, settled into Ashley's classroom. The president called to let them know Colonel Mitchell was ready. He asked if Fritz would come for him as soon as Tony arrived. Fritz instructed Al about George's usual jobs. None of them had keys to the cafeteria, though. "We may have to break in later."

Tony set up the generator. Fritz and Ashley had posted signs identifying each room's use. Major Barclay huddled with Colonel Mitchell. A truck backed up to the doorway.

Al said, "Fritz, this looks like they know exactly what to do. It's so quiet."

"It'll get louder in a minute."

Al gasped when he walked past the classroom labeled HOSPITAL.

Colonel Mitchell motioned to Fritz to join him. Fritz eyed Tony as he passed. Tony stuck his thumb in the air. The colonel said that the president was ready. When he grabbed the doorknob and pulled, the president and half-a-dozen secret service agents were waiting.

"Thanks, Fritz." By the time the door closed, the president was already talking to the colonel and Major Barclay. "Fritz, I have

President Putin's floor plan. He's here." The president pointed to what appeared to be a living room. "We'll get him first." Handing Fritz a second map, he said, "His troops are ready. Here."

"Mr. President, do you want to get him right now, or bring in our guys first?" asked the colonel.

"I want him here while we're unloading. He'll see we're ready to help. I don't want an incident, so he needs to see this unfold. The president stepped to the doorway, Mel Zack right behind. "Be ready. Keep the door open. Let's go." Waiting on the other side, President Putin was startled.

"I was expecting you at my door, Mr. President." They shook hands as the translator spoke. Putin interrupted. "I speak and understand English. Some things are better to be unknown."

"There was no other way. If you will come with me, you will walk into the United States."

Putin stared at the rectangle in the middle of his living room and at the faces watching him. The president reassured him that everything would be fine. Slowly, as though his feet weighed tons, he crossed the room and into a granite hallway with tan lockers lining the walls. "Where am I?" he asked.

"A school in America, Mr. President." With a subtle nod from Mitchell, the outside doors opened and soldiers entered.

"Mr. President, Colonel Mitchell will lead our troops into the area with your men. We are tracking the thieves by satellite. We believe they are headed for an airfield."

"Mr. President, this is most unusual," replied Putin. "You are saying you want to go into Russia to stop them. From here?"

"Yes. We'll go together, bring your troops, cut off the road, get the nuclear device, and bring it back here." He pointed to the truck at the door. "We are running out of time. If you agree, we can go now."

Putin hesitated, watching the soldiers line the hallways with almost no noise. "A joint effort?" he asked. The president nodded. "Who are these thieves?"

"I don't know. I'd like to capture them if possible. In any event, the warhead will be safe. We will dispose of it. But I need your agreement."

Putin examined the president with a penetrating stare. "How did you know?"

"We can discuss that after." He nodded to Fritz. With the paperclip on the map set at the outside of a barracks complex, the two chiefs of state returned to Russia.

"Heads up everyone," said the colonel. "You've all done this before. This time, it's a joint op with the Russians. We want prisoners, but we don't want casualties. They will shoot back, so don't give them a chance. Any questions?" No hands, no comments. "Remember, the Russians have no idea how this works. They may be jumpy. All the Russian speakers should go in the first group. You can help keep the Russians calm. Good luck."

When the door opened, the president and Putin led a line of men through. The Russians followed the example of the Americans in line, standing next to them in two lines. Heads nodded, hands shaken, the message had passed they were all working together. The Russian president introduced Colonel Mitchell to Marshal Kirinyenko, who said in almost perfect English, "To stop this truck, rocks may be our only form of road block. All my men have flashlights."

"Marshal, we want to avoid shooting if possible. We should line the road, take out tires. I hope we can take prisoners. But I've told my men not to get shot."

"I have told mine the same." While they were talking, Fritz had set the map, leaving a twenty-mile cushion along the road where the truck was headed. "You only have a few minutes, Colonel. You should go now," said Fritz.

The soldiers entered Russia on the run and kept running, flashlights showing the way, as Fritz held the door. The sound of boots crunching on stone and soft commands in two languages came through the portal as the hall emptied.

"Mr. President, the truck turned off, heading north," said Major Barclay, holding the computer for the presidents.

"What should we do?" asked Putin.

"Hold up, Fritz," said the president. "Come here."

"Ash, take the door."

The president told Fritz that the truck had turned off about three miles before the insertion. He asked if Fritz could change the map. "We need to get our guys back quickly."

"Hold this," the major said, handing the computer to the president. She ran to the door, grabbed a rifle from a startled soldier still in the hall and ran through. They heard her calling, "Colonel Mitchell."

Fritz looked at the computer image. The truck moved along a straight line but seemed to be slowing down. President Putin said, "Yes, they slow down. But it is dark there. Can you make the picture better?"

"Lin, can you work this thing," Fritz asked. She handed TJ to him and enhanced the picture as the soldiers started to file back.

"Gentlemen, they turned off and are slowing down. We're going in hot," said Major Barclay, wearing trousers and a sweater. Marshal Kirinyenko looked at her and then at Mitchell, who said. "I'll explain later, Marshal."

"Fritz, maps," said the major. "We're guessing. If there's a road there, they will be about here," Jane pointed. "Let's go." The entrance began again. Major Barclay directed the troops in three different directions, telling them to form a perimeter.

"THEY'RE COMING back," called the president.

"Ash, direct traffic," Fritz said. "Al, would you tell the truck driver they're coming."

The soldiers began to appear. The Russians spoke quietly among themselves. Moments before, they had been somewhere in Russia and were suddenly standing in a hallway. Between groups of returning troops, Captain Dolan led soldiers carrying a box labeled with the international symbol for radiation hazards. A couple of soldiers moved to the doors and placed the box in the open truck. Everything had happened quickly and smoothly. Putin merely observed.

Trailing the last soldiers, Colonel Mitchell and Major Barclay came back, her arm slung over the colonel's shoulder. Jane's right pants leg was stained with blood and torn at the knee. "Medic," Ashley shouted and followed Jane to the hospital room. The colonel walked to the presidents and Marshal Kirinyenko. Fritz heard the colonel say, "Mr. President, none of them would give up. Sorry sir." Kirinyenko nodded to his president.

"Mr. President, if you would like, we can send your men home now," said the president.

"That is acceptable, Mr. President. But if I may, I have questions."

The two presidents went into Ashley's classroom. When they returned, President Putin waved Marshal Kirinyenko over, and whispered to him. The officer nodded, saluted, and told his men to prepare to leave. At Fritz's door, Colonel Mitchell thanked his Russian counterpart.

"All set, Colonel," said Fritz.

"Nice to have met you, Marshal Kirinyenko." Still grappling with the strangeness, the Russian shook hands with the colonel, saluted, and signaled his men to move to the door. With Tony beside him, Fritz watched as the column of Russians marched single file back to their own country, some smiling or nodding heads as they passed. Next to the door, one of the Americans who spoke Russian listened for comments he could relay to the colonel. When the portal cleared, Fritz removed the map from his desk and reset the portal to Putin's home.

"THANKS, FRITZ," said the president. "I told him about our new technology that affects atmospheric pressure. We can cause wormholes and walk inside from place to place. It's secret for now, I told him, but we want to use it to reverse climate change. I suggested a joint study with their scientists. It will keep him wondering. He asked where we were. I told him Oklahoma. Tornado country. I think the portal is safe."

"Not bad, Mr. President. That's as implausible as time travel, so he's sure not to believe you."

"Sleight of hand. Colonel, time to go home." The immediate increase in hallway echoes reminded Fritz that his students would soon return.

As if this mission were daily routine, the machine went into motion. The truck with the warhead left, the buses began to load, and the clean-up crew waited outside. Linda and Ashley, alerted by the activity, left the hospital room.

"Where's TJ?" asked Fritz.

"Jane has him. They're wrapping her legs, so they're both sitting still," said Linda.

Ashley was frowning. "She must have a four-leaf clover or a rabbit's foot or something I don't know about." Since they had met in September, Jane had been wounded three times. In November, she had been shot when terrorists attacked the president's car in Washington. His wisecrack that Jane had a better scar than he did hid a touch of envy.

"Time for me to go home," said the president. "Sorry guys, but New Year's Eve is postponed. We still have the ship bombing to figure out. And now this."

* * *

"THE RUSSIANS must have followed our comrades. We heard the gunfire but lost contact. I don't think any of them survived. The warhead was captured, I think."

"Don't concern yourself. Stolen nuclear material gives the Americans and the Russians something to think about in the new year. Besides, we've saved enough to buy more men. We don’t need to pay that lot. Just get more. Oh, and Happy New Year.”

Chapter 5

"**THANKS FOR** your help, Al," said Fritz.

"I didn't do much. Can you tell me what just happened? It went so fast."

"Come to our place," Fritz said.

Before they reached the house, Jane had the president on the phone. He had called to thank them once again and to tell her he needed her in Washington the next day.

Al joined them at the crowded kitchen table. Fritz made coffee and brought out pound cake. Everyone listened as Jane talked to the president. She handed Fritz her phone.

"Mr. President, if Tony's here, why don't you come here?" he said. "No interruptions. Bring anyone you need with you." He listened and said, "No problem. See you tomorrow then." He handed the phone to Jane.

Placing the phone on the table, Jane said that everyone who was needed to discuss both the ship bombing and the summit would come through the portal at ten the next morning. It would likely be the secretaries of state, defense, and homeland security, General Beech, Admiral Davis, the heads of the CIA and FBI, and of course the president and vice president. She looked around the table with a blank stare, still thinking. "I think that's it. Fritz, we'll use a classroom to meet. Okay? You know, he likes it here.

And it will get him away from the vultures. Oh, and the NSA chief. How could I forget her?"

Fritz asked, "Would this be a good time to add the Speaker?" Yanked from her reverie, Jane said she would ask the president.

Ashley suggested that they disguise the classroom. "People in the government were behind the attack on the school," he said. "Koppler. That Navy guy, Wixted, the one who fed information to Koppler. How do we know they didn't tell others?"

"We don't," said Jane.

Ashley said he thought they should get to the school early and set up across the hall from the portal. That classroom was not being used. He said it should be easy to set up like a meeting space.

"We're collecting equipment and uniforms in the morning," Al said. "We should be done in about two hours. I told them I would open the doors at 9:30. They'll only be able to use the locker room entrance, in and out."

"Before you leave, stop down and let us know everyone's gone."

* * *

BY NINE THE next morning, Tony, Colonel Mitchell and six soldiers had arrived from the secret airport. At quarter to ten, Tony hooked up the generator and called the planes. Colonel Mitchell lined up his men to form an aisle from room to room. At ten sharp, Jane signaled Fritz. He pulled the door and looked at surprised faces. The Oval Office occupants emptied into the room across the hall. The president came last, winked, but didn't speak. James and Mel stood aside as Jane and the president disappeared behind the closing door. He told the group that he wanted to discuss the explosion in San Diego and his proposal for the Middle East.

The desks were arranged in a circle. The president asked the Director of Naval Intelligence for a status update on the ship bombing. Admiral Davis told them diving teams were searching for telltale debris on the ship and at the bottom of the mooring. At least four bombs had been set near the ship's munitions, where they would cause the most damage.

"Any progress on the video cameras?" the president asked.

"We spotted what you guessed, Mr. President," said Doug Glassen, the FBI Director. "Four divers climbed over the seawall on Friday morning. We followed their movements to an SUV, but the plates were stolen."

"Were you able to get faces?"

"All we can say is they appear to be Asian. They have their wetsuit hoods on in all the film we've reviewed so far. Sorry, sir."

"Thus far, no group has claimed responsibility. And nothing has shown up in our internet or phone surveillance," said the national security advisor.

The Speaker interrupted. "Where are we?" The president glanced at him, and continued his questioning.

"John, have you had any response from the North Koreans?"

"They haven't denied it, Mr. President. But they haven't actually responded to my inquiries." The Secretary of State frowned.

"What about the original film, the eyewitness?"

"Mr. President, I have personally spoken to Mr. Burke and Mr. Griffin," said the FBI director. "The NBC group said they'll get back to me. But they're stonewalling."

"Why? Don't they understand we may have a war on our hands?"

"They're protecting a source, Mr. President."

The president's jaw muscles rippled, and his eyebrows lowered. After the flash of anger passed, he asked everyone for suggestions about next steps. Only the Speaker, arms crossed and scowling, had nothing to contribute.

In the classroom down the hall, Fritz, Linda, and Ashley listened closely. Ashley and Jane had an audio connection between their computers. Linda took notes while TJ napped in his swing.

"No wonder the president has problems," Ashley said.

"Fritz, which of them know about the portal?" asked Linda.

"The veep does, the secretary of defense, but I don't know about the rest, or how he'll explain where they are. Obviously they know they're not in the White House."

"If he's going to talk about the summit, they'll all know by the end of the meeting," said Ashley. Colonel Mitchell walked in and sat down. He asked what had been discussed.

"So far, only the ship explosion. Do you know the agenda, Colonel?" asked Fritz.

"Jane briefed me last night. He's still got the Middle East to discuss."

In the room down the hall, the president said he had heard from leaders throughout the world that they had had enough of constant crisis. "I don't know about any of you," the president said, "but I'm convinced we have a chance, maybe our best chance, to stop it."

Fritz said, "He's going to explain why. He's going to tell them." He didn't expect the president to say, "Fritz, would you come here please?" Linda gasped. Ashley and the colonel just looked at him.

"Did you know he would do this?" asked Linda.

"I had no idea. I'll be back."

As Fritz pulled up a chair, Jane's eyes said it would be okay. He took a deep breath.

The president said, "What I am about to tell you will remain here, not be discussed or even dreamed about." He looked pointedly at the Speaker. "Last spring, our ambassador to Eledoria and his family were taken hostage. Our troops rescued them." He paused and looked from face to face. "In September, the Narian nuclear program was terminated, not by the Narians or the Israelis, but by a joint special operations mission of the U.S. military." He stopped again. Fritz could feel the tension grow as fast as his anxiety. "In the aftermath, Eledorian soldiers attacked an

Israeli settlement in the West Bank. The same unit rescued those taken hostage."

"I don't mean to be rude," said the Speaker, "but what's your point?"

"My point, Mr. Speaker, is that you don't know the full stories. And if you'll let me finish, you'll understand why you can't talk about how these missions were accomplished." No one could doubt the president's anger. He continued with the stories of stolen nuclear weapons in Pakistan and Russia that American soldiers had recovered. The vice president, whose serious look hid a devilish twinkle, had a tough time not smiling.

"Ladies and gentlemen, I've asked Fritz to join us because his research and subsequent practical application have made it possible for you to get here so quickly." The president cut short the Speaker's interruption, holding up his hand. "We are now sitting in New Jersey."

"Oh, come … on. You don't expect us to believe that," the Speaker said. The vice president began to chuckle. The others looked at each other. "Fritz, would you like to show everyone the trophy case?" The president nodded to go ahead. His look, like Jane's, said everything would be all right.

"OH, MY GOD," Linda said. "I can't believe he said that." They heard the squeak of chairs on the floor and the door opening as the meeting adjourned for a walk down the hall.

Fritz led them past the rows of lockers and the green tiled walls. Shoes tapping the granite floor made the only sounds. At the end of the hall, a glass-enclosed case exhibited a variety of sports memorabilia and trophies. On the wall above it, a sign said, "Riverboro High School. Congratulations New Jersey Division 3 Football Champs."

"Look at the trophies, closely," said the president. The group spread along the case, still not speaking. Footsteps announced someone's approach.

Dressed in his coach's jacket, startled, Al said, "Sorry, Fritz. I didn't know anyone would be here. Hi, Mr. President."

"Mr. Kennedy," the president acknowledged. "I'd like to introduce you all to Al Kennedy, Riverboro High's football coach. Congratulations on your fine season, Coach."

"Thanks, Mr. President. I didn't mean to interrupt. Sorry." Al looked closely at the crowd. He recognized people he had only seen on TV. "Holy mackerel." The vice president finally laughed and introduced himself. He shook Al's hand and said, "Nice to meet another Irishman."

"This is pretty elaborate, Mr. President. How much did this cost the taxpayers? This doesn't prove anything to me," the Speaker said.

Al looked over the vice president's shoulder and got mad, rising to his full, intimidating height. "It didn't cost us taxpayers anything. This is Riverboro High School in New Jersey. I know who you are. Fritz has done things to make this country safe. The portal's real. Last night, we captured a stolen nuke, and..." Al stopped. "Sorry, Mr. President."

"Couldn't have said it better myself, Mr. Kennedy. I think we should go back to work." The return to the classroom wasn't as quiet. Al gripped Fritz's arm. "I'm really sorry, Fritz. Would you tell the President? I hope I didn't screw anything up."

"It'll be okay, Al. You may have done him a favor. Talk to you later."

The president waited for him at the door. "That wasn't planned, but it couldn't have worked out better. Thank him for me. I'm going over the Middle East outline next. You can go back to Linda. Later, we'll take the Speaker home first." He removed a sheet of paper from his jacket pocket. "The Speaker's house. We'll go to the living room. Here." He tapped the floor plan. In small print in the corner was a GPS icon "It'll be a while yet."

The president began again. "One reason we're here was to show you a momentous discovery that gives us the carrot and the stick we need to get the world's attention. Now I want to discuss a proposal to end the Middle East conflict."

"When do we see this new discovery?" asked the Speaker.

The President gritted his teeth, glanced briefly at the Speaker, and asked Jane to pass out the folders. She handed them to each person individually and smiled at the Speaker, taking more time in front of him than necessary. The president asked them to open the packet to page five.

"You will see two maps. The top is the current Middle East. On the bottom is a new map that adds a State of Palestine." He waited for them to look it over. "Without a nation of their own, the Palestinians will continue to be used by other countries to perpetuate conflict."

General Beech said, "Mr. President, we've had this discussion before, you and I. I can't help but wonder if Major Barclay put this together."

"She did, General, but not alone."

"Then I want to say something on the record. Dr. Barclay and I have argued about this for seven years. And I have reached a conclusion. Without reading a word, you can depend on the data, the analysis, and the conclusion."

"Thank you, General," said the president.

The Speaker scowled, having expected the general to scoff. "I can see I'm outnumbered here. I'll take this and look it over, but I see no reason to stay." He pushed back his chair and started to stand.

"Sit. Down." Angrier than anyone except Jane had seen him, the president said, "I need you, and our country needs you, to be here now. You'll leave when I'm done." Not happy with being publicly humiliated, the Speaker resumed his seat.

ASHLEY SAID, "Wow. He's really pissed."

"This is too important to play politics. The Speaker hasn't had enough of a shock yet," said Colonel Mitchell, chuckling.

Chapter 6

"**NOW. THE** bottom map," said the president. "We've created a country for the Palestinians and a buffer zone between Israel and the other countries. Remember that the Brits and the French did this in the early twentieth century, but didn't account for all the cultural issues. The culture and history are all outlined inside."

The meeting continued, but few seemed convinced. The concept of a U.S.-driven nation-building effort, even with massive development programs, seemed like it would be an impossible sell to the leaders in the Middle East.

The president knew he needed to push harder. "Fritz, will you all come in please?" He waited for them, Fritz, Ashley, Linda with TJ, and Colonel Mitchell. Before the door closed, he asked James and Mel to come too.

"General, Admiral, you both know Colonel Mitchell. Colonel, would you describe the missions you have performed."

"Certainly, Mr. President." He made eye contact with everyone before he spoke. "The President has already told you what we accomplished. What he didn't say was that we entered Naria, Israel, Pakistan, Switzerland, and Russia through the door across the hall. Mr. Speaker, you asked what the new discovery is. It's a tunnel that allows us to move anywhere in the world, and from what I've heard, it's also a portal into the past."

"From what you've heard?"

Fritz stepped forward. "I've met with Robert E. Lee six times, witnessed the Triangle Fire, met William Shakespeare, heard the end of the Gettysburg Address, rescued the president from the Geneva meeting attack, and..." He hesitated and looked at the president. Ashley didn't wait. "I helped rescue the Israelis from the settlement, and last night, I saw President Putin standing just outside this room." The meeting erupted into chaos.

"The night we went to Israel, Jerry Burnett died," said the colonel, looking at General Beech and Admiral Davis. "We carried him from this room. We killed the thieves who stole the Russian nuke and brought it back through that door."

The president said, "Gentlemen, ladies, Mr. Speaker, this isn't a theatrical production. Last night, the Russians saw what we can do. The Israeli Prime Minister knows. The Narians have never figured it out. You were sitting in Washington and now you're in New Jersey. The portal is our stick. We can go anywhere, at any time. That's real power."

"Why have I not been told?" asked the secretary of state.

"Would you, would any of you have believed it? These people," pointing to Fritz, Linda, and Ashley, "have put their lives on hold and on the line for the country. At Thanksgiving, the existence of the portal was leaked, and they were in danger. The leaker is dead." He looked squarely at the secretary of state. "You haven't been told until today because this is as much a secret weapon as the atomic bomb was when even Vice President Truman wasn't told of it."

The room filled anew with indecipherable noise, questions, and comments. Only when TJ began to cry did the cacophony subside.

"Why is a baby here?" asked the Speaker.

Before the president could answer, Linda said, "We didn't have time to find a babysitter and we wanted him to have company. We figured you'd do fine."

The vice president broke out laughing.

General Beech said, "Mr. President, I'd like to ask Dr. Barclay a question." The president gestured for him to go ahead. "I'll read the details later, but how do you plan to make this work?"

"General, that's the easy part. Another summit, including the leaders of each country in the region plus the Chinese, Russians, Japanese, Germans, French, British, Turks, Brazilians, Indians, and South Africans. In this room. It will be renovated for the meeting. The president will show them the portal. The carrot and the stick. We expect the countries with resources to share them. They'll all get the message."

"And what if they don't?" asked the Speaker.

Jane looked at the president. He waved his left hand as if to say keep going. "Mr. Speaker," she continued, "there are maps and floor plans of pretty much every building in the world. They're pretty easy to get." The President handed her a folded sheet of paper. She opened it and handed it to the Speaker. "This is your house, isn't it?" He looked down, and then raised his eyes to meet hers. "We have access to every location in the world."

Fritz said, "I worked on an experiment with General Lee to pinpoint exactly where we go, and we've had occasion to need that accuracy. Like getting the president out of Geneva or putting Colonel Mitchell's troops into underground nuclear facilities. This is real, Mr. Speaker." Fritz looked at the president, an apology on his face.

"Maybe it IS time for you to go home, Jack. The rest of you can stand in the hall. Fritz."

"Yes, sir." He winked at Linda, patted TJ on the head, and walked out. Tony waited on a chair, reading. Fritz told him to get ready. He set the paperclip and returned to the hall as the group assembled. When the president entered the hallway, he motioned to Fritz and told the Speaker to look through the window in the door.

"It looks like a classroom. So what?"

"Fritz," prompted the president. The cabinet members and advisors gathered by the doorway. Fritz twisted the knob and pulled. The president guided the Speaker through the door. Audible inhaling and soft comments broke the suspense. "Wow," said the secretary of state as the scene changed to a living room. The president waved to close the door. His classroom reappeared in the window.

"How does this work?" asked Admiral Davis.

"Sorry sir," Fritz said. "I'm not sure you have the clearance. You'll have to ask the president." The vice president laughed again.

"What's so funny, Joe?" asked the admiral.

"He's messing with you, Admiral, and unless I'm way off, he's enjoying it." The vice president continued. "Folks, for the past eight months, we've put these people through hell. We've asked them to do things we couldn't have done without them. In spite of the danger, these two gentlemen put on body armor and rescued the president with a couple of local cops. They brought out James and Mel also. You need to know this because they're civilians. Teachers."

"Mel and the late Tom Andrews rescued the ambassador and his family," the secretary of defense added. "I found out about the portal during the summer, but this is the first time I've seen it."

"And now, you all know about it," said Fritz. "I worry every minute of every day that someone's going to spill the story. My family is in jeopardy. For us, it's not a political toy. So, Admiral, I'm not being a wise ass. And clearance is determined by me, not the president. So you all better help him make this happen. It'll be about time." They all looked as if they had been slapped.

When the door opened and the president returned, the Speaker followed a few steps behind. Before he crossed the threshold, he looked over his shoulder at his living room. "Fritz, close the door," said the president. "Everyone stay here for a second." The president mouthed "open it" to Fritz and told everyone to follow him. When everyone had entered, he asked Fritz to tell everyone where they were.

"Mr. President, as you know, this is my classroom. Mr. Speaker, if you look out this window, to that wall, the school name is on the building." A few of the others crept closer to look out the window. "Mr. President, if you don't mind, would you get your meeting going. I spend too much time here already. This is Christmas break."

The president patted his arm and whispered, "You're the tough guy now. Good job. Set the portal to the Speaker's bedroom. He'll go home first when we're done."

ASHLEY GLANCED at his watch. "Jeez, it's already lunchtime. Should we get some food?"

"I don't know what the president wants to do," said the colonel.

"I'll go ask," said Fritz, and he walked down the hall. "Sorry, Mr. President. I just wanted to know if you wanted lunch."

"It's that late?" Fritz later said that the president was looking at the Speaker when he said, "Time flies when you're having fun. Excuse me for a moment."

In the hall, the president said, "I thought it might take this long. Sorry Fritz. I told the kitchen to make up platters, but I planned to eat at the White House. But since we've made some progress, I'd rather eat here." The president scratched gently behind his left ear. "We'll have to get it. I don't know what they prepared, so we might need a couple of trips."

"Mr. President, I'll get Ash. And maybe these guys?" Fritz said, pointing to the soldiers in the hall.

"I have a better idea. How about we ask our guests to help?" A sly grin sneaked out.

"That works for me. I'll set the portal."

Fritz went into his classroom and the president asked for help. The Speaker was the first to volunteer and sped out the door.

Fritz opened the portal and the Speaker, the CIA director, the secretary of state, and three soldiers followed the president back to the Oval Office. The rest of the officials waited by the doorway, staring at their morning's starting point.

"Hmmm. Looks like the President's office to me," said the vice president. "I thought we just saw a classroom, or was it a living room?"

"Subtle, Mr. Vice President," said General Beech. Then he turned to Fritz and asked, "You really met Robert E. Lee?" Fritz nodded. "How did he react?"

"General, it's a long story. But I will tell you he was more receptive and curious than what I've seen today. I'd be glad to tell you more some other time."

"What's your name?"

"Don't answer, Fritz." The vice president jumped in and said, "General, right now we're still establishing security protocols for these folks. You'll find out later."

"We're the good guys, Joe,' said General Beech.

Fritz interrupted. "Right under the nose of one of the people here," Fritz looked at the admiral, "a conspiracy almost succeeded in killing the president." The vice president said to drop it.

The door remained open, and in minutes, a parade of food platters walked through the Oval Office in the hands of leaders of the government, including the president. "The bread is fresh, and I recommend the corned beef and pastrami," he said.

The group ate at their desks. Linda, Ashley, and the agents and soldiers were invited to join them. Everyone glanced from time to time at Fritz.

"Let's get back to work. Jane will explain the details." For the next half hour, she laid out the plan. The non-participants had followed Linda to Ashley's classroom and settled in front of Ashley's computer. TJ watched from his swing.

Jane rattled them when she presented the proposed finances. The multi-trillion dollar cost of a variety of projects started a discussion about who would pay. The president looked to the Speaker but said nothing. In short order, dead silence replaced the conversation.

"Mr. President, this borders on foolhardy," said the Speaker. "Congress will never approve even a portion of this amount."

"Mr. Speaker, if some of your members need convincing, I'm sure I can help. The minority leader is already on board. These costs will be shared. Will be."

"Can you guarantee that?" asked the Speaker.

"At this moment, no. I haven't asked. But I think Fritz has a way to convince the recalcitrant. Wouldn't you agree?"

The battle of wills echoed mythological battles of the gods, lightning flashing from eye to eye. When the flames died, the president said, "Jack, you have a century of peace, or war, in your hands. I know where your campaign funds come from. It will take courage. I also know, from my conversation with Putin last night," he pointed at the door, "that he can be convinced. But this has to be a united effort. Now once again, America must lead. We've done it before. It's the right thing to do. It will pay for itself. No country can match us if we gear up to make it happen. Jack, I need your help." The president sat down. Fritz thought, *If silence is golden, this is Fort Knox.* "I think we have a good start. Please read the folder. I am going to ask you each to swear to protect the secrecy of the portal," and he went person to person for a verbal answer. "Got that, Fritz?" An email arrived, which Jane shoved in front of the president. Lips pursed, he said, "Fritz heard every word."

The president adjourned the meeting, and Fritz returned to the hall. The portal opened, the president and Speaker crossed the threshold, and Fritz shut the door. In a short moment, the president returned. "Sorry Jack, I forgot your car is at the White House." The Speaker glared at Fritz, who grinned in response.

With the portal properly reset to the Oval Office, everyone now returned to where they had started the day. As he left, the vice president squeezed Fritz's arm and winked again. The president whispered, "Wait here. I'll be right back." Fritz let the door close. With his phone in his hand, he remained by the door, his neck and shoulders relaxing. The others joined him as fingers of afternoon sunlight reached down the hall. Linda was about to pass TJ to him when his phone rang.

"Hi, Mr. President. Give me a second."

"GOOD JOB, EVERYONE. That last little maneuver, the Speaker's bedroom, shook him up. He's alone. His family is out of the District. I asked him if he had plans for New Year's Eve. He said no." A devilish grin shown on his face. "Let's go sit for a bit."

When the soldiers had departed, Tony entered the classroom with James and Mel. The president exhaled, "It's been a hell of a year."

"How do you think it went?" asked Linda.

"Only one person needed to be here. Everyone else provided camouflage. Those who didn't know would have had to be told shortly." The president looked at his watch and took out his phone. "Lily, please call the Speaker at home. I just want to know if he's there. If he answers, tell him to expect a call from me in a couple of minutes." He grinned.

"What are you up to?" Fritz asked, as the president's grin widened.

"One more trip. I'm going to invite him to the White House for a New Year's Eve party. If he accepts, it's back on despite the ship bombing. I want him to see me just pop in and then disappear into the glowing box. So far, he hasn't seen that. I think that will be a perfect final touch."

In less than five minutes, the door opened. The president sported a smaller grin. "He's coming." Everyone laughed. "So," said the president, "what're you doing New Year's Eve?"

"I know that song," said Ashley. Jane shook her head.

"Seriously, I outsmarted myself. Can I convince you guys to come, at least for a while?"

Linda shook her head. "Honestly, I can't believe you boxed us in after all. Do we use the portal?"

"Fastest way. Bring TJ. I ordered a crib ready for him."

She looked at Fritz and sighed. "What do we wear?"

Chapter 7

WHEN ASHLEY had said he would bring his sneakers, Jane hit him.

"I'm serious," he said. "What better way to end the year than one-on-one?"

James greeted them when they entered the Oval Office. Pointing to a suit draped over a chair, he told Tony that his roommate had dropped it off and ushered him to a place where he could change. When the president and First Lady welcomed them, a gym bag hung from Ashley's arm.

"I couldn't talk him out of it," Jane said.

The First Lady laughed. "Are you going to do this before or after?"

"After," they said together.

"Let's celebrate," the president said, leading them into the heart of the White House. "Let's hope next year will be better." The president's gaze swept the hall, a distant look on his face. "This time next year, we'll be getting ready to move." They reached the center hall and headed into the State Dining Room.

"We're using the Blue and Red Rooms, too" the First Lady said. "Check out all the Christmas decorations." Ashley excused himself and went to say hello to the vice president. As they shook hands, he whispered in the vice president's ear, which brought a loud guffaw. TJ, in Linda's arms, made a noise that sounded like a laugh, and General Beech said, "Sounds like a vice president in the making."

Fritz spotted a number of the morning's attendees. Standing on the periphery with Linda and Jane, he understood why they had been invited. The president and First Lady walked the room. When he reached the Speaker, they whispered to each other, and Fritz saw the speaker glance at him. The president waved for him to join them.

"Come on, Lin."

"I'll stay here with Jane."

"I'll be back," Fritz said in his best Arnold Schwarzenegger voice. Linda sighed.

Fritz approached the president cautiously.

"You remember Jack, don't you, Fritz?"

"He's vaguely familiar, Mr. President. Mr. Speaker, I'm a news junkie, and I think that's the first time I've ever seen you smile."

"Well, Fritz, it's either smile or be afraid of you. You gave us quite a demonstration."

"Mr. Speaker, this is a party. But everything we told you really happened. If you're scared, well, you should be in my shoes." The Speaker, hearing one of the president's standard phrases, looked at the chief executive.

"Must be rubbing off," said the president, tilting his head. He turned to the rest of his guests, who were standing around the table. "Hey, everyone, this is a party. The food's great. Please help yourselves.

LINDA SMILED as she followed a volley between the general and Jane.

"Telling a story, General?" asked the president.

"I was just telling Linda, sorry ma'am, those of us who know your last name have been asked not to use it. Well, I was telling her about my first meeting with Jane. You were one stubborn young woman, let me tell you."

Fritz listened as General Beech reached the punch line. In the middle of a briefing, Jane had told him he didn't know his ass from Israel. "I was furious. And I told the president. When I got back to my office, a folder on my desk contained enough analysis to sink a ship and prove Jane right." Jane smiled as Ashley came back and took her hand. "Jane and I have argued about tactics ever since. I looked at your plan when I got home. It'll be hard to make work, but it's brilliant."

"Thank you, General. Let me introduce my fiancé, Ashley Gilbert." She closed her eyes, realizing her mistake.

"Congratulations! And don't worry Jane. I know a thing or two about classified information." He smiled, still shaking Ashley's hand. "Nice ring, by the way. You should know, Ashley, a lot of smoke from extinguished flames will be floating all around Washington."

The president returned with his daughters and a woman, who would watch TJ in the Red Room. A swing and a crib had been placed in a dimly-lit corner.

"I want you guys to have some fun tonight. Ms. Davis will watch him, and you'll be right nearby."

Linda handed the baby to her. "First time out?" she asked. Linda nodded. "We'll be in the next room." Fritz and Jane stroked his head, which he had put sleepily on the babysitter's shoulder.

James walked in with two women, followed by Mel Zack, barely recognizable with her hair down. The president welcomed them and pointed toward Fritz and Linda. James's wife, Lucy, smiled and waved.

"Everyone," the president said as he took the woman by the hand, "I want you to meet Sharon Andrews, Tom's wife. Sharon, this is Fritz, this is Ashley. Guys, Sharon knows the story."

Fritz shook her hand and introduced Linda, whose eyes were suddenly puddled. Ashley, instead of shaking hands, hugged her and held on for a minute. "We're all so sorry. Tom was a great guy. Please accept our sympathy."

When she stepped out of his grasp, Sharon had tears on her cheeks. "Thank you, Ashley. Tom could never tell me the whole story, but I know the two of you saved him in Geneva. He spoke about you both as superheroes."

"Well, Fritz isn't. But I am," Ashley answered with a smile.

"Tom said you were a wiseass. He couldn't laugh at you when he was working, but he told me some stories. So did James. Thanks. I needed a good laugh."

"Sharon," Fritz said, "stick around. He's on a roll."

"Maybe I will. Hello, Jane. I understand congratulations are in order. You too, Ashley. Thanks for inviting me, Mr. President."

"Glad you're here, Sharon. Let me introduce you to some others."

When the president left, Linda said, "Can't the two of you behave, just for one night. Honestly! Lucy, don't let James spend too much time with them. I think they're contagious."

The First Lady, with a daughter on either side, introduced them to the growing crowd in the corner. "Where's TJ?" asked the younger.

"He's in the next room," said Linda, winking at her. Linda had met both of them when she was hiding at the White House for a couple of days at Thanksgiving.

"Can I hold him?"

"Sure. Let's go see if he's still awake."

The First Lady sighed. "They've grown up so fast. They were both little when we moved in. It's going to be quite a change for them, living somewhere else.

Fritz asked, "Do you know where you might move?"

"My husband keeps talking about Riverboro, but probably here or Chicago. Or maybe Hawaii."

FRITZ, LINDA, AND ASHLEY wandered from room to room. Linda kept checking on TJ, asleep in the Red Room. They looked out the Blue Room windows and admired the spectacular decorations. They said hello to the secretary of defense, whom they had first met in September. Everyone who had been at the morning's meeting stopped to say hi.

The good time froze when phones around the room started ringing. The president asked Jane to join the crowd moving toward the hall. "Another attack," he told them. "This time in Norfolk. Four ships." The president thanked everyone for coming, apologized that some of them would be heading to the Situation Room, and asked Fritz and Linda to hang around.

One woman said that the attacks were like Pearl Harbor. Creases appeared on Linda's brow. Ashley's worry ruts appeared. He asked, "Do you think he'll need us?"

"Probably not tonight," Fritz said. "The damage is done. I hope no one was hurt."

A short while later, the president returned. When he joined them, he said, "Sorry Ash. No game tonight. It appears to be the same deal as San Diego. We'll know more when we can see what happened." He frowned as he went to say goodnight to Washington's powerful.

"We should get TJ," Linda said.

"Lin, let's wait until we can leave. No point in making him wait."

"It won't be long," said Ashley. "But where's Jane?"

"I didn't see her come back," said Linda.

The president and First Lady had said goodnight to most of their other guests. When James started to move toward the door, the president held up his hand.

"Hang on a minute, James. Jane and General Beech are calling to get info. I'm really sorry about this. I wanted everyone to have a nice evening."

THE AGENTS LEFT from the North Portico with Sharon Andrews. The First Lady shooed the girls up to the residence. Ashley and the Russells followed the president and First Lady back to the Oval Office, where Jane and Tony were waiting. General Beech was on the phone in the outer office.

"One of these days, I'd like to look around here when everything's not nuts," said Fritz. "Does that ever happen?"

The president exhaled sharply. "It doesn't feel like it sometimes. What's up, Jane?"

Jane told them the MO matched the San Diego bombing, with greater damage. Four ships had sunk. "The admiral said they got a carrier, too. Still afloat, but a lot of damage."

"Casualties?"

"They don't know. Some injuries on deck. Most of the crews are on shore leave, but they'll have divers out at first light. The Admiral said he didn't want them back yet. But every diver in the area is being contacted." The electric glint in her eyes conveyed her anger.

THE PRESIDENT BALLED his hands, told the First Lady he'd be a while, and told Jane to stay near a secure phone. She said she'd go to the airport with Tony. Then he pulled Fritz and Linda aside. He said he didn't know what plans they had for childcare, but he would like a secret service agent to go back with them. He wanted them to have someone with them at all times. Mary McElroy was great with kids and would be happy to take care of TJ. Shaken and grateful, they agreed. Although they had chosen a very reputable agency, they had not picked a particular nanny yet since Linda didn't have to go back to school until two days after Fritz's classes began.

"Let's get you guys home. Mary has suitcases." A clock chimed midnight. The president shook his head, and they left for Riverboro High. "Happy New Year," he said, but nothing in his voice sounded remotely happy.

BEFORE TJ was born, Linda could plan a schedule. School during the day, work at home. She was planning to finish her MBA in the spring. Her boss at the publishing house had sent her a steady flow of work, and she had gotten it all done. But she'd fallen behind. She realized it would be a huge help having Mary there a few days earlier than they'd planned to bring a nanny in.

Chapter 8

IN A GREEN leather recliner, the man glanced at his watch and returned to the annual report on his lap. It was just past nine. It had been a great year, and his greeting proclaimed it when the phone rang.

"They sank four missile cruisers. You were right. They also have the *Bush* listing. I don't think she'll go down, but they'll have a problem moving her."

"Make sure we get the pictures to the right people." He hung up. He raised his glass in a toast to the empty room, "Happy New Year." He left his report, went up a fifteen-foot-wide staircase, and began dressing for his guests. The steps heard "Auld Lang Syne" as he climbed.

* * *

"HAPPY NEW YEAR. NOT," Fritz said. Linda frowned in response. Fritz turned on the TV as soon as they got in. Linda put TJ to bed and showed Mary the guest room.

"Fritz, this smells like the fall all over again." He scanned for reports, but all the stations were carrying New Year's shows. Anderson Cooper was still in Times Square. There was no crawler. The news hadn't yet become public.

He said, "Let's go to bed. We'll have all day to watch."

"THANK GOD FOR coffee makers." Fritz yawned. Linda was booting her laptop, her coffee at arm's length. She glanced up at his slurp. "Sorry. It's hot."

"Fritz, start scrambling eggs, and I'll look for news." As he went to the refrigerator, Ashley and Jane walked in wearing their previous evening's clothes and with dark circles under their eyes. They grunted their greetings and went straight to the coffee. A wide-awake TJ gurgled in Mary's arms. Jane told them about the damage.

"What time did you get home?" Fritz asked.

"A little after the sky was bright enough to see," answered Ashley, taking a sip. "They got a carrier. And an eyewitness filmed it again."

Jane rubbed her eyes. She said she had talked to the president at seven. Once more, NBC had the pictures. Another exclusive. "This is all wrong."

"NBC. Not the others?" asked Fritz. "Are they going to give up the film?"

"I don't know yet. A cabinet meeting is starting at 11:30. The president ordered all nearby videos to be confiscated. The Navy probably won't have all of them until tomorrow."

Jane watched the TV with her usual intensity. In the NBC film, the underwater explosions were loud thumps, but no significant fireworks were visible until the *USS Bush*. That explosion was at water level.

Thinking aloud, Jane asked, "Why did they only have one device?" She took out her phone. "Good morning, Lily. And you, too. Is he available?

"Mr. President, we may have spotted something on the *Bush*. We need to look at the shore videos as soon as they come in. I think we'll see the divers again." She listened and then said, "I can if you want. Tony's up." She asked Fritz if he could get her to the Oval Office.

Fritz shrugged. "I'll go get ready."

* * *

TONY PACED by the school door. Jane said, "Fritz, I won't be back until later. Maybe not until tomorrow. Tell Ash I'll call." Before the classroom door closed, the president, in shirt sleeves and wrinkled pants, called out. His eyes revealed a weariness that came from more than just lack of sleep.

"Fritz, are you going to be home?"

"I expect so."

"I may need to visit New York. NBC's still giving me a hard time."

"Call me. We'll be there."

"Why don't you come for dinner?"

"Thanks, Mr. President, I'll ask Linda."

"I know. You don't want to come, so you are setting up to blame her." He laughed. "Talk to you later."

WHEN FRITZ ARRIVED home, he told Linda they had been invited to dinner.

"I haven't made anything. Jane will be there."

"So, you want to go?"

"Might as well."

Fritz asked if any new stories had been reported.

"Not yet," she said. "Call about dinner."

They watched planes removed by crane from the aircraft carrier, which was listing to starboard. The NBC film of the explosions, complete with audio, showed rescue boats shuttling around the harbor in the aftermath. After the explosions, searchlights combing the water furnished no new information.

* * *

THE PRESIDENT was waiting when they crossed the threshold at dinner time and flashed a knowing smile at Fritz. "Glad you could make it," he said. "Nothing fancy. Some of the stuff that was left from last night and a casserole of something. Jane's upstairs." They ate in the residence with the First Lady, the girls, and James. The crib and swing had been moved to the family dining room, and TJ napped while they ate. The president bantered back and forth with Ashley about the bowl games. Heads swiveled as the debate continued. Fritz thought that it was incredible that the president could be so engrossed given all the problems confronting him. He shook his head. The president noticed. As if he had sucked the thought out of the air, he said, "Compartments, Fritz."

"You really can do it." Fritz recounted their November conversation about compartmentalization. It seemed so long ago. "It's magic."

By the end of the meal, Ashley and the president had made a ten-dollar bet.

Once dessert was served, Linda asked, "Are you planning to use the portal tonight?" The president shook his head. She was touched they had been asked to the White House just to socialize.

* * *

THE NEXT MORNING, Ashley and Jane arrived with five bags of groceries. Fritz jumped to hold the door. "What's all this?"

"Good morning to you, too," said Ashley.

Ashley and Fritz made eggs, bacon, and toast. Jane and Mary joined them in the kitchen. "Time to fill you in." Jane said. "The president spoke to the president of NBC. In light of the second attack, the network agreed to release the film from San Diego. The eyewitness was taken into custody early this morning. They checked her out, and she was in Washington on New Year's Eve. She's not talking."

* * *

"WHAT?" HE WALKED around his office, listening. "OK, where is she?" He looked out at the Mall, a bleak gray etching. "She works for you. Is there any trail?" He listened again. "If they find out she was in Norfolk…" He stopped and leaned on the door jamb. "I'll take care of this."

* * *

"COME QUICK!" Ashley was pointing at the screen crawler. It said the eyewitness who had filmed the San Diego ship attacks had been found dead in her home.

"I thought she was in custody," said Fritz.

"How does the news have it already?" Jane asked. Her hard stare reminded Fritz of aiming at a target when he had gone shooting with Jim Shaw.

"A leaker?" asked Ashley. Jane nodded. She was lifting her phone.

"Do you know anything else?" asked Ashley when Jane put her phone down. Jane told them that the FBI still had the eyewitness in custody. "Someone's playing games."

Chapter 9

ASHLEY SHOWED up early with more groceries. Another full house for dinner. When Mary helped unload the food, Fritz noticed a bulge in the small of her back.

"Mary," he asked, "are you carrying?"

"Of course."

Jane's return a few hours later sparked an explosion of questions. She answered as many as she could. The feds still had no idea who was responsible for the attacks, and all military resources were on alert.

Jane was pacing. "Why is the Navy being targeted?" she asked. Ashley suggested that the Navy targets were easily accessed, that no one guarded underwater. Fritz agreed. He said the attackers could take their time if they knew when routine checks were scheduled.

"Easy targets," Linda mused. "Jane, what was the Navy's general response after Norfolk was hit?"

"Increased surveillance. Moved ships. Called off leave."

"Right. Motion with no strategy. And what about the eyewitness?" Linda asked.

"Oh, she's dead all right. Her lawyer blocked the door and gave her poisoned soda. I don't know if he knew what he had, but they were both dead in three minutes." She shook her head.

"We have video. It was gruesome." The woman, Caitlin Morgan, had been a computer analyst for National Digital Communications, a leading cyber-security company.

Investigators were looking for more information on her, and agents were collecting security film. Finding the people involved would be hard without someone claiming responsibility. The North Korean government had responded to the secretary of state. They said they were not responsible, but seeing the second attack, wanted to assure the president he would receive their cooperation moving forward. A representative had actually flown in from North Korea.

* * *

THE PRESIDENT went on TV that night. He assured the nation that the military was prepared to act. No claim of responsibility had surfaced, and all law enforcement agencies were investigating.

* * *

ASHLEY WAS ALREADY at his desk when Fritz arrived at school, wondering aloud if vacation had skipped them. Only when he spotted Ashley's sweater did Fritz realize he was cold.

"Doesn't feel like we've left," he said. Eric Silver poked his head in and told them that the script was written through the 1930s. He handed them copies.

"Good job, Eric," said Ashley. "I'll talk to Jean later and try to read it tonight."

"Thanks, Mr. Gilbert. I'll see you later, Mr. R."

"They didn't have a vacation either," Ashley said.

The first class, his tenth graders, set the table. They were grumpy and worried.

"Mr. R," said AJ, "I've been reading the news and watching reports for a week. It wasn't a fun vacation."

"AJ, what are you thinking?"

“I watched the president last night. I don’t think he knows what he’s doing.”

Mary Ann jumped him. “How can you say that? He has a hard job. Do you want a war?”

The play distracted the next class. Fritz thanked them for taking time to work so hard during vacation. As the period wound down, Bob Bee asked, “Mr. R, do you think we’re going to war again?” By lunch, Fritz had heard questions about war in each class. Ashley told him the same had happened in his classes.

After lunch, Fritz talked about the French and Indian War and England’s rise to international power. But the kids still asked about the news. In seventh period, he started by congratulating Johnny Clayton for having been chosen for the all-state football team. His class on the history of work was discussing wartime production during World War II, so the news gave them an incentive to talk about the military-industrial complex. His ninth graders were chafing in their seats and questions flew. They barely mentioned the tournament.

“HI, HONEY, I’m home,” said Fritz. “Anything new?”

Jane said, “Nothing that’s been released. The president said nothing is conclusive, but the chemistry indicates the same explosives were used in Norfolk and San Diego.”

* * *

“WE’VE CREATED A CRISIS,” the younger man laughed, raising a glass of bourbon. “I salute you. They’ll be busy for a decade figuring it out.” His host sipped a dry martini and withheld comment. “A great idea, absolutely perfect.” The young man’s effusive reaction brought tremors to his companion’s well-honed sense of caution.

“The girl and the lawyer are traceable,” said the man. He walked to the windows, watching a wave smash the rocks below. “You need to be watchful and silent. You will be questioned, more likely sooner than later. I recommend a trip, one that began two weeks ago. Can you arrange it?"

"No problem. I was on my boat," the younger responded with an off-handed impertinence.

The man knew then his associate was lucky, not smart. "And where was your boat?"

"Just driving around. Didn't stop anywhere."

The man nodded, recognizing a weak link that jeopardized everything.

* * *

THE NEXT WEEK, Linda went back to school. She was taking three courses, one involving a major project. She thought she could begin to think about setting up her bicycle store. Finding the money would come first, but she knew what she was doing. In addition to her graduate coursework, her father, an innovator in corporate financial management, had begun teaching her about his work when she was very young.

"I'll have to buy a bike so we can race, Fritz," said Ashley. "How about a buck a minute? I'll design the race course. Lin, I'll be your first customer."

* * *

THE PRESIDENT was frustrated by the investigation's lack of progress. No one had claimed responsibility. The videos disclosed unidentifiable divers. The military and law enforcement teams had no reports. A dead woman and her dead lawyer formed the only tangible connection. A single link. Three weeks after the San Diego bombing, the president faced another Sunday of talk-show critics. *No man is an island?* he thought. *Yeah, right.*

Jane spent most of the week with General Beech and the CIA Director. The facts pointed to a single set of perpetrators. Friday afternoon, Jane sat at the Russells' kitchen table, looking at the snow-covered lawn through the bay window. Her phone had been silent all day. Startled by the ring, she jumped.

"Yes, General?"

"Jane, you were right. There's a definite link. It's the Eledorians."

"General, there's a link, but it's not them. It was mercenaries, bought and supplied by someone else. This ties back to Koppler. I'm sure of it. Someone is pulling strings. And spending a lot to do it. General, I don't know if you know, but I worked with the colonel saving the Israeli settlers."

The general interrupted. "I didn't know. The portal?"

Jane continued, "Um-hmm. The troops that attacked the settlement had no identifying markings. The planes were stolen, and we captured no prisoners." She spotted two cardinals in a tree. "General, you are already sworn. You know I have to report this discussion to the president. He's got a list of everything to do with the portal. I want you to know that I trust you, but the president requires it. Nothing personal."

General Beech laughed. "Jane, everything with you is personal. But don't worry. I get it. You know, Fritz and Ashley have a lot of guts. Those guys handled the Speaker and Admiral Davis. I don't think they know how hard that was. And the football coach couldn't have done a better job."

Jane knew the mercenaries could have been Eledorians fighting for funds rather than country. Facing terrible shortages of food, shelter, and medicine made them eager for cash. Whoever was paying them was still hidden, though, and Jane wanted to look for large, unusual bank transfers that might lead them to the puppeteer.

* * *

FRITZ AND ASHLEY had planned to play ball Friday afternoon. Liz Chambers found Fritz in his classroom, already in shorts and tee shirt. He had given her the list of questions he had prepared and the tentative schedule for all the games.

She said, "Some of the teachers are already working with the kids. They don't want to lose. They're going to have fun, but they'll be competitive. We may need to set up the cafeteria for the overflow."

"The kids amaze me. Thanks for your help, Liz."

"George will have a full house when this gets started. Do you know what Susan Leslie and your kids did over the holidays?" Fritz said they hadn't told him. "Well, she corralled her sisters and their friends to go door-to-door with flyers about the tournament. Every flyer had a form for a scholarship donation. They've raised nearly $20,000. They're at the office now opening envelopes. George is beside himself." Fritz started to laugh.

He and Ashley surprised the twelve students sitting on the office floor. Stacks of unopened envelopes surrounded them. Susan, Mary Ann, and Pat were collecting the checks and cash, recording the proceeds, and writing receipts. A crew of kids was addressing outgoing mail.

"Hi, Mr. R," said Susan. The other kids looked up, said hello, and returned to their tasks.

"So. Holding out on me, huh?" Susan smiled and said they wanted to surprise him.

George poked his face out his office door. "Mr. Russell, may I speak to you please?" Fritz winked at Susan, grinned at Ashley, and said he was on his way.

"This is amazing, isn't it, George?" He closed the door.

"Did you know about this?"

"I just found out. They did all this over the holidays."

"There's all sorts of money here. This is very irregular."

"How do we set up an account for the scholarship fund? What did you do with Liz's check?"

"It's in my desk. Don't worry. It's safe. Fritz, they went all over town. I keep getting calls. Every time I try to get something done, it's another call. This has to stop. I can't even go home."

"I can't believe you sometimes. Liz told me she thinks we'll need the cafeteria for the crowd at the games."

"This is out of control."

"George, calm down. We have time to work out the details. If it's too much for you, ask for help."

"You're going to have to cancel this, Fritz. I'm sorry. You're just going to have to."

"No."

"What do you mean, no?"

"If I have to do it without your cooperation, I will. We're not canceling. If you want to go home, I'll move the kids to my room. And I'll tell them to use it from now on."

A knock on the door interrupted them. Ms. Sweeney said that the superintendent was on the phone. "See, now look at the trouble." George picked up his phone. "Hello, Mr. Chatham." George glared while he listened. "Well, of course I know. In fact, Mr. Russell is right here." Then, like a scolded puppy, he sat down. "Thank you. That's very kind." *His face suddenly looks like library paste*, Fritz thought. "I'll tell him. Yes, you too. Bye, now." George set the phone in the cradle. "That was the superintendent."

"I know." Fritz waited.

"He said he's been getting calls about the tournament and congratulated us for a wonderful idea. He said he'll be here for the games."

"Still want to cancel, George?" Bewildered, George shook his head. "Then I'll go move the kids to my room."

"No, don't bother. I'll stay a little late. Let them finish up today. You can move them on Monday."

Fritz thanked him and snorted softly after he left the office. He caught Ashley's eye and shook his head.

"Kids, on Monday, we'll move all this to my room. Okay?"

"Mr. Russell," said Ms. Sweeney. "May I speak to you for a second?" Fritz sat by her desk and leaned forward. She whispered, "You should know they've been exceptional. They've stayed out of the way and cleaned up. They're so excited that all the teachers are commenting. You should be proud of them."

"Thanks, Ms. Sweeney. I am. I'm sure George will be too when we get started."

"You know, I can't wait."

Fritz and Ashley offered to help, but Susan said that they were okay, they had a system.

"You're turning me down?"

"Well, yes. We're doing fine." Ashley laughed.

Chapter 10

KOPPLER'S BOXES held full address books, most in code. They also discovered a list of names under the heading *Caballeros,* with numbers and letters. At dinner, Jane moved the food around her plate and stared at the far wall. She was sure she'd heard the name *Caballeros* before.

* * *

THE PRESIDENT SAT with a stack of yellow pads and the to-do list Lily Evans had left on his desk. He spread them out and read the headings. He reached into a desk drawer and took out Colonel Mitchell's and the Israelis' reports about the rescue mission. Jane had said she had a feeling. She wanted to follow the money, but he was reluctant to start a search through bank accounts without something more to go on. Then again, he knew that if he had listened to her feeling in October, Geneva wouldn't have happened. So he read everything again and scribbled in the margins. Sucking the top of his pen, he recalled a voice. "Where was I?" he asked himself. The scene returned. *The elevator in Switzerland.* He picked up his phone.

* * *

"G'MORNING, MARY," Linda said, taking a mug from the shelf. "You're up early." Mary McElroy stood at the counter with a full mixing bowl and an eggbeater. It was barely seven. TJ was in his swing. A frying pan sat on the stove.

"I'm usually up at five, so this is like sleeping in. Pancakes okay?"

"Great. Not sure if you'll have a lot of customers though."

"The batter will keep, but I think it'll be busy. Jane called. She's already talked to the president. She and Ashley will be here soon. Something's up."

"Should I get Fritz started?"

"I'm already started," he said, yawning in the kitchen doorway. "What's the early bird special?"

"Mary's making pancakes, and Jane and Ash are on the way."

"Did something happen?" he asked, pouring a cup of coffee.

"We don't know what yet. Jane's already spoken to the president."

JANE AND ASHLEY arrived with more food. "What's up? Why so early?" asked Fritz, before Ashley put the bag down.

"I figured you were a poor, lonely, forgotten soul, so we've come to lighten your burden."

"Putting up with you is my living purgatory."

Jane said, "We need to talk, but coffee first. Hi, Mary."

"Mary's making pancakes," Linda said, "or do you want a bagel?"

"Sure, bagel, toasted," Ashley answered, "with butter and cream cheese. And some cold grapefruit juice. No, better, half a grapefruit."

Linda shook her head. "No problem. But put your coat back on. The grapefruit is next to your section at the store. You know, the nuts."

"Don't get him started. He's already in rare form," said Jane. "Turning to the serious, the president called. The head of NDC was found dead. By himself. That big boat of his. Just floating."

"His name was Jonathan Hartmann," said Mary. With all eyes on her, she held up her phone. "Text message. Caitlin Morgan worked for him."

"The woman in Los Angeles." said Linda.

"So there is a connection," Fritz said.

"Only NDC, so far," Jane answered. "Somewhere we're going to find a money trail. Fake Eledorians, I'll bet fake Koreans, explosives, and weapons purchased, travel for a bunch of men, or hiring a lot of mercenaries in different locations." Jane scanned their faces. "This is all tied together. I'd bet on it."

"But who? Why?" asked Linda.

"Right now," Jane shrugged, "the name is a blank."

The toaster popped as Tony and Mel opened the back door. Linda asked where James was. Mel told her he would be along shortly. He had to go shopping. "It's Lucy's birthday, and he hasn't been home."

Jane asked, "Mel, how hard would it be to find the file about the Caballeros?"

"No trouble. I know exactly where it is. But it's in Washington."

"Fritz, Tony, could you set it up? I think it ties in."

Ashley asked, "What do you remember about the Caballeros, Jane?"

"Someone said to watch out for them. Maybe the president will remember something."

* * *

"MR. PRESIDENT, have you ever heard the name Caballeros?"

"Rings a bell. Hang on, Jane." He called Lily Evans and asked her to step into his office. Although it was cold, he led her outside. "Lily, do you have a file on Caballeros? I don't know why, but the word makes me queasy. I don't want it even mentioned inside."

"I understand, Mr. President. I'll check."

"Jane, Lily is checking her file. I can't pinpoint anything in my memory. Let me think about it."

* * *

Once James arrived, Jane, Mel, Fritz, Ashley, and Tony headed to the school. Over the previous couple of weeks the portal had turned the Oval Office into a transit station.

"Good morning, Mr. President," said Jane. "Mel is picking up a file."

"Hi, everyone." He stood, but Jane told him they would be leaving right away. "Jane, until we remember, don't mention that name in here, okay." The President held a finger to his ear and gestured around the room.

"Got it," she said. The office door opened, and Lily Evans and Mel came in.

"Good morning, Jane, everyone," she said, smiling. "Mr. President, this was all I could find." She handed him a single sheet of paper. He read it and held it out to Jane, who glanced and then looked up at him. It said, "Bill Clinton."

"Can you call him, Mr. President, and let me know what he says?" He nodded, and waved to Fritz, who was holding the door open. At the door, Jane asked, "Sir, do you know if General Beech is in his office this morning?"

"He is. I spoke to him about an hour ago."

"Good. Talk to you later," she said.

* * *

"LINDA, CAN I spread this out on the dining room table?" asked Jane, holding up the file folder.

"Of course. Do you want help?" Jane nodded.

Slowly, a full file box was emptied on the table and turned into fourteen separate piles. Linda scanned each piece. Jane began turning pages, her soundless lips moving. The note reading "Caballeros" sat in front of her.

The others watched TV, scanning the news for any updates or interviews. The main story was the tragic yet suspicious death of NDC founder, Jonathan Hartmann. CWN host Alan Carter was interviewing former colleagues, who expressed surprise and sadness that "such a brilliant mind had been lost." A senior employee, Penelope Wise, said it was terrible to lose them. Carter sat up, his brow wrinkled and asked her who she meant. "Why Caitlin and Jonathan, of course." Jane was in the doorway before another word was said, her phone in her hand.

"Mr. President, we need to get to Penelope Wise from NDC. She's on CWN with Alan Carter. Right now. Can we get someone to New York City?"

"Fastest way is the portal. I'll call CWN." He hung up.

* * *

THE PLANES were flying before they reached the school. Jane asked the president where she should go. He said CWN had a meeting room set up. "Just tell them who you are at the reception desk. They know you're coming."

"Jane, we should close the portal when you go in. When you're ready to come back, I'll open it again. Otherwise, someone in New York might see it or just walk through. They don't pay attention to where they're going."

Chapter 11

THE ARRIVAL OF two Secret Service agents and an official from Homeland Security, all carrying weapons, afforded a new experience for the security team at CWN. Alan Carter was informed of their presence only when his guest was removed to a small meeting room and told not to leave.

Penelope Wise, a senior vice president for NDC, rubbed her hands and cleaned her glasses.

"Ms. Wise," Jane said.

"Call me Jen."

"I thought your name was Penelope?"

"It is, but would you go around being called Penny? Penny Wise?"

"I see your point."

Jane introduced herself and the agents and told Wise she might have information needed for an ongoing investigation.

Puzzled, Wise said, "I think you have the wrong person."

"You mentioned a relationship between Caitlin Morgan and Mr. Hartmann moments ago."

"Yes. It's a tragedy."

"Ms. Wise, Jen, do you know how many people watch Alan Carter?"

"Not really."

"I don't either, but your interview will be replayed, and others exist who won't want that link made public."

"I don't know what you're getting at, but I don't like the sound of it. Are you arresting me?"

"No, protecting you." Jane faced her, staring hard at the blue eyes glaring back, and said, "What I need to know is everything you can tell me about the two of them."

"Why?" Her eyes narrowed. "I should get a lawyer."

"Caitlin Morgan had a lawyer," said Jane, knowing she had an opening. "He was killed with her. Did you know that?"

Behind her glasses, Wise's smugness transformed to wide-eyed shock. In a shaky voice, she said, "I didn't know they were killed. Just that she died. We were told it was an aneurysm."

Jane said, "Jonathan Hartmann died, alone on that big boat floating unmanned like a ghost ship. It's under investigation. We know Ms. Morgan worked for NDC, but until you spoke, we had no link. We're here now at the order of the president. Will you help us?"

"Am I in trouble?"

"No, but you may be in danger."

Clearly agitated, Wise said, "I want a lawyer."

Jane turned to James, who was standing by the door. "James, will you get Alan Carter in here, please. Ms. Wise, we have reason to believe Ms. Morgan was involved in a conspiracy to assassinate the president. We're asking you to tell us what you know."

"Not without my lawyer." She folded her arms and turned away.

Jane took out her phone and nodded to Mel, who left the room. "Before I make this call, Jen, I want you to understand that I hoped this would be straightforward. I know you think you need to protect yourself legally, but by refusing to answer, you're forcing me to consider your possible involvement." Jane smiled at her. Jen Wise turned to Jane, bemused by the smile. She shook her head.

"Okay." Jane spoke softly, but her intention was undisguised. "You leave me no choice." She walked to the door and asked the agents and the anchor to come in. She dialed a number.

"Mr. President," Jane said so everyone could hear, "Ms. Wise is refusing to answer without her lawyer." She listened to his instructions. "Do you really want to do that? Alan Carter is here, too." She handed her phone to the newsman. "The president wants to talk to you."

He raised his eyebrows, and his wrinkled forehead activated. "Hello." He listened to the president's instructions and handed the phone back to Jane.

"Yes, sir. I'll set it up. You'll be there? OK, see you shortly." She took a deep breath. "James, will you stand at the door, please?" She said, "Miss Wise, you are under arrest for withholding evidence in a Federal criminal investigation." She recited the Miranda rules and said Wise would be able to call her lawyer later. "Mr. Carter, you will join us." Surprised, he agreed.

Jane called Fritz and told him to get the president, who would explain. "Then, give us about three minutes. I'll call you to tell you we're ready."

"Can you tell me what's going on?" asked Carter. "This is pretty weird stuff."

"Mr. Carter, my name is Jane Barclay. I work for the president. Mel, will you cuff Ms. Wise?" Wise gasped and began to complain about her rights being violated. Jane told her she had had her chance and blew it. "Let's go."

James led the way through the lobby to the street. As they left the building, a rectangular outline appeared down the sidewalk, a soft light-brown fluorescence. Jane walked to it, pushed what appeared to be blank space, and ushered everyone through. Before she joined them, she glanced at the bystanders, including a CWN security guard, and waved.

"He's in there," said Fritz. Standing by what seemed to be school desks was the President of the United States.

"Take the cuffs off, Mel," he said. "Ms. Wise, I'm sorry we had to do this, but you need to know why it's important that you help us. Mr. Carter, nice to see you again. Please have a seat."

"Where are we?" asked Wise.

"I'll explain later. First, I want you to know you are in possession of vital information. Are you aware that Navy facilities were attacked and over three-hundred men and women killed?" He waited until she nodded. "Ms. Morgan was present at the ship bombings in San Diego and Norfolk. She took the only eyewitness film of both attacks. We also know she had an unusually large bank balance, money deposited over the past month." He stopped. He looked at Wise with a withering stare that chilled her. "Until you spoke to Mr. Carter this morning, we knew of no link between Morgan and Jonathan Hartmann. Other people now know you know. Dangerous people."

With her upper lip raised, Wise asked if they were calling Morgan responsible for the bombings.

"She took those pictures on someone's orders. She had received a great deal of money. Jonathan Hartmann's death is suspicious." The president pulled a chair in front of her and sat. "Ms. Wise, in my world, one and one still equals two. You can help make the equation work. Right now, it doesn't." The president stopped, allowing her to absorb his statement. She glanced through the window at the parking lot.

"All I know is that Caitlin was in love with Jonathan. She and I were friends. She had been offered promotions but turned them down. She traveled with him, so he told her to stay in her position because she could work remotely. But I can't believe she had any involvement with the ship bombings. She met him in Washington for New Year's. He kept his boat docked somewhere around San Diego."

"Did she ever mention any of the people she met with him?"

"Sure. He had parties, and she went to them. He took her everywhere." She brushed her hair back over her right ear. "I think he loved her too. But he was always busy."

"Where did they go together?" the president asked.

"They spent a lot of time on his boat. He always had guests. But he went all over the country. And all over the world. Caitlin went with him when she could take time off."

"Did she ever tell you about any unusual meetings or people?"

She frowned and took a deep breath. "I know what you want me to say, Mr. President, but frankly, I'm a little intimidated and nothing is coming to me right now. And I'm not in New York City. Where are we?"

The president ignored her question. "Mr. Carter, what brought Ms. Wise to your attention?"

Taken aback by the abrupt change of direction, Carter said that one of his staff members had seen her name on Facebook. "We were trying to get some personal information about a woman who died in government hands." The president nodded and frowned at the implicit criticism.

He asked if she had ever heard Caitlin mention the Caballeros. Her head jerked up, and she gasped. "Yes. They were his special buddies, Caitlin said. That's what she called them. She met them more than a few times."

"This could be important, Ms. Wise. Did she ever mention any names? Or say anything about them?"

"No." She hesitated. "But she did say they all had girl friends or women other than their wives with them. And they apparently came from around the world. They were wealthy. That's no surprise."

The president scratched gently behind his left ear and considered what had been said. When he didn't ask another question, Alan Carter asked, "Mr. President, can you tell me where we are? We're not in New York."

"Mr. Carter, Ms. Wise, we have discovered a new technology that allows us to connect locations. It's classified at the highest security level and before we're done, you will be sworn to secrecy."

"Mr. President? Am I in trouble?" Wise asked.

"Ms. Barclay is going to ask you some additional questions, and then you'll be free to go. You will be returned to Columbus Circle. Mr. Carter, if you would like to leave now, you may." Carter stood, knowing he had been dismissed. The president took two folded sheets of paper from his jacket. He handed one to the newsman and the other to James, who walked out. James handed the sheet to Fritz. "Carter's residence. Same as the Speaker."

"Got it," said Fritz. He went into his classroom.

The president and Alan Carter entered the hall at the same time as Fritz. The president waved for him to open the door. Carter stepped across the threshold with the president right behind. When the president returned, he said, "Fritz, reset it. I'm going back to his place." He remained longer and returned with a confident smile on his face.

"He got the message," said the president. "I don't think I'll need to do it with her." A couple of minutes later, Jane and Wise came out. Fritz had changed the map, so he opened the door, and Jane ushered her companion onto the streets of New York.

* * *

"MR. PRESIDENT, you know she's in danger now," said Jane, her lips tight.

"Can't be helped, Jane," he said.

"Why did you bring Carter?"

"We needed to move quickly. From what you'd said, I thought she would be unresponsive if she was alone. With him sitting with her, she had a buffer. I don't think he'll be saying anything that's believable."

Fritz listened to the conversation, unhappy that more people knew about the portal. "Did you get information you can use?" he asked.

"Yes. We need to concentrate on Hartmann and Morgan. We need good police work. And fast. James, you and Mel get teams set up. Put those devices in both their houses."

"Yes, sir. We'll need to find out all the locations." He paused. "Mr. President, that means not being in Riverboro." He glanced at Fritz.

"Get it started. Mary is there. Jane, you stay too. James, Mel, get the best, regardless of agency. Get them reassigned to temporary duty at the White House. This is 24/7, starting now. Go ahead." He gestured with his right hand. "Fritz, I want to talk to you."

With the agents gone and Jane and Tony waiting, Fritz and the president went into his classroom. The president asked if he could visit Robert E. Lee.

"Mr. President, I haven't tried since our dinner, but I don't think we'll be able to. In his time, five days after you met him, he had a stroke. He died two weeks later. Let's see."

Fritz located the book that had first brought him to the general at Appomattox. They returned to the hallway. Fritz said they were going to look for Lee and opened the door cautiously. The Civil War wasn't over.

"Mr. President, we should leave. The trees are whole, like the battle hasn't started. I don't know what day it is, but he's not here. Let's try his office." Turning to leave, a volley of cannons sent them running through the portal. Fritz reset it to Lee's office, but again, Lee wasn't there. They looked around the sparsely decorated room, where dust and cobwebs appeared to be the newest decoration.

"Mr. President, I think he's gone." His eyes moist, he felt his chest tighten. "I'd go further back, but you'd be in danger. Do you want to go somewhere else?"

"You know, Fritz, I think I'll go home. I just time traveled to the 1800s. That's enough excitement for now. Maybe some other time."

On the way home, Jane asked where they had gone. When Fritz told her, she shook her head. "He takes too many risks."

Chapter 12

"**DID YOU SEE** the interview?" asked the man. On the other side of the country, his associate stared at the top of the Washington Monument and said yes. "Does she know anything?" the man asked.

"She was a close friend of the Morgan woman. If CWN found her, there are bound to be other leaks."

"No names." The order was sharp, tinged with anger.

"Sorry."

Silence, then the disconnect. The man had two more problems.

* * *

JANE RETURNED to the files and her long-distance stare. At the kitchen table, Linda held TJ while Fritz told her about the president, Alan Carter, and the trips to find Lee. "He asked me, Lin."

"He's as bad as you. I'm glad Ash stayed here."

"Why?" asked Ashley, walking through the doorway.

"The three of you together would be out of control."

"Me? I'm a reliable, quiet, stay-at-home kind of guy."

"Shut up, Ashley" came from the dining room.

"And I always do what I'm told."

Jane read and reread throughout the afternoon, looking for anything that would match the Caballeros list. Fritz looked through each of Koppler's address books and compared each phone number to the list in front of him. In the fourth book, he spotted the name Boatman under H.

With the TV on in the next room, Fritz prepared lesson plans for the rest of January. With the presidential primaries beginning at the end of the month, the tournament only five-weeks away, and all the intrigue surrounding them, he wanted to be prepared as far ahead as possible. Engrossed in his work, he jumped when James tapped his shoulder.

"Sorry to startle you," James said. "Can you get me home?"

Fritz set down his pen. "Sure. Every year when I read about the lead-up to the Civil War, I get sucked in. It seems so obvious now, but it's hard to remember that the country was only fifty years old and still feeling political growing pains." He had just reread his notes on John C. Calhoun, the Tariff of Abominations, States' Rights, Nullification, and the Tenth Amendment. "Where are we headed?"

"My car's at the White House."

"Are you coming back tonight?"

"Not tonight." Catching Fritz's eye, he said, "This is going to be harder, a lot harder, than Koppler."

Already falling behind on another project and with three classes to prepare for, food for the multitudes wasn't on Linda's agenda. No new clues on the attacks had been found. To make matters worse, twelve inches of snow were predicted for the next day. Fritz, Ashley, and Tony had returned James and arrived home with dinner. Before they could remove their coats, Jane, with tears streaming down her cheeks, said, "TV."

A report from New York showed a blanket-covered body surrounded by policemen and flashing lights. The anchor, Alan Carter, paler than usual, stated that the woman had been his guest earlier in the day. Penelope Wise had fallen or jumped eight floors. She had left a note declaring her misery at the loss of her friend and partner, Caitlin Morgan.

Stunned, Fritz said, "That doesn't make sense."

"They didn't waste time. James has already sent a team to her apartment. I want to speak to anyone who knew her—parents, siblings, friends. Especially ex-boyfriends. I don't think she was Caitlin's partner. Wise said Caitlin had been involved with Boatman. I want to go myself and look."

"Jane, let's eat first," said Ashley, sitting in front of the TV.

"Maybe Alan Carter can help," said Fritz. Jane took her phone out and called the president. He told her he would set it up.

* * *

THEY MET CARTER at Penelope Wise's apartment. Ashley went with Mel and Jane.

"What are we looking for?" Ashley asked.

"Some indication that she and Caitlin were more than friends," Jane said. "Just in case the story about Caitlin and Hartmann was disinformation. Check especially for photos or other personal things." She turned to Carter. "Mr. Carter, I'd like your reporter's eye to see if you spot anything unusual."

"You mean more unusual than the rest of today?" he sighed. "I don't know what you expect to find."

The spacious two-bedroom apartment was furnished with Persian carpets, antique furniture, and solid walnut dressers. The closets, which had been fitted with built-in drawers and shelves, housed expensive clothing. But not one picture of Caitlin Morgan sat on tables or hung on walls.

They found a photo album in a closet drawer. Jane placed it on the antique secretary and turned to the back, looking for the most recent pictures. Again, no picture of Jen Wise and Caitlin Morgan, although she had photos of vacations, parties, and holidays.

“This is very strange,” said Carter. “Not a thing. And it doesn’t look like anything has been disturbed. It’s like she flew out the window.”

Jane stared at Carter with the look that meant she was about to make a call.

“Mr. President, I know the M.E. is far from finished, but can you have the mayor ask if she was dead before she hit the sidewalk.” She listened. “Mr. Carter made an observation.” She turned to the anchor. “Yes, sir.” She closed the connection. “He said to say thanks.”

“Jane, no sign of forced entry, no struggle,” Mel said. “We have the security camera film. Let’s go.”

“How come I’ve never heard your name before?” Carter asked Jane as they headed for the door.

“Mr. Carter, I’m a forensic analyst. I thought you might have a sense of Ms. Wise given that you spent some time with her. You’re a pretty good interviewer.”

She smiled. Ashley could almost see ropes or tentacles extend to wrap up her prey. He watched the CWN anchor lean slightly forward and smile back.

She has him. Does he have a clue? Did she do that to me?

* * *

THEY SAW CARTER home and called Fritz to reopen the portal. Driving from the school, Ashley said, “With so many details floating right now, it’s almost impossible to sort them.”

“That’s why I make lists,” Fritz said, navigating slowly through the large snowflakes that had begun falling. Turning into the driveway, Fritz slid sideways. Jane bumped her head on the window. “I’m fine,” she said. Ashley told her again that she was accident-prone.

Fritz sat at the kitchen table telling Linda how crazy things were. She said she didn’t see normal returning any time soon. Leaning back, he sighed, longing for a cigarette, a feeling that had come more frequently in the past month. Ashley joined them. He asked if Jane could leave the papers on the table because they were going home. Mel and Tony were going with them. When Fritz opened the front door, the swirling snow had piled calf-deep on the walk. He hated to disturb it.

The house had a residual hum. Fritz brought his laptop and a yellow pad to the kitchen. Thumbing through the folders, he scribbled a new note for each class. Linda focused on the latest manuscript from her publisher, trying to speed up her review. Behind her on the counter, two stacks waited patiently for their turn. She looked like she was smoking her pen.

"Stop staring at me," she said. "You're distracting me." They both remembered other times when they stared at each other and wouldn't have stayed in the kitchen long.

"I'm not staring. I'm thinking."

"If I didn't have so much to do, I'd ask what you were thinking." She smiled.

"I can tell you. I was thinking I love you and tomorrow's Sunday." They drifted into their own thoughts. Saying that he loved her was easy. It was true. He had fallen for her at their second cup of coffee, but he didn't say it for a long time. He was afraid of chasing her away. She had felt his hesitance. She knew his stint with Teach for America would end, and then he'd be gone. But she didn't give up easily. He was comfortable to talk to. And he was cute. This one had the potential to be a keeper.

He rose early when he heard the baby cry. On a clear day, the sky would be visible, but the snow reflected all available light back to the clouds. "Come on, buddy." He changed TJ's diaper, took him to the kitchen, and turned on the coffee. With TJ on his lap, he headed to a news website. A story about Penelope Wise quoted her parents. They said they had never heard of Caitlin Morgan and had no idea, as her father said, "that she liked girls."

Fritz looked for other stories, bookmarking them all. They sat in the window seat, watching the blowing snow.

Chapter 13

AS SUNRISE APPROACHED, the president studied the white blanket on the lawn. He had read the story of another dead woman. His jaw tight and lips pressed, he knew he was partly responsible for her death. He should have moved her out of harm's way. He put his cup to his lips not knowing that Fritz was doing the same.

* * *

WITH TJ IN the swing, Fritz spread his yellow pads on the table. He breathed deeply and closed his eyes. "Compartmentalize," he said to himself. He started with the tournament, now less than five weeks away. With a random number generator, he paired the forty-four teams to determine the schedule. *That was easy.* He made a note to collect the team names. *I'll bet the kids already have them.*

Not knowing who might show up for breakfast, he took out the waffle iron and began to mix batter. He was enjoying the quiet time. His thoughts drifted, like the snow on the window ledge. He was startled when Linda said, "Good morning."

"Hi, Lin. I was wandering."

"I know. I've been here for three minutes. Good smells woke me."

"Sorry. I was getting hungry, so I figured I'd get started. Want a waffle?"

"Not just yet." She kissed TJ's head and looked out at the winter portrait. "I don't think there will be much going on today."

Mary McElroy in jeans and a sweatshirt poked her head around the corner, rubbing her eyes. "Sorry, folks, I overslept." She gazed at the backyard. When Fritz asked if she wanted breakfast, she said, "Just coffee for now. I haven't seen this much snow in a while, at least not without skis."

Fritz asked, "Mary, do you want to go home? I mean to Washington?" Linda glanced up, wondering why he was asking.

Mary shook her head. "This is like a vacation. I mean, look at me. I couldn't be wearing jeans. Don't get me wrong. I love my job. But the long hours. And always, a gun." She gently patted her sweatshirt.

"FRITZ, WHAT are you up to?" Linda asked.

His eyebrows raised in feigned innocence, he said, "Me? Nothing." The crunch of waffle took her eyes off him.

"That sounds good. I'll make myself one," said Mary. "Linda?" Linda nodded.

The thumping of a snowplow reminded Fritz to get the snow blower from the garage. He parked the thought in the list of things called "Later." When the doorbell rang, he set down his fork. Ashley and Jane had trudged up the walk. A moment of snow-flecked wind blew past him when Jane opened the storm door. Red scarves covering red cheeks, they hustled into the warmth.

"It's cold out," said Ashley. "Some people bother to clear a path."

"It's only eight o'clock," said Fritz. "Come on in, Jane." Fritz turned toward the kitchen. "Jane, toss your stuff in the family room. Leave him there."

"Well, then, I won't make the snowman I planned," Ashley responded.

"Shut up. Breakfast is waffles. Why are you out so early anyway?"

Jane said, "The president called at six-thirty. He said to watch the TV news shows. He thinks something is cooking."

Ashley told them that he and Jane had shoveled for half an hour to free their car. "We have a while. Get some coffee and tell us," said Fritz. She cloaked her warm cup with her cold hands, and related her conversation.

Before Fritz sat down again, he got dressed and called Jim Shaw, inviting him for breakfast. He took over the waffle iron and made a stack, brown and crispy, and put them in the oven. Waffles took him to childhood, when his mom taught him to maneuver in the kitchen. He wasn't much help now. Linda made meals that looked like magazine photos. Fritz helped sometimes, peeling potatoes or carrots, or grating cheese or cabbage, but mostly he stuck to making breakfast. Still too early for the news shows, Fritz donned his down coat and prepared for a tussle with the still-blowing snow.

"Save me one," he said.

He shivered at his first step into snow almost up to his knees. High-stepping to the garage, he was able to get the snow blower started right away, and he pushed his way to the street. He had to lift the machine to get through the pile where the driveway had been plowed in. The first run created a walkway, and as he finished the path to the front door, Jim Shaw pulled up in his own car.

"Hi, Jim. Follow me to the back door while I do the driveway."

"Mr. R, you need to cover your face. You're getting frostbite."

"I think I'll go in for a bit. Do you know what the temperature is?"

"Below ten, and with the wind, maybe below zero. You're totally not dressed for this."

"Maybe my ears will fall off." He smiled and regretted it when his lips stuck to his teeth for a moment.

"Hi, Jim," said Linda, shivering as the cold blew in with him.

"Hi, everyone," he said, looking around the table. Seeing a new face, he stopped short.

"Jim Shaw, meet Mary McElroy," said Linda. "Mary, Jim Shaw." Jim reached out his gloved hand, but pulled back and took the glove off.

"Too cold to do it all at once," said Fritz. "I'll have another waffle and finish after."

"Some of us are hardier folk," Ashley said. "You'd never have survived prairie winters. We put you to shame."

"I forgot. You're supposed to be out on the front landing. Why did I let you in? Remind me."

"To try to poison me with your cooking? Just a guess."

Linda took Jim's coat, told him to sit in the corner seat. "Make Jim a waffle, and then have your second breakfast, Frodo."

Ashley raised his hands, fingers wiggling at Jim. "Poof. You are now a waffle."

Mary walked to the counter, and said she would make them. Jim watched every movement she made.

"Mary, Jim is one of the officers who helped rescue the president in Geneva," Linda said. Jim frowned. "Mary is a Secret Service agent, Jim. The president wanted us to have extra protection."

Jim nodded, not taking his eyes off Mary. She watched and then smiled. "Oops." Batter missed the waffle iron. Jim and Mary sneaked peeks at each other. Fritz stared at Linda, and her grin made him think he had done the right thing.

* * *

THE SPEAKER WAS on two of the major Sunday programs. He noted his concern about the slow pace of the inquiry into the ship bombings and that the administration had not yet found the attackers. Later, he said he fully supported the president's planned summit agenda and hoped for a solution to the Middle East conflict. He said he expected all the governments of the region to participate.

"Why do you think that?"

"The president can be very persuasive."

On the second show, asking his reaction to the death of Jonathan Hartmann, the host noted that Hartmann had been an outspoken supporter of the Speaker and a significant campaign contributor. Jane reached for a pad.

The snow continued, and the plows blocked the driveway again. Another street plow came by, but the driver saw the dirty look Ashley gave him, and placed the blade at the edge of the pile and pushed it all out of the way. Ashley waved, put the shovel over his shoulder, and followed Fritz back and forth up and down the driveway.

"You're just gonna follow me?" Fritz asked.

"I'm done," he said, pointing to the cleared entrance. "What's taking you so long?" Fritz turned the chute and covered him with snow.

As Ashley shook off, Fritz said, "Ash, this place is a zoo. I'm worried about how we're using the portal. We won't be able to use it again, fortunately, until this snow stops."

They came in to a very quiet house. The TV was background noise, and TJ was gurgling in his swing. Linda looked up from her books and told Fritz to mop the floor.

Jane was holding the list in front of her, her head swiveling, and her lips moving. "This is a numerical nightmare," she said. "If I can match any of these with one of Hartmann's phone numbers, we have the key. But I'm not sure these are phone numbers." She turned back to the table. Ashley said it scared him when she did that. "It's like she's talking in her sleep," he said.

Mel was watching a repeat of a talk show. Jim and Mary were talking in the sunroom. Ashley said, "Greetings, Professor Falken. How about a nice game of chess?" By the late afternoon of the most uneventful Sunday in what felt like months, Fritz realized he hadn't had lunch, nor had anyone else. Linda sat at the kitchen table, talking with Jane, a copy of the Caballeros list in front of her. Jane's eyes were bloodshot, but she managed a tired smile when he came to the table.

"You found something," Fritz said.

"I think so. Actually, Linda did. These are phone numbers, all right. Each one on the list has its own number also." Linda pushed the sheet over so he could see. "It's a formula."

"How did you figure that out?"

Linda said, "It's from a spy novel. A writer I worked with. Jane showed me where she got stuck. Fritz, I can't believe we could be that lucky. I only read the book to get a feel of how he wrote. And it wasn't a big seller."

"Do the numbers match up?

"I called," said Jane. "Got an answering machine or voice mail. A woman's voice. I called the president. We can track the number, and I'll bet that it was Caitlin Morgan's voice. We're getting tapes of the interrogation. Maybe voice analysis can tie them together."

Chapter 14

"**YOU'RE EARLY,**" Ashley said, walking into Fritz's classroom on Tuesday morning.

Fritz returned his gaze to his notes. Ashley interrupted him again.

"Jane was up most of the night. I think she wants to be in Washington." Fritz lifted his head when he heard the tone.

"Is something wrong?"

"I don't know. She's distracted, and I think she misses the action. It's almost too domestic here." Sadness was speaking, the same sadness that Fritz had seen briefly each time a woman had left Ashley's life.

"She's got a lot on her plate, Ash. And she's tired. So are you. That's probably all it is."

"This is what I was afraid of. That she'd get bored here."

"Ash, sit down. Look at me. How can she be bored? We, all of us, haven't had a quiet moment in almost half a year. But if it worries you, you need to tell her what you think. You can't be a loner when you're married." Ashley's droop-eyed misery stunned Fritz. "You're still getting married, aren't you?"

"I don't know."

"Maybe you need some time by yourselves. No bombings, no babysitting. Just you and Jane. Ash, talk to her."

His World History classes had already reached the 1800s. His train of thought about European wars continued as he discussed Napoleon. But he enjoyed most the discussion of the westward movement in his U.S. history course—wagon trains, steamboats and railroads. The rest of the year would be busy, but fun. At the end of the day, after a discussion of *Marbury v. Madison*, his ninth-graders didn't leave at the bell.

"What's up, guys?"

"We have a surprise, Mr. R," said Susan. "Then we'll get the mail." Heads turned to Ted, his pale cheeks turning a deepening pink.

"I spoke to Mr. Montgomery last night. He said the Phillies would donate $10,000 and that he had told a bunch of Phillies sponsors and will let me know how much they'll donate. Mr. R, he didn't say if, but how much!" Reserved clapping told Fritz the story wasn't complete. "He said he'll have a surprise for the final game. Some Phillies will be the pitchers. The class erupted. They were so loud, Ashley yanked the door open and ran in.

"What happened?" he asked.

"Ted, why don't you tell him?" Before the story could be repeated, George scurried through the door.

"I heard noise. What's going on?" The door opened again. Tom Jaffrey and Liz Chambers came in.

"Looks like you have an audience, Ted." Fritz smiled.

"Does he have a fever?" George asked. The kids laughed.

"He's fine, Mr. McAllister," Fritz said. "But he has a good story. Go on, Ted." When the story reached its punch line, the class cheered as loudly as before.

"I could hear you in the office," said George. "I guess that's very good. I'm glad everything's all right." He turned to leave, but Liz Chambers grabbed his shoulder.

"George, did you hear the story? The Phillies and their sponsors are donating."

"Yes, well, um, uh, I must have missed that. I'm glad everything is all right."

"George," Liz said, "the kids did this. No teachers."

"Yes, that's very good." He waved at the class staring at him.

"I'll tell you about it later," said Fritz. "See you then." The principal left. The teachers looked at each other and started to laugh.

Fritz turned to the kids. "Thank you all. This is great for the school and the whole town. You know what? I think you should all go home now. The mail will be here tomorrow. And no homework."

The teachers formed a greeting line and all four shook hands with the students as they left.

"What is wrong with that man?" asked Liz.

"Don't worry, Liz. When has he ever been different?" Ashley said.

"I better go down and explain it to him," said Fritz.

"George, what's wrong?"

"I thought someone was hurt, or worse. That cheer came down the hall like a tsunami. Lockers were rattling."

"I think the kids scare you George. Why is that?"

"Just getting old, I guess. I've been in schools now for almost forty years. And I worry about everything. Lois knows. She'll tell you. Did you say the Phillies have donated?"

"Ted O'Neil spoke to the Phillies chairman, who told him the Phillies would donate $10,000. He told Ted that he had roped in the team's sponsors, and he would call Ted to tell him how much they would give." George was listening, wide-eyed. "And for the championship, our pitchers will be Phillies players."

George whispered, "This could be big, Fritz."

* * *

WHEN FRITZ REACHED home, he watched the flakes gather and melt on the windshield before going in. A line of cars fronted the house, so the usual suspects greeted him when he walked in the back door. Ashley was in the middle of a story. Linda followed him to the hall closet.

He whispered, "Hi honey. I'm home."

She smiled and kissed him. "They all like being here, Fritz. I'll never get anything done."

"I'll pick up dinner and keep them occupied. Can you work in a bedroom? I think we still have an extra. Or the sunroom?"

"I don't want to be rude."

"Lin, they know how much you have to do." He cocked his head. "Is anything going on?"

"The voices match. Hartmann appears to have been one of the Caballeros. Jane sent the other numbers to the NSA this afternoon. A puncture on the Wise woman's neck was detected, like a needle. No autopsy results yet."

"Did anyone mention the summit meeting?"

"No.

"Fritz, do you know what's wrong with Ash?" she asked in a low voice.

"Fear of losing Jane." Whispering, he filled her in.

"He really is nuts. I see her almost as much as he does. We talk. She's crazy about him. But don't tell him."

* * *

WHEN THEY GOT home, Ashley said, "I need to talk to you."

"Sure. Go ahead." Jane sank into a cushion. "We need a new couch, Ash. This one's shot."

"We?" he asked.

"Of course, we. You'll need one to sleep on when we fight. Isn't that how it's supposed to work? So what's up?"

Ashley took a step back. "I want to know if you still want to marry me?"

Her eyes widened. "Why would you think I wouldn't?"

"You just seem so distant. You stay up half the night, and you're at the computer before I'm awake."

"Ash, I've never needed a lot of sleep. You know what's happening now. It's my job." She gazed deep into his eyes. "Of course, I want to marry you. But you have something else you want to tell me. Out with it."

"I've lost girlfriends before. I mean, they died."

"Have you ever told Fritz and Linda?" she asked, tears lining her cheeks, his pain so palpable.

"You're the only person I've ever told." He wiped his right eye. "That's why I get scared every time you go into danger. Jane, I don't want to lose you, and you have so little regard for your own safety."

"And you, who faced terrorists and rescued me, twice, not to mention saved the president, are the epitome of caution?" She put her arms around his neck, and drew as close as she could to kiss him with a passion that lifted his spirit and his toes. When she loosened her hold, the sparkle in his eyes had returned, a gentle smile on his face. "Ash, I love you, and when this craziness is over, we'll get to spend some real time together. I think it's time you met my mother."

Chapter 15

THE PRESIDENT STOOD in front of the mirror examining his hairline. "These weren't here yesterday," he said, poking at some new gray hairs.

As he entered the hall, the vice president exited the elevator. "We have pictures from San Diego," he said. "They stopped in a strip mall. A motion sensor camera caught them with hoods down." The facial analysis was still sketchy, but one person had been identified as a North Korean colonel tied to a trade delegation in Cuba."

"Who else knows?"

"John, Charlie, Jim Beech, and the FBI."

"Does anyone know where this colonel is now?"

"Charlie said the agency is on the ground, looking for him in Havana."

Before opening the door to his office, the president said, "I think we have another job for Fritz."

* * *

THE PINK OCEAN portended the kind of news the man disliked. *Sailor, take warning,* he thought. He hated puzzles. When puzzles turned up, the most persistent would battle to solve them. To safely cloak his anonymity, he had learned from his grandfather when he was very young to leave clues that went nowhere. His father had taught him to leave no loose ends. They had left him the money to do both. But to maintain his invisibility, he was forced to rely on so many lesser beings. Too bad about the women, he thought, but then shrugged. Loose ends gone. A soft vibration in his pocket disturbed his reverie. "Where did you find him?" he asked. He gritted his teeth. "Bring him to me." He stared out at the glimmer of the waves as the sun split the horizon.

* * *

FRITZ TOLD the second period class that he considered the Berlin Blockade and airlift a highlight event in the Cold War. Its success reflected on that entire generation. "Let's review it quickly, and I'll add some details. You read about how Germany, and Berlin, were split into four sectors." He pulled down one of the old maps hanging over the blackboard. "Russian, French, British and American. Berlin was cut in half since it had been the capital, but it was completely inside the Soviet sector. West Berlin couldn't get food or anything else when the USSR cut off all the roads leading into the city." He tapped the map with a yardstick. "Beginning in June, 1948, the Allies flew cargo planes into Berlin. The first day, thirty-two planes brought in eighty tons of food and supplies. When it became clear that the blockade would last, they flew in heavy equipment and built two new airports. Once they got going, they could load flights so fast they took off every four minutes. The ground crews in Berlin competed and a ten-ton cargo was unloaded in under six minutes. The airlift was so successful, and so embarrassing to the Soviets that they lifted the blockade in May '49. By the end, more supplies arrived in Berlin every day than had come by train and truck before the blockade began." He leaned against his desk.

"Mr. R," said Eric. "I read that we would have helped the Russians rebuild Berlin and East Germany with the Marshall Plan, but the Russians refused."

"True, Eric. They were unwilling to accept the terms we insisted on in exchange for loans. I have a couple of handouts for homework. One is about the Marshall Plan and the other is about the blockade and airlift."

When the bell rang, Fritz thumbed through his notes for his next classes. Looking through the textbook, he flipped to pictures of the Alamo and thought about the movies he had seen. He placed a paperclip on the page. The face in the window came in and asked, "Where are you going?"

"Hi Ash. Nowhere. Just marking the Alamo. I have a lecture about the Mexican War in the next couple of weeks.

"And you're going to try to see the Alamo. I know you, Fritz."

"I hadn't planned on it. Wanna go?"

"You're proving you're crazy."

* * *

ANXIETY BANGED on past the middle of January. The investigations continued. Fritz avoided baseball in class since the tournament was so close. Ashley worked with Eric and Jean to finalize the scripts for the play and supervised the first rehearsals so Fritz could go home early.

"Linda," said Mary, "Jim has asked me on a date. He wants to take me to the range and then for dinner."

"Now that sounds really romantic. When does this torrid affair take place?"

"He kind of left it up to me. An evening or a weekend, whenever Jane can be here."

"We'll be fine, either way. You really don't need to be here all the time, Mary. It's not like we're a national secret or anything."

"Aside from the fact that you are, the president gave me explicit instructions. Until the bombing case is solved, I'm supposed to watch like a hawk and be sure someone else is here when I'm not."

"A few hours can't hurt. Why don't you tell Jim that Saturday night is fine. At least it's a date night. Tell him you talked with me, and I suggested the Old Lion Inn for dinner." She chuckled. "That'll set the bar high enough for him."

"Is it nice?"

"Nicest around. Food's spectacular."

* * *

"NEXT WEEK, THE Iowa Caucuses will begin the presidential selection process," Fritz said to his ninth graders. "Two weeks later, we'll have the New Hampshire primary. What's important about them?"

Ted raised his hand, and his face grew pink. Fritz smiled and pointed to his formerly diffident student. "I don't think either of them are important this year."

"That's an interesting take, Ted. Explain, please." Everyone listened to their new class leader.

"Well, so many people are running, on both sides, that the votes are going to be split all over the place. Also, neither New Hampshire nor Iowa is large enough to make a difference, except maybe for getting people to drop out. Then it's about raising money."

"Good answer, Ted."

"For homework..." The boos were loud. "Stop it," Fritz chuckled. "For homework, two things. I want you to read about the changes in the election process, pages 232-241, and I want you to predict the winners in the Iowa Caucuses and the New Hampshire primary. Have a nice weekend."

* * *

FRITZ ARRIVED HOME to what appeared to be a fashion show, with one model, Mary McElroy. Linda and Jane were smiling. Mel was studying.

"Hi, honey, I'm home. What's going on?"

"Mary's got a date tomorrow with Jim, so we went shopping," said Linda.

Mary's black dress reminded Fritz of Jane's cocktail party dress getting ruined in the Israeli rescue.

Jane's phone buzzed.

"Jane, have you heard of Georg Badenhof?" asked the president. "He just landed at the bottom of a fifty-story building."

"International chemical business. That's the second rich guy in a month, sir. I wonder if he had any connection to Hartmann," she said, speaking mostly to herself.

"A dead man was discovered on the roof of the building too. Shot. Unregistered gun, no ID. No fingerprint identification yet. The bureau is checking the guy out."

"A rich guy jumps off a tall building after shooting another guy. Mr. President, that doesn't make sense. I think we have a third person involved. Just a feeling."

"A feeling or a logical conclusion? I'll talk to you later."

* * *

WHEN FRITZ WALKED to the kitchen, Jane called Ashley, and they both sat at the table. She asked Fritz and Linda to sit, that Ashley had a story to tell them. They could tell he was reluctant, staring at his hands. "Ash, this is more important than a football game. Tell them."

He looked from Fritz to Linda, took a deep breath and said, "I've never told this to anyone. I only told Jane a few days ago." He took a long breath. "You know I haven't had long relationships. Well, when I was in high school, I was in love with a girl who I had known since third grade. She was killed waiting to cross the street. When I was in college, I had a girlfriend, who was shot and killed coming to meet me. You remember Andrea Porter. She left teaching because she had cancer. She died, too. All those other women over the years … I was afraid something would happen to them, so I kept it short."

"I'm glad you told us," said Linda. "That explains a lot. It also says just how important Jane is to you."

With the floodgate opened, Ashley told the whole story, including details he hadn't yet told Jane. Tears, waiting for years, spilled. Fritz grabbed the tissue box.

"There's something else," Jane said. "Get it out, Ash."

"No easy way to say this. I killed my brother. On that hunting trip, I'm the one who shot him." He told them that his brother had separated from them and was playing in some bushes. Ashley had called out, but before anyone could stop him, he'd pulled the trigger. "My parents haven't really ever forgiven me."

Fritz dabbed his eyes with his shirt sleeve. With TJ on his lap, Fritz looked at Ashley and then at Jane.

"Jane, you're the best thing that's ever happened to him. Do me a favor? Let someone else jump in front of bullets from now on."

"Yeah," said Ashley, smiling again.

"Not married yet, and you're already trying to change me," Jane said.

A LITTLE PAST midnight, they heard the key rattle in the front door. No one left the table. Most of the lights were dimmed or turned off, but Mary knew everyone was up. She invited Jim in, and they headed to the kitchen.

"Hi, Mr. R," said Jim.

"Have a good time?"

Mary said they did.

"I'm on tomorrow early, so I better get going," Jim said. He and Mary went to the front door.

"I guess we'll be seeing a lot more of Jim Shaw," said Fritz.

* * *

"FRITZ, IF IT'S okay, Ash and I will bring breakfast." Jane's calling so early had his immediate attention. "The president called an hour ago. He's on Alan Carter's show this morning. He's announcing the summit for early March."

"Sure. What time did you get up?" he yawned.

"He called at 6:15, but he's not on until eleven. A half-hour segment. Exclusive."

"Payment for the kidnapping." On a new pad, he wrote "Summit—Early March." He took out his pad for the tournament. The beginning of March, he thought, the second round. But because he didn't know the exact dates, all he could do was wait. Or call the President.

"Good morning, Mr. Russell," said the cheerful voice of Lily Evans. "How's TJ today."

"He's doing fine, thanks. Having breakfast right now." Fritz grinned. She always asked. "Does he have a minute?"

"I'll tell him you're on the line. Hold a moment, please."

Fritz said he wanted to know about the dates for the summit because the tournament would be going by then.

"Fritz, I expect an invite to the finals. The summit will be on Saturday and Sunday. We can use the school without overlapping."

"Mr. President, I want to say something." He paused to make sure it came out the way he wanted. "Ms. Evans has to be the best mood setter for anyone who calls you. No one could be upset after talking to her."

"Home-court advantage, Fritz." He laughed. "I'll tell her you mentioned it."

As concerned as he was about the approaching tournament, Fritz was unable to avoid the Sunday interviews with primary candidates from both parties. For the first time in eight years, both parties had candidates in the Iowa caucuses. The three-year build-up had produced multiple candidates, including two women, one a business executive, the other a former U.S. senator and secretary of state. One Sunday host said that by the time he had a chance to interview them all, half would already have dropped out. Another story was the death of yet another very rich man. The guest said he wondered if the ninety-nine percenters had finally gone too far.

* * *

A FILLER STORY just before a commercial mentioned the strange deaths of two businessmen heavily involved in the global economy. The man listened as the guests expressed sorrow and condolences for people they didn't know. Not a regular viewer, he was waiting for the president's live interview. He had been alerted earlier that the president had a major announcement.

* * *

AFTER THE TV FANFARE, the theme song, the neon introductions, Alan Carter introduced the president, live from the White House. Carter asked if the president had good news.

"Alan, I certainly hope so. For the first time, the world truly has a chance to see peace in the Middle East. On March 5 and 6, the United States will present a comprehensive approach to ending more than a century of warfare. Leaders from around the world will be attending." The seriousness of his statement was followed by a smile.

"Mr. President, can you tell us yet who will be attending?"

"Not yet, Alan, but we will release the schedule of events in the next couple of weeks. The response thus far has been very positive. I look forward to making the program public."

"Mr. President, I can say from personal experience, you can be convincing."

* * *

THE BEAUTIFUL DAY IN California didn't interest the man. As soon as he heard the dates for the summit, he made a phone call. "Get them ready. Plan a meeting and social gathering. Golf bags. The Hay-Adams. February 28 to March 7, eight rooms on the same floor. The higher the better. Do it now." *How can I be so fortunate?*

Chapter 16

JANE WAS SMILING. "Fritz, he just put the world on notice. The questions were a plant. Alan Carter was willing to help."

"What's he doing, Jane?" asked Linda.

"Setting up the NSA phone surveillance. They have the numbers I gave them. If someone is trying to mess with him, the phones on the list should get busy quickly."

"You mean he wasn't just announcing the summit?"

"We already have the invitations out, and everyone has already responded. The president suggested putting a prefab room inside the classroom. It could be assembled on Friday night and taken down on Sunday."

"George will have a canary," said Ashley. "How are you going to do that?"

"Lois," Jane said. "We've already set up a weekend vacation for them. Flying in family from Austin and California."

* * *

FRITZ NEEDED to deal with the portal and the room across the hall. Each project needed George's approval, and then he would need to coordinate. More of his time, and it was running out. "Compartmentalize," he reminded himself. He headed to the office as soon as he got to school. The principal didn't give the week an easy start.

"Fritz, how can you ask me to do all this? I'm as busy as you are. How do you know we'll need the cafeteria? Maybe no one will come."

"You saw the kids. They filled the auditorium. We may not have a full house every game, but the parents and the sponsors are likely to show up for the final rounds. My ninth graders have already started an advertising campaign for the entire schedule."

"You can't let them run wild. Advertising, charging admission, using the school all the time. I'll never get home. The phone barely stops ringing now."

"It's not easy for either of us, George. Say yes or no, but I need to know. I'll take care of the details. We're out of time." Fritz realized his voice was louder than it should be, and George was already turning crimson. "Sorry, George. I need to know."

"I have to think about the cost and review the legal issue of charging admission. I'll talk to you later."

"Dammit, George. We charge to get into football and basketball games. What's the difference?"

"I have things to do right now. If you'll excuse me."

Fritz slammed the door as he left. After the last bell, he returned to the office to apologize to George.

"I accept your apology."

"George, I'm juggling time, and I don't have much. I have to give the kids information about where the tournament stands and the president needs to set up for the summit. We need to let the workers get started. I'll take care of it. But you have to decide on this stuff."

"Okay, but the costs for the cafeteria, the auditorium, and the room can't come from my budget."

"The president said he would take care of the room. If we collect admission, we can use it to pay the other costs of the tournament." Fritz hurried back to his room, trying to remember when he wouldn't have been bothered by any of this. David Jewels was waiting for him.

"Hi Mr. R. Can I talk to you for a minute?"

"Sure, David, what's up?" He was talking to a student who was now taller than he was.

"I wanted to ask about General Lee. I saw you with him at Starbucks. He was real, Mr. R. That wasn't any projection. Did we really time-travel?"

"Sit down, David." *Now what do I do?* "How old are you now, David?"

"Seventeen."

"Two-hundred years ago, that would be old enough for you to be on your own, get married, have a family, maybe move to the wilderness. Open a store or study a profession or a trade. Today, you're a student in school, getting ready to go to college. And you're old enough to go to prison as an adult." David listened intently. "David, wait for me in the hall, please."

Fritz took out his phone. "Hi, Tony. Can you come to the school now, with the equipment?" He listened to a quick response. "Tell you when you get here. Thanks." Then he dialed another number. "Hi, Mrs. Evans, is he available?"

When the president picked up, Fritz said, "A student cornered me. He saw me with Lee at Starbucks. He's old enough to go to prison, if you get my meaning. Can you help? Will you be there in a half hour? See you then. Thanks."

From his window, Fritz saw the new SUV pull into the parking lot. When he left the room, David was waiting. "Are we going to see the general, Mr. R?" David's freckles looked like they were jumping. They walked to the parking-lot door, now locked for the evening, as Tony pulled to the curb.

"No, David. How's the tournament coming?"

"My team's doing really well. We practice a hundred questions a day. We're not telling anyone. We think we can win."

"Hi Fritz. What's up?" Looking sideways at David, he raised an eyebrow.

"Tony, this is David Jewels."

"Hello, David."

"Hi, Mr. Almeida."

Tony checked the parking lot before unloading. "I guess I'm not so unforgettable."

Fritz told Tony he had been caught this time. They were going to see the president. Tony set up the generator and hooked up the doorknob. Fritz and David went into the classroom. David stood by as Fritz placed a paperclip on a brochure for a White House tour.

"Come with me, David." Once in the hallway, Fritz pulled the door open and took a step. In front of him, the president was crossing the Oval Office.

"Come in, come in. Happy you could stop by."

"David Jewels, I would like to introduce the president." David held his breath as he shook hands.

"You look a bit startled, David. I know how you feel. I felt the same way the first time Mr. Russell walked through the portal and found me here. Won't you take a seat?"

Although David was speechless, Fritz said, "Sorry to take your time, Mr. President. David was in the class that met General Lee. He saw him again when Lee came to Riverboro and was asking how that happened."

"Pretty cool, huh, David?" Seeing the student's obvious confusion, he patted David's shoulder. "Now, you and I need to discuss national security. You're the only student who knows, David. And I am going to ask you to swear an oath that you will discuss this with no one, not parents, not friends, not anyone. Mr. Russell will be giving me your address and phone number. Do you agree?" Still stunned, David nodded. "You need to say it out loud."

"Yes, sir, Mr. President."

"Good. Now that we've taken care of business, can I get you a soda?"

David looked again at Fritz, who shook his head. "Mr. President, we won't keep you. But if you would allow it, could David talk to me about this?"

"Good idea. David, you may talk only to Mr. Russell, who I give permission to tell you more. David, you have just portaled through space. Kind of like surfing. Except you don't get wet. Now if you'll excuse me, I'm planning to save the world." Leading them to the door, he shook David's hand again and told him he was a member of a special group of people.

"Mr. President," said Fritz. "Indulge me a moment. David, take a look around and absorb it all. This is **the** Oval Office. That is **the** Resolute desk. I'll tell you more about that later. That document on the wall is **the** Emancipation Proclamation. David, this is a special place." David was too stunned to look very hard. "Time to go."

Dazed by his encounter, David said goodbye. Ashley was talking with Tony in the hallway when the door opened. He waved to the president but said nothing.

"Let's go in, David. Tony, Ash, come with us."

"Mr. Russell, did that really happen? Were we really at the White House?"

"What do you think, David?"

"It sure felt real. He looked like the president. He even felt real."

This was the moment Fritz had dreaded. Did he continue lying to his student, or tell him the truth? "David, you remember what Mr. Almeida told you last spring? About the projection system." David nodded. "And you remember we discussed time-travel as one option?" David nodded again. "David, what you just witnessed—" Fritz could feel his insides churn, "what you just did, was real."

"Mr. R, does that mean," he paused, "I spoke to Robert E. Lee, really?"

"David, last year, I was hit by the lightning that hit the school. Remember?" David nodded. "The day we went to Appomattox, I got a shock when I grabbed the doorknob. We found out later that some kind of connection lets me open a portal to the past or a tunnel in the present. Tony works for the government, not Hollywood. And that's all the truth."

"Mr. R, how have you kept this secret? It's cool, but how do you know when it's going to happen? Does it only work at school? Have you gone anywhere else?" The questions poured out.

"David, those are all good questions. I appreciate how quickly they came to you. Some of them I can't answer, and the rest will have to wait. I will tell you that I saw John Wilkes Booth at Ford's Theater and met William Shakespeare. That was General Lee at Starbucks. And you just shook hands with the president." David rubbed his hand.

On the way home, Fritz called the president to thank him. "Mr. President, I had to decide. I hate lying to the kids, and David is impressed and scared enough to be quiet. The story is still so unbelievable that no one would swallow it."

"I'm not concerned about him, Fritz. We're looking at the phone traffic after my interview. So far, there hasn't been much. But we have a line on one of the ship bombers. If we can find him, I may need your help again."

* * *

WHEN HIS STUDENTS were gone, a stranger entered. "Are you Mr. Russell?"

"I am. Can I help you?"

"Sir, my name is Milt Chelton. I'm in charge of refitting the room across the hall. We want to start on the floor as soon as possible. I was told to speak to you."

"Have you seen Mr. McAllister?"

"He's the one who said to see you. Mr. Russell," he looked around, "Tom Andrews was my friend for twenty years. I'm an agent. The crew is mainly from the service or the ops group at the airport. I know. The president said I should tell you."

"Thanks. You understand that I can't help you do it. And it can't be done when the kids are here, Mr. Chelton."

"Call me Milt."

"Thanks, I'm Fritz. We have a wrinkle. Next week, we start a tournament, so people will be here until early evening. That leaves you nights and weekends."

"We'd planned to do it at night."

"Starting when?"

Tomorrow, if possible. We want to get the supplies inside."

Fritz shook his hand and headed to the office. George frowned when he saw Fritz coming.

"I was leaving."

"I know. I'll be quick. The construction guys are going to start tomorrow. And we're going to need the auditorium every day." George was quiet. "We'll have two or three games a day. About an hour each. That will clear the school by dinnertime. I've spoken to Joe Pettinelli. He agreed to help."

"I hope this works. I keep getting calls from other schools. I don't want to be embarrassed."

"George, when this is done, you'll be a hero to these kids for letting them do it. Stop worrying. The teachers have your back."

Chapter 17

THEY FOUND THE BOMBER in Cuba. Jane and Tony were on their way to the school. By the time Fritz arrived, Tony was set up. Fritz set the paperclip on a satellite photo Jane handed him—a house outside Havana.

Jane and six heavily armed men waited. "This won't be easy. Our suspect isn't alone, but we don't know how many are with him. We'll surround the house."

"Do you have enough guys for this?" Fritz asked.

"More are on the way, but we can't wait. Send the rest when they get here."

He opened the door. The fragrance of an ocean breeze drifted through the doorway. A tan, beachside bungalow reflected the sunset, and the gentle sound of breaking waves harmonized with the calm, a calm that would soon end.

Within only minutes, Captain Dolan and thirty armed men in Kevlar vests ran through the portal. Fritz told him the area was wide open. Gunfire met them. Jane kneeled near the entrance and waved them to her left.

Minutes after Fritz closed the door, Ashley arrived.

"They're in already. Jane went. There's shooting."

As before, Tony, Fritz, and Ashley stood in the now-empty hallway, watching as the last light of day slithered down the granite floor. Fifteen minutes later, the door opened. The salt air wafted through with the first soldiers, who led a single blindfolded prisoner. Dolan said the surprise attack had left four men dead in the house with no American casualties.

"Captain, take him into that room," said Major Barclay, pointing. "Fritz, get the man."

"Take off the blindfold and take out your pistol," the president told Captain Dolan. "Colonel, you are charged with multiple counts of murder." The president spoke calmly to the North Korean officer, but his pointed words left no doubt what would happen. "Your diplomatic immunity matters not one bit to me. Who are you working for?" The prisoner sat motionless. "Colonel, you know who I am. I know you speak English." Dolan cocked the pistol. "You were one of the bombers of our ships in San Diego and probably involved in the other bombing. Your government has disavowed you. Who hired you?" No answer. "Colonel, I don't have a lot of time today. I'll be leaving shortly. You don't want me to leave you in their hands. You have a minute to answer my questions." The president waited, an eye on his watch. "Do you have a family we can notify?"

The colonel blinked. "I have a wife and two children," he said, with a barely noticeable accent.

"Where are they? So we can let them know you won't be coming home."

"They remain in North Korea."

"Give him something to write with." Jane took a pad and pen from the desk. "Colonel, the address, please. Colonel, time's running out."

The captive met the president's stare, glanced at the others surrounding him, and lifted the pen. Dolan removed a large serrated-edge knife from the scabbard on his belt. "I'll be leaving now," the president said.

"Wait."

"Wait for what?"

"We were hired by a man, I don't know his name. He paid cash."

"What information do you have? Did you do both bombings?"

"One of my teams did each. We had no other contacts. Money was left for us." The president nodded to the soldiers, who released their holds, though Dolan's knife remained close.

"Bind his hands. Then we'll have a conversation." The president sat and gestured everyone else to do the same. "We'll be here a while."

Jane turned on her computer's recorder. When asked where the money was now, the colonel said, "In the bank. We were paid half up front, half when done." When asked how the money changed hands, he told them a woman delivered a briefcase. She waited at public benches at bus stations. When he sat down, she left.

"How many teams? How many men?"

The colonel said he knew of four teams, eight men each, but he had no control over them. They had each been assigned different missions. "I only met with their leaders once. I do not know where they are now."

"Do you recognize this picture?" Jane asked. She showed him a picture of Penelope Wise. He said no. Then she showed him a series of random pictures, like a police line-up. He peered at each and pointed to Caitlin Morgan.

"Have you ever heard of the Caballeros?" asked the president. The North Korean said no.

* * *

MILT CHELTON and his crew arrived just as the interrogation ended. "Fritz, get me home. We'll talk tomorrow. Jane, I'll talk to you later too. We have a link, but we need the bank records."

"Milt, would you mind having your guys clean up this room? It's been a busy night."

I know. Half my guys were involved."

On the way home, Ashley broke the silence. "Do you think the president would have shot him?" A reply was slow in coming.

"Every time I see him, he's angrier," Jane said. "When Dolan took off the safety, I thought he might. But I think it was a stall so he didn't have to. Still, if the colonel hadn't talked, I don't know. Now they're taking him for more questioning. No, I don't think he would have shot him. He wants answers. Dead men don't talk. And he remains a Constitutionalist, even though this guy is an enemy combatant. And if word ever got out … He cares about his legacy."

"He's getting to be a badass," said Fritz.

"Not getting to be. He is, Fritz. I've said before, he's always sold short. This is far from over."

Chapter 18

FRITZ SHUDDERED AT the thought of the week ahead. The tournament would start on Monday. Linda had a test on Tuesday. Ashley's Aristocrats were in Wednesday's second game.

A call from the president interrupted his class preparation. He said he wanted to speak to the Israeli prime minister face-to-face before the summit. "I want to use the portal to remind him and to get his input on how he thinks the rest are going to react. Want to come with me?"

"Mr. President, my tournament starts tomorrow. When do you want to go?"

"How about next weekend? It shouldn't be for long."

As busy as she was, Linda took a moment to complain that the portal was nothing more than convenient transportation. "He could make a phone call."

* * *

"WHAT DO YOU MEAN, they're gone," yelled the man. He listened to the description. An empty bungalow, four dead men, and empty cartridges found around the perimeter. "Did they get away? Were they arrested?" Once again, he had assigned a simple job that had not been done. "Find out and call me back."

* * *

THE START OF the Phillies spring training topped the morning news on the car radio. The tournament pounded in Fritz's head as he walked in. Liz Chambers waited at his door.

"Morning, Fritz, I think we'll need the cafeteria today. My last class will set up everything. On Friday, I asked a couple of seniors to set up the video cameras."

"Thanks, Liz. I hadn't even thought about that."

"Will George introduce everyone today?"

"He said he would."

With his thoughts floating elsewhere, Fritz chose topics to engage his classes and free him to think about the week ahead. In the first class, he listed some inventions of the mid-1800s and let the class discuss which were most important. He included Samuel Colt's revolver, the sewing machine, pasteurization, Morse code, and the daguerreotype. While the class argued, he made notes on questions about the summit. Second period, he discussed the use of fear to polarize the electorate. He listed the 1919 red scare, the post-World War II red scare, and terrorism in the Middle East. For his American History classes, he handed out "The Sentiments" from the Seneca Falls convention, and the classes discussed the beginnings of the women's rights movement.

"Mr. R?"

"Go ahead, Fran."

"The Sentiments sound a lot like the Declaration of Independence. Was that intentional?"

"Yes, I believe it was. When it was written, America had had time to become the country the Founders wanted. The Sentiments emphasized that the same reasoning used to gain independence from England argued that women should have the same rights as men. Elizabeth Cady Stanton and Lucretia Mott, the primary authors, were abolitionists and believed that equality should be for everyone. In 1848, they wanted laws changed."

"Like how?"

"Just a couple before the bell. Women couldn't vote, but if they were single and inherited a house, they had to pay taxes. So, taxation without representation. Also, if a woman had income, it belonged to her husband, as did her personal property."

"That's not fair."

Fritz leaned against his desk. "Women's rights have developed slowly. It took from 1848 when the Sentiments were signed, until 1920 for women to get the right to vote. So yeah, it wasn't fair. How is it now?"

The class lit up for the remaining few minutes. No hands were raised, and the points the students threw into the air included pay inequality, women's healthcare, and domestic abuse. When the bell rang, Fritz congratulated them on an enlightened discussion. "Remember all this when, not too long from now, you're making decisions about your world."

At lunchtime, he refocused on the tournament. Cruising through to last period, he welcomed his excited ninth graders with a discussion of the Eighteenth Amendment, which prohibited alcoholic beverages. They discussed how to fix bad laws.

With only a few minutes remaining, he asked, "So, are you all ready?"

Susan asked, "Mr. R, does Mr. McAllister know that we already have a traffic jam outside?" She pointed out the window, where a line of cars headed for the parking lot. "All the kids who are in the first games have asked their parents to come. We even have rolls of quarters, so we can give change."

"It seems you've thought of everything. Well done. Anything I should know before we start?"

Ted said, "You should know that next year even more kids will want to play."

Waiting by Fritz's door, George paced, his nervousness undisguised. As Fritz entered the hall, George was visibly shaking. "Mr. Chatham is here."

"Relax, George. He wants to see what all the fuss has been about. Liz has the cafeteria all set. Do you have your introductions ready?"

"Yes, but I didn't know he was coming." At the end of the hall, the superintendent walked in and waved. Lois was walking with him.

"Everything will be fine. Remember, you're on the team." He waved and met Lois and Mr. Chatham, pulling George with him. "Hi, Lois. Mr. Chatham, I'm Fritz Russell."

"So you're the culprit." He chuckled as they shook hands. "My office staff will be here in a little bit. They want to meet the man who has had our phones ringing off the hook."

"Sorry. This is much more than we had expected."

"Nonsense. I'm looking forward to it. No reason to be sorry."

Standing in the middle of the corridor, Liz Chambers directed the traffic into the cafeteria. She smiled at the approaching group. "Hi Bob, glad you're here," she said to the superintendent. "Fritz, the auditorium is full. Bob, we saved you a seat up front." While she talked, she waved kids and parents to the line that had formed to buy tickets. "By the way, Bob," she said, "adult tickets are $1.00." George snorted.

At the lectern, George waited for quiet. But the loudspeaker boomed, "Everyone, please rise for our national anthem." Fritz gleamed at Susan. When the music ended, the announcer said, "Play ball." Cheers filled the auditorium.

George welcomed the superintendent, parents, and students to the first Riverboro High School History-Baseball Tournament. The two teams for the first game waited backstage. He introduced Rosenberg's Scorpions and their captain, Bob Bee, and Lucas's Logarithms, led by David Jewels. Like the rest of the audience, Fritz saw the team tee shirts for the first time. The cheers exploded. George introduced Susan and raised his hands to his ears. Bob Chatham gave George a thumb's up.

Susan thanked everyone for coming and Barking Tees for donating the team uniforms. "I hope everyone will go there to buy their Riverboro sweatshirts and jackets." She turned to Fritz, and said, "I'd like to present today's pitcher, Mr. R, I mean, Mr. Russell." The whoops drowned out her correction.

Both teams had worked hard. Although the Scorpions scored first, Barb Lucas' kids got hit after hit and led 6-1 after the first inning. Joe Rosenberg stood in a corner of the stage, deflated. His students scored twice in their second at-bats. The score at the end of the second inning was 6-3. With two men on and two out, Bob Bee asked for a home run. If he made it, he'd tie the score. Fritz asked, "What year did California become a state?" Bob closed his eyes. "Eighteen…" A low buzz filled the stage. "1852." The Logarithms all whooped. Fritz said, "Sorry, Bob, 1850, as set up in the Compromise of 1850." Bob hung his head and smacked his forehead.

Susan returned to the microphone. She introduced the next teams' teachers Shelly Rapstein and Ellen Berg, and their teams, Rapstein's Raptors and Berg's Behemoths. Again, George covered his ears. In a close game, the Behemoths beat the Raptors, 3-2. The two language teachers, who were sisters, hugged and then shook hands. The first day's play had ended. As the auditorium emptied, Jay Bennett walked up to the principal and the superintendent, carrying a grey metal box. Jay shook the superintendent's hand and headed for the stage.

"Mr. R, Susan, we collected four hundred-eighteen dollars. The cafeteria was packed."

Several teachers had been waiting to speak with Fritz. "What we want to know is if you'd allow other teachers to be the pitcher. We might want to try this in our own classes."

"I'd have to show you how it works. I'd love to have a rotation of relief pitchers." He suggested they spread the word. He would meet with them before classes on Thursday.

Ashley was a nervous wreck by Wednesday afternoon. At lunch, he couldn't eat or stand still. Between classes, Fritz overheard students commenting that Ashley hadn't taught anything all week.

"I want to win this thing."

"Are you making things worse for the kids?"

Mid-step, Ash stopped. "I don't know."

"Then, my friend, you'd better calm down. Your team, in case you didn't know, has practiced without you. Matt told me on Monday they were all at his house on Saturday for six hours."

"Really?"

"They want to win too."

When the final class ended, George waited in the middle of the hall. "Here he is now. Fritz, this is Natalie Johnston. She's writing about the tournament for the Riverboro newspaper."

"Nice to meet you. I'm afraid I can't talk now, but if you want, you can call me."

"That's fine, Mr. Russell. Mr. McAllister has filled me in. I'd like to watch."

"Come on in then. I have to get ready." Ashley had disappeared when Fritz stopped. When Fritz found him backstage, he asked, "You ready?"

"I dated her."

"Who?"

"Nat Johnston."

"I thought the name was familiar. Pretty woman."

"Long story. I gotta get my kids."

The first game came down to the last question. Then Ashley's Aristocrats battled Larsen's Lunatics. Ashley's worries fizzled. Matt had set a strategy of "all or nothing." Singles and home runs. By the end of the first inning, the Aristocrats were ahead, 6-0. Matt had the lower grades try to get on base with singles, and the seniors answer home-run questions. Johnny Clayton and Matt both drove in three runs in their first at-bats. Ashley's team won 12-3.

As the auditorium emptied, George told Fritz that the cafeteria had been standing room only. Jay and Susan announced they had collected over $800. "Mr. R, I think every kid in school was here." Ashley was beaming. "Bye, Mr. Gilbert." The twin voices of Nicole and Rachel carried over the surrounding noise. Rachel, who was on Ashley's team, had hit well.

"Bye, girls. See you tomorrow. Good game, Rachel."

"Ash, I think that's the first time you haven't been scared of them," said Fritz.

* * *

CARS LINED THE street in front of his house. Fritz waited for Ashley, and they went in the back door together. In his jammed kitchen, he greeted Linda, and then asked if something had happened. Jane told them the president had just called. The North Korean had been killed trying to escape on the way to another interrogation. He had grabbed a gun and shot six guards before they got him. "The president is furious," Jane said.

"How did the games go?" Linda asked.

With a wide grin, Ashley said, "The kids were great. We won, 12-3."

When the house was finally quiet again, it was past nine o'clock. Linda told Fritz that she had aced her finance test and had another piece of her term project completed. He told her that he had an early meeting with teachers who wanted to be pitchers.

"Did the president say when you're going to Israel?"

"No, but I'm guessing Sunday."

"Why does he want you to come?"

"Lin, honestly, I think he wants company. But I really don't know. Should I invite him for dinner?"

"Not unless you have to. We already have too many people hanging around."

Chapter 19

TEN TEACHERS WERE waiting by his door when Fritz arrived. He invited them all inside.

"Wow. So, you all want to be pitchers?"

"Fritz, I've heard about your classroom games for years," said Liz Chambers. "My kids haven't stopped hounding me to try it."

"I may not be much on history," Joe Rosenberg said. He was excited to have a new tool for chemistry. "I'm going to try it."

The door opened and Ashley and four more teachers came in and sat. Fritz could tell from Ashley's frown that something had happened, but it would have to wait. "Ash and I prepared the list from the textbooks and related readings, and we found some great sources on the internet." Fritz explained how he chose questions, and Liz suggested letting them try. She offered to pitch the three games the following day. Fritz said he would show them all what to do after the first round ended.

Ashley waited for the teachers to leave. "Jane flew to Washington early. There's a money link. She said it doesn't make sense. It ties the Korean to Eledoria. She said it's a wild goose chase. The president disagrees."

The afternoon games pitted Jaffrey's "Gyroscopes" against O'Malley's "Ordeal" and Ben Cumber's "Batch" against Oaks' "Blokes." Tom Jaffrey's team won the first game, 7-3, and Ben Cumber's kids eked out a win.

As he was leaving, a man came up and introduced himself as the proprietor of Barking Tees. "Mr. Russell, my name is Mark Witcannon. I dropped by to see the tournament in action."

"Nice to meet you, and thank you so much for our uniforms. The ninth graders were ecstatic when you offered."

"I was glad to. This is so cool. I've been telling the Chamber of Commerce and the Riverboro Business Council how much you've done to get all our businesses involved."

"It wasn't me. Really. It was the kids. You can see from the turnout that they've been very busy."

"I saw the cafeteria when I came in. Jay Bennett let me in the auditorium, but he said it was standing room only. Some showing!"

"I hope it met your expectations."

"It sure did. Nice meeting you, Mr. Russell."

"Name's Fritz. I can't thank you enough. See you again."

Ashley waited until Fritz's conversation ended. "Let's get out of here. I just spoke to Jane. She and the president have been going at it all day."

* * *

AS SOON AS he got home, Linda told him the president had called and sounded upset. "You left your phone on the counter this morning."

When he called back, the president asked him to set the portal so Jane could come back to New Jersey.

Jane related her argument with the president between bites. An Eledorian bank had been the source of funds for the terror attacks through an account in the name of Caitlin Morgan. The Eledorian government continued to disavow knowledge or involvement. She said that one point of contention was that the Eledorians always denied involvement. The argument had peaked when Jane reminded the president that Colonel Mitchell didn't think the soldiers at the settlement were Eledorian. She pointed out that Eledoria gained nothing from the bombing. Neither did Naria. The United States had no grounds for an attack, and a misdirected attack hurt us as much as its targets. He still thought the straight line from the bank to the terrorists was evidence enough.

She asked him where the money had come from. "Is it like God, it always has been there? Was it in the Garden of Eden?" He didn't like the sarcasm. "All due respect, sir, are you forgetting Geneva? The assassination attempt? Are you forgetting Koppler? He was tied to this. He's dead, but it's still happening. So he wasn't alone."

"Jane, WE DON'T KNOW THAT. We have no evidence of it."

"THEN LET'S GET SOME."

General Beech brought them back to basics. "What can or will we do? Are you suggesting an attack, sanctions? Turning the Israelis loose? We don't have good options. If we do something that starts new warfare, what happens to the summit?"

"Jim, what do you suggest?" the president asked.

"Keep looking for evidence. Activate our naval forces in the Mediterranean. Announce maneuvers with NATO so they are not surprised. And call the Eledorians and Narians first and let them know we're not on a war footing."

"Did he mention what he's going to Israel for?" Fritz asked.

"Yeah. To hold them back and make sure the Prime Minister remembers we can just show up."

"Why does he need me?"

Chapter 20

"**I WISH TODAY** were over," said Ashley. "I was just grilled about ship bombings." Fritz agreed. His first period had been the same. By the end of the day, Fritz had accomplished almost nothing in any class. Liz Chambers met him at his door, and they walked together to the auditorium. Their route was clogged with students. A group of men in ties waited with Mark Witcannon.

"My friends here are from the Chamber of Commerce. They've come to see what I've been talking about."

"Glad you're all able to take the time," said Fritz. "This is Liz Chambers, head of our history department. She'll be the pitcher for today's games."

"We better go get our seats before you have another sell-out," said Mark. "See you later."

The first game pitted Jim Wayne's "Pistols" against Bob Fortune's "Outrage," the name stemming from Mr. Fortune's supposed favorite word, outrageous. The Pistols whipped their opponent, 8-3.

"I think you've got the idea, Liz," said Fritz after the last call. "Good luck with the next ones. Remember, you're the umpire. You can decide any answer. I'm going to head home."

The second game was a slaughter. Cynthia Lee, another social studies teacher, had prepared long and hard with her team, the

"Virginians." Their opponent was Charlie Webb's "Spiders." The Virginians scored eight runs in their first at-bats. The Spiders tried unsuccessfully to catch up with home runs.

Before he left, Fritz waved to Susan, who was ready to announce the next teams. He found Ashley and said, "See you at home. I'm going."

"Jane's at your place. She texted me. News."

* * *

THE SKY SPIT some rain on his windshield. Hearing a siren, Fritz pulled over as the police car door opened.

"Mr. Russell, your rear light is out."

Fritz focused on the officer. "Sorry, Chief Dempsey. I'll take care of it."

"Jim Shaw has been telling me a lot's happening." Fritz's worried look prompted, "Don't worry. I swore not to say anything. Say hi to the president for me. And get the light fixed. No ticket."

"Thanks, Chief. See ya."

Starting to drive away, Fritz stopped again. *The car's new. Why would a bulb be out?* Dempsey was a block ahead, but backed up when Fritz got out.

"Something wrong?" asked the chief.

"I don't want to sound paranoid, but I bought this car in November. I'm just wondering if someone tampered with it."

"Do you want me to call someone?"

"Can you hang around a minute?"

"Sure."

Fritz called home and told Linda where he was. She put Jane on.

"Fritz, leave the car. I'll get the forensics people to check it out. Do you want me to come get you?"

"Hang on. Chief, someone's going to come check it out. Can you give me a lift? And maybe have someone keep an eye on it?"

"I'll have someone here in about ten minutes." The chief radioed for help. "Mr. Russell, park it at the curb and hop in."

Fritz told Jane he had a ride. When he walked through the back door, Linda was pouring a soda, her cheeks tracked.

"Why are you crying?"

"Fritz, this is too soon to forget. I'm scared."

"It's probably nothing but a blown bulb, but I was just being cautious. It's okay." He hugged her. "I'm home safe." Jane said the car was going to be transported to the warehouse where his other car had been investigated. She had also called the president.

"He said to call him when you got home."

"Ash said you have news."

"Call the president," she said. "Have your soda, then I'll tell you. Ash will be here soon."

While he was hanging up his coat, the doorbell rang.

"Come on in, Jim."

"Chief Dempsey called me, Mr. R. What's going on? Hi, Mary."

"Probably nothing, but a light bulb blew so quickly on a new car. Just taking precautions. It's a good thing it was the chief who stopped me."

"One of my friends is watching the car. I'm going to join him."

"Someone is coming to tow it. Do me a favor. Let me know when they have it."

"Sure. I'll be back. See you in a few minutes, Mary." Mary was holding TJ, and Fritz bent to kiss him. They went into the kitchen.

"Jim is watching the car. He'll be back in a bit."

"Sit down, Fritz," said Linda.

"So what's the news?"

"Did you call the president yet?"

"No, not yet."

"Call him first."

After the now-routine greeting and TJ comment from Lily Evans, the president got on and said he was sorry they were going through all they were.

"Mr. President, this isn't your fault. I just hope it's a manufacturing defect."

"It is my fault, Fritz, that too many know about you and the portal. We don't know how many people Koppler might have told, but hoarding information was his way of doing business. Not sharing. So we have another trail to sniff out. Maybe."

"Is there anything you want me to do on Sunday? I have a couple of questions for the prime minister."

"Write them down and send them to me. They may be better coming from me, or maybe not. You may get answers I wouldn't."

"I'll email them this evening. I'll see you at eight on Sunday morning."

FRITZ ASKED, "So what's the news? He didn't say anything."

"Ash and I set a date."

"When?"

"August twentieth. That gives us a couple of weeks for a honeymoon before school starts. And it's enough time for my mother to overdo everything. We decided we wouldn't have any time, so we are letting her plan stuff. I hope we're not sorry."

Fritz reached across the table, squeezed her hand, and then kissed her. "Why didn't Ash say anything to me?"

"I asked him not to."

Banging at the backdoor preceded Ashley, who had his arms wrapped around bags.

"Congratulations, old friend," said Fritz.

"Who are you calling old?"

"You. What's in the bags?"

"I don't know. I was told to pick up an order, so I did. I always do what I'm told."

Chapter 21

FRITZ PULLED THE door, and they stepped into Israel.

"Welcome, Mr. President, Mr. Russell. Have you had your breakfast?" asked the prime minister.

"I haven't," said Fritz.

"Nor I," said the president.

"Good. Good. Then please sit. We'll eat and talk." Fritz appreciated the prime minister's thoughtfulness. It was mid-afternoon in Israel.

Trays filled with a variety of foods were place on the table by four men who looked very much like soldiers, not waiters, in spite of their white jackets. The president noticed, but Fritz asked, "Mr. Prime Minister, are they soldiers? They look familiar." Fritz had seen the faces of all the soldiers who had been in Riverboro during the settlement rescue.

"Good memory, Mr. Russell. They were at your school. I thought it best not to have new faces to know about your, shall we call it, transportation."

"Is this pastrami?" asked Fritz, serving himself.

"Straight from Brooklyn. My favorite. It comes once a week, fresh. So is the rye bread. It arrived this morning while you were sleeping."

The prime minister seemed too jovial for this meeting.

Fritz asked how the settlers they'd rescued were doing. The prime minister said they were all well. "We are a resilient people. We have been survivors for thousands of years."

"And what did they think about New Jersey?" Fritz glanced at the president.

"Frankly, Mr. Russell, they were more relieved to be safe than they were concerned about how it was done. I told them our government had found a way to pass through space, but we used it only in a limited way. Your secret is safe, not to mention unbelievable."

Fritz took a bite of his sandwich. The prime minister asked if something was of particular concern. The president was direct. He said he wanted the prime minister's vocal support for the plan he'd announce at the summit, whether he liked it or not. If he was reluctant, the others would have a reason to balk.

"I don't even know what it is."

The president reached into his jacket pocket and passed the outline to the prime minister. "The second thing I want is your thoughts on bringing each leader to the meeting using the portal. This is business, not diplomacy. It's not a party. I am prepared to use the portal to achieve agreement. You and I are elected to represent our countries, but not all our participants can say that. I am prepared to stay until they are convinced."

Fritz said, "Mr. Prime Minister, since I discovered the portal, I have been involved in actions in Pakistan, Naria, Russia, and Israel, as well as the summit in Geneva in October. Your fight to survive has been going on since before I was born." The prime minister nodded. "It's time for level heads to prevail. I may be out of place, but I have put my life and that of my family at risk to help the president. The world has to change."

"Mr. Russell," said the prime minister, "I too would like an end to this madness. Agreements have been made. But people change, people die, and old accords are forgotten."

"Not if people benefit," said Fritz. "Your neighbors live in poverty and have no hope of escaping it. If a road out is available, don't you think the people would take it?"

The president took over. "Mr. Prime Minister, the outline of the meeting addresses how to build that road. But my second question, using the portal, matters. Do you think we should bring them to Washington using the portal or show them later?"

The prime minister pondered the question. "Mr. President," he began slowly, "if you bypass the usual transportation and accommodations, you will alert every country to the portal's existence. Do you want to do that before they know your plan? Some things are best left for demonstration."

Although the sun shone through high windows and the casual décor indicated a sunroom, the prime minister said it was not. He pushed a button. Fritz thought that was how he summoned his staff. But within seconds, a dozen soldiers entered, and the room began to sink. The windows disappeared. Within thirty seconds, a pleasant sunroom converted into an armed bunker. "This is a secure room. The only entrance is opening doors from the inside. We have full communications, a kitchen, sleeping area, and food for a year. Almost no one knows about it."

The president looked around and said, "We're even." The prime minister unfolded the outline.

* * *

"SO WHAT DID the president need you for?" asked Linda.

"Actually, I think I was the opening act. For the first half hour, I did all the talking. He just nodded a couple of times, as if he wanted me to keep going."

"So the prime minister is on board?" Jane asked.

"He said he wanted to consider the possible ramifications, and he asked what would happen if the Arabs don't agree. The president told him about his episode with the Speaker. By the time the story ended, the prime minister was laughing. He said if the Speaker could be convinced, he was sure the disagreeable could be turned. Ash, I forgot to ask. Is everything good for the tournament?"

"Liz was fine with the last game. By next Friday, we're half done. George told me other principals are coming. Honestly, if he had feathers, he'd be a peacock."

"That's one big headache gone. What about the play?"

"Eric is drilling them to learn lines and stage directions. Jean has recruited my entire class to write the parts, advertising, website posts. Your ninth graders are contagious. All my kids want the same recognition. They even got Abby Anderson's art classes to help with the scenery. They've added crowd scenes and extras. A lot of the extras are kids who didn't sign up for one of your teams. Dana Goldsense told me that next year every kid might want to be in the tournament."

Fritz inhaled deeply. "At least tomorrow is a day off."

"Not for me," said Linda. "I have classes early, and I'll be gone most of the day."

"I'll be here. Unless you want me to get anything. Should I make dinner or get something?"

"I have a shopping list, but you still don't have a car."

"I forgot. Have we heard anything yet? It was supposed to be done yesterday."

Jane said, "I spoke to the head of the team earlier. This morning, they found a wire that shouldn't have been there. He said it wasn't attached to anything. Anyway, he said they might have it completed by tomorrow."

"If you need a ride, I'll take you," said Ashley. "Problem solved."

* * *

FRITZ'S SUV was parked in the driveway when they returned. Jane and a man in overalls were waiting. Jane introduced Mike Morgan.

"Mr. Russell, you had a loose wire that we followed into the door. That's all it was. We called the company and spoke to a technician and an engineer. Apparently, it's a known defect. We fixed everything, and you're all set. This car is okay, not like your last one."

"You worked on that?" asked Fritz.

"I was amazed no one was killed. What they did was clever and would have been hard to detect in a routine investigation. Acid on the axle and an electrical charge to open the seal. Just enough to be a slow leak." Jane and Ashley listened, Jane with a faraway look.

"Want some coffee?" Fritz asked. "I assume you need a ride back."

"Love some. My ride will be here in about twenty minutes."

As they walked up the driveway, Jane raised some questions. "Mike, there are a lot of different acids. They needed the right container so it wouldn't burn, and the right acid to slowly eat through the axles. It had to be strong enough to cut through while the car was moving. That had to be hard to figure."

"It was also expensive. Whoever put it together spent a lot to get the containers designed. They resisted the acid enough to survive the accident, but if they weren't discovered quickly, in this case by us, they would have disappeared."

"Disappeared?" Fritz opened the door and waved to Mary.

"Yeah. If the accident had been somewhere on a country road and had been left for a couple of hours more, the acid would have eaten through and the containers would be gone. The acid burns would still show, but we would never have figured it out. We needed a strong alkali to counter the acid when we saw the containers evaporating."

They sat at the kitchen table. "Mr. Morgan, you said they spent a lot," said Fritz. "Who would have that kind of technology?"

Morgan sipped his coffee. "Mr. Russell, in my opinion, the design work, metallurgy, and chemistry were industrial and military. You can't buy that stuff at a hardware store. It was specially made. And whoever made it knew it was for no good deed." A horn sounded, and Morgan said, "My ride."

"Thanks for checking it out. I just felt it was too coincidental."

"No problem. After Thanksgiving, I would be concerned too. Any questions, or if any problems, give me a call." Morgan handed Fritz a business card. "Don't give that to anyone."

Ashley's worried look returned when the back door closed. He cleared his throat. "We already know Koppler was behind your crash. But if that guy is right, someone funded him. Jane, you have a money tie to Eledoria. Maybe there's another connection."

"Not maybe," she said. "Caballeros. The German, Badenhof, ran a major industrial research company, among other things. We have no proof, but it fits." She took her phone from her pocket. "I have to get the report Morgan filed after your accident, Fritz. Pass me that business card." She dialed Mike Morgan and asked for a copy of the report. He told her that it was still in progress.

"I called Mr. Koppler with a preliminary," he said, "but we're still trying to figure out the pieces. Jane, the metal and the acid were custom-made. Koppler told me to file a report when we knew what we had. With him dead, no one else asked. I'll check to see what's happening, if you want."

"If you would, Mike, please. You have my number."

Jane sucked in her lips and stared at the table. "He told Koppler about the initial findings, and Koppler told him to find out what the components were. I bet Koppler knew it would take a while, and no one else asked. I'm trying to decide if I should call the president."

"He'll want to know I got my car back, Jane, so one of us should call him."

"I don't think he's at the White House. He went to a President's Day event somewhere. I'll call later."

Ashley thought she should call anyway and leave a message with Lily Evans, who told her that the president would be right with her. The vice president had gone to the event instead. She told the president about the conversation with Mike Morgan and that Fritz had his car back. He said he hadn't seen a report, but wasn't surprised. "Jane, I don't know if this gets us closer to an answer or farther away. It's so elaborate, so evil. Are you with Fritz now?" She passed Fritz the phone.

"Hi, Mr. President."

"Glad everything's okay this time, Fritz. I wanted you to know that I spoke to the prime minister this morning. He said he was glad you came and offered you and Linda a vacation, his treat, whenever you want."

"Thanks, Mr. President. Is he on board with the summit?"

"He will be. Believe me. But you really can't blame him for being skeptical. The Israelis know how hard it will be to convince the Arabs. Both sides have to win to make this work. He also knows that if we don't stop all the wars, it's only a matter of time before the whole region explodes again."

"Then we'll make it work, Mr. President."

"Let me talk to Jane. Bye for now."

He told her that the money link looked solid. They had gotten into the bank's computers.

"Mr. President, I think we should check if Georg Badenhof or any of his companies had ownership or accounts there. We should look for large transfers within a couple of months before Thanksgiving, especially if his chemical company has an account. It's just another clue, but it may tie him to Koppler."

"Noted, Jane. Let me think about all this. I'll talk to you later."

When Linda arrived home, she told Fritz to move his car. Not hello. A sour look at the crowded table pushed Fritz from his chair. "What's wrong?"

"I had an argument with a professor who told me my business plan wasn't well thought out. So I asked him what he thought wasn't working. He went through my outline and criticized it line by line. When he was done, I told him it had been reviewed by one of Daddy's friends at Harvard Business, who said when I was ready, he had financing lined up. The professor said he didn't believe in Harvard. I thanked him and walked out, only to drive right into a traffic jam all the way home. So how was your day?"

Chapter 22

LINDA'S FLIGHT departed for Cleveland at 6:20 p.m. Her break allowed her to go home to talk to her father. At the terminal entrance, they were met by Charles Dougherty and three security officers.

"Ms. Russell, a friend has asked us to get you safely to your plane." Fritz smiled, said hello, and introduced Linda and TJ to the airport security director. "Mr. Russell, we'll have an escort for you back to the bridge. Our friend told me what happened last time. He asked for our help to keep you safe. How could I refuse?" Fritz thanked him, grabbed Linda's bag, and kissed her.

"I'm going to miss you. Call me when you land. And say hi to your folks."

"I love you. Stay out of trouble."

"See you soon. I love you, too."

* * *

AS CHARLES DOUGHERTY WAS escorting Linda and TJ through the terminal, eight men arrived at the Hay-Adams Hotel in Washington, D.C. They unloaded eight golf bags from three taxis.

"We have reservations for Nakamura Industries. I will register for all of us." He spoke to his companions in a language that the desk clerk didn't understand. When the paperwork was completed, the man said, "We requested rooms as high up as possible, with a view."

"We have reserved four suites for you, sir. Two bedrooms in each. Is that satisfactory?"

He nodded. "And we have a meeting planned for Saturday evening."

"We have everything arranged." The man handed $20.00 bills to each of the available bellhops as the carts were wheeled to the elevator.

* * *

"DID JANE SAY when the leaders are arriving?" Fritz asked.

"Most are coming on Friday. She said the president might be having informal talks with some of them. She tried to talk him out of it. She said he shouldn't give them a chance to get mad."

"I think she's right."

Ashley had his phone to his ear when Fritz returned with a new yellow pad. "Jane," he mouthed. "Then the whole meeting schedule has changed? I'll tell Fritz. Do we need to do anything? Okay, see you then." He refilled his soda and said, "The meeting will start Friday night. Saturday morning they'll have breakfast. Here. Colonel Mitchell's guys will be the waiters. He's keeping them in the meeting."

"That means I can't be home. I might need to be gone Friday night and all day Saturday."

"No problem," Mary said. "Jim's off Friday and Saturday. If it's okay, I can ask him to come over. Will Jane and Ashley be with you?"

"Jane will. Are you coming with me?"

"Hadn't planned on it."

* * *

FRITZ DIDN'T sleep well with Linda away. Friday morning, he and Ashley arrived together, both with dark under their eyes. Milt Chelton had already arrived.

"Fritz, you know the schedule has changed. Timing is really tight. My guys need to be here right after school. They're bringing the walls and floor that will disguise the hallway. Then they have to change to be waiters. Oh, and we put veneer on your door, a couple of screws and Velcro. Can't tell."

"That's good. I'll warn George, have an announcement that this corridor will be closed, and get signs made."

"Then I'll see you later."

* * *

"HOW MAY I HELP you, Mr. Nakamura?" asked the concierge.

"Our plans have changed. When will Ms. Porter arrive?"

"She's already here. I'll find her for you if you would like to wait at her office."

"Yes, thank you. I will meet her in half an hour, after I have breakfast." Nakamura bowed slightly and walked to the dining room.

Ms. Porter greeted her client, who told her he wanted food set up at 7:30 that evening. "We wish privacy. I will notify your staff when you may remove the food. We will serve ourselves."

When he left, she went to the hotel manager to explain the change in schedule.

"Margaret, this is one of the strangest groups I've seen here. They brought golf clubs and haven't used them. In fact, we've hardly seen them all week."

"I know. He planned the whole thing before he got here. I scheduled eight people to serve. Now I don't need them. He's spending close to $10,000, and they'll serve themselves?"

"Well, at least we've got his credit card number."

* * *

"CLASS, KEEP working. I'll be back in a minute." Susan raised her hand. "I'll talk to you after class, Susan." He left the room and pulled his phone out of his pocket.

"Mr. President, sorry I'm late on this. I forgot to call."

"No problem, Fritz. We've been busy too."

"Sir, when do you want to start the meeting?"

The official start would be at eight o'clock in the Oval Office. But the real beginning would be at six. Food would be sent through the portal at 5:30. The leaders would arrive at the Old Executive Office Building and take the tunnels to the president's office. "At eight, a procession of limousines with imposters will arrive at the North Portico. We're trying to disguise the arrivals, just in case."

"Milt and the guys are outside now. They'll have to hurry to set up."

"I'll see you in a couple of hours."

He returned to his classroom and was struck by the quiet. But all eyes were on him, not the test. "What's up, guys. Are you all done?"

"Mr. R," said Susan, "I wanted to tell you before. We got a $5,000 donation from the Business Council."

"And we've collected over $4,000 from ticket sales," Ron added.

"Mr. R," Ted said, "we have almost $55,000, and we still have the rest of the tournament."

"Guys, that's fantastic. You're doing great work. No homework. Now finish your essays." The class settled back into their answers, and Fritz returned to his yellow pad. He envisioned the crowded section of hallway between the rooms, with no way to get into the rest of the school. The only direction would be into the Oval Office. As he glanced at his students, a face appeared in the window of his door. He waved Tony in, but Tony shook his head. With only five minutes remaining, Fritz told the class to finish up and put their papers on his desk.

"Hi, Tony. What's up?"

"I just talked to Jane. She wants to come home right away. She said she needs some stuff for tonight."

"As soon as we clear the hallway. We weren't expecting this. Do you know they're starting early?"

"Yeah. Do you have your uniform?"

"He wants me in a uniform? What uniform? What am I going to do?"

"I hope Jane thought about it. You can't be here like this. I hope they figured out how to hide the wires."

"More to do. Just what I need."

As the hall began to fill with students and teachers, Fritz grabbed Ashley, told him Jane was coming, and asked him to tell the teachers to remind the kids they wouldn't be able to get into the hallway. Seeing Tony, Tom Jaffrey asked Fritz where he was going.

"Tom, do me a favor and move the kids out. I'll tell you when they're gone." The Friday afternoon din of shouting students and slamming locker doors rose to a noisy crescendo and quickly subsided.

As quiet returned, Milt Chelton walked toward them, accompanied by Colonel Mitchell, looking every bit the civilian he wasn't. Coming from the opposite direction, Tom Jaffrey arrived and greeted Tony.

"Tom, you're not involved, so I can't say more than there's a meeting. I don't know yet what the president wants to do."

"Are you talking about the summit?" Tom saw the sideway glances around him. "Wow. That's it, isn't it?" Fritz nodded. "Then I better get going. If you need me, call. I can keep a secret."

"Thanks, Tom. You'll be home tonight and tomorrow?"

"Yeah, I'm reviewing the tournament questions. My team has practice every afternoon until our next game. Good luck."

MILT SIGNALED to start. A door, gate and frame, and folded cloth led the procession. From the truck, tool boxes and a generator followed. Two men carried the gate to the end of the corridor, and more men with a heavy load appeared at the exit.

"Fritz, which room should we use?" Milt asked.

"Fritz, we need to get Jane," the colonel interrupted. Fritz started to feel stretched.

"Use Ash's for now. We need to get this figured out."

With the generator connected and the fake walls being set up crossing the hall from his room to the meeting room, Fritz set the paperclip on the Oval Office brochure and called the president. Almost before the door was open, Jane ran past him, straight to Ashley. All she said was "Let's go." The president waved Fritz in.

"NSA picked up potential threat warnings, Fritz, but we don't know how serious. We need everything set up when the leaders arrive. The good news is we may have another Caballeros link."

"That's great, Mr. President. I have a problem, though. I don't have a uniform."

"It's ready for you. Colonel Mitchell will have one of his guys help you dress."

Fritz stared and shook his head, "How?"

The president chuckled. "Your shirt and pants labels and a good tailor, sergeant. I'm hoping that Mr. Putin and our Israeli friend don't recognize you. I doubt it, but they won't say anything. Now get going and come back right away. You're the only one who knows if we have a problem."

Back in the hallway, the colonel touched his arm. "Fritz, we should go." As they reached the exit, the first fake wall was lifted into place.

Chapter 23

“**HI FRITZ. DON’T** you look nice?”

“Thanks, Jane. So do you.” Jane had changed into her dress blues, her left jacket pocket covered with ribbons. “So, you know what’s happening?” Two curtains blocked any view from the parking lot. “How does it look?”

“It’s a perfect disguise. They’re finishing up now.”

Milt Chelton and three other men walked through the wall opening. “Hi, Fritz. Come take a look.” They stepped into the fake passage. Milt tapped the opening, and as it clicked, Fritz thought he knew how Alice felt when she arrived in Wonderland.

“We already have the Cheshire Cat, so I must be the Mad Hatter. Jane, that would make you the Queen of Hearts.” He ran his hand over the three-paneled walls on each side. The soles of his patent leather shoes almost slid on the high gloss of the new hardwood floor.

“Where’s your cover, Fritz?”

“Huh?”

“Your cover, soldier,” the colonel barked. More gently, he said, “Your hat, Fritz.”

“Oh. In the car.”

“From this point on, you need to be in proper dress, sergeant. Understood?”

"Yeah, sure. Okay."

"Fritz, you say, 'Yes, sir.' "

"Yes, sir."

"Go get it. And give your keys to someone else. You can't jingle here."

"Ash, get his hat, please," said Jane.

Fritz tossed him the keys, rattling through the air. "I see what you mean, Colonel."

Ashley placed the hat in the colonel's outstretched hand. Mitchell put it on Fritz's head, wiggling it to find the proper angle. "We're short on time, Fritz. Do you have a mirror nearby?"

"Only in the boys' room." He looked around. "Milt, can we get through the gate for a few minutes."

Facing the mirror in the bathroom, the colonel said, "Fritz for the next couple of days, you'll need to concentrate. This disguise is pointless if you don't play the part."

"I know. It's hard."

"Your answer, soldier, is improper," yelled the colonel. Fritz jumped and saw a drill sergeant from every movie he remembered.

"Yes, sir."

"Look at the uniform, look at how the hat sits on your head. When the president comes into the hallway, you'll hear 'ten hut.' Even holding the door, you will stand straight. He won't salute you. He won't want to draw attention to you. When he's gone, someone will say 'at ease' or 'as you were.' If the president comes out of the room, even to talk to you, you are a soldier in the Army. When he approaches, you salute him."

"Got it. Oops. Yes, sir. Sorry, sir."

"I know this is an adjustment, Fritz. When we leave this room, you are on duty. Is that clear?"

"Yes, sir."

"Atten-hut." The colonel laughed. "Fritz, this will be the shortest basic training in history. Put your heels together, knees locked, chin up, stand straight." Colonel Mitchell laughed again. "I hope you don't pop any buttons."

"Yes, sir."

The colonel took a couple of steps back and looked at Fritz from head to toe. "Good. Let's go back."

"Yes, sir!" The colonel smiled.

Chapter 24

FRITZ FELT HIS PHONE vibrate. "Yes, Mr. President."

"We're ready to set up, Fritz. Tell the colonel and open up."

"Yes, sir."

The doorknob buzzed. Ten soldiers wearing white jackets, black pants, white shirts, and black ties marched into the Oval Office. Moments later, they returned carrying trays and pushing carts filled with covered containers. Plates, silverware, and glassware were set on the conference table. Colonel Mitchell had changed into waiter's livery, except for a slight bulge under his left arm.

The president walked into the hallway. "Atten-hut" flew to Fritz's ears. With the president staring straight at him, Fritz saluted. "Well, this is a little different, huh, Fritz?"

"Yes, sir," he said, still saluting. The president returned the salute.

"Fritz, you end the salute once he has saluted," said the colonel.

"Yes, sir."

"At ease, Sergeant Russell. A word, if I might."

"Yes, sir."

The president put his hand on Fritz's shoulder. "We're not using the trophy case tonight," he said. "Here are floor plans for all of their homes. We'll try a couple tonight. The ones who object the most. I won't know until we start. They'll be arriving in a couple of minutes, but they'll all come together through the tunnel. We'll have a formal picture taken. That's all set. No press. Then I'll call. Open up right away."

MAJOR BARCLAY was speaking with Colonel Mitchell as they walked around the raised platform. The room had been decorated in keeping with White House style, complete with drapes covering artificial windowsills. Fritz felt the tension of previous missions replace the pressure of his snug attire. Jane placed packets at each place. She and the colonel stepped off the platform to the food carts. She pointed to a waiter's visible bulge and he adjusted his jacket. Fritz stepped back and looked through the opening of the false wall.

"Everything okay, Tony?"

"Ready to go, Fritz."

He looked at the soldiers in their dress uniforms. "Who's in charge here?"

"I am, sergeant," said a captain, who winked at Fritz. "How much time left?"

Fritz looked at his watch and told him any second. Fritz saluted, and said, "I think you should line up."

Fritz checked for Tony's thumbs-up, and Milt closed the panel. When the phone rang, Fritz said, "Here we go," as the president said, "Open it."

* * *

WITH THE EVENING festivities arranged, Margaret Porter sat back and sighed. Two hours before, Mr. Nakamura had told her he wanted to inspect the roof top. He was concerned about his guests being injured when they went out to see the view. Although she assured him that railings, chest-high fences, and a reinforced ceiling below would protect his guests, he had insisted on a personal inspection. They walked around the roof.

Mr. Nakamura checked the doors to the roof and wrote some notes that he slipped into his pocket. Before they returned to the lobby, he stood at the front and looked across Lafayette Square at the White House.

* * *

"LADIES AND GENTLEMEN," said the president. "We will keep this evening informal. I have asked our waiters and servers to leave us so we can speak openly and frankly. In front of you is a proposal to end the fighting in the Middle East, to establish economic and social well-being for us all, and to bring an end to the terrorist acts which have plagued the world. We will discuss the concepts and your countries' roles, and I expect that we will find agreement."

"Mr. President," said the Saudi king, "even if I were to agree, I must discuss this with my advisors."

"Your highness, let's not start with disagreement. You know as well as I that your opinion will be the final decision, so allow me to continue, please. When I've told you what we propose, I will show you how we will succeed." The president made a small check mark on a sheet in front of him. "You will understand why I believe you will see this my way." A subtle smile appeared on the Israeli Prime Minister's face.

"The first map shows current political borders and the second shows how much of the region remains undeveloped after thousands of years. The next chart outlines water and oil resources. You will note their wide disparity across nations. The third map presents average incomes as well as the range of wealth in the top ten percent of each population."

"Mr. President, that gap is certainly visible in your country, as well. What point is there in assigning blame?" said the Bahraini.

"Mr. Prime Minister, this is not about blame. You are viewing data provided by your governments. Unless it is incorrect, a marked chasm has grown between your wealthy and the rest of your citizens.

"As is yours, Mr. President."

"Mr. Prime Minister, I assure you, of that I am well aware. But again, that is not our current topic. The fourth map shows the new Palestine." The president pushed a button and a larger projection appeared on a screen disguised as a wall panel. The room began to rumble as if a storm were on the way.

The Palestinian president said, "We did not know that we would be present as you dissect the Middle East. What I see is you have taken territory from us, but not from Israel."

The president looked hard at the Israeli Prime Minister, the power of his glance stopping a response. Touching his chest, he said, "Mr. President, as of right now, your people live where others in this room allow. You, more than anyone, should accept that this proposal provides a permanent home that will be called the State of Palestine. Your own land."

"There are no resources. Water is scarce. We gain nothing."

"Mr. President, have you read the proposal? Have you glanced even a bit?" said the President of the United Arab Emirates. "I have looked at some of it, and although I do not agree with much of what I have read, you should see what we are asked to forfeit to give you a new address."

The Emirati smiled at his host. "Thank you, Mr. President," said the man who had called them together. "I hope you will find more agreement as I continue."

In Ashley's classroom down the hall, Jane took notes. The soldiers in the white jackets sat quietly, and Colonel Mitchell stared at the blackboard.

The president moved to the economic plan that Jane had prepared. To irrigate the desert, desalination plants would be constructed on the Mediterranean and pipelines would be connected to water storage facilities. Public works projects for roads, bridges, housing, schools, and hospitals addressed the need for temporary employment, putting disposable income in the hands of people living at a subsistence level. That would jump start the economies that needed the push. A deep-water harbor would be constructed in southern Gaza to provide access to shipping. The president discussed the need for educating young and old to meet their countries' needs.

"You need to bring your people into this century. We will begin by training your brightest to teach the rest. You will be able to build a middle class and make upward mobility possible."

"This is a very American plan, Mr. President, quite similar to your Marshall plan," said the King of Jordan.

"And you know, Your Highness, that the Marshall Plan succeeded in rebuilding all of western Europe," said the German Prime Minister.

"That is all well and good, but our societal structures are dissimilar and are not addressed."

"Your Highness, they are integral. I am not proposing changes to your society. I hope you will see the benefits for yourself, but a section further on discusses those issues. They apply not just to Palestine but to the entire region."

"He's on an island by himself," said Fritz.

"He's been there a lot, Fritz. He's doing fine. So far, no one has tried to leave.

"What's next?"

"The fun part. Paying for it."

* * *

HE IS ONE COLD, unfriendly SOB, Margaret Porter thought.

At 7:15, two men entered the hotel lobby. One, in a well-tailored blue pinstripe suit, had the patrician look of a diplomat. His companion, an Asian, stood behind, not moving. The concierge pointed to the express elevator to the roof.

At 7:30, the hotel wait staff arrived on the top floor with carts filled with a variety of hot, aromatic foods. Nakamura was alone except for the two men who had just arrived. More carts arrived, with plates and silverware. The man in the pinstripe suit noted the efficiency and glanced at his watch. Their tasks completed, the hotel staff left.

Nakamura followed the second hand of his watch and then nodded to his first guests. The Asian walked to the stairway exit and held the door. Nakamura's companions, carrying their golf bags, went straight to the roof. The older gentleman followed and stood looking down at the White House. A parade of limousines discharged their passengers and quickly moved away.

* * *

"ONLY ONE WAY does this move ahead. And since the whole world will benefit from the end of your wars, the whole world should participate in making these changes a reality. The United States is prepared to invest one trillion dollars over the next ten years in supplies, equipment, and manpower. We expect those of you with oil to match our financing and other resources. We expect those who will benefit most to provide the necessary political and social environment to allow this to happen. And to those of you who allow or facilitate the perpetuation of terrorist organizations, you must stop immediately. In return for our commitment and our resources, you will all agree to end your war against Israel." The president's words sparked a room full of loud refusal.

"Stop. All of you. Stop," said the Kuwaiti prime minister. "A growing economy helps each of us. We have already seen the damage of lost opportunity. I am an old man. It is time to end it. Stop the wars, stop the terror, behave like men. We believe in one God, all of us. Praise Allah, we should want him to be proud of us." The shouting started. The president laughed. He stood and cleared his throat.

The Iraqi president said, "Mr. President, we have had our differences. They will not be resolved here. I wish to leave." Shouting began again. The president held up his hand.

"We have barely begun."

"And you'll be gone in a year."

"And I intend to leave office with this project well under way. You want to leave. Give me a moment to arrange it." He left the room.

"FRITZ, GET out there," said the colonel. Already afoot, he ran into the false hallway just as the president also entered it.

"Ever been to Baghdad, Fritz?"

The president escorted the Iraqi across the hall. Fritz opened the portal. The president walked so close behind that the Iraqi president had to keep walking. They remained through the portal for three minutes until the president came back alone. "Reset it, Fritz. Quick."

When the president reappeared, the Iraqi president looked like he had been awakened from a bad dream. The president held the door and ushered him back to the meeting. From the open door, Fritz could hear the continuing arguments.

* * *

AS HER LAST stop for the day, Margaret Porter decided that one last check with Mr. Nakamura would suffice. Then she could go home. She had arranged for the room to be cleared once the time for use had expired. She had two wedding receptions to prepare in the morning.

Stepping from the elevator, she saw men with golf bags going through the door, shook her head, and went back to the lobby. The manager on duty was passing as the elevator doors opened.

"Hi, Margaret. Still here?"

"I don't know, John," she said, shrugging her shoulders. "I'm not sure where I am."

The look on her face made him ask if something was wrong. She told him what she had just seen.

* * *

FRITZ TOOK OUT his phone. "Hi Lin."

"Where are you?" she asked.

"At school, the summit." He saw Jane and the colonel each take out phones. "What's up?"

* * *

THE MEN TOOK THEIR GOLF BAGS to the roof. Five hid metal tubes. The Asians slid rockets from them, attached legs, and placed the tubes on metal bases that moments before had been golf bag bottoms.

"All of you, stay down. We can be seen," said Nakamura. "We have one minute to complete our mission. You have the range. Check where your first round hits, adjust, shoot, and leave. When the fireworks shells explode, it will distract them for only seconds. You must fire immediately." Nakamura walked to the front, ducking. "We have ten minutes."

The man in the pinstripe suit watched the men prepare. His companion stood in a concealed corner inside. When a bell sounded to indicate the elevator had reached the roof, the Asian removed his silenced pistol. Margaret Porter and her boss took two steps toward the roof. They never heard the two rapid pops. The Asian dragged the bodies to the corner and walked to the man in pinstripes.

In front of him, four mortars were aimed across Pennsylvania Avenue and one toward the southeast. "Mr. Nakamura," said pinstripe, "you go in thirty seconds. Earplugs." Each man placed a plug in one ear, waiting for the final moment.

* * *

“LADIES AND GENTLEMEN, my friend from Iraq and I have just found a reason to agree, which makes me very happy,” said the president. “As you can see, he has decided to stay. And I’m sure he will have some positive suggestions to add.” The Iraqi nodded.

“Now shall we get more specific? One of the two water plants we suggest is on the Turkish-Syrian border. Tanks will collect the water, and pipelines will stretch to the east and south, where more water tanks will be located. As progress continues, pipelines will reach further. Water-tank facilities will be at the ends of the pipelines. To pump the water, we propose development of solar and wind farms. You all know where the best places would be for each of you.”

Throughout the room and down the hall, cell phones began to ring.

* * *

SOUTHEAST OF THE White House, two star shells exploded, a fireworks display, turning the heads of the White House rooftop security. By the time they looked for the source, four rockets had been fired. Within seconds, more explosions had destroyed sections of the executive mansion.

* * *

“DON’T YOU KNOW?” asked Linda, fear climbing through the phone. “The White House is being bombed.” Jane’s face paled as she and the colonel headed for the door.

“I’ll call you back, Lin. No one here knew. I love you.”

“Fritz, be careful. Call me back.”

One of the soldiers asked him what was happening. He told them what he knew and took off with armed soldiers and waiters on his heels.

* * *

RADIO TRAFFIC WAS emphatic, "Move the first family." Spotters on the roof saw the smoke trail, and within minutes the Hay-Adams was invaded by angry soldiers.

* * *

MEL RUSHED THROUGH THE portal, not stopping for the soldiers, and pulled the conference-room door open. Heads turned at the unexpected disruption.

"Mr. President, the White House is being bombed. You need to stay here. All of you."

"Mel, what's happening? Where's my family?"

"They're safe, Mr. President. In a bunker. James is hurt. He's buried under the rubble. Sorry, sir. The Oval Office is gone. Troops are already in place."

"Get the guys, Mel. Everyone, please stay here."

The president ran right behind Mel. Jane and Colonel Mitchell were waiting in the school hallway.

Jane asked, "Mel, have the bombs stopped?"

"I don't know. I ran out as the roof fell in. When the bombs started, James called the residence. Then I came here."

The president said, "There's only one way to find anything out. Fritz, get me in." The portal had been held open, so he pulled the door. A secret service agent fell flat as he tried to grab the president and missed. Other agents raced through the portal.

* * *

ALARMED STAFF AND frightened guests avoided the soldiers, but the concierge stepped out and said, "May I help you?"

"The White House has been attacked from your roof," said the captain. "Take us up. The hotel is locked down. No one in or out." With weapons at the ready, soldiers blocked the doors.

The concierge was unruffled. "Of course, sir. As you wish. But our guests must be treated appropriately." The captain grabbed him by his lapels and lifted him off the ground.

"Get us up there now. For all I know, some of your guests did it. Now move!"

"Of course, sir. Any assistance we can provide." The concierge smoothed himself. "A moment please, so I can have our people accommodate you. We have an event in progress on our roof."

No one was visible. The surprised concierge led the soldiers to the door, where red splatter adorned the lace curtains of French doors. The soldiers ran in ahead. In the corner to his left, two bodies lay in bloody pools. The captain returned from the roof, a radio in hand. He reported five mortars and nine dead bodies, all apparently Asian. "Yes, sir. Right away." He looked straight at the now-stunned concierge. "Some party. Follow me."

* * *

FRITZ OPENED THE DOOR and Jane led six soldiers into a pile of rubble. Mel pointed to where James had fallen, and the soldiers began to dig. In the doorway, the president stood silent. Behind him, the conference attendees began to file out.

Fritz watched a metamorphosis occur. First, the president's jaw set, and he lowered his eyebrows. A quick brush of his left hand over his left ear. He balled his hands and pivoted to the filled hall. "Stay here." Fritz grabbed his arm as the president stepped to enter his office.

"Fritz, I want to see about James, and I want to check on my family. I'll be fine."

"Mr. President, please take someone with you. You don't know what's inside." Colonel Mitchell had worked his way through the crowd.

"I'll go with him, Fritz. Let him go."

Under the collapsed roof, soldiers had freed James from the debris, gravely hurt. Stepping through the rubble from the school, the President of Eledoria walked to James. "I am a doctor, Mr. President. I will do what I can until your doctor arrives."

"You're an eye doctor," said the colonel.

"Yes, but any doctor can help, and I was an Army doctor for four years. Do you have an oxygen tank nearby? And will someone get me water and a cloth?" While the Eledorian knelt to care for James, the president ran over broken glass and fallen ceiling into the main section of the White House. Surrounded by Marines and secret service agents, a crowd had collected—the imposter arrivals for the conference. And in the hall coming toward him were his family and Jane Barclay.

MEL WAS ON A PHONE when the first EMTs arrived with a doctor. Relinquishing his position, the President of Eledoria told the arriving doctor that the agent had a severe head wound but no other external wounds were apparent. James's respiration was shallow, he probably had broken ribs and punctured lungs, and he had a severely broken leg. The soldiers nearby cleared enough space for a stretcher and helped carry the agent to a waiting ambulance.

Fritz asked, "Where are you taking him."

"GW."

Climbing over the windowsill, which only moments before looked placidly out to the South Lawn, the vice president spotted Fritz. Before he could speak, Mel reported that Pennsylvania Avenue had been blocked off, and D.C. police and military units had moved on the Hay-Adams. "I'm talking to your team now, sir."

"I know. I walked two blocks to get in. Pissed off my agents, I can tell you. Is the president okay?"

"He's in the White House, Mr. Vice President. We were in the conference," Fritz cleared his throat, "across the hall."

"How was it going? Any progress?"

"A little, I think. Then this. No one knew until we got calls."

"Looks like you did it again, Fritz. Saved him. If we were doing the usual, they would all have been in here."

"Mr. Vice President, the leaders are standing in the doorway. What should I do?"

"Do any of them know about the portal?"

"He showed the Iraqi president his own living room. President Putin, the Israeli. That's it as far as I know."

"Well then, let's get them settled down. Come on."

"Wait." Fritz stepped gingerly across the room, bent over, and picked up a picture frame. "We should take care of this."

Chapter 25

AS THE ONLY uniformed person remaining, Fritz shepherded the leaders back to the meeting. The vice president took over. Once they were settled, Fritz walked through the panel to check on Tony.

"Glad to see you remembered me. Milt went back to the airport to get more guys. Can you tell me what's happening? I didn't want to move." Hard knocking down the hall delayed the answer. Fritz brushed the curtains aside, and looking in at him were Ashley and Chief Dempsey.

"Come on in. What brought you here?"

"We were watching TV," Ashley said. "When the attack started, they went live. The reporters were on the street when the fireworks started. Jim called the chief. Here we are. I brought my computer so we can check what's going on."

"We're camped in your classroom, Ash. The president is in the White House, the vice president is running the meeting."

"Where?" the chief asked.

"Just the other side of that wall."

THE VICE PRESIDENT knew every phase of the proposal. He assured everyone that they were completely safe and told them to get comfortable. "If anyone would like food, help yourselves. Then let's get back to work."

"Mr. Vice President, this seems a bad time for us to continue," said the British Prime Minister.

"Mr. Prime Minister, we have just suffered an attack on the center of my government. If we had kept to our original schedule, you would all have been in that room. What better time to talk about stopping this?" His piercing blue eyes crossed the room like lasers and left no doubt that he was in charge of the meeting.

"We could still be in danger. We don't know if they will attack again," said the Narian President.

"Mr. President, where you sit could not be safer."

"I must protest."

The vice president held up his hand. "Right now, while the White House is being checked, you are sitting far away. I know the president was saving the best for last, but no time like the present, my mother always said." He walked them back to the hallway.

"Sergeant, I want you to close the door in a minute." Turning to the leaders, he said, "Look closely at what was the Oval Office." He nodded to Fritz. When the latch clicked, Fritz pulled again. The vice president said, "If you will all follow me." He stepped into Fritz's classroom. As they gathered in front of the room, Robert E. Lee reached out to his memory. The current occupants shared the same bewildered looks. The vice president continued. "You are standing in a classroom of an American high school. Now, would anyone like to go somewhere else?"

"I would like to go to my home," said the Israeli Prime Minister, smiling.

Fritz reset the portal, and the Israeli invited everyone to join him. As the hall emptied, President Putin, the last one in line, caught his eye. Ashley joined Fritz.

"Ash, do you have your phone?"

"Yep."

"Go with them in case there's a problem," Moments later, Fritz's phone rang. He looked at the ID screen.

"Hi, Mr. President. Is your family okay?"

"We're all shaken. Fritz, what's going on? I can't get back."

"Everyone is in Israel. I'll come get you in a minute. They're with the vice president."

The door opened and the leaders were talking softly, some to themselves.

"Mr. President, they're coming back. I'll see you in a minute."

Ashley led them out and opened the door to the meeting room. The vice president and the Israeli leader were the last to come through.

"Mr. Vice President, I may be wrong," said the prime minister, "but I think you have convinced them."

THE PRESIDENT hurried across the hall. "I'll talk to you later, Fritz." Holding the door open, Fritz and Ashley stared at unimaginable destruction. Shovels and wheelbarrows were already removing debris. Two men with paint brushes were whisking a flat surface. Although covered with rubble and surrounded by it, the Resolute Desk had survived. Covered in dust, tracks on her cheeks, Jane walked into the remains of the Oval Office with Colonel Mitchell. With small, careful steps, they reached the school hall. She hugged Ashley.

Colonel Mitchell said, "At least seven are dead, and James is in bad shape. The bombs were mortar shells, apparently fired from the hotel. Whoever is responsible killed all their own operatives."

Jane said, "The president wants to keep going. He doesn't want another Geneva. He was doing so well."

"The vice president picked up the meeting. He's already taken them to the Oval Office and Israel and let them see my classroom. He beat them over the head. I think it might work."

“He has to keep them quiet though. Fritz, if word gets out, the bad guys will know.”

“Too bad we can’t bug them all.”

Jane said quietly, “Thanks, Fritz.”

* * *

IN THE MIDDLE OF Key Bridge, a man in a pinstripe suit took a camera from a small travel bag set on the paved walkway. Pretending to take pictures of the Lincoln Memorial and the lighted Lee-Custis mansion at the top of Arlington National Cemetery, he removed a silencer from his pocket and tossed the metal tube into the Potomac. When a lull in traffic gave him the opportunity, he tore the molded plastic from his face, wrapped it securely around the pistol and dropped them to the churning water below. Satisfied, he repacked the camera, climbed into his car, and headed for his waiting plane.

Chapter 26

"**MR. PRESIDENT,** in spite of all we have seen and all that has happened tonight, I need time to absorb your proposal. You expect much, perhaps more than is possible," said the Lebanese president. "You cannot appreciate how limited my authority is. Hezbollah can veto anything we might decide."

"Mr. President, you have just witnessed what we can do. Some of you have already seen it first hand, though you may not have known it."

"That was YOU?" proclaimed the Narian president. "But how? They were underground." The president smiled but said nothing, watching his audience exchange glances.

"I am committed to our collective success," said the president. "You have heard our proposal. Perhaps you need to consider it in some quiet. We'll stop for now and resume tomorrow morning. Same travel arrangements. You will all be picked up at 8 am. In light of tonight's attack, the location for tomorrow will be adjusted. To keep us all safe, you are all sworn to secrecy. I ask for your words of honor. I will consider any breach an act of bad faith, and depending on what comes of tonight's attack, perhaps an act of war."

The vice president suggested another demonstration before they adjourned and left the room. Before the others followed, he said, "Fritz, can you set us up to go to an open field somewhere?

Colonel, I need a weapon and someone to shoot it." Stepping into in the Oval Office debris, he brought out a seat cushion. Fritz shut the door. In the bottom drawer of his desk, he had the map for the open field where the Israeli settlers had gone after their rescue from the Eledorians. The paperclip was already in place.

"Where are we going, Sergeant?" the president asked.

"Mr. President, perhaps the prime minister would help here." He looked at the Israeli. "He's been here before." Fritz opened the door, and the vice president and Colonel Mitchell led everyone out.

"Where are they, Fritz?" the president whispered.

"Where the settlers went." They watched the vice president stage the assassination of a seat cushion. They heard him say, "Now if you will all wait here." He walked into the hall. "Fritz, shut the door."

Fritz quickly reset the portal.

"Let 'em wait a second. Let it sink in," said the vice president. "The Israeli PM is telling them where they are." His head bobbed, as if he were counting down, and then he said, "Okay. Let's get them back."

As they returned, they all looked squarely at the vice president. He smiled at each of them. The president stood to the side, holding back a snide remark.

With everyone in the meeting room again, the president asked them to be seated for a moment. They were being reconnected to the White House and their rides, he said. "Please look over your packages. We have an opportunity now that has been squandered for years. Think of what you have seen, and we will find agreement tomorrow."

Crossing into the debris field of the Oval Office, the president escorted them to the White House exit. In the empty school, now quiet, Fritz began asking questions. He asked Jane how James was. She said he was in bad shape. He asked about the others. Twelve people, including Lily Evans, were wounded by the explosions or falling plaster. Seven were killed: three from the housekeeping staff, a secret service agent, and three soldiers.

"Have you spoken to Linda yet?" Jane asked.

"Only earlier. I ought to call her." He ran down the hall. The vice president waited for the president's return.

Tony asked, "Are you done?"

"Almost." The vice president continued to watch through the portal.

"NICE SHOW, JOE," said the president. "I intended to wait until tomorrow."

"Hope I didn't spoil it for you, Mr. President. At least they'll all have a night to think about it. But where will we do it to-morrow?"

"Well, not here. That's for sure. We need to talk to Fritz." He opened Ashley's classroom.

In the meeting room, Jane backed up all the meeting segments, and in the hall, Fritz spoke to Linda.

"The newsfeed was live," said Linda. "Two explosions were in front, and two seemed to be behind. But four hit the building. It looked like it came from across the street."

"It did. The hotel. Lin, James is badly hurt. The Oval Office is a mess. The president just signaled me. I'll call you in a bit, when I know what's next."

"Fritz, be careful."

"SORRY TO PUT this pressure on you," the president said. "I'm not going to let this end in a disaster. We're going to do more tomorrow. I'm going to make this work."

Fritz looked him in the eye. "Then do it, Mr. President."

Jane had wandered in with her open laptop. She reported that two hotel employees and nine Asian men were found shot to death on the roof, along with eight empty golf bags. Surveillance video for the past week had been taken for analysis. "Apparently, the shooters checked in on Monday. Some guy named

Nakamura arranged everything. He's dead, too. No evidence of a fight. They fired their shells and then someone executed them."

* * *

FRITZ REACHED HIS classroom at quarter to eight and grabbed the White House brochure. Disturbed by banging in the hall, he stepped through the fake wall and saw Tony with Jane and Ashley. The leaders were running late after their long night reading, but the president wanted Fritz to get him at eight.

"Where are the generators?"

"The colonel is bringing them," said Tony. "They left a couple of minutes behind me."

Fritz called the president, who answered his cell phone before the first ring was done. "Are you ready, Fritz?"

"Not yet, Mr. President. We're waiting for Colonel Mitchell. Have you decided what to do?"

"I have maps and photos of the tunnel entrance from the Old Executive and Camp David. We'll gather in the meeting room and then head to Camp David." Fritz heard a touch of sadness in his voice.

Four cars stopped by the door. "The colonel's here. What time do you want to do this?" Fritz saw the soldiers leaving the cars. "They're dressed like waiters again."

"Fritz, hand me over to Mitchell." Fritz held out his phone.

"Morning, Mr. President. Yes, sir. We can try. Can we get through your office? Okay, yes, sir. We'll be right there."

The colonel handed the phone back. The president told Fritz to come to the Oval Office as soon as he could and asked to speak to Jane. Fritz called down the hall.

Jane took the phone while the generators and power cords were being set. "If that's what you want, no problem. Camp David has all the recording devices we need. Are you going to need the colonel? Okay. Tony just signaled he's set. Okay. In a minute."

She gave the phone back and said, "He's ready." The open door displayed a clear sky where the ceiling had been. As the president crossed the room, Fritz was astounded by the desk, cleaned and polished, sitting in its prominent spot, an anchor of American resilience.

Ashley held the door as the previous night's dinner carts were shoved through the Oval Office and out of sight. Colonel Mitchell came out smiling. "Thought you might want this, Mr. President."

A reserved smile crossed the president's face. "The Proclamation. You saved it. Oh, thank you."

"Fritz grabbed it last night in case of another attack."

The president squeezed Fritz's shoulder. He tugged up his jacket sleeve, checked the time, and crossed the hall. "Almost done?" he asked.

Colonel Mitchell, standing at his right, said, "One more trip and everything's out. We don't have time to make it neat and pretty for them, sir."

"Push in the chairs. They won't be here long enough for it to matter." His phone rang. "Hi, Joe. Really? Already? Give me a second to set up. I wasn't expecting them yet." The president listened. "See you in a minute." Facing his companions, he said, "He's hearing positive comments. Fritz, let's go."

Colonel Mitchell called his men, who had taken off waiter white and put on their service uniforms.

"Here's the tunnel. And this is where we're headed at Camp David."

With the hallway returned to perfect camouflage, the leaders entered the hall. The Israeli prime minister winked, and Putin actually smiled.

Jane kissed Ashley and joined the dignitaries. Fritz reset the portal, knocked on the meeting room door, and reopened his classroom door to their new destination, a conference room at

Camp David. Jane, wearing a skirt, blouse, and heels, waited with the president. Directing the group through the door, the president wore his battle face. The leaders glanced at Fritz as they passed. After Jane and the president entered, the vice president said, "And away we go. Who wants breakfast?"

Monitoring the portal wasn't necessary while the meeting proceeded. Ashley and the vice president went to Hoffmann's and returned with trays of sandwiches. Ashley told Fritz he thought Mr. Hoffmann was going to faint when they walked in. Conversation ate the morning. When Robert E. Lee's visit was mentioned, questions abounded. One soldier asked where else Fritz had been. Ashley checked on any breaking news on Jane's computer.

The conversation changed when Linda called. She had called Lucy Williams. Linda choked up. James wasn't expected to survive, and Lily Evans had died. She wondered if the president knew.

"He didn't say anything, Lin. About either of them." Everyone was looking at him. "But he doesn't look like he slept much. I'm sure he knows." Fritz hung his head. "The meeting is still going, so we're just hanging around." They said goodbye, and Fritz told the group what Linda had told him.

Finally, Jane called to say they were adjourning. "She said to open the door in five minutes so everyone could go into the school meeting room."

Everyone played their parts. The president emerged with an unidentifiable look on his face. Fritz looked for tell-tale signs of agreement but saw only poker faces. The president said, "I'll call you when they're gone." The colonel and the soldiers accompanied him.

"How did it go?" Fritz asked Jane.

"I'll let him tell you."

"Does he know about Lily Evans and James?"

"I'll let him say, Fritz. This situation is above my pay-grade."

Within five minutes, the president called. Saying nothing, he nodded to Tony and walked to Ashley's room. Although Fritz had questions, he waited for the president to speak. He told them to sit down.

"This hasn't been my best day." With a quick glance at the late-afternoon sunlight dancing through the window, he took a deep breath and turned back to his waiting audience. "Fritz, will you set up for dinner. We covered a lot, but they're not all convinced. I know they suspect some of what we've used the portal for, but I haven't said outright." His grimace reflected his frustration. "I know they want to talk to advisors, but they need to agree first or this will get mired in excuses. They're stalling. I can't help but think some of them are happy about last night's attack."

"Do you think one of them is the perpetrator?" Ashley asked.

"I don't know. I think so, but who?"

Fritz asked, "What do you need for tonight?"

"Same as this morning. But Fritz, I may need you to set up to take them to their homes. Like the Speaker."

"I have the maps ready. It'll be the middle of the night."

"So much the better. If you can find bedrooms, that would be best. Drop them, leave, and then show up again."

"Mr. President, they don't know where we are, do they?"

"I haven't said anything. They only know it's a school. I'm still concerned about your safety, Fritz. I should go now. I want to check on my family, and I need to check on James and Lily's families." His eyes began to fill up.

"Could this be the Caballeros, Mr. President?"

"One thing at a time, Fritz. I asked Mel to get as much info about the attack as possible. So pick me up at six. They'll be ready at 6:15." He returned to the hall and through the panel with Fritz right behind.

Reaching into his jacket pocket, he withdrew a picture, yellowed and old. "Hang on to this for me. Keep it safe."

“Sure.” In the photo, a young woman stood on the porch of a house. He reset the Oval Office, and the president stepped into the White House.

* * *

AT QUARTER TO SIX, they met in the parking lot. Jane had her laptop in her satchel. Once again, she was Major Barclay.

“You’re a chameleon, Jane,” Fritz said.

“I’m not important, Fritz. I don’t want to be a distraction. My job is to record everything. The president is trying hard to contain his anger, and he’s very upset about James and Lily.”

“How long do you think he’ll go tonight?”

“It could be late. Even those who know what he’s doing are keeping quiet. No one wants to be the first to agree.”

At six, the president came through the portal. He was biting his lip. He told them James had lost his battle. “Jane, we need to find out where these attacks are coming from.”

“We will, sir. I have a feeling.”

The president looked at his watch. “Game time.” Fritz reached out and felt the buzz. It ran through his fingers, up his arm, and into his head. Though he didn’t know why, he knew everything would work out. He blinked and saw how it would play out.

“Are you okay?” the president asked.

Fritz met his eyes, and smiled. “Yes, sir. And we’ll all be okay. Go get ‘em.”

When the door clicked, Ashley asked, “What happened?”

“I don’t know. But I could see it. Like a gigantic sunrise.”

Uncommon for him, the vice president frowned and said nothing. The stifling quiet on a hum of whispers made Fritz uneasy. He wondered if his vivid image was wrong. Could the bright light be something other than sunrise?

“Sir, what do you think is going to happen?

The Vice President looked around, licked his lips and inhaled. He was trying to choose the words. “I’ve spoken personally to most of those guys over the years. And for years, they've been afraid that a solution will take them out of control. Some of them are greedy. Some like the power. They all like their cushy lives. Some aren't willing to change." He looked down at his hands. "Fritz, they're all smart people, playing the odds. The portal is a game-changer. They're measuring the cost to them personally. If all of them had thought about their countries before, you wouldn't have to ask."

"Do you think the president will get an agreement tonight?"

The vice president put his hand to his chin, and a cautious smile reached his face. "I don't know, but he'll scare them for sure. They'll be on the spot. He'll force them to say yes or no." Then he shook his head and said, "And woe to them that vote no." He checked the wall clock. "It won't be much longer."

"Do you know how long it will take to fix the Oval Office?"

"You ask a lot of hard questions, Fritz, but I guess I should expect that. You are a teacher." Quiet chuckles filled the room. "A few weeks for repairs, maybe."

Fritz wanted to ask every question that came to mind, but the vice president turned away. Ashley touched Fritz's arm and shook his head. Quiet returned, but not for long.

Cell phones rang together. Fritz didn't have time to say hello. "Fritz, get us out of here. Quickly." The president was shouting. Everyone was moving. Fritz reset the portal and the push to exit was magnified by the background explosions. Ashley stood by the door, ignoring protocol, waiting for Jane. The president said, "Ashley, I don't know where she is."

Pushing through the doorway, he ran in, calling her name. Fritz kept the door open watching explosive flashes and hearing accompanying booms. Between concussions, he could hear Ashley calling.

"Call her phone," Fritz yelled.

His phone to his ear, dodging broken furniture and fallen ceiling slabs, Ashley rounded a corner. When he reappeared, he was carrying Jane and led a dozen men. Colonel Mitchell ran in to help. Finally, Fritz shut the door.

"Open your door, Fritz," said the president. The classroom appeared. The portal was shut. The president moved the meeting back to the original meeting room.

* * *

"I'M FINE, ASH," said Jane. "I got hit on the head." She started to stand. Fritz pointed to blood running down her left leg.

"I'm taking her out of here. I'll talk to you later."

* * *

"SOMEONE IN THIS room is responsible for this attack," the president said. "You may not have ordered it, but one of you told someone we were meeting at Camp David." He looked around, staring from his lowered brow. "Only four people on my staff knew. They are all beyond suspicion. Which of you gave our location away?" Four reluctant hands went up. Saudi Arabia, England, the United Arab Emirates, Israel. The president's anger hid his disbelief. *These are the wrong guys.* "Anyone else?" No hands. "Wait here."

"Fritz, set up Saudi Arabia, the Emirates, England, and Israel. We're taking a trip."

"Yes, sir." The Saudi king was the first stop.

"Your Highness, if you would." Fritz opened the door to a dark room and shut the door. The president returned alone. Fritz reset the portal and yanked the door open again.

Two men returned. "But, Mr. President. Please." The president waved his hand to cut the king short. Next, the president of the United Arab Emirates was escorted through, and once again, the president returned alone. Fritz repeated the process for each man. When they had seen the extraordinary stealth and the precision, the president herded them back to the meeting.

* * *

"MR. PRESIDENT, please, I only told Massoud in case I was needed."

"And you told me that you could keep a secret, so we have a problem." The president pounded on the last word. "I know you all have others who you would like to tell. I can't stop you. I trusted the honor of your word as enough. I was wrong. And all of us were in mortal danger."

"But Mr. President…"

"We have been attacked. Again. Like we were in Geneva. U.S. navy bases have been attacked. I have been clear about what the United States hopes to achieve here, and what we are willing to do to help you make life better in each of your countries. All of you have seen firsthand what we are able to do. We are not here for politics or diplomacy. We are here to stop your endless wars and petty arguments. Addressing the needs of your countries is our goal. Stability with economic development is the only way you can remain in power. Tomorrow morning we will meet again. I hoped we could do this tonight. I will have an agreement sent to each of you. Be prepared to sign it tomorrow." He headed to the door.

"Mr. President, I will sign it now," said the British Prime Minister.

"Thank you. Tomorrow." No one doubted his anger. "Now it's time to leave."

Fritz held the door as the leaders silently returned to the Old Executive Office Building. Only the president, the vice president, and Fritz were left in the fake hallway.

"Can you handle one more day, Fritz?"

"I can, but I need to get Linda at the airport at dinnertime."

"We'll be done by then. By noon, I hope. How's Jane?"

"I don't know. She's with Ash. I think they went to the hospital."

The president pushed the panel, but it didn't open. Fritz hit the release, and they went to Ashley's empty classroom. Tony told Fritz that Ashley had said to call him.

"We're done, Tony."

"Not yet, Fritz. I still need to go home."

"Sorry. I keep forgetting you don't live here."

"It feels that way sometimes, doesn't it? I'll go now. Oh, and I'll call Mr. Dougherty. They'll get Linda."

"Thank you. I'll tell her." He hesitated. "Mr. President, do you think it worked?"

"We'll know in the morning. Let's go, Joe. I have something I want you to do."

When the president was gone, Fritz went into his classroom and sat at his desk. Tony came in, and Fritz motioned to a chair.

"You know, Tony. I thought for sure this would work, that he'd get them to sign." Fritz rubbed the back of his neck as he looked up at the president's picture on the wall. He opened the buttons of the uniform jacket. "That's better," he said, and rubbed his stomach and chest. "Tony, is Milt Chelton at the airport?"

"Uh-huh. They plan to break everything down when the meeting is over. Why?"

"I had a thought the other day. I think I have the perfect place for the walls in the hallway. Bring him with you in the morning, okay?"

Tony nodded and said, "Call Ashley."

Chapter 27

JANE LIMPED into the kitchen with Ashley just behind. Fritz caressed a glass of amber liquid. "Want a drink?" he asked.

"Tonight, yes, I do," she said. "What happened after we left?"

"Another meeting tomorrow morning. I don't think I've ever seen him so angry. He walked four of them through the portal, the way he did with the Speaker. Blank stares when they came back. I could hear him in the meeting. He was, let's say, purposeful."

"Good. But something else is going on. I can feel it. Remember the Korean talking about his teams. What if one of them was the group at the Hay-Adams? What if another was at Camp David? What if it's not terrorists from the Middle East?" Mary and Jim walked into the kitchen. Jane looked at Jim and said, "Who stands to benefit?"

"Jane, even if you're right, the president thinks it's someone from the meeting," said Fritz. "We still don't have any proof. Only random links."

Jane shook her head, her long-distance stare returning. "Caballeros."

The president called at midnight. "Nine o'clock, Fritz. Okay?"

"Sure. Same routine? Where are you going this time?"

"Death Valley."

Fritz chuckled and shook his head. "See you then, Mr. President."

"WE'RE READY, Mr. President." The door opened to the Oval Office, the missing ceiling now made up of tarps. The debris had disappeared, and the Presidential Seal was visible again on the rug.

"Morning, everyone. Last shot to make my point." He handed Fritz the Death Valley map. "No one knows except us. Let's go."

Fritz set the map. The hallway filled quickly, and the heads of state were gone. The president returned almost immediately.

"Let them sweat a bit. Maybe then they'll know I'm serious."

"Mr. President," Jane said, "I think it's the Caballeros."

"I've been thinking about that too, Jane. But how would they know? We'll talk later. Fritz, Linda will be at Dougherty's office. They traced her reservation for me."

"Thanks. I'll tell her."

"Let's bring them back."

The portal opened, and the hall filled and emptied again. Fritz didn't need a cue.

"Thanks, Fritz. You're done for now. Talk to you all later."

* * *

ONCE THE PRESIDENT had gone, Fritz found Milt and asked when they planned to take down the fake walls and clear the hallway.

"We'll start as soon as the guys get here. Had to wait until everything was done."

"What are you going to do with these walls?"

"Take them out and probably break them up for scrap. They don't have any other use."

"I had an idea the other day. I think they'll fit in George's office. Would you consider a remodel job?"

"Why not? Shame to waste all that hard work making them. Let's take a look."

"Jane, why don't you go sit in my room?"

"Fritz, I want to see what you're thinking," said Ashley. "George will have a fit if you mess with his inner sanctum."

"He hasn't even painted that room since I've been here. It's time to redecorate."

Getting into George's office was easy. Milt took a tape measure to the bare walls. His experienced eye visualized the finished product. "We can do this. They will just fit. Do you want us to paint too?"

"Do you have gold paint?" asked Fritz.

"No, but I can get some. Want us to do it today?"

"Don't do it, Fritz." Ashley warned. "Ask him first."

"How long before your guys get here, Milt?"

"I haven't called yet. If they stop for paint, a half hour maybe. The trucks are already loaded."

Fritz took out his phone, hesitated, and then dialed George. Lois answered.

"What are you up to, Fritz?"

"You amaze me constantly, Lois. Do you think George would like his office remodeled? And painted?"

"We'll be there in fifteen minutes." She hung up.

"Call the guys, Milt."

George was huffy, not happy about another disturbance in his life. Lois, on the other hand, looked at the panels and told him it would add stature to his position. "White won't work in here though," she said. "You need some color. Something bright." She turned to Milt. "Could you add some shelves? George, you can get rid of those ugly metal things." When Milt said they could, she said, "George let's go home and let them get to work." As they were leaving, she said yellow or gold would be good.

* * *

"I DO NOT KNOW WHERE they will be this morning. He did not tell me. In fact, he went straight to his room."

The man gazed at the sunrise hitting the Pacific as he listened. "IM, we've disrupted them successfully. Thank you for keeping me informed. I assume you are returning home with your people. I will see you here in two weeks." He hung up. *Excellent orange juice this morning.*

* * *

"FRITZ, I THINK we need to spend some time on the play this week," Ashley said.

Fritz yawned and ran a hand through his hair. "It's hard to change gears. You're right, but I'm not ready yet. I could use a day off."

"Hey, pal, we don't have a day off until school ends. Suck it up."

"We've just been a part of what may be the most important event of our lives, and we're talking about school. What an absurdity."

"I understand. I was thinking how weird it is that your door opens to the world, literally and figuratively."

* * *

MEMORANDA HAD BEEN sent to each leader. Doubts and questions resonated in the conference room. The agreement they were about to conclude would mark the end of conflict and notify the world that a new economy was coming to the region. The president told them they had two words from which to choose—yes or no.

"Mr. President, I need to discuss this with..."

"No, you don't. You can agree or not. What you say after that, and to whom, won't matter. We will have a press conference when we're done. It will be broadcast around the world, either for or against. Yes or no."

The four-page agreement had been reviewed by the cabinet, the state department counsel, and the four congressional leaders. "You all have seen the development documents and the agreement. Here it is. I've already signed and dated it. Lunch is in the next room. If you will, sign it and join me." Surveying the faces around the table, he rose, and left the room.

* * *

ANOTHER NON-STOP weekend caught up with them. Jane spent the afternoon waiting for news and discussing the reports on the two attacks. The details about what had happened at the Hay-Adams were more readily available, but the security videos from Camp David were too far away to spot the attackers. At 5:30, Fritz said he was heading to the airport and asked if anyone wanted to come. Jane said she was waiting to hear from the president. Ashley said he'd pick up dinner. He was on his own. He drove over the bridge and south on I-95, the same route he had followed at Thanksgiving. When he reached the spot where his wheels came off, his wandering into a vision of the crash brought honking from the car he almost cut off. *Just what I need, another one.* On the downslope of the bridge, he watched a plane approaching the runway until the road curved and the plane disappeared from view. He parked and went looking for Charles Dougherty's office.

At 6:30, Linda and TJ arrived, escorted by two security guards. Dougherty said the two men would escort Fritz and Linda to their car. Linda had protested that it wasn't necessary.

"Ms. Russell, our mutual friend asked me to be sure you got home safely. We've arranged an escort across the river. He asked me to call him when you're on your way."

Fritz said, "I appreciate it, but I think he's probably a little busy right now. He's had a bad weekend."

"Ya think? I wouldn't want to be in his shoes. But he insisted, and he's not someone I want mad at me."

"I know what you mean. Well, then, thank you."

With two police cars as company, one in front, one behind, the Russells crossed the bridge to New Jersey. Fritz watched in the rearview mirror as their escort peeled off and headed back.

"I'm glad you're home," said Fritz.

"Glad to be home. I have a lot to tell you. I had a long talk with Daddy. But I was busy, too. Mom asked me to make lasagna and wrote down everything I did." She told Fritz that she spent each meal giving her mother tips on how to cook dinner. "Daddy said he hadn't had a good homemade meal in years. Not in front of Mom, though."

"We have company for dinner, Lin. Jane and Ash. And Jim has been with Mary pretty much all weekend."

"You weren't in the attacks, were you?" She frowned. "Fritz, too many people know now for us to be safe."

"I wasn't. Ashley went into Camp David last night. Jane was hurt again. He brought out a bunch of people after the attack."

"And now more people know. Is she hurt badly?"

"Fortunately, no. At least it doesn't seem like it. She was hit by glass and something hit her on the head."

"He's as bad as she is. Rushing into an attack. They're both nuts. Made for each other." Fritz looked sideways for a moment. Although her comment was innocuous, her tone was angry. He wondered what she was holding back, but he let it pass.

Dinner was ready when they walked in. "You've had a quiet weekend, I hear," she said, looking around the table. "Jane, are you okay?"

"A little sore. But I've been worse."

Fritz looked out the window. Behind him, the whoosh and soft bang of the closing oven door signaled dinner. The clink of glasses, the clank of pot and serving spoon, and the clunk of the platter on the counter was prelude to the meal Ashley had collected.

"Have you heard from the president?" Fritz asked. Jane shook her head, glancing at the clock. "I wonder if the meeting's done?"

"He said he would call. If it had gone well, we would have heard by now, I think," Jane said.

"I was so sure this morning. Is anything being reported on the news?" Jane shook her head again. "Any news about the attacks?"

"Fritz, nothing's changed since you left." She stopped. Though she had more to say, she shook her head, and took a bite of chicken. The only sound was TJ chittering in his swing.

Dinnertime passed into evening and pressed into night. Jim left and Jane and Ashley had their coats on, when finally Jane's phone sounded, "Hail to the Chief," her new ringtone for the president.

"Hello, Mr. President." Her frown became a scowl. "You're kidding. Sorry, but that just makes no sense. Okay, talk to you then." She handed the phone to Fritz.

"Hello, Mr. President."

"Fritz, I just wanted to thank you again. I know it's been a long weekend for you. We'll talk again soon." The abrupt click prevented further questions.

"Jane, what happened?"

"He didn't want to talk. Only the Israelis and British were willing to sign. He knows he can't force them, and he can't keep them here."

Fritz leaned on his elbows and pressed his fingers together. Looking through the bay window, he said, "It's not over. School ends before dinner. Maybe we have another shot to make it work." He turned to Jane. "Jane, call him back. Tell him to keep them in town until tomorrow night. We need to come up with one more demonstration. Let's figure it out. I have an idea."

Jane's call went unanswered. Linda stared at Fritz as if he'd lost his mind. He ignored the questions, took out his phone, and called. His call wasn't answered either.

"Jane, do you have Mel Zack's number?" She found it and handed Fritz her phone.

"Hi Mel. It's Fritz Russell."

"I know, Fritz. My phone is magic."

"Sorry. Do you know where the president is?"

"Fritz, he's on his way to see Lucy Williams. He said he won't take calls until he gets back."

"Can you get through?"

"I don't know. He's on an emotional rollercoaster. Been a bad weekend."

"Mel, I have an idea, and it can't wait. Will you try, please?"

"James is dead, and he's upset and angry about the outcome of the meeting. I want to help, but I can't overstep my limits. I'll let him know you said it was urgent, but I can't promise."

He hung up and picked up a pen and tapped, staring at the tabletop.

"What's your idea?" Ashley asked.

"It won't matter if I don't talk to him." He sucked his lips. "Linda, don't we have James's home phone?"

"It's with TJ's stuff. The gift list. I'll go get it."

"Fritz, maybe now's not a good time to pursue this," Jane said. Linda agreed.

"Look, we've all had a long weekend, and it certainly didn't go well. I know he's rattled. But he can't quit now. I've seen him face adversity. He's embraced it, shaken hands with it, and even invited it to dinner. Then, he choked it out of its misery. He can't stop now."

Linda grimaced. "I'll get the number."

"Lucy, this is Fritz Russell. We're so deeply sorry. Linda wants to talk to you, too. But I really need to talk to the president, and

I was told he was on his way to see you. I think I have a way to make this weekend not a waste. Would you tell him?"

"That's a mouthful, Fritz. He's right here." Fritz heard a momentary pause as he came to the phone.

"I got your message, Fritz. I have a lot to do. I'll talk with you tomorrow."

"Tomorrow's too late." Fritz yelled to keep the president from hanging up. A sigh, and the sharp tone that followed bit into his ear.

"All right, Fritz. What is it?"

"Mr. President, I have an idea that might shake them up. But you have to keep them here."

A dispirited voice asked, "What's your idea, Fritz?"

"The past."

Fritz's answer summoned the Cheshire Cat. Ashley knew the leaders hadn't seen the portal at its best and asked, "So what did he say?"

"He'll call when he gets back to the White House. He wanted to know if I have something specific in mind. We need to come up with something."

Linda said, "A Christmas Carol."

Chapter 28

WHEN THE PRESIDENT finally called, the printer was running, Linda and Ashley were doing research, and Jane was making calls.

"So you think you can make this work?"

"I do, Mr. President. I was thinking—the past. But Linda suggested we make it personal. We already know we change the future, but you can certainly make a point about changing the present. If being in their bedroom didn't get the message through, maybe this will."

"That's pretty devious, Fritz. You missed your calling. I should have been more wary of you last spring. So what's the plan?"

* * *

EXHAUSTED, Fritz and Ashley met in the hall after third period. Fritz said he had talked about the War of 1812 in class, the last time the White House had been attacked. Ashley told him all his kids wanted to talk about was what had happened over the weekend. He had them write news stories and read them aloud.

"Did they stay?" Fritz asked.

"Jane said only two left. The president told them to come back, or he was coming to get them."

Fritz told the ninth graders he would have the next round matches ready to post by Wednesday. "We already did it," said

Susan. "We used a random number generator, like you did." She waved a sheet of paper. "Here it is." The list was set up like the brackets for March Madness.

"Good. Go ahead and post it. You might ask Mr. McAllister if you can announce the games."

"We did that too," said Jay. "Tomorrow morning." *I should be getting used to their competence and impressive thinking*, Fritz thought.

Before heading out, he went to see George and let him know another mission was coming. Ms. Sweeney accompanied him to George's doorway, a cheerful twinkle in her eyes. George was rearranging his office.

"Looks nice, George."

The principal looked at his new bookcases and the paneling and grinned. "Thanks, Fritz. It makes me feel brand new. Even the paint smell doesn't bother me too much." The side chairs were empty for the first time since the fall.

"Looks like you're getting organized. I'm going home, but I wanted you to know we'll be back later. The summit's not over yet. We have one more idea to use."

"Do you want me to come?"

"Not necessary. Just wanted you to know."

"Well, I'll be here a while, so stop by if I'm still here. Oh, by the way, Mr. Chelton said the president asked him not to dismantle the classroom." He went back to work, singing under his breath.

No argument, no fuss. Fritz scratched behind his left ear. *The portal at work?*

* * *

"HI HONEY, I'm home," he said, stepping into the kitchen.

"Hi honey, I'm glad," said Ashley.

Linda said, "The president called. He wants you to get him at 6:15."

"Okay. Where's Jane?"

"In here, Fritz," she called from the dining room. "I'm finishing up the locations."

"We've been doing research all day," Linda said. He draped his coat over his chair. "If this doesn't work, nothing will."

Jane joined them, a file folder in her right hand. "We have a bio and a map for each of them. I put them in order of most susceptible. Putin's first."

"Wow. You've really done a lot of work. The maps are really detailed. But I have to think about how to make the times match up."

Ashley said, "When you first saw General Lee, you paper-clipped a section of the book. We think if you clip the bio and the map together, you'll get the same effect."

"That might work. These maps all look like floor plans."

Jane responded, "Each childhood home, with a GPS. We thought you should go to the outside so they can see where they are. But you'll have to play it by ear."

"It'd be useful to have a practice run." Turning pages, Fritz rubbed his forehead. "But I don't imagine we'll have time."

"Fritz, we thought you should end with a big event, so they all could see it together," said Linda.

"What?"

"We made a list of possibilities and then tried to find the supporting materials. Mary suggested Christ's crucifixion or Hiroshima," said Linda.

"Either of those would take the starch out of their shorts," Ashley said.

"Won't work. We'd be guessing about Jerusalem, and Hiroshima would be too dangerous."

"It'll be the middle of the night in Paris. We figured the Louvre will be empty and locked down," said Linda. "Go see the Mona Lisa. It's not exactly time travel, but they'll all know it. You emphasize the ability to be precise, that way. And if you take the colonel and some soldiers, no guard will be a problem."

Fritz grinned. They had thought it through, step by step. "Did you tell all this to the president?" he asked.

Jane said, "He's impressed, Fritz. He was almost giggling. He said he couldn't wait to see their faces."

At a quarter to six, Fritz grabbed his coat and the folder. Only Jane joined him. Linda saw his confusion and told him that she and Ashley were staying behind. "Too many extras, Fritz. And here's the picture the president gave you. He asked if you would bring it." He kissed her, waved to Mary, and patted Ashley on the shoulder. Two SUVs were waiting when they arrived. Everyone was so used to the routine that conversation was unnecessary. The colonel and five members of his unit waited for them. The idling police car meant that Jim Shaw had been alerted. Fritz set up the White House brochure, fetched the president and Mel Zack, and crossed the hall to the meeting room.

"They are all back and I had very little difficulty arranging tonight," the president said. "They've had all day to discuss the plan with their advisors. Jane, you have an itinerary, you said?"

"Yes, sir. First stop. Russia."

"Fritz, is there any way to gauge the time you walk out of the portal?"

"I've been thinking about that all day. We've used current time up until now, but we tried to adjust the time when we experimented with General Lee. I think I can swivel the paperclip as if it were the hand on a clock, starting with our time now. Going clockwise, and calculating the time zones, I think we get to tomorrow morning in Russia. So, with the nine-hour time difference, right now it's three in the morning in St. Petersburg. If I move the clip ahead by what would be five hours," Fritz twisted the paperclip in the air so they could all visualize it, "then it should be eight in the morning when I open the portal. But I'm just guessing."

"Maybe this isn't such a good idea."

"Mr. President, now that I've gone through this, I think our first stop should be Israel. If we screw up, it won't be so bad. And if we do, we might be able to adjust."

Jane said, "I think Fritz is right, Mr. President. This is too important."

Knowing that time was short, the president looked from Fritz to Jane and back. He asked if Fritz had brought his photograph. Fritz handed it to him. "Let's go here, Fritz. Four o'clock in the afternoon, Central Time." Fritz twisted the clip counterclockwise. "Come with me. We won't be long."

* * *

"LET'S JUST STAND here for a few minutes." They saw a young woman on the other side of the street. The president pointed. "That's my grandmother. My mother's mother. Look how young she is. My mother hasn't been born yet. I'm guessing, but I think she's coming home from work. That it's World War Two." They stood and watched as the woman walked up the front steps and look around the yard. When she saw them, she smiled, then opened the door and disappeared. His eyes filled up. "Your guess appears sound, Fritz. Thanks. Let's go."

* * *

AS SOON AS they returned, the president checked the time. "They're going to be in the Old Executive Building again, so let's go get them. First stop, Russia."

The colonel lined up his men to block the hall to the trophy case. First through with the president was Putin, who again nodded to Fritz. Single file, they all returned to the room across the hall, looking both ways at what they thought was a new arrival point. When the door closed, Fritz set the paperclip to arrive in St. Petersburg around eight in the morning. He reminded himself that they were actually going to Leningrad in the Soviet

Union. St. Petersburg wouldn't be its name again for another thirty years.

Waiting for him in the hall were the two presidents.

The Russian president said, "I have not spoken to you, but I remember you. Are you well?

"I'm fine, thank you, sir. And you?"

"Perhaps I will have a better answer momentarily." The slight uptick of his lips was the closest Fritz had ever noticed him smiling. Fritz opened the portal to what appeared to be a school and a street of apartment buildings. The two presidents entered, and the door shut behind. Absolute silence filled the hall. Fritz crossed his fingers.

They had been in the portal for more than ten minutes when the door opened, and a shaken man, quickly wiping his eyes, followed him to the present. Putin glanced briefly at Fritz and returned to the meeting.

The president returned immediately with the President of the United Arab Emirates. Another prolonged stay in the portal turned Fritz's attention to Tony. Without words, Tony stuck his thumb in the air.

One by one, the president escorted each of the leaders through the portal. None returned unmoved. Jane and Linda had done the research well. As the last trip ended, the president told Fritz to reset for the Old Executive Office Building and to get the vice president. We'll go to Paris in ten minutes, Fritz."

The vice president asked, "How's it going, Fritz?"

"Almost done, sir. Next stop, the Mona Lisa room."

"Then we'll bring them back here and get them on board."

Fritz reset the portal to the Louvre. As the leaders gathered in the hall, they all stared at him with a variety of emotions. He opened the door and a large, dimly-lit gallery opened before them. Colonel Mitchell signaled his men and winked at Fritz as he passed. Only Jane, Tony, and Fritz remained behind.

"Can you tell anything, Jane?"

"Only that the room has grown quieter with each trip."

"Everything okay, Tony?"

"Fine. Working perfectly, knock wood."

Then even they were silent, looking from one to the other, waiting. Ending the quiet, the door opened and feet scuffed across the hall again. Last back, the president flashed a quick smile. "Thank you all, and Fritz, thank Linda. Some saw their parents or childhood friends, and some even saw themselves. A real-life Christmas Carol. Right now, I'd like to go thank Charles Dickens. It worked."

* * *

FRITZ TRIED TO REGROUP for his classes. "Today is Super Tuesday," Fritz reminded his students. The reporting of primary results would mean many people in the United States would be watching TV when the president came on to speak. As the day progressed, students and teachers became more animated. Speculation about the outcome increased, with hope that the extra day of the summit led to a positive result. At lunch, teachers circulated, discussing the possibilities. Al Kennedy stopped Fritz and asked if he'd been part of it.

When Fritz nodded, Al said, "Wow. Can I ask you about it sometime? This is sure turning out to be an interesting school year."

* * *

LATE-AFTERNOON SUN bounced off the Pacific. His stocking feet on an ottoman, the man said, "We have disrupted. We have destroyed. Yet we have not delivered. We will see what he says tonight. When we meet, our next step must succeed." Listening again, his face grew hot. "I am not the only one who needs to think." He disconnected, flung his phone across the room, and knew he had a problem he hadn't had only moments before.

* * *

SCATTERED AROUND THE family room, they watched TV as the first polls closed. All pundits agreed that the night would pare down the candidate list, perhaps by as much as half in each party.

The president had called earlier and told Fritz the idea of taking each leader back in time was brilliant. He said that he had merely mentioned "changing the future by altering the past" and the message had been received. "I have to finish up my speech for tonight, but do me a favor and take notes. I'd like your impression."

Jane said, "I was surprised when he told me that he was increasing the number of people who would be working on the investigation. With the summit complete, he had already moved on to his next priority. The speech only puts the exclamation point at the end of one story."

"You're awfully quiet, Ash," said Fritz.

"Partly tired. But I was reading about the attack Friday night. A comment from one of the hotel employees has me thinking. A party was scheduled on the roof. Two guests showed up. One was a tall white guy. The police reported only Asians were found dead."

"Maybe he escaped when he saw what was happening?" Fritz suggested.

"Or maybe he's the killer," Ashley said. "Remember Badenhof and the other guy in Chicago?"

Picking up the thought, Fritz said, "And then maybe he's behind the attack. Another Caballero? And the white guy sticks out," said Fritz.

Jane said, "I've asked for copies of the hotel security footage. We'll have it this week. Ash, I think you guys are right."

ALL THE COMMERCIAL stations and every cable news channel covered the president's speech. No advance copies had been distributed. He wanted everyone listening to hear the details from him, not through a filter. He said, "We have a signed peace accord which will end the wars in the Middle East. Here is what 34 nations have agreed to." With charts, maps, and diagrams, he took forty-five minutes to describe a developing and growing Middle East. When he discussed costs and the creation of jobs in the Middle East and at home, he said the ten-year program would ultimately pay for itself and showed how that would work. He smiled throughout. And just as he signed off, he said, "Thanks, Fritz."

Surprised, Fritz looked up from his yellow pad, glanced at Linda's frown, and returned to his last note. Leaning back, he read the details aloud. "He hit everything, except when it would start."

"He has to get Congressional approval first," said Jane. "He has a discharge petition ready if the Speaker reneges. But it could get tied up in committee, so he may need your help again."

"I thought this was a done deal," Ashley said.

"The president plans to meet with every senator and representative who has any say. All committees, the leadership on both sides." Jane said. "He said he expects little opposition, but they'll all have questions. I'll be there. So will General Beech. The president said he's planning a very nice lunch. And he's taking names."

Chapter 29

JANE RETURNED TO deciphering Koppler's files. Or trying to. For someone so well-connected, he had left a barren trail. "Fritz, we have connections that don't connect. We have people who communicate and no records to follow. All the phone numbers we have are from disposable phones, and even the purchase records are for people who don't exist, credit cards that are used once, and accounts we can't trace, including Nakamura Industries. Every clue takes us nowhere. All we have is dead people."

"Whoever is behind this has a playbook. Just like Koppler did. What I don't get is why."

Ashley stood in the doorway, listening. "Money, maybe?"

"Someone with money, lots of money, is certainly behind this," said Jane.

Fritz said, "Or more than one someone. But if they already have money, what do they really want?"

"To get rid of the president? But that doesn't make sense either," said Ashley.

"He'll be out of office in ten months. All they have to do is wait," said Fritz. "So what do they really want?"

* * *

THE TOURNAMENT'S NEXT round was announced, so Fritz was expecting a noisy Monday. When he arrived, a group of teachers was waiting.

"Good morning, Fritz."

"Hi Liz." He continued to his classroom as they trailed behind.

"Sorry to jump you but the kids will be here soon. We all want to be pitchers. With the new schedule, you can take it easy."

"That's great. Do you have the questions?"

"Susan gave them to me," Liz said. "Do you want to pitch any games?"

"I'll pitch one. I don't want the one with Ash's team though. And I'll be here if you need help."

WITH NO GAMES to worry about, Fritz focused on his classes. Normally by mid-March, he was so far behind that he started skipping sections and increasing homework. Now, he was able to spend more time on subjects he had always wanted to discuss in depth. In his World History classes, he would cover economics after World War I, the Nazi and Japanese militaries' rise to power, and how the world responded. With the seniors, he would be able to discuss the 1960s in more depth and add some fun readings. For his third and fourth period classes, he would cover the Civil War and Reconstruction in greater detail.

At lunch, he talked about how far ahead he was. Ashley said, "You're lucky. You don't have after-school work to do. I, on the other hand, am an overworked machine."

"Do you want me to work with the kids on the play?"

"Nope. They know what to do until the tournament's done. You can just go home."

"Fine with me. Or even better, I'll call Tony and go visit some places." Ashley looked like a puppy begging to go for a walk. "I'll go visit some martyrs and bring you some tips."

"I have a suggestion for where you can go."

FRITZ WISHED HIS ninth graders good luck. He and Ashley walked together into the growing crowd. Taking a detour, they bumped into Natalie Johnston.

"Hi, Ashley. You didn't really think you could avoid me forever, did you?" Fritz tried to slide past, but she said he was the one she wanted to interview.

"Hi, Nat. Been reading your pieces," Ashley replied.

She chuckled. "You still blush. It's cute. Mr. Russell, I wanted to ask you if the tournament was meeting your expectations." Ashley tried to slip away. "You can stay, Ash."

"Well, Ms. Johnston..."

"You can call me Nat."

"Well, Nat, your articles have done a lot to get the story out. But, mostly, my ninth graders have done all the work. I think they've done a great job."

"I understand you have guest pitchers for the final."

"That's what they told me. I'm looking forward to it."

"They told you? They really have done this on their own?"

"For the most part. They put everything together and told me later. I'm really proud of them."

She turned to Ashley. "And what have you been up to?"

"Oh, you know, the usual."

"I hear you're getting married." She laughed at his surprise. "Ash, I'm a reporter. I ask questions. I got it from your fan club."

Fritz started to laugh. "Now he has a fan club." Ashley scowled.

"Rachel and Nicole."

They stood together in the back, behind the packed rows, just below the mezzanine seats. After the first game ended, the predictable visitors arrived.

"Hi, Nat," said Rachel and Nicole together, and then, "Hi, Mr. Gilbert." With Ashley trapped between a former girlfriend and the Dough Twins, Fritz bailed out his friend.

"Rachel, Nicole, how do you think the games are going?" he asked.

"Everyone's excited, Mr. R," said Rachel. "But we're going to win, so no biggie. Mr. Gilbert is a great coach."

"You're not going to win. We are," Nicole said. "Mr. R, did you know that Johnny Clayton and I are Charleston partners?"

"For what, Nicole?" asked Natalie.

"The play. It's gonna be cool. You should come. Mr. Gilbert is directing."

"Thanks, Nicole. Maybe I will. Ashley, I'll need to talk to you more about your extracurricular activities."

"Maybe you'll meet Jane," said Nicole. "See you, Mr. R." And, together, "Bye, Mr. Gilbert."

In the second game, a stunning comeback tied it up. With two outs in the bottom of the fourth, Dylan Lake homered. The question was "What general directed Operation Overlord, in what year, and in what country?" Dylan hesitated for a moment, and said, "The overall commander was General Eisenhower, but he wasn't the only general. Operation Overload was the plan to invade Europe. The date was June 6, 1944, D-Day. The Allies landed in Normandy, France." His team won, 12-11.

"Ash, why don't you let me buy you a drink, and you can tell me about your play."

"Love to Nat, but Jane, well, she has a gun. You understand." Fritz turned away covering his snickers with his hand.

* * *

FRITZ WENT home early the next day. As he prepared for classes, he realized that on Friday, his U.S. history class would discuss Appomattox. He told Linda.

"You miss him, don't you?"

"Lin, it's strange to think about it like that, but I do. Everything seemed to build up to bringing him here, and then, poof, he's gone."

"That's kind of what history is, isn't it. Moments of such importance they leave a lasting impression. And you want to go see if you can find him, don't you?"

"I've only tried once, with the president. I would like to see him again, or at least try. Wanna come?"

"Fritz, I'll never be happy with this, but I know I can't stop you. Why don't you ask the president and Ash to go with you?"

"Seriously?"

"At least you won't be alone."

"What's going on in here?" asked Ashley, poking his head around the corner.

"Wanna go in search of Robert E. Lee?"

"When did you become Leonard Nimoy?"

* * *

By Friday, the only surprise was students in third period asking Fritz if they would meet Robert E. Lee. Sad eyes, as if they had been denied a treat, followed him for the entire class. His next class argued that they had been gypped.

When classes ended, Tony Almeida was waiting in the parking lot. He clawed through the exodus to let Fritz know he was ready. Fritz retrieved the president, and then set the portal for Lee's office. Fritz told them that if Lee wasn't in his office, they should go toward his grave. He showed them the map.

Ashley, the president, and Fritz entered an office as empty as the last time Fritz had tried. They walked from the chapel on to the college grounds. All around were reminders that they were in the late-1800s. Dirt and stone paths, wooden buildings rather than brick, horses and wagons, no one walking while looking at a cell phone. As they approached what appeared to be a gravesite, a voice spoke from behind.

"Mr. Russell?" Behind them, an old woman approached.

"Mrs. Lee?" Fritz asked.

"Robert said you might appear one day. We talked for years about your visits. He did so enjoy them. And you, sir, are you the president?"

"I am, Mrs. Lee. It is an honor to meet you." His smile radiated warmth.

"Before his illness, right after he went with you, Mr. Russell, he spoke fondly of his visit, and of how very glad he was to have seen how the country will grow. But he prattled on about his automobile ride and seeing aeroplanes. And are you Mr. Gilbert?"

"Yes, Mrs. Lee. I was honored to have met the general."

"Is there a reason that you've come? May I be of service?"

"Mrs. Lee, to be honest with you, I was hoping to find the general. The material I am teaching today is the same I was teaching last year when I first met him. I miss our conversations."

Tears welled in her eyes. "I miss him too. It's been almost two years that he's been gone." Fritz shook his head. "Is something amiss, Mr. Russell?"

"Mrs. Lee, in our time, it's been only five months since he visited us. I'm just surprised and confused by how time moves."

"Robert told me about your experiments. He was so excited to have been a participant. Over dinner one evening when our son was with us, Robert told him about your flying machines. Rooney laughed at him."

"It must be difficult to know and not be believed," said the president. "Is there anything we might do for you?"

"Thank you, sir. That is most kind. But seeing you gentlemen and knowing how happy you made my husband is enough for me."

"Mrs. Lee, if I may, I'd like you to know that General Lee's office will remain an historic site into our time. And people from everywhere will come to pay their respects."

Her tears flowed freely. Ashley characteristically, yet a surprise to her, embraced her. "Mrs. Lee, I met your husband a few times. He was a great man." Ashley stepped back.

"Robert liked you all. And so do I. I'm so glad he believed in you and confided in me. And I am so grateful that you have come. Robert died a happy man, and I shall tell him in my prayers that I have met you." They said their farewells and returned to Lee's office, where a rectangle glowed, waiting for them to return to their own time.

"Fritz, every time we go somewhere, I want to keep doing it," said the president. "Think of all the places we could see."

"Believe me, Mr. President, I have." Remembering a trip, he said, "Did I tell you I was at the Gettysburg Address, only the end, but I was there. And you know we met William Shakespeare."

"Are you planning to go anywhere else?" the president asked.

"Well, I can't just go. If Tony's not here, I need a helpful storm. But I've thought about a couple of places that I might take my kids. And there are tons of places I'd like to go, just to see."

"Like what?"

"First, Ben Franklin. I'd love to tell him about his experiment. Watching the Berlin Wall come down, the early space launches. I don't know how far back I dare to go. We still don't know how much going back can impact us today. And it would be hard to watch Booth approach Lincoln and not do anything."

"Or maybe one of us could take a shot at Hitler," Ashley said.

"See, Mr. President, even with the best intentions, we could make the world a very different place, and we don't know if it would be better. Or, and I realize this is selfish, if we would ever have been born."

"Well, if you plan to go somewhere, and I can come, will you take me along?"

"Honestly, I'd be afraid something might happen to you. Then I'd really be in trouble. But I'll let you know, and you can decide."

Tony added, "Mr. President, we have some control when I'm here, but if you leave Mother Nature in charge, who knows."

Fritz said, "That's a good point."

"For you too, Fritz," said Ashley.

Chapter 30

THEIR ANXIETY GREW over the weekend. Despite Jane's persistence, no name could be linked to another. The phone numbers were empty leads. Ashley wondered if they were approaching the spider web in the wrong way. The only tie to every incident was Koppler, and they knew he had help. But maybe more than one person was at the top. Or had been since Koppler's death. "Did anyone check the Navy guy's stuff?" he asked. "Not like what I'm doing," said Jane. "They may have collected his stuff, but maybe we need to sort through that, too." She left the kitchen and called General Beech, whom she asked to check with Admiral Davis.

"BLESSED MONDAY," Fritz said on the way to school. He took time to admire the flirting colors of earliest spring. The week's games would end Round Two, and the next week was spring vacation. On his way inside, he glanced at the clouds. *Storm coming*. He was the pitcher for Tuesday's second game. His ninth graders said they needed to calculate the run totals on Thursday but would have the final round announcement ready before spring break.

* * *

AS FRITZ WALKED TO the auditorium, seven people in a mansion overlooking the Pacific discussed the attacks on the White House and Camp David.

"This room seems larger," said one, the owner of an import-export conglomerate, also known to the group for his weapons dealing.

"The furniture is rearranged," smirked the oil man.

In a harsh tone, the man said, "There are fewer of us than at Christmas." He opened the jacket button on his suit and sat. "Though we have done well, more yet remains to do. But we are enough."

"Are you gonna replace those guys?" asked the South Dakota banker.

"We will, but not yet. We must consider our new members carefully."

"We have two openings. Why not our friends in Texas?" asked the Dakotan.

"No, not ever," said the man. "They are too visible and draw attention faster than maggots to Badenhof." None had seen him so emphatic. "We will replace them after."

"After what, Thomas? After we kill the president? That's what you're trying to do, isn't it?" asked the California congresswoman. The silence froze the air.

The man stood and shrugged as he arranged his suit coat. "When you joined us, we expressed the need for anonymity and avoiding names. Your increased public persona is a disadvantage to us. The media pays attention to you. You will take a less aggressive attitude. For our safety."

"Your safety, you mean," LW, the arms dealer, said. "Why should we worry? No one's gonna talk. Our congressional friend gets us things we want. I'm not concerned."

"We have agreed to abide by the rules set down long ago. Now is not the time to forget them," the man said.

"Now, then, whatever. What is it that we've accomplished? I didn't agree to an assassination," said the congresswoman.

"Chaos." The man's voice boomed. "We have achieved disruption. The more disturbances, the greater the gain. Peace in the Middle East is counter to our interests."

"Do you have something more in mind?" asked the man from the Emirates. "Your government has a new technology, but even in private conversation, my president would not say a word. He was afraid."

His eyes slits, the man looked at each face. "None of you know about this?" His eyes grew wide, his jaw clenched. "You all have contacts. Use them." He looked at the congresswoman. "You are placed to find out about these things. Why don't you know?"

"Don't raise your voice at me. Your vast network hasn't told you either." Her sarcasm slapped his face. "We don't even know if there really is some new technology. Just what he says."

"I have kept you in Washington for two decades," said the man. "If this exists, we need to know. FIND OUT."

"If I may," said the oil man. "What is our next action? We seem to be losing our operatives with each one."

"An election is coming."

* * *

AFTER THE FIRST game, Fritz climbed the steps. Looking into the auditorium, a full house waited for the next game.

"What's wrong, Ash?"

"Nothing. My team is up tomorrow."

"Are they ready?"

"I hope so. I'm not. Fritz, they've worked hard. I want them to win."

"So have the other teams, Ash. It's a game. We have other things to worry about. Tonight's a primary night, and you still have the play. And you have a wedding to plan."

"Yeah. Jane and I are going to her parents' house for a few days."

"No wonder you look so happy." Ashley grunted.

A day later, a newspaper in hand, Fritz told his ninth graders to grab their books. He started to speak, but his class sat immobile. "What's up?" Restrained grins gave way to giggles.

"Mr. R, we have news." Fritz glanced around the room. They were about to explode.

"Tell me."

"I've heard from a bank president in New York. James Sapphire. He said he had heard about the tournament and wanted to know more. He's coming today after his meeting in Philadelphia."

"Did you look him up?" Fritz asked. "More important, did you tell Mr. McAllister?"

"We didn't tell Mr. McAllister yet," Susan said.

"Maybe business news isn't your focus, yet, but he's not just a bank president. He's one of the most influential people in domestic and international finance. Did he say when he was getting here?"

"He said he would try to get here when school ends. We're gonna meet him at the front door."

"One of you better go tell Mr. McAllister. Now. Jay, you and Ted go. Tell him you just found out and then come right back. GO. Hurry. I'm sure Mr. McAllister will be visiting us in less than four minutes." He looked at his watch.

"Are we in trouble, Mr. R?" asked Susan.

"You would be if we didn't tell him. Does anyone know how Sapphire found out?"

"Jay said he heard about it from a customer. But that's all we know," said Samantha.

Jay and Ted weren't smiling when they walked in. They said the principal shouted.

"How far behind you is he?" The door opened. George had already hit scarlet on the irritometer.

"Mr. Russell, would you come out here, please?" Fritz smiled at the class as he stepped out. "You can't keep doing this, Fritz."

Fritz started to laugh, which made George angrier. "George, he's coming to see the tournament. If the kids hadn't told you, you wouldn't even know. He's just another spectator. I'm curious about why he's even interested. Do you want to meet him?"

"I'll meet him after the games. I wish this was over." As he turned to go back to his office, Jay stuck his head out the classroom door. "I think he's here. A limousine just pulled into the driveway."

"He's here, George. We should go meet him. Let's find out what the kids have arranged." He opened the door to a class of window gazers. "Kids?"

Jay said, "I said we would meet him in the lobby when classes were dismissed."

"Then, class is dismissed. Let's not leave him in the driveway. Come on, George."

Beating the bell by a couple of minutes, Jay and Susan went to the limo. Four people climbed out. The last was Natalie Johnston.

After they introduced themselves, the students brought Sapphire to the door, where Fritz waited. "Mr. Russell, nice to meet you. I've heard quite a bit about your tournament. Thought I'd take a peek."

"Happy you could make the time, Mr. Sapphire. Please, all of you, come in. Our principal is waiting to say hello." Fritz held the door, but before she could get by, he snagged Natalie's arm. Before he could ask, she said, "I interviewed him a few years ago. When I called him, he already knew about it, but said he'd like to see for himself."

"He read your stories about the tournament?"

“No, at least that’s not why he’s here. Someone else called him, I don’t know who. Yet.”

“Let’s go kids. Jay, you stay with Mr. Sapphire.”

“Mr. Russell, I’d like to talk to you when you’re free afterwards.”

“My pleasure. And we’ll get you a seat now.”

The first game went back and forth, but Jim Wayne’s Pistols overwhelmed Copley’s Characters in the last inning, 14-10. Fritz watched Ashley pace. His team was facing Lee’s Virginians. Liz Chambers had told Fritz she planned to bump up the difficulty.

The Virginians, coached by a social studies teacher, scored three runs in the first inning, but Ashley’s Aristocrats caught up when Rachel and a tenth grader got singles and Johnny Clayton clubbed a home run. The Virginians scored four more in the second to Ashley’s team’s one. In the third, Lee’s Virginians got three more, giving them a six run lead. Ashley placed his hands over his ears, rubbed them through his hair, and stood with his face cupped in his palms. Fritz recognized the questions. Liz was asking hard questions. Ashley’s team had huddled before their ups. One after another, each batter asked for a double. Before the first out, seven doubles had tied the score. Matt told the next three batters to ask for singles, and two were outs. He was the next batter and asked for a triple. Liz asked, “What movie depicted the Nazi War Crime trials?” Matt had done his homework. “Judgment at Nuremburg,” he answered, and without waiting for Ms. Chambers to tell him, he trotted to third, driving in the go-ahead run.

With the score 11-10, the Virginians scored three more runs in the top of the fourth. With two singles to lead off, the audience waited as Johnny Clayton asked for a home run. Ms. Chambers took her time finding a question. “Which constitutional amendment established Christianity as the official religion of the United States?” Johnny stared at her and rubbed his chin.

"That's a trick question. There isn't one. The first amendment guarantees freedom of religion. 'Congress shall make no law respecting an establishment of religion, or prohibiting the free exercise thereof.' " The Aristocrats had won, and the room cheered as Johnny circled the bases. Ashley ran on stage and jumped up and down with his team.

Natalie grabbed Fritz's arm and told him to follow her. James Sapphire waited by the front door. He told Fritz that he had enjoyed the games and that more schools should have these tournaments. "Nat's told me you're building a scholarship fund from the proceeds. I have to go now, but let me see if I can help." Fritz shook his hand and thanked him. The limousine merged into street traffic.

Fritz said, "Thanks for bringing him. Do you need a ride?"

"I think I have one," she said, as a beaming Ashley walked up.

"How about those kids," he said.

"Congratulations, Ashley. How about giving me a lift to the office? I have a story to finish."

His excitement turned cautious. He took a small step backward. "Sorry, Nat. I have a previous appointment, otherwise I would."

She shrugged. "I guess you really are getting married. Fritz, how about that ride?"

The next day's round went well, and on the way home, Fritz got a call from Natalie Johnson telling him that the next day's *Wall Street Journal* would have a short op-ed about the tournament.

"Thanks for letting me know. I guess we'll see you for the final rounds?"

"At this point, my editor wouldn't let me miss it. I may even convince him to stop by."

PEOPLE WAITING AT his door was no longer a surprise, but students waiting was brand-new. The next morning, half his ninth grade class was in the hall, and half of them had newspapers.

"Good morning all. What's brought you here so early?"

"It's only ten minutes early, Mr. R," said Ted.

"Have you seen the Wall Street Journal?" Jay asked.

"Not yet. I was planning to get it later." He opened the door. "Come in."

"It's a great article, but it's not about us. Well, it is, but he doesn't mention the school," said Susan.

"May I see it?" Four copies were offered. "Who Says Schools Don't Innovate?" Fritz read aloud. "On Wednesday, I had the pleasure of witnessing a baseball doubleheader. Not baseball as you might expect, but baseball games that teach. A history-baseball tournament. Correct answers with different degrees of difficulty count as different kinds of hits; wrong answers are outs.

"The school auditorium sold out. Almost half the student body is involved, and more than a third of the faculty has volunteered as coaches and pitchers.

"It was as exciting as being in a stadium.

"Our teachers have been dragged through the political mud for a long time for a variety of unfair and inaccurate reasons. This single innovation is a sample of the possibilities our teachers bring to the education of our children. To which I say, 'well done.' "

"That's terrific," said Fritz. "Kids, it doesn't matter that he didn't mention us. The message is what's important. Besides, we live in a viral age. The story will probably get out in more detail."

As they left, Ashley walked in. "Want to play golf next weekend? I need to do something besides watching the news."

"I thought you were going to Jane's parents' place."

"We're going tonight and coming back by mid-week. We may stop in Washington on the way home, but we'll be back for sure by the weekend. So, you wanna play?"

"Sure. If it's nice. What are you doing about your team and the play?"

"My team has informed me that they will be practicing without me, and Jean and Eric are taking turns going through the scenes and rehearsing at their houses. Fritz, they're incredible."

"The portal, I think."

"Could be. I wouldn't be surprised anymore."

The kids were already in vacation mode, which made keeping their attention more difficult. Fritz talked about how the atomic bomb changed the nature of war as well as the bomb's influence on international relations. "Tomorrow we'll talk about the Cuban Missile Crisis."

The next class discussed independence movements in Africa and the battles for influence between the Soviet Union and the United States. He showed them maps of Africa in 1950 and the present.

"Mr. R, it seems like Africans were better off in a lot of ways under colonial rule," said Bob Bee.

"That's just wrong, Bob," said Cheryl. "No matter what happened, they made choices for themselves. In their own countries."

"And how many people were killed in all the revolutions. They're still fighting," Bob fought back.

"Hold on a minute," said Fritz. "These arguments have been around for more than sixty years. Africa has vast natural resources, which the Europeans claimed, and the Russians and United States also wanted. Under European rule, much death and brutality were commonplace."

"Mr. R, couldn't the president have a plan for Africa like the one for the Middle East?" Dan asked.

"Dan, I think the president hopes his Middle East plan will be a blueprint. Let's hope it works in the Middle East and then elsewhere."

Chapter 31

BY THE TIME the day had crawled to an end, Fritz had surrendered to vacation. "No homework," he told each class. But he reminded them that another primary was coming and to pay attention.

When he arrived home, Fritz was surprised to find Jane at the table. He figured she and Ashley would be on the road.

"Hi, honey, I'm home. Hi, Jane. When are you leaving, and do you want me to do anything?"

"I was just telling Linda that Mel will be bringing Wixted's files. You remember him."

"How could I forget?"

"Sort them like I did with Koppler's stuff. The president told me he thinks it's better to keep it away from Washington for now. Insiders might still be involved."

"If that's true, the portal is in jeopardy again," said Linda.

With his usual bang, Ashley entered frowning. "Hi. Jane your phone is off. Call the president." She walked to the dining room.

"Are you driving straight through?" asked Fritz.

"Depends on all this. If we get out of here much later, we'll hit traffic all the way, so we'll probably spend the night in Washington and go the rest of the way in the morning."

Jane returned, shaking her head. "The NSA picked up a phone call, but he didn't want to talk. He sent me a message." She lifted her laptop to the table and read the note. "The sender is a big shot and was here during the summit. They're trying to find out who he called."

"Another Caballero?" Fritz asked.

"The president is having him checked out. Ash, let's go, or we'll be driving until midnight."

"I was naïve to think the people at the summit would be scared silent," Fritz said.

* * *

JANE AND ASHLEY spent the night at her apartment and went to the White House in the morning. The president was digging through a desk drawer, his lips pressed tight, when they entered his office. He told them to sit as he dug through a pile of yellow pads on his desk.

"I can't tell you how much I miss Lily."

"You said you found a link to a phone call from the Emirates to California." He was poring over the pile in front of him.

The president handed Jane a sheet of paper. "They traced the call to another disposable phone. The guy is close to the head of state, and he's rich. Oil."

"Who's working it?"

"Mel." He motioned them to step onto the walkway outside the Oval Office. "An analysis of the Hay-Adams films showed two men entering the elevator just before the attack. He said the men avoided the visible cameras, but another was disguised in the floor-button panel." The president said he saw photos, but didn't recognize the face. "It's in an envelope. Whoever he is, he is part of this. He didn't touch anything we could see or say anything. But he looked like, I don't know, like he had an attitude. Like the Asian was a servant."

"Mr. President," asked Ashley, "could the IRS help?"

"I'm not ready to open that door yet. Too many people would be tipped off. Especially in Congress. When we get closer, maybe."

* * *

ON THE DRIVE south, Jane looked out her window and gave only grunts and one-word answers to Ashley's continuous talking. As the road curved west, the Blue Ridge rose up along the horizon. When he asked if the mountains in front of them were the Rockies, she said, "Uh-huh." He abruptly pulled off the highway.

"I've been chattering for an hour, and you're not here. What's wrong?"

"Sorry, I've been thinking."

"I figured that out. What?"

"Ash, I'm going in a hundred directions. The president, my mother, the wedding, but mostly the attacks. We can't even use the tools we have. We can't trust them. And everywhere we go, we hit another dead-end. I don't think the attacks are over. I really don't want to be here. My mother will be another distraction."

"It's only for a couple of days. It might be fun. And we could use a break."

"And you think we'll get one? With my mother? Ha!"

"Jane, we have to do this. So don't make it harder on either of us. We'll be there in less than an hour. Want the top down?"

Jane leaned over and kissed him. "Yeah, let's get some fresh air."

A few houses away from her parents', she said, "Oh no," and pointed. "I can't believe she did this."

"What?"

"See those cars. She invited everyone. You're on the spot, bucko. I'm gonna kill her."

"Relax, Jane. I teach teenagers. This will be a piece of cake."

"Listen up, Yankee. You are in the midst of what some locals still call the War of Northern Aggression. Lee and Stonewall Jackson are alive in these parts."

* * *

FRITZ WROTE "What's Happened." On a second pad, he wrote, "What Do We Know." Side by side, the blank sheets began to fill. He titled a third pad, "The Portal," leaving room for notes by skipping lines. When he listed the names of the victims, he stopped at Lily Evans and looked at TJ, who returned his smile. "You'd have liked her, TJ. She always asked about you."

Jonathan Hartmann, Georg Badenhof, the North Korean, the Asians at the Hay-Adams. Colonel Mitchell had said the soldiers weren't Eledorians. The attack on Camp David and the White House. No survivors in Geneva. What about the guys who worked for Koppler? And his car-accident report, where was that? The money trail. The pads were yelling, but in what language?

"TJ, don't ever smoke. It's hard to stop. I could use a cigarette right now." TJ blew him a raspberry. While he stirred sweetener into a newly poured second cup, he remembered the business card he had. He lifted TJ from the swing and said, "I need my wallet, buddy," and he wrinkled his nose. "And you need a fresh diaper." He taped the new one, grabbed his wallet and phone from the dresser, returned his son to his comfort zone, and called Mike Morgan.

"Mr. Russell, I was just thinking about you. We aren't done with the report yet, but we have confirmed the chemicals are foreign-made. By a company in Poland owned by a German conglomerate.

"Mr. Morgan, can you tell me the name?"

"I'd like to, but I can't. I'll let Jane know. Chain of command, need-to-know, that kind of thing. You understand."

Fritz said he did and that it was time urgent. He asked Morgan to call her right away.

Fritz returned to his yellow pads. "TJ, I smells a rat." The baby just looked at him. "Sorry, buddy, I'm used to talking this time of day." He tapped his pen on the table. When he added the bank transfer to the list of events, he said, "TJ, someone is financing these attacks. Why?"

Another pad appeared.

His fingers massaging his forehead, Fritz stared at the title. "Why?" he said. He wrote, "1. To kill the President." He shook his head. "They didn't try hard enough." Then, he added "2. Money. Who makes money by blowing up hotels, ships, the White House? Builders." He underlined the word. *Big builders, he thought. International? Ships and planes? People with government clearances? People who make explosives? People who can afford to hire mercenaries?*

He jumped, disturbed by the doorbell. "Let's go see who's here, TJ." With the baby in his left arm, he opened the door. Mel and stacks of storage boxes. "Do you need help?"

"No, Fritz, just a couple more." Fritz offered her a cup of coffee. In the kitchen, she draped her jacket over a chair and grinned at the yellow covering the table.

"I've seen this scene before," she said. "You too?"

"He told me about it last fall. It works pretty well for organizing your thoughts."

"I think yellow pads may become an endangered species in Washington."

"Have you looked at the stuff you brought?"

"Sorry, Fritz. We've been doing other things."

"Yeah. I haven't had any down time, either. So I just started making notes. It's like a spider web. You can see the thread, but where's the spider?"

"It sure has a lot of twists and turns. I hope we find the spider soon."

Fritz brought a new box of folders to the dining room. He thought they should go piece by piece and make folders when they were done.

"Hi Mel. You've got a lot done. Did you scan the papers?"

"Hi Linda. Not yet. It'll be easier to keep it together once it's out of the boxes."

Linda brought her laptop and scanner to the table. "How much is left?"

"About half a box." Linda said she would wait to scan until the boxes were empty.

Fritz carried the empty boxes to the kitchen. From one, a small note fluttered to the floor. He took it to Mel, who put it in a folder.

Tuesday clicked forward. Fritz and TJ returned to their conversation of the previous morning. Fritz hoped that maybe they would have a little time to finish what they had started.

"Now where was I?" TJ gurgled. "Thanks, TJ. I think you're right." Fritz spread the pads on the table and stared at them. He took out a new one. "What country?" he wrote. Resting his cheek on his fist, he wrote a list, including each country associated with the various events. "Eledoria, Naria, Switzerland, North Korea, Israel, Pakistan, Russia, Cuba, the summit countries. What am I missing?" TJ chirped. "Thanks again, buddy. USA." Sucking his pen, he whispered, "Hmm, maybe." Staring at him, Mel's empty boxes lay on the floor behind the backdoor. "Right." He went to the folders, opening each until he found what he had ignored earlier. Stuck at the top of a file marked "Miscellaneous" was the piece of paper that had fallen when they were putting the boxes aside. He wished he'd glanced at it then. A list of initials and numbers vaulted from the fragment. One set of letters was underlined, JK. "Jim Koppler."

"I'm back, TJ. Didn't go far. But I think we have another connection." He looked at the other sets of letters, TR, JH, GB, DI,

MA, LW, SI. JH, he thought, was Jonathan Hartmann. "We already knew that." There were ten sets, three he knew were dead. "Ten little Indians. But why?" He reached for his phone and dialed Ashley.

"Hi Fritz," said Jane. "Ash's driving."

"Hi Jane. I probably should have called you anyway. Wixted's papers have a list like Koppler's. When are you coming back?"

"We're on our way now. ETA around noon."

"I'm glad, but why so soon?"

"We'll tell you when we see you."

"We're having company, TJ. Uncle Ash and Aunt Jane are on their way home." TJ squealed. Fritz wondered if the baby understood what he was saying. "So let's get back to work." He reread his pads, put his head in his hands, and closed his eyes. "International, rich, industry, finance, weapons." He sat up. Linda had talked to her father about money trails. "I should have paid closer attention. What did he say?" The doorbell rang. Fritz sighed and took TJ with him to the door. Natalie Johnston waited on the landing holding a piece of paper.

"Hi, Fritz. You're not in school, so I don't need to call you Mr. Russell, do I?"

"No, that's fine. I'm not in school, so can I call you a wiseass?"

"Yup." She grinned and held the paper out for him to take. "I have something for you. From James Sapphire."

"You didn't need to bring it. Next week would have been fine."

"Actually, I didn't want the responsibility. Here." She handed him a check for $25,000. "He said he would have some friends help out, too."

"Wow, Nat. This is fantastic. Thanks. Want some coffee?"

"I'd love some. I have another story to write that I'm avoiding."

Fritz realized the tables were filled. "Uh, the place is a mess. Sorry." She marched by him toward the kitchen.

"Not much of a housekeeper myself. This isn't bad."

"Uh-oh," he said to himself.

"Where do you keep the cups?" she asked, opening cabinets.

"Next one," he said.

"You want a cup?" she asked.

"No thanks. Milk's in the fridge."

"I should hope so. But I drink it black. So you didn't go to Florida for spring break. What do teachers do when their kids are off?"

"I'm just working on a project." He put TJ back in his swing.

"So no break for you." She sat in his chair and inspected the pads spread across the table. "Hmm. This looks like some very un-school-like project, Fritz. Looks more like detective work."

"I'm outlining a book plot." He hoped the lie would be enough.

"Yeah, and I'm the Easter bunny." She continued to scan his notes. "What's the portal?"

"The title."

"Okay, Fritz. I'm a reporter, and I've interviewed a lot of people. I can tell when they're uncomfortable and, usually, when they're lying. You're both. So, tell me."

"Sorry. I can't."

"That's even more interesting. Can't? Maybe I can help with your story. Can't? Why not?"

She had so surprised him with the assault, he blurted, "National security."

"Really? Well then, call the president and get me clearance," she said, a smirk appearing. "Seriously. This looks like the naval base bombings and the attack on the White House." She gestured to the pads.

"It is." *God, I'm easy,* he thought, trying to blame it on exhaustion. "Look, Nat. You can't say anything or report anything. It really is national security. Hang on." He picked up his phone. "Hi, Mr. President. I have a problem. I have a reporter named Natalie Johnston sitting across from me. I was working on our project when I offered her a cup of coffee, but I hadn't put the stuff away." He listened to the response. "Okay." He handed her the phone and gave her a pen.

"Hello?" She looked at Fritz. Her face moved in all directions. She wrote a number. "Was that really him?" Fritz told her to make the call. The voice of the White House operator made her groan. When the president answered, her face blanched.

"Yes, hello, Mr. President." She listened to what Fritz knew was a request for silence. "Yes, sir. I understand." She handed Fritz the phone.

"Sorry, Mr. President. I was caught off guard. I can? If you think so. Sure, I'll talk to you then." Directing his attention to his visitor, he said, "The president said I should tell you everything. He asked me to get your phone numbers and address first."

"You know the president? You called him direct. What's this about, Fritz?"

"Phone numbers and address first, Nat." She wrote them on a yellow pad.

He started to type. "Thanks. Oh, and he said that you'll get a visit from a member of his secret service detail." He told her he was sending her info to the president. Her complexion reminded Fritz of the view from the window last winter.

"Last year," he began, "I walked into my classroom, except on the other side of the door, we were at Appomattox and met Robert E. Lee the day after he surrendered."

"Oh, come on, Fritz. I'm a reporter, not an idiot. That's ridiculous."

"Now do you believe I'm writing a novel?"

"No," she said over the cup at her lips. "I just talked to the president. But time-travel?"

"It's real." For the next few minutes, he told her what had happened, how the portal had been used, and why he was trying to figure out all the connections. "You can see why we want this to be a secret. Also, anyone who knows can be in danger."

"This is unbelievable. This is the biggest story of the century, and I can't say a thing."

"Not a word. Nat, dangerous people engineered this. We just don't know who. They've already killed people to cover their tracks." She asked who he meant. "Remember the story about Jonathan Hartmann and his girlfriend." She nodded. "They killed her and her lawyer. Cyanide cocktail."

She glanced at her watch and then at the kitchen clock. "Fritz, I've got to go, but if I can do anything to help, please ask."

He walked her to the door and thanked her again for the check. "Nat, the president means business. So do the bad guys."

She headed to her car as Linda turned into the driveway. Linda rolled down the window and called. "Hi, Nat. What are you doing here?"

"Hi, Linda. Wait, Linda Russell?" She pointed from Linda to Fritz, standing on the front steps. "He's your husband."

"I know. But why are you here?"

AS THEY WALKED in the back door, Linda looked at the table and understood immediately what had happened.

"You left all this stuff out?" Linda barked.

"The doorbell rang. Nat was delivering a check for the tournament. I offered her coffee. I'm exhausted. That's my only excuse for not thinking."

"Linda, I figured out that something was going on. But the portal!" Natalie pointed to the yellow pad.

"Do you want another cup, Nat? I need one. Fritz, get two cups, will you please? She lifted TJ, kissed him, and grimaced. "Fritz, he's soaked, again. Don't you pay attention? You change him while I get the coffee."

Fritz sighed, put down the cup, and took TJ. "Come on, pal. Looks like our quiet time is over."

Linda ignored him. "Sit down, Nat. Tell me what happened." When Fritz returned, Linda was talking about the summit and the attack on the White House.

Fritz said, "I don't think it was terrorists. At least, not from the Middle East. How do you know each other?"

"Fritz, sometimes I wonder about you. Natalie lived down the hall from me in New York. You met her at a party. She also dated Ashley. Twice, if memory serves. Four or five years ago."

"You knew about that?" asked Nat.

"Only the name. I didn't make the connection until just now."

"Ash and Jane are on their way. Should be here soon, in fact," said Fritz, looking at his watch. "The president said it was better to let Nat know than to have a reporter asking questions. He made her swear to secrecy."

"He means it Nat, not a word. Not even to yourself," said Linda. "The more people who know, the more dangerous it is for us."

Natalie asked, "What's Robert E. Lee like?" Before either could answer, Ashley stepped through the back door and stopped like his feet were in wet concrete.

Chapter 32

"**WHAT ARE YOU** doing here?"

"Nice to see you too," Natalie said. Jane pushed in behind him. "And you must be Jane." She reached out to shake hands. "I'm Natalie Johnston."

Jane peeled off her jacket and handed it to Ashley, who draped it over a chair in the dining room. "Hang it up," Linda called.

"You're the reporter? So what's going on," asked Jane. Fritz explained. "So the president is okay with this?"

"He is, Jane. I spoke to him."

"And how do you know Ashley?" she asked.

"We had a couple of dates a few years ago. He stopped calling."

Their conversation traveled through the afternoon, and Natalie asked one question after another and took notes, which Fritz said she would have to leave with them. Linda asked her to join them for dinner.

"I'd love to. Even if I can't write about this, it's a fascinating story. No one would believe it, but I'd love to see the faces of readers if I could write about it."

"Some of those faces are killers," Ashley said. "And you're not safe now, either." Looking at Fritz, he said, "It would be better if you hadn't found out, Nat."

While Fritz and Ashley picked up dinner, Ashley questioned Fritz's judgment, his sanity, and his ability to protect himself. He said that Natalie was extremely nosy. And a talker. “How could you have invited her in with all that stuff out?”

“So how was your trip?”

“Something that even H. P. Lovecraft couldn’t imagine.”

After Natalie left, Fritz asked again about their trip. Jane laughed. She let Ashley start. He said that Jane’s mother had invited more than seventy people, who were all waiting when they arrived. People spilled into the backyard, men and women intent on grilling him about anything they could think of, but especially politics and religion. He’d been dragged from person to person, like a sack, and he stood for almost eight hours as his audience drank and ate, in that order. Jane’s mother kept her going in opposite directions, so he had no rescue. His gracious host thanked him for taking her spinster daughter off her hands. They all laughed when he said her mother whispered that she had wondered if Jane was, Ashley leaned in to imitate, “you know, gay.”

“And I spent the day refighting the Civil War. I heard about ancestors who fought in this battle or that and who was killed by Yankees. I finally excused myself to go to the bathroom. They followed me.”

“That was just the start,” said Jane. “Most people didn’t leave until after dark. Mom ran out of paper goods, so they started using plates and glasses and left the stuff everywhere. And get this. She said she was exhausted and went to bed. Told us to clean up. ‘Well, it was your party, you know.’ So at ten o’clock, Ash and I were scouring the yard with flashlights. I didn’t know there were so many places to leave stuff.”

“Why not wait until morning?” Fritz asked.

“You don’t know my mother. She’d have flipped.”

“I’m glad I put my top up,” said Ashley. “Six plates were stacked on my roof and six glasses were leaning on the wipers. That was just Saturday. It started again on Easter. The food was good, but another crowd showed up.”

"My uncle came with a hangover and started drinking right away. Then he started railing about Yankees stealing 'the best of our southern blossoms' while Ash and I just sat like we were invisible."

"We decided yesterday to come back today after we discussed the wedding with Jane's mom and four, what were they? Relatives? Anyway, the five of them argued about every single thing on the list, and no one asked Jane what she wanted."

"So let me get this straight," said Fritz. "You were outtalked for three days?"

"Shut up. I told Jane we should just get married."

"I couldn't do that to my family, Ash. They've been planning this for ten years."

"And they still can't agree."

"I'm the only girl left. My aunts have been after me almost as long as Mom. And this is only going to get worse. Mom knows what she's going to do. She'll have to argue with the aunts until at least three months after the wedding."

"How did it feel to be home with all that's going on," Linda asked.

Ashley answered with a description of Jane's childhood bedroom. "My favorite was her prom picture." Fritz imagined the room as Ashley described it. A gun collection seemed so out of place with the chess club, but not for Jane. Pink he couldn't see, but oil and rags and the smell of gunpowder somehow fit.

When Ashley finished, Jane snorted.

"In answer to your question, Linda, it was nice to visit, and very nice to leave. When Ash's parents visit, knowing my mother, it'll be another circus. And she loves being the ringmaster."

"Jane, I hate to interrupt the fun, but I have two things to talk about," said Fritz. "Did you speak to Mike Morgan? And I found another list."

"Fritz, this can wait until tomorrow," said Linda. "Let them unwind."

"We're fine, Linda," said Jane. "I want to compare the lists. Then we'll go. It's been a long day for all of us." Fritz was on his feet in a flash and brought both lists from the folders.

After a quick scan, Jane looked up. "The initials are the same, but we have different phone numbers." She studied the lists, her tongue between her teeth. "Here's another one. IM. The president said they picked it up on a phone call. Ibrahim Massoud. His initials are on both lists too. But this will be tricky. He's rich and well-protected. We'll talk about him tomorrow."

* * *

FRITZ'S WEDNESDAY started late. Linda was scanning the new documents, a cup of coffee on her left and TJ in his swing on the right. Filling his own cup, Fritz asked how far she'd gone. She told him she was almost half done.

"I'm going to the library when I'm finished," she said. "We need food too. You can do that when I get home."

"Okay. I've been trying to remember exactly what your dad told you about the bank transfers. We have the puzzle pieces, but it has only one color, blank. I was close on Monday and yesterday. Everything links to a person or group with money." He took a sip. "But it's a maze with constant dead ends. Maybe the new name will shed some light."

"He said that bank transfers are hard to pin down unless the countries are willing to help and force the banks to cooperate. You need political pressure. Many large depositors use couriers, not electronic transfers.

"Money mules."

"Uh-huh. We're looking for one needle in multiple haystacks. It would help if we had pictures, so we could tie people together."

"If we had pictures, we'd know who we're dealing with." Knowing they were no closer, he dug out the other pads from his desk and started to read his notes. The sunroom, warm and bright, was the opposite of how he felt.

"Fritz, I'm leaving," said Linda. "I won't be long, but do me a favor. Check TJ's diapers before I get back."

"You should check how many diapers are in the trash. He just times it well. I changed a bunch while you were gone yesterday." He snatched up the pads and moved to the kitchen. "See you later," she said, after she kissed TJ. Fritz blew her a kiss.

With pen in hand, he stared at the pad labeled "Why?" At that moment, the president sat alone in his private office staring at a yellow pad amid the bangs of hammers and the whirs of electric tools.

"TJ, how would you like to go for a walk?" Fritz lifted the baby. The warm dampness shouted that he had a job he needed to do first. *A walk around the block on a nice day. Maybe that will shake something loose.* He needed a new idea. Not expecting answers, he asked TJ questions, but he could see his classes, kids raising their hands. Then he heard the question that mattered. "Thanks, kids," he said. "TJ, let's go." TJ squeaked his agreement.

When they entered the kitchen, Jane and Ashley, sat at the kitchen table.

"The door was open," said Ashley.

"I know. I live here."

"You should lock your door."

"Then you'd never get in. Any coffee left?"

"Jane made me make more. She treats me like a slave, but then, you know where her home is."

"I had a thought. What is it that's different about rich people?" said Fritz.

"They have more money," Ashley said.

"You're annoying. We're not dealing with people who are comfortable. These people could buy all the comfortable people in the world and still have plenty to spend. So money can't be the motivation. What makes them tick? And what would be so important that they would kill, even each other."

"Good question," Jane said. Fritz flipped a yellow page. "What Makes Rich People Tick?" he wrote. On the next line, he added, "besides money."

"Power," said Jane. "Most people in Congress are rich. More than half in the Senate and the House are millionaires."

"That explains a lot," said Ashley.

"Control?" asked Fritz. "Keeping things the way they are. No surprises. For themselves and everything in their world."

"Good point. And they have big worlds that overlap," Jane said.

"Things," said Ashley. "They can buy anything they want."

"Want, not need," Fritz said. "Like what?"

"They may think they need them," said Ashley. "Like expensive cars, big houses, planes. Go anywhere, anytime. Like us with the portal. Does that mean we're rich?"

"There has to be more than that. It's so superficial," said Fritz.

"Then let's pretend. If you had twenty million dollars, what would you do?" asked Jane. "Differently."

"I've thought about that when the lottery gets high. What would I do? I'd give a lot of it away," said Fritz. "We don't really need much. I'd pay off debts, put money away for TJ's education. Maybe take a sabbatical."

"You'd keep teaching?" asked Ashley. "I don't think I would."

"Then what would you do all day, bother me?" asked Fritz.

"I don't know. Fly around the world and have lunch and dinner in fancy restaurants."

"And make trouble because you can, so people will call you eccentric."

"And I'm eccentric because I'm rich. Then you couldn't call me weird anymore."

"Hold on," said Jane. "You're on to something. 'Cause trouble because you can.' "

"Who's causing trouble?" asked Linda, coming through the door.

"We're talking about the rich, how they're different," Fritz said.

A moment later she was on the phone. "I'm fine, Dad. We're trying to figure out who's responsible for the attacks. No, we're not. We already know that someone with money has to be behind it." She covered the phone. "He thinks we're guessing. Stop. All we want to know is what character traits are different in the very rich that would motivate them, besides money. All right, then call me back. Love you. Bye."

Fritz decided to say nothing more.

* * *

VACATION RUSHED by, and the tournament and classes took over. On Sunday, the president called. "Hi, Fritz. If my calculation is correct, your tournament should wrap up next week. Am I still invited?"

"Are you sure you want to come? With all that's happened, you might not be safe here."

"So I'm not invited?"

"Of course you're invited. I'm just worried. So many people know about the portal's being here. It doesn't take a genius to figure one plus one. And we still don't know who's behind the attacks."

"You might be right. Let me think about it. What day is the final game?"

"Thursday. The fourteenth."

"OK. Fritz, I also wanted to let you know that we have your accident report. There are three possible sources, one of which is Badenhof's company. I think we can say it's him. It's another connection. Gotta run. Talk to you later."

Linda asked, "What did he say?"

"He wants to come to the tournament final, and he said he thinks Badenhof's companies supplied the metal and chemicals for my accident." Fritz bit his lip. "I'm not comfortable with having him at the game."

Linda scrutinized his face. "I don't like that you're worried. That's the first time you've looked like this."

"With so much to do, I can't afford a distraction. I don't like that some rich guy who doesn't know me tried to kill me. And I just don't understand why."

"They've left a trail of bodies," said Ashley.

"Yeah. And they don't seem to care much whose they are."

* * *

BEFORE HIS LAST class on Tuesday, while Fritz looked over the Supreme Court cases he wanted to discuss, his door opened and the class marched in. A big picture of himself smiled back from every student's tee-shirt. His name on the front sparkled, and on their backs were the words *Riverboro High 2016 History Baseball Tournament.*

"Ladies and gentlemen, you've outdone yourselves."

Ted said, "They're selling like crazy. Mr. Witcannon said he would trust us to pay him back. We make ten dollars for each shirt."

"We sold two hundred on Saturday, downtown." Susan said. "Mr. Hoffmann let us set up outside his store."

"We have a special one for you," said Ron. At that, Susan handed him a wrapped box as the class applauded. He removed the red ribbon and tried to avoid tearing the paper.

"Come on, Mr. R," said Don. "Rip it."

"Okay guys, here goes." With a single smooth stroke, he stripped the box bare. Inside was a yellow tee with his picture and the signatures of each member of the class. He lifted the shirt, unfolded it, and put it on. Moments later, Ashley walked in, looked at Fritz, and started laughing.

“I wasn’t sure, but I had a feeling.” He waved to the class. “I’ve got mine ready for game-time.”

“Thanks for the picture, Mr. Gilbert,” said Susan.

“Susan,” he said, “I can’t express how welcome you are. See you all later.”

“Well, we’re certainly not going to get done all I wanted to do today. Let’s see how much we can.”

The class discussed the cases and jumped when the bell rang. “We’ll look at variations on the interpretation of free speech tomorrow.”

The way to the auditorium was decorated with extra-large tee-shirts. Even George, who was waving the students into the auditorium, wore one. In the first game, the answer that the Supreme Court upheld the Fugitive Slave Act in the Dred Scott decision won the game. Fritz pitched the second game. Between games, he announced the donation from James Sapphire and noted that the scholarship fund had collected over $80,000.

On Wednesday, Ashley’s team ran up an early score to win. The principals of four local high schools were spectators, and Natalie Johnston was a member of the standing-room-only crowd. As the auditorium emptied, she approached Fritz, holding papers in her hand, smiling. “Hi Fritz. Got a present for you.” She handed him two checks. “Sapphire twisted some arms, looks like.” Each check was for $10,000.

“Thanks, Nat. This puts us over $100,000. Too late to announce it, but I will on Friday.”

“Fritz, I have a question. Have I earned a shot at seeing the portal in action? I’d love to meet an early Mark Twain. He was a believer, you know. *Connecticut Yankee*.”

“Nat, I don’t want to flat out say no, but right now, I’m afraid the portal is getting dangerous. Until we get a handle on these attacks, we really don’t know who’s on our side. So let me say maybe. And let’s not talk about it except in my house.”

* * *

FRITZ WALKED in the back door still wearing his tee-shirt. The usual greeting was preceded by a snort and a laugh.

"They are a terrific bunch, aren't they?" Linda asked.

"Lin, they haven't missed a trick. By the way, Ash's team won big today. And Natalie Johnston gave me two more checks."

"How much?"

"Twenty grand."

"Oh Fritz, that's fantastic."

"My mind has been elsewhere. We had clues that led somewhere with Koppler, but this feels like digging holes and filling them in again. I'm trying to picture a group of men working to disrupt the country, maybe the world. I don't get it."

Linda looked out the window at the birds in the yard. "Maybe that's a way, Fritz. Get a picture."

"I don't remember seeing any in the files."

"You said Koppler's office was full of pictures. What happened to them?"

"Mel will know."

When Ashley and Jane showed up, they brought dinner. Ashley was almost strutting. Fritz told him to knock it off. He hadn't won yet. "My pitching days are done. Tom Jaffrey and Liz Chambers are pitching the next two games."

When Linda mentioned the pictures, Jane said, "They're still in his office, I think. We only wanted papers. Good idea." Her phone appeared, now a routine. "Mr. President, sorry to bother you." She told him about the pictures and hung up with "yes, sir."

"What did he say?" Fritz asked.

"He'll call you shortly. He wants to use the portal to get them. He's working on something else, but he said he'd get everything ready."

"Why the portal?" asked Linda.

"He doesn't want anyone seen going into the building or the office. If anyone is watching, it won't be safe."

The president called a little after ten. He said he had arranged for three agents to go in and that Tony was on the way. "See you shortly, Fritz."

* * *

THEY WEREN'T gone long. Although Fritz had the clip on his old photo of the Oval Office, the room was obscured by scaffolding and tarps. The president walked to the portal, grimacing as he looked at his office.

"Let's see what we left behind," he said. The president introduced the agents with him, Bill Sharp and Lou Masanelli.

Fritz took out Koppler's office floor plan and opened the portal. While they waited, he said, "Mr. President, I've got a bad feeling about what's been happening. I feel like the answer is at my fingertips, and it slips away. But it feels like time's not on my side. Still, everything leads to one conclusion—someone is trying to keep you from getting things done."

"It comes with the job. My concern, my question, is whether they're after me personally or are trying to prevent policy from working."

The three agents returned with full boxes. Before Fritz left, the president told him he would have to skip the tournament final but was sending the secretary of education. "Talk soon. Good night."

A police car in the far corner started toward them.

"Hi Jim. What's up?"

"I heard you were on another adventure, Mr. R. I'm just making sure everything's okay."

"Thanks, Jim. This one was easy."

Chapter 33

EVENING RAIN HAD curtained the ocean. Only the relentless crashing of the waves and the salt smell remained to keep him company. The man picked up the buzzing phone.

"Do you know who this is?" asked the caller.

"I do."

"You know the office where the man shot himself?"

"I do."

"I check it daily. Tonight, the pictures are gone. No one came through the lobby. No alarms for the rear door. Nothing on video. Just thought you should know."

"Thank you."

The man peered into the darkness and wondered what else he didn't know.

* * *

THE TOURNAMENT semi-finals intruded on classes for the rest of the week. Nail biting, hand rubbing, and other fidgeting broadcast which students were still playing. Ashley was the worst. Between classes, he fluttered from wordlessness to verbal waterfall.

"You know you're more nervous than the kids."

"I just wonder if I've done enough. I don't want to let them down."

"At this point, there's not much more you can do, except calm down. If they lose, you don't want them to think they've let you down. Losing is not the end of the world, and they need to learn that, too."

The ninth graders were more excited than anxious. "We've sold out of tee-shirts. Two thousand already. Mr. Witcannon said he would make some more and have a special one for the finals," said Jay. "This is so cool."

"Everyone is proud of you. Especially Mr. McAllister."

"Mr. Harkness at the UPrint shop is making a program for the championship round," Susan said. "He's going to put in all the teams. And pictures. We gave him a list of everyone who donated. Mr. Hoffmann is making trays of sandwiches, and Pluto's Pizza is making forty, not thirty, pizzas for after the game. We told Ms. Chambers we needed room in the cafeteria. And more trash cans."

Fritz leaned on his desk, beaming. "Did you tell Mr. McAllister?"

"He said he'd make sure everything was ready. He didn't even turn red," said Jay.

Susan asked, "Mr. R, can we sell stuff at the play?"

"Wow. You don't quit, do you? I don't see why not, but you need to ask the boss."

"He's used to us now," Nancy said. Fritz marveled at how his class had matured during the year. The bell sounded. Ashley was waiting, and they headed down the hallway. Before they reached the cafeteria, Ashley turned into the backstage entrance. As Fritz reached the cafeteria, he poked his head in. The first rows of seats were already taken. At the far door, Jay stood with Ms. Bergstrom, selling tickets.

"Hi, Mr. R."

"Hi, Jay. Hi, Brenda. Looks busy."

"The auditorium is full." She pointed behind him. "We may fill the cafeteria. Thank you, Fritz. This has been great fun. I don't think I've ever enjoyed teaching more. A lot of us feel that way."

In the auditorium, Lois was glancing around with an approving head nod. "Well, Mr. Russell, you certainly have everyone's attention. Eight school principals are here today as well as eight members of the business council. And parents everywhere." She leaned in and whispered, "George even bought me a ticket. Imagine."

"Lois, I would never have guessed. George, when this is done, please make a speech of sorts. The kids have earned our enormous thanks. The auditorium is full, the cafeteria is filling. They've sold two thousand tee-shirts."

Lois looked at George. "Tee-shirts? You didn't buy me one?"

"The kids are selling them in the hall, George. Mark Witcannon made more. He has a special one for the final game."

"Let's go, George." Lois took a step and stopped. "Never mind. I'll go. You go get this started."

When she had her back to him, George rolled his eyes and walked to the stage. His presence was not enough to quiet the crowd. He tapped the microphone and a roar stormed the stage. As he had for most games, George covered his ears. He welcomed the VIPs and introduced the teams for the first game and the pitcher, Mr. Jaffrey.

Tom turned pages on the list, and Fritz knew he was altering the questions. Curveballs. Studying the lists would not have helped the hitters. Fritz glanced at Liz Chambers, who was watching and taking notes. She worked her way past the teachers lining the wall.

"He's changing the questions, Fritz."

"I know. Pretty clever, don't you think?"

"I didn't know I could do that. That spoils all the memorization. I'm going to try that."

"You're the pitcher, Liz. Go get 'em."

A home run brought the abrupt conclusion of the first game when Tom Jaffrey asked, "In 1945, a former artillery officer was the president of the United States. In August, he ordered an air attack. Who was the president, what weapon was used, what date, what location, what was the plane named, and who was the pilot?" Fritz grinned. *That's not a curve, that's a knuckleball.* Liz was laughing. Johnny Autumn asked Tom to repeat the question and answered each part. "Harry Truman was the president. The weapon was the atomic bomb. August sixth, Hiroshima, Japan was bombed." He scratched his head, closed his eyes, and said, "The pilot was Paul Tibbets, and the plane was named for his mother, Enola Gay." The auditorium went wild.

The second game promised to be close. Fritz knew what Ashley's kids had done to prepare, but Dr. Nesbitt, a history teacher, had drilled his team hard on the hardest questions and made the easiest ones more complex. Liz changed every question Fritz had given her. At the end of the fourth inning, the score was tied. Ashley's team was up first, and the last inning's lineup was stacked. The first four batters answered correctly, and one run scored. Matt was the next batter. Liz asked, "The Civil War ended in 1865. In what month?" Fritz saw a wide smile bloom on Matt's face. He had asked for a home-run. "November," he said. "You're out," said Liz. An argument began. Fritz let Liz and Matt go for a minute as the crowd egged them on. He walked to the microphone and said, "Instant replay." The crowd was whooping and yelling. He hastened to Liz and told her that Matt was right.

"Fritz, that's not what the answer sheet says."

"That's not the same question, either. The answer to your question, the one you asked, is November, not April. The Confederate ship, *Shenandoah*, surrendered in November. He's right."

Liz turned to Matt and said, "Instant replay says it's a home run." As he crossed the plate, Matt said, "1963, Ms. Chambers. That's when the instant replay was introduced." The few who heard, laughed. The Aristocrats scored two more runs and led by seven when their rivals finally got their last ups. They couldn't catch up. Ashley high-fived his team all the way back to the classroom.

* * *

DINNER AND NEWS greeted Fritz and Ashley when they walked in. Before he could greet them, Linda said her father had called and Jane said the president had called.

"Ash's team won," Fritz said, digesting their welcome. "Hi, Mary."

"Dinner's ready, Fritz."

"What did your father say?"

"I'll tell you while we're eating."

Turning to Jane, he asked, "What did the president want?"

"I'll tell you while we're eating."

"Then, let's eat," said Ashley.

Mary took two bowls from the oven. The first was filled to the lip with mashed potatoes. The second, bigger one, was piled with fried chicken.

"Move over," said Ash. "You all can have what's left. He spooned half a plate of potatoes and took three pieces of chicken. "Any gravy?"

"On the stove. Use the ladle."

"So your kids won?" asked Jane.

"Yeah, they were great. We won by two runs."

"You beat Bill Nesbitt's kids, right?" asked Linda. "English beats history. Pretty good."

"He's up against Andy Slate's crew in the finals. You remember Sean Little, Lin. He's their captain."

"Isn't he the kid that was so shy he blushed if someone said hello?"

"That's the one. Big change this year."

Mary came down, wearing a dress and conversation was put on hold.

"You look nice," said Fritz. "Where are you going?" The doorbell rang. Mary brought Natalie Johnston into the kitchen.

"Oh, sorry. Didn't mean to bother. Fritz, I have another check. I'll just leave it."

Linda said, "Have you eaten? Want some chicken?"

"It's another $10,000 from one of James Sapphire's fellow Wall Streeters."

"This is very generous. I'll have to thank him."

"You can. Next week. He's coming to the final game. Fritz, I don't think you know how big this is."

Linda asked, "What do you mean?"

"*The Wall Street Journal* and *New York Times* are sending reporters."

"The Secretary of Education is coming," said Jane. "The president called to say a videographer is coming with the secretary so he can watch later."

"Wow," Fritz whispered, with a deep inhale. "I hate to say it, but I better warn George tonight. He'll be impossible if he finds out Monday."

Jane's thousand-yard stare returned. Ashley asked why. "Pictures. Maybe, Natalie, you'd be willing to look at some?"

"Sure. Of what?"

"People who might be involved in all this. And your oath is operative." Jane waited for an acknowledgment.

"Jane, I don't know how much help I can be, but I'll look."

Jane started to get up, but Ashley grabbed her arm, held her in place, and said, "Eat."

When they finished, Jane took Natalie to the boxes in the dining room, while Fritz and Ashley cleared the table and Linda went to feed TJ. Natalie studied the photos and frames piled on the table.

“He knew everyone. Some we don’t know.” Jane gave her a couple of pictures. She recognized them as Wall Street people.

“Nice suit. You can smell the money from here.”

Fritz said, “We need to check his closet.” Jane already had her phone out. “Thanks, Nat.”

Startled by the reaction to a throw-away comment, she said, “Sure, but I didn’t do anything.”

“Mr. President, we need to get into Koppler’s house and check his suits. We need to find his tailor. Was he referred by anyone? Or did he refer others. He was part of a pack.” She listened again. “I’ll tell him.”

When she looked at him, Fritz asked, “When?”

“Now. He’s calling Tony.”

“Can I ask?” Natalie glanced from face to face, not understanding.

“We’re going to use the portal to get the names of all tailors he used,” Jane said.

“Linda, bring TJ. We shouldn’t be long, and you shouldn’t be here without Jane,” said Fritz.

“Can I come?” Natalie asked.

* * *

WITHIN FIVE minutes of their arrival, the president entered the hallway with two agents. When the door opened to the Oval Office, Natalie’s gasp echoed. Jane said, “Mr. President, this is Natalie Johnston. She’s the reporter you spoke with.”

The president shook her hand, hugged Linda, and said hi to Tony. “I brought the floor plan, Fritz. Let’s get this done.” Jane showed the agents what to look for, told them to check all the labels, and said not to disturb anything.

The president warned them to get out fast. Fritz told them to expect a second floor entry. He opened the door, and Mel led the other agents into the portal. They were back in minutes.

"The labels were all the same," Mel said. "Lipton and Son, London". I went downstairs to see if anything had been moved. Looks like it did when James and I were there before."

"Okay. Let's get out of here. Natalie, I enjoyed your articles on the tournament."

Natalie said, "Thank you, sir," in a soft voice the rest of them hadn't heard before.

"Thanks, Fritz. Good luck in the final, Ashley." Then he was gone.

Nat slapped her face and pinched her arm. "Did that just happen, or am I in a trance?" She looked at the lockers and the soft green of the walls. "This sure looks like Riverboro High."

Chapter 34

JANE LEFT before dawn. The president had sent a plane. Ashley was at Fritz's door a little after seven, a bag in hand. Ashley sliced a bagel for each of them, popped them in the toaster, and wiped the crumbs into the sink.

"You're up and annoying early," said Fritz. "Any news?"

"Yup."

"What?"

"Jane was up most of the night looking at info about the tailor. The suits are hand-sewn from custom-made wool. $5,000 each. Minimum. She said the president wants her to go to London."

"You've seen her when she charms men. They'll tell her anything she wants to know."

"Fritz, do you get the same feeling I do, that we're in over our heads. That we don't belong." The toaster popped.

In answer, Fritz handed his stack of pads to Ashley, with *Why?* on the top. He spread them out and went from list to list. Glancing out the window, Ashley said, "It's like they're daring the president to do something, double-dog-daring. Pushing every button. Or maybe warning him to back off. And not caring about what he does or its ramifications."

"What scares me is how many people know about the portal. If they don't care about the damage, none of us is safe. They've timed the attacks to create distraction and disruption. Who the hell are they?"

"We keep finding clues, so we'll find them eventually." Ashley pushed onion flakes around his plate as he read the lists again.

"Assume Mitchell is right about the Eledorians. We know the North Korean didn't answer to North Korea. So this is all a stage production. Did Jane find out anything about IM?"

"With the suit thing, she was going in another direction. I didn't ask."

"Hand me a new pad, will you?" Fritz wrote a title: Things to Ask Jane.

* * *

WHEN JANE ENTERED THE president's office, General Beech was already seated on a couch. The president frowned deeply. He pointed to the coffee tray and motioned for her to sit.

"How soon can you go to London, Jane?" asked the president.

"I need to talk to William Carey and see if the Brits have any info on Lipton and Son, but I can go today."

"Lipton and Son?" asked the general. "What's up with them?" Both heads turned. "I have a suit from them. Got it when I was at NATO."

"We found the name in one of Jim Koppler's suits," the president answered.

"In all of them, Mr. President. We want to know if they remember him, General, and if they might have any info on referrals he made. Or who referred him."

"That's the only way they make suits, Jane," said Beech. "You need to be recommended by another client. They don't have walk-in customers. They don't have a store, only a fitting room where they also cut and sew. Their showroom is full of rolls of cloth."

"Mr. President, I really need to talk to William if I can't just walk in. He'll need to find a reference for me. Or just tell them we want information."

"You can't just barge in, Jane. They work by appointment only. They all look like Swiss bankers and are just as secretive about their clients. This has to be for queen and country."

"Who referred you, General?"

"Florian Declercq. He owns a large shipping company. Moves heavy equipment. I met him when I was at NATO. We needed to get the big stuff for building roads and railroads into Eastern Europe."

Jane was already on the phone. "Fritz, can you do me a favor? Check the lists for the initials, FD."

"Sure, Jane. Hang on. Want to talk to Ash?" He handed Ashley the phone and went to get the lists. The initials were on both lists.

"Thanks, Fritz. Talk to you later. Mr. President, General, those initials are on the Caballeros lists."

"Do you suspect him, Jane?" the general asked. "We've been friends for more than a decade. He's a really nice guy."

"All we have are initials, but he fits a profile." She stared at him and glanced at the president. "General, could you use a new suit?"

* * *

IN FRITZ'S DESK, a pad contained a list of places he wanted to visit. With storms on the way, the pad was out before he took off his jacket. Under the pad were books, already paperclipped. He stacked them.

"Where can I go and not be in a crowd?" he asked the empty room. "Kitty Hawk. The Wright Brothers. I've already been to Ford's Theater. Maybe I can just go in that back door. If I set the time, Pearl Harbor. In and out. I'd like to talk to Gandhi." At the bottom of the open drawer, he saw a program an older friend had given him. It was for a Yankees-Red Sox game at Fenway Park. "I wonder if Ash wants to go to a real game?" He placed the program on top of the stack. Then he took off his coat and put his desk key in his pocket.

Thunder began at noon, but no buzz on the doorknob made him growl. Midway through the last period, lightning brightened the sky and his afternoon. He discussed *Plessy v. Ferguson* and *Brown v. Board of Education* with his ninth graders. He told them that in his opinion, the most important reason to vote for president was judicial appointments.

After the classroom emptied, he put the key in the lock and placed the Ford Theater book on the left side of his desk. In the hallway, a buzz tingled his fingers. He gently opened the door and walked onto a landing in an alley. A man holding a horse's reins stood outside a door, which Fritz opened as gunshots rang out. He moved to the wings of the stage as a man leapt from a box seat, collapsed on the stage shouting, "Sic semper tyrannis," and ran toward him. As tempting as it was to stop him, Fritz stepped back as John Wilkes Booth limped by. Fritz followed him out.

Taking two steps forward, Fritz stepped back into the hallway and saw Ashley ambling toward him.

"You okay?" Ash asked. "You look weird."

"Portal's open. I was just at Ford's Theater."

"Are you out of your mind? The kids are still here."

"I know, but I had to see. Wanna come?"

"Where?"

"Kitty Hawk. We won't be long. The first flight was only twelve seconds."

Ashley shook his head. "You know, you are nuts. You've already met Wilbur. What if he remembers you? Then what? But I'll come just to keep you out of trouble."

Fritz switched books and returned to the hall. Stepping through once again, his feet hit flat sand surrounded by dunes.

Waves crashed behind them, sending salty spray into the air. He and Ashley climbed to the top of a dune and looked around in time to see a small biplane climb off the ground with a man lying prone in the middle.

"Duck," Ashley said.

"Nah, he'll be past in a second." Two small propellers puttered by.

"I thought you said he was up only seconds."

"They did four flights that day. This must be the last one. He's been up almost a minute." A gust blew sand in their faces.

"I thought Kitty Hawk was a town."

"It's about four miles from here. We're at Kill Devil Hills."

When they returned to the hallway, Ashley brushed his head and then his shoulders. A scattering of fine sand collected around his feet. In the classroom, he took off his shoes and tapped beach into the trash can.

"That was cool," said Fritz. Lifting the program, he said, "Wanna go to a ball game?"

"Where?"

"Fenway."

"Sure, why not. Who's playing?

"Yankees and Red Sox."

"Perfect."

They stepped through the portal. The crowd cheered as Ted Williams kicked some dirt around the batter's box. Fritz and Ashley stood in an aisle in the upper deck along the third base line. The Yankees pitcher turned to look at the outfield.

"Is that Whitey Ford?"

"Yup." On the fifth pitch, the crack echoed through the evening, and the ball shot to right-center field for a long single. The centerfielder throwing the ball back in was Mickey Mantle.

"Let's go, Ash."

Back again on familiar ground, Fritz smiled. He had grown up loving the Yankees. Ashley was a lifelong Red Sox fan. But

Mantle, Ford, and Williams were legends before either of them was born.

Ashley said, "You know, if we didn't have so much bad stuff happening, this could be fun."

"I know. How about one more?"

"Sure."

Fritz set another book on the desk. He grabbed the door and stepped onto flat concrete. Sunny warmth surrounded them, but an explosion to the right jerked their heads. The high pitch of an approaching plane turned their attention from curious to terrified. Muzzle flashes surrounded them, and concrete dust rose high. They were in the direct path of hits that were yet to come. Ashley grabbed Fritz's shirt and dove through the outline behind them. They heard pings on the door as it shut.

"I thought we were going to see Babe Ruth or something. Are you crazy?"

"Pretty scary, huh? That was Pearl Harbor. Sorry, Ash. The paperclip must have been in the wrong spot."

"Wrong spot?" Ashley yelled.

"Sssh. What if someone walks by the door?

"Wrong everything. What was that explosion?"

"I think it was the *Arizona*. I meant for us to be overlooking the harbor." He looked at the book. "See, this is where I marked." He turned the page. The clip sat directly on the runway on Ford Island with Battleship Row to their right. He showed the book to Ashley.

"Paperclip caught two pages."

"Your head's screwed on backwards. And your shirt's ripped."

"So are your pants."

Fritz started to smile until he looked closer at his friend's leg. "Ash, are you okay? That's not a rip. It looks like a bullet hole."

Ashley reached down and patted his leg, then stuck his fingers through the hole and rubbed his leg. "You're an idiot. It missed, but not by much. Wait till I tell Linda."

"Now that's low-down. I didn't do that on purpose. C'mon, Ash, she's already starting to worry again."

"She ought to."

Chapter 35

"**LIN, YOU'RE NOT** going to believe this. I have to prepare more class sessions." She looked up from her computer. "I've outrun myself this year."

"I can't talk about it now, Fritz. I have to get this book finished. I told them it would be my last until after school ends. Go do what you need to. Who knows what's going to happen next?"

She turned back to the laptop and waved him away.

At his desk, he set up new pads for each class. His World History classes had never gotten deeply into the post-World War II world. American History had never done more than skim once they got to the 1980s and the Reagan era. Work in America, his labor history class, was almost at the end of his usual plan, so he could talk about the demise of organized labor and teach some more advanced labor economics. Already so far ahead, finals had been prepared for a couple of weeks. He thought he might have to add questions to the exams.

* * *

HE STOPPED at Ashley's classroom first thing Thursday. Ashley was already at his desk and wearing his worry ruts.

"Hi. What's wrong?"

"Final game, the play, finals."

"And Jane's not here. So what's really the matter."

"I spoke to her a few minutes ago. She'll call later, but it sounds like she and the general are in a viper pit. The tailor set off her alarm. The general felt it too. When she asked about the history of the company, they all clammed up."

"That's weird. People usually love to talk about their businesses."

"I know. And they're having dinner with that friend of the general. The one Jane thinks may be a Caballero."

"It fits the call I got from the president. They may need the portal to get into the tailor shop. You can guess how happy that made Linda. Anyway, let's get through today. Good luck. To your team. And your opponent."

All day, classes vibrated, hallways buzzed, and teachers and students were in overdrive. Fritz congratulated each class for making him have to prepare more material to get to the end of the term.

"Mr. R," asked Johnny Clayton after second period, "can we talk? I got into all my schools. I have two football scholarships and some serious financial aid offers."

"Can't do it today, Johnny. How about tomorrow after school? Where do you think you want to go?"

"I couldn't believe it, Mr. R, but I got into Harvard and Princeton, Penn State, Rutgers, Nebraska, and the University of Virginia. It's a hard decision."

"Let me think about it, and we'll talk tomorrow afternoon. Congratulations. That's a very impressive indication of your intelligence and your athletic skill."

"Thanks, Mr. R."

At the start of the last period, his ninth graders told him they were going to be busy, so he shouldn't teach anything. Susan had designated greeting committees for all the celebrities. By the middle of the period, traffic had begun to back up on the street. Groups of people trooped toward the school from all directions. Half his class had already disappeared, and the rest were just looking out the window. When a limo turned into the driveway, the stragglers went to watch.

"That's Ryan Howard," said Don, pointing at the first to emerge.

"Boy, he's big," said Judy.

"And that's Vince Velasquez. He won't be pitching for a few days, except here. And that must be Cameron Rupp. Cool." Ted, Ron, and Emma hustled out to greet them.

The next out was an older man. "That must be Mr. Montgomery," said Fred.

The ball players stood by the limo while Ted and Mr. Montgomery talked. Fritz watched joyful faces and the ballplayers' concentration when Ted handed them each the list of questions. Ted pointed to the classroom window, blinds now raised. The Phillies waved.

Another limousine parked behind. First out was Natalie Johnston, who saw the faces and also waved. Behind her, James Sapphire, another man, and a woman, both in suits, climbed out. Susan, Samantha, and Todd LeMaster greeted them, and they were introduced to the other limo group by Ted. Fritz smiled at the remarkable confidence that the students had developed.

The bell rang, and in a flash, Fritz was alone. He lowered the blinds, cleared his desk, and daydreamed about summer. His reverie dissolved when Ashley tore in.

"Are you okay?" Fritz asked.

"Jane just called to wish me good luck. But she said she guessed right. I'll tell you later. Let's go."

When he entered the auditorium, an ovation greeted him. He looked around for George. The noise soared as he reached the stage. After his third attempt to quiet the crowd, the cheering subsided. Susan said she didn't know where Mr. McAllister was and wondered if they should begin. He paused a moment and decided to go ahead.

"Thank you all for coming to the championship game." He had to wait for the first volley of cheers to die down. "We'd like to welcome all our special guests." From the corner of his eye, he saw George step from the other side of the stage, carrying a box and followed by a man he recognized from the news. "I'd like to introduce our principal, George McAllister."

Fritz started to leave the stage, but Susan pulled him back. George took the microphone and said, "Mr. Russell, I have a special presentation. But first, I would like to introduce the United States Secretary of Education." A tsunami of sound flooded the room.

The secretary shook Fritz's hand and stepped to the lectern. "Thank you all for the invitation. On behalf of the president, I would like to commend you for one of the most innovative events we have seen. He sends his greetings to you all." Once again, the roar sent the principal's hands to his ears.

George then thanked everyone and introduced the other special guests. Before he finished, he said, "Mr. Russell, this is for you." Handing him the package, he said, "Open it." Fritz tore through the gift wrapping. In the box, a new tee-shirt featured his picture across the front. He held it up. On the back, "Our Champion" jumped off in gleaming gold letters. Signatures of the faculty covered every bit of available fabric. From the audience, Al Kennedy shouted, "Put it on, Fritz."

Fritz returned to the microphone. Looking first at his ninth-graders and then toward the crowd, he put the shirt over the one he had on and said, "Thanks, but the real champions are my ninth graders, who have done a remarkable job to get us to today's game. So let's get started."

George announced that three pitchers would be on the mound for two innings each. "But first, our national anthem." After calling out "play ball," George introduced the two teams. Andy Slate smiled and waved. Ashley was pale, flexing his fingers and rubbing his hands together. Bill Nesbitt, the umpire, walked to the microphone and said, "Batter up." For the final round, George had allowed stage lighting and spotlights. The coaches had flipped a coin to determine which would be the home team. Slate's Economists were up first. Each pitcher had been given a fresh list of questions, edited to eliminate those already used. Liz Chambers had changed the difficulty level when she made the list.

The first batter asked for a single, and the first pitch was "The Star Spangled Banner was written during the War of 1812. What was the original title?"

Jack took a deep breath and said, "I don't know."

Dr. Nesbitt shook his head and said, "In Defence of Fort McHenry. One out."

Ashley's Aristocrats followed their routine of asking for singles, but the questions were harder than they were expecting. The score after the first inning was tied at zero. Ashley stood in the shadows of the stage curtain, pacing two steps up and two back. The second inning ended with the same score. As he left the pitcher's chair, Ryan Howard waved to the cheering audience and then high-fived both teams. Cameron Rupp took the mound.

In their next at-bat, Slate's Economists scored three runs. Matt again rallied his team. So far, they had only one hit. But he had stacked the line-up, figuring that the last at-bat might make a difference. A ninth grader was up first. She singled. Rachel was next. Her question was "What was the largest construction project of the twentieth century?"

Rachel went to first base when she said, "the Panama Canal."

Matt was next. He asked for a single. "During World War II, which meeting of the Allied leaders defined post-war Europe?"

Matt, usually confident, began to wiggle. He twisted from side to side, shrugged his shoulders, and put his hand to his chin. "Yalta."

Dr. Nesbitt said, "Correct. Take first base." Johnny Clayton strode to the batter's box and looked at Matt, who drew a circle in the air. Johnny asked for a home run. "Franklin D. Roosevelt served in office using a wheelchair. What famous organization did he found?"

A large grin lit Johnny's face. Everyone could tell he knew. "The American Red Cross."

Dr. Nesbitt said, "No. March of Dimes. You're out." Johnny stood looking, his mouth open, his face blank. Gasps came from his team. Johnny shook his head and walked to the end of the line.

The next batter, Steve Christopher had planned to start the routine again. Instead, he asked for a home run. "Winston Churchill coined the term, 'Iron Curtain'. He was replaced as prime minister by whom?"

Steve shook his head. "No idea," he said.

"Labor won the general election, and Clement Atlee became the new prime minister," said Dr. Nesbitt. "Two outs."

With the bases loaded, the next batter asked for a single. He was asked which president established the Environmental Protection Agency and said, "Theodore Roosevelt." Dr. Nesbitt said, "You're out. It was Richard Nixon."

Ashley's team was rattled. Starting the fourth inning, with the score, 3-0, the "ohs" and "ahs" were almost as loud as the ones at the ball park.

The Economists scored twice and led 5-0. Ashley's Aristocrats scored twice. At the end of four, the score sat at 5-2.

The new pitcher entered the stage as Cameron Rupp followed Ryan Howard's example and high-fived both teams when he left. Vince Velasquez shook hands with George and Dr. Nesbitt and took the pitcher's chair. He glanced at the questions list when the next batter was called. "The Fugitive Slave Act was upheld by what Supreme Court decision?"

Tom Wyle answered, "Dred Scott" and took first base.

"The Fugitive Slave Act was part of what piece of major legislation?" the pitcher asked Sam Olberman.

"It was one piece of the Compromise of 1850," said Sam. He had a hit. The next batter was out.

"Two men, a scientist and a cartoonist, are known for working with peanuts. Name them." Looking for a triple, Sarah Bright bounced on her toes. "Um … Charles Schulz was the cartoonist and um, I know this one … um." She sucked in her lower lip. Her eyelids twitched open and closed. "George Washington…" she closed her eyes. "Carver," she shouted. Her team and the audience cheered as two more runs scored. Ashley was staring at his feet. The next two batters answered incorrectly, but the Economists now led, 7-2. The Aristocrats scored one run and the Economists scored three runs in the top of the sixth.

With a 10-3 deficit, Ashley waved for Matt. He told Fritz later that he had told Matt they had done well and their formula worked. He patted Matt's back and said, "You can do it."

The first batter was out. The second reached first by answering, "What was the first state to ratify the Constitution?"

"Delaware," said Linda Plum. Next up, Rachel asked for a single. Fritz looked out and saw the audience beginning to stand.

"Only one Constitutional Amendment has ever been repealed. Which one?"

Her crisp answer came quickly. "The eighteenth, Prohibition." Matt took his spot in the batter's box. George asked the cheering crowd to sit down.

Vince Velasquez asked, "What infrastructure project connected New York City and the Great Lakes?"

Matt said, "The Erie Canal," and the bases were loaded.

Johnny Clayton came to bat. Again, Matt signaled for a home run. "What American financial asset surpassed the value of all the banks and industrial production combined in 1860?"

This time, replacing the smile from his last at-bat, Johnny's eyes narrowed. His lips were tight. "The dollar value of slaves."

"Home run," said Dr. Nesbitt. The score was 10-7. As it was when the game ended.

Andy Slate shook hands with Ashley and joined his team's celebration. Ashley congratulated his downcast kids for a great effort. "Listen up," he said to some teary-eyed students, "you all got us here, and we almost made it. You did a great job. An amazing one. Somebody had to lose this game. Be proud."

Then George awarded the trophy and said, "The year and the winning team's name, The Economists, will be engraved on this. With plenty of room for future team winners." Cheers took over. Susan directed a group of ninth graders to hand the champions their winners' tee-shirts. She waved to Mark Witcannon, who waved back. No one was sitting, so George invited everyone to the cafeteria for snacks.

"You almost made it, Ash," said Fritz.

"They did great."

"Now that the tournament is out of the way, I can help you with the play."

"Fritz, I feel bad for the kids. I should have worked longer with them."

"Ash, Johnny knew the right answer was The March of Dimes on that first question. But even he got the jitters. If he had answered that right, the game might have gone the other way."

"Let's go to the cafeteria and get out of here."

"You can go. I have to stay for a while. You know, thank everyone and all that. I'll meet you at my house. I still want to hear what Jane has to report."

Everyone wanted to talk to him. Students and teachers, the secretary of education, the special guests, and the reporters all followed him to a corner. He couldn't get away. The secretary whispered that the president would call later. Natalie introduced Fritz to some reporters, including one from a Philadelphia TV station. He spoke to Mr. Hoffmann, whose sandwiches had disappeared in minutes, and he greeted James Sapphire and the two other bankers he had brought. He thanked them for their donations. Sapphire told him he was surprised that the game was actually exciting. Mark Witcannon waited for the crowd to thin and said, "Your tournament has inspired the business council. They're all talking about other things we can do, especially when I told them how my business has increased." The Phillies and Mr. Montgomery were surrounded. Fritz wanted to thank them, but all he could do was wave.

As the cafeteria started to empty, George and Lois appeared in front of Fritz. Lois said, "Well done, Fritz. George has been bragging to the other principals about the increase in school spirit and student focus, too. He agreed to help them set up tournaments of their own. I'm sure he'll be talking to you about it."

"Lois, let me tell him," said George. "Fritz, they were impressed by the turnout and our guests. We have a hit."

"Yes, George, we do."

Chapter 36

HE WANTED to be home. The lightning always promised he could go again. Fritz leaned back, the bucket seat cocooning his thoughts. *The tournament's over and a success.* With a moment to himself, he thought about the past year as the thunder rumbled overhead. He bumped over the curb as he entered the driveway, imagining Robert E. Lee sitting on a tree stump, waving to him. *I really miss him.*

"Hi, honey. I'm home." Linda was standing at the door when he came in.

She kissed him and said, "Hi, honey. You don't know how glad I am." He was taken aback by the response. "Can't I be really glad you're here?" At the table, Ashley and Mary were watching them.

"Sure, but you sound like an alarm went off."

"Jane called again. You tell him, Ash."

Jane had told him that Declercq was worrisome, and the tailor shop seemed like a set in a movie from the Cold War years. "What do you mean?"

"Jane said she expected a fancy lobby, lots of pictures of famous clients, maybe refreshments. For the prices they charge, she didn't expect threadbare carpets and beat-up chairs. It was like they didn't want anyone there."

"What did the friend say?" asked Linda.

"She was cautious with him. But she said he was very open. And very aware of our problems here. He asked the general if we had any leads on the attackers. When the general said we were still working on it, Declercq said he didn't think it was terrorists. He thought someone was trying to overthrow the government."

"Jane must have been really suspicious then," Fritz said.

"She's having his phones tapped, and she alerted the NSA. But she doesn't think he's the one. They're going back tomorrow to fit the suit. She'll try to find where they keep their customer records. They may need some hackers and maybe will go in at night."

"So, they want to use the portal. When?"

"I don't know. She said the president will call you."

"I think Declercq is the key. He knows the tailor, and he's got the bucks and the influence. If he's not a good guy, we'll find out in short order. I bet he's already heard something. 'Overthrow the government' he said."

With anxiety already on the rise, when Fritz's phone rang, they jumped. "Hi, Mr. President." After he listened for a minute, he said that Jane should just let him know when she wanted to enter the shop. The president said to expect to go the following night and that he had heard great things about the tournament.

Fritz and Ashley went out to pick up dinner. When they returned, Natalie's car was outside. As soon as they walked in, Natalie handed Fritz another check.

"Wow." He passed the piece of paper around the group.

"James talked to some of the other foundations about how you have changed the educational environment at the high school, and they all wanted to help. He said to tell you he enjoyed his visits, and he wants to talk to you."

"Did he say about what?"

"A job, I think. He mentioned setting up a new non-profit to look for programs like the tournament."

“You’ll have to think about that, Fritz,” said Linda. “It’ll mean the portal would go away.”

Her comment came like a gut punch. “We’ll see if he actually calls. Thanks, Nat.” The tournament had now raised more than $200,000. Natalie asked if she could stop by the next night. She had made a list of questions for Declercq. If he was on the level, he could be very useful. He did seem to know everyone.

* * *

AT THE END of the day, Fritz’s phone rang. The president wanted to get into the tailor shop. Jane had snooped around while the general had been trying on the suit. She felt uncomfortable pretending she was tagging along to a fitting. She’d found a card file, so it wouldn’t be enough to hack their computer. They would need to go in for paper before dawn in Europe.

“Natalie Johnston will be with us,” Fritz said.

“Hard to keep a good reporter from asking questions. Come get me first, say 10:45?”

NEXT AFTERNOON, AS they headed for their cars at day’s end, the fields behind the school called out. Ashley angled off to the fence to watch. In the far corner, dust rose from a play at second base. The starting gun reverberated on the far right where a track meet was in progress. In front of them, boys and girls in helmets, pads, and gloves ran up and down the lacrosse field.

“I miss this stuff, Fritz.”

“Yeah, I know. I can feel it too. Look.” Fritz squeezed his waist. “I’m getting flabby. Ash, let’s go.” Fritz headed toward his car and stopped. “Let me ask you something. The president is telling us about everything that’s going on. Don’t you think that’s strange?”

“Not really. We’re part of this, like it or not. He trusts you, for good reason. You saved his life, you never ask for anything. And maybe most important, you think about how to solve problems he's facing and tell him. You really are a terrific analyst. Jane says he talks about you all the time. He worries about you and Linda. He likes you, although *that* I don't understand."

At 10:30, Fritz put on a jacket. Linda said she was staying with TJ because Mary wanted to talk to the president. A security car would be stationed outside the house. Ashley, Natalie, and Mary piled into Fritz's SUV. Tony was talking to Jim Shaw when they arrived.

Tony said, "Hi, Fritz." He greeted the others, but looked at Natalie a second time and smiled.

Fritz grabbed one handle on the generator, Tony took the other. In his classroom, Fritz explained the way the portal worked to Mary and Natalie. He called the president and a minute later, shook his hand. Mel and a stranger followed.

"Fritz, this is Tom Andrews, Jr. He is a first-rate hacker. But a white-hat. Only for good."

Fritz shook hands with the surprised young man and thought how striking the resemblance was. "I'm so sorry about your father, Tom. I liked him a lot."

"Fritz, let's get Jane at her hotel. She has the tailor shop map."

A thought hit Fritz. *This has become routine.* He pulled the door open, and Jane and General Beech walked into New Jersey.

"Here's the tailor shop layout," Jane said. "We need to be exact. It will probably be pitch black. Mel's coming with us."

Fritz asked, "Do you have any idea how long this will take?"

"Not for sure," she said. "Maybe a half hour if everything goes smoothly."

"Okay. If you're done sooner, we'll be in Ash's classroom." He got a buzz and the intruders were in London.

"Jim, I want to talk to you about your friend," the president said to the general. "Let's go sit." The president waved everyone to follow. He told Tony and Jim Shaw to join them. "I think you all know each other. This is General Jim Beech. He's chairman of the joint chiefs, and he and Jane set up tonight's entertainment." He introduced all those who the general had not yet met.

"Mr. President, shouldn't we speak privately? No offense, everyone."

"We can count on everyone here."

The general shrugged. "As you know, I've known Florian since I was at NATO. We've developed a close friendship over the years. He's even offered me a job when I retire."

"You know that the initials FD have appeared on Koppler's and Wixted's lists. We don't know they refer to Declercq, but we have to be very careful with him." The general leaned forward while the president explained his plan. Jane's quick return startled them. They were done. It had been too easy.

They found what they were looking for, and Tom put a device on the USB port that was virtually undetectable. The tailors would have to throw out the computer to get rid of the connection. "I'll check the files when I get..." Tom said, "home. This is really weird. Dad couldn't say anything, but I thought something like this. I just didn't believe it."

Jane had found their client file cabinet and photographed every name that fit the initials. She had seen a folder label for Georg Badenhof. Natalie who had been silent, said, "Mr. President, I don't mean to be rude, but I've been doing research on some of what I've been told. I found another FD who fits the description. Powerful, rich, and influential. In our government."

The president's eyes narrowed. "Thank you, Natalie. That's an angle we haven't looked at. Is that on your list of questions?"

"It is, Mr. President. Along with some for Declercq that might allow you to distinguish between the two names."

Fritz hooked up London, then Washington, and moments later, the locals were on their way home. In the parking lot, Natalie asked Tony if he was going anywhere near her office. He said he would be glad to give her a lift. They arranged to meet Mary and Jim for a drink at midnight.

* * *

SHE WAS ON HER way to a fundraiser with two campaign donors. An accident ahead brought the limo to a stop. The car started to roll. Abruptly, the rear door opened, and a man wearing a kefiyyah and robe pulled her out. The barrel of a silenced pistol was aimed at her forehead.

* * *

GENERAL BEECH picked up his suit. They were meeting Declercq for drinks and dinner that evening. "What took so long?" Jane asked when he got back to the hotel.

"The pants were too tight. They fixed them on the spot. I told them I needed it for tonight. They were very accommodating."

"Do you like it?"

"For $6000, I'd better like it. Do you think I can get a tax write-off as a business expense?" He grinned. "Florian is sending a car for us at 5:15. I'll meet you in the lobby."

As Jane dressed, she wondered what her computer contained. When she returned to London from Riverboro, she had planned to nap for a couple of hours but was fooled by a comfortable bed. A call from the general had her up and running. Now, preparing for dinner, she couldn't read the computer and put on make-up at the same time. As she was doing her eyes, her phone rang.

"Hello, Mr. President."

"Jane, you have to tell General Beech not to wear the suit to dinner. Tell him to wear his uniform."

"What's wrong?" she asked, tensing as she spoke.

"Jane, your feelings are scary. These tailors aren't OUR bad guys, but they are bad guys. Tom called. The suit is bugged. Pants and jacket. Tell him someone is meeting you, and he needs his uniform to ID you both. Tell him I said so. Don't say anything about the bugs. In fact, write him a note, just in case. You're coming home tonight by portal. I'll call later with the details."

"Yes, sir. What about Declercq? He's taking us to dinner."

"He's coming with you. He doesn't know it yet. Colonel Mitchell will go through the portal to pick you up. I'll call you in about three hours."

Chapter 37

FRITZ LOOKED up from his computer. "We keep finding more clues. I wish we could see where they lead."

"And even more people know. If Koppler even hinted about the portal, someone's going to put those pieces together. Frankly, at this point, I'm glad Mary's here." Linda sighed. "I didn't tell you, I polished up the plan presentation. I'll hand it in next week. Then, it's just classes and finals."

"That's great. How soon do you want to open the store?"

"No rush. Let's get this next month behind us. I'd like to go talk to Charlie in New York. Mostly to ask if he sees any big changes coming. To me, Bicycle Habitat is the Vatican of bikes." She smiled at the thought. "I guess that makes him the Pontiff of Pedaling. I'll have to tell him."

* * *

AT 2:30, THE president entered the hallway outside Fritz's classroom.

Fritz asked, "What's in the box, Mr. President?"

"Nothing yet. Superman couldn't see through it, though."

"For the suit?"

The president nodded and told them to put it down. The clang resonated down the hallway. Both Mel and the colonel rubbed their shoulders. The president said he didn't know yet if Declercq was a friend, but he planned to find out. He wanted Declercq to send a note to Massoud and sign it FD. "If Declercq is FD, he'll know that we know. He'll want to leave so he can make contact. If there's another FD, then it may lead us to the rest."

"If we're right about the murders of the rich guys, the rest must be afraid," Fritz said.

"Whoever's at the top of their operation is ruthless." The president checked his watch. "Fritz, get me to London."

* * *

CONVERSATION AT DINNER had included the president's development plan, but also the attacks on the navy, the White House, and Camp David. They touched on the strange deaths of some of the world's wealthiest businessmen. The general hinted he thought they were all connected and that the plot was unraveling. Declercq absorbed the conversation with a poker face. When the general told him a visitor was coming to talk to them, Declercq yielded to curiosity.

"Who, Jim?"

"Not here. We should be leaving. He's on a tight schedule."

"I am getting the feeling you suspect me of being involved in the matters of which we have been speaking. Do you?" His voice rasped, enough to make Jane look. He noticed. "Jim, I'm not involved. I don't know what's going on, and I can't figure out what anybody, much less me, would have to gain from killing a bunch of wealthy men and attacking your government. And how do you know those are related?"

"Florian, we may need your help. You knew Badenhof. And I'm sure you know about Hartmann and his boat. Shall we go?"

Declercq looked at Jane. "Your smile has deserted you, Major. I think maybe you are not what you portray. You look too sharply."

"Mr. Declercq, we can discuss this elsewhere. But I am an Army major, and I work with General Beech every day. Perhaps you see things that aren't there. But you see these?" She pointed to her decorations. "They are real, and I earned them all."

* * *

FROM A SHOP ON Savile Row, where their conversation was heard and recorded, a message immediately flew to an office in Abu Dhabi. What nobody in the shop or Abu Dhabi knew was that the Andrews kid's tinkering meant that it also went to a computer in Maryland.

* * *

SITTING BY THE window, the president glanced at Big Ben and Parliament and watched the traffic on the Thames. Colonel Mitchell sat across from him. His phone buzzed. "Mr. President, this is Tom Andrews. Declercq's suit is wired. A message just went to the Emirates."

Grateful for secure phone lines, he thanked Tom, disconnected and called Jane. "Don't talk," he said before she could say more than hello. "Just listen. Declercq is bugged. Is he with you?"

"Yes."

"Try to alert the general. I'll see you in a couple of minutes." He swiveled to his companions. "Colonel, get the box back."

Everyone was surprised to see Colonel Mitchell return to the hallway. He asked Tony and Ashley to bring the box into Jane's hotel room.

"What's up, Colonel?" asked Fritz.

"Declercq's suit is bugged." He stepped back to London when Tony and Ashley came out.

The president had to make a quick choice. He wanted to talk to the man but not to anyone who was listening. He called Jane.

"Just listen. Yes or no, does the general know?"

"Yes."

"I want you to meet me in your room. Leave Declercq with the general in his room. I'll have a note for you to give him."

MAJOR BARCLAY, GENERAL BEECH, and Florian Declercq stepped from the elevator. The general opened his room, and Jane headed for hers next door, saying she would be right back.

The president handed her a note for Declercq. "I hope we can trust him. We need to hurry though." His phone rang. "Yes, Tom."

"Mr. President, you need to get out. Now. They've sent a hit squad. I'll tell you everything later. Get out."

"Go, Jane. I'll be a minute behind. We're about to be attacked. Colonel, get Mel." Again, the colonel poked his head through the portal. He and Mel returned. "Let's go."

The colonel checked the hall. Mel stepped past and took the president's arm. In the general's room, a befuddled Florian Declercq stood in his underwear. The president pressed his finger to his lips and waved for everyone to follow. Mel and the colonel took the box. Mel whispered, "Gun, Jane."

A bell at the end of the hall rang. Jane saw a rifle emerge from the elevator. Black gloves and a mask followed. She followed everyone into her room and shut the door. "They're here."

* * *

THEIR UNEXPECTED return, with a man dressed only in his underwear, led George to cover his eyes. *Ears, eyes, it's all the same, I guess,* Fritz thought.

The president said, "Ashley's room." He looked at George and then at Declercq. "George, could you run home and get Mr. Declercq a shirt and pants. A robe, even. We'll be waiting for you."

Lois said, "We'll be right back."

"Mr. Declercq, we haven't met." The president held out his hand. Confused and embarrassed, Declercq shook it.

"Nice to meet you, Mr. President. Normally I would be more presentable. Where am I?"

"Please take a seat. Everyone, please. Mr. Declercq, I hope you will accept my apology. We found out only moments ago that your suit is wired. We'll find out how later. It appears your tailor is a front for funding terrorists. I had wanted to ask you if you would be willing to help us. But with this information, I think you already have."

"I'm afraid I do not understand."

The president explained the original intent of their meeting and that he believed the attacks, including the assault on the summit, were related. "We discovered a link to Abu Dhabi today."

Declercq looked to the general for confirmation on each point. He had been concerned about the attacks because his business might be disrupted, but he had no idea that organized terrorists had been involved. He told the president that he had believed a foolish group of American "wingnuts, I believe you call them," was responsible.

Before the president could respond, George and Lois walked in. Over her arm, Lois carried pieces of George's wardrobe. "We brought a few things that might fit. I'm always on a diet, so I have a few different sizes."

"Thank you, sir." Turning to the president, he asked, "Mr. President, where am I, and who are these people?"

"Mr. Declercq, what I'm about to tell you is top secret. Our scientists have discovered an atmospheric anomaly. You are now in a high school in America." *That was a great non-answer,* Fritz thought. "These people are a combination of our technicians, intelligence operatives, and as you obviously can see, our military. We pulled you out of Europe because we had learned your suit was capturing your dinner conversation. It seems your very expensive suits have been providing funds to terrorist organizations. And information, too. Perhaps others are also such victims."

So, young lady," Declercq said, "you are in fact not what you seem."

She said, "Sir, I'm a major in the army, as I told you. My area of expertise is the Middle East."

"Major, I have been a world traveler most of my life. I have met and spoken with many people. You may be what you say, but there is much more you are not saying. Perhaps it doesn't matter at this time. But rarely am I wrong. I cannot afford to be."

"Florian," said General Beech, "I've been arguing with the major for the past seven years. You're aware of the proposed program to develop the Middle East." Declercq nodded. "She designed the overall plan. You're right. She's much more than a random major. And our world may become safer because she doesn't give an inch when she thinks she's right."

Declercq smiled. "Thank you, Jim. I knew I was correct. Again. Now if you will permit me, let me put some clothes on."

* * *

"SAY THIS AGAIN. They saw a woman enter a room. They broke in, and no one was there? Did they go in the right room? Did you hire escapees from Bedlam?" he yelled.

* * *

"NOW THAT YOU KNOW all this, are you willing to help?" asked the president.

"Certainly, Mr. President. But you said you rescued me earlier. Do you think I am in danger? How can I go home? Or conduct my business?"

"If we get you back to London, will you go home, to a hotel, where?"

"I have a flat in London. And an office. When I go back to Antwerp, I will fly. My driver flies with me."

"I'm sending you back with an escort, straight to your car. Colonel, we need a dozen men here, in civilian clothes."

Jane interrupted. "Mr. President, let's use the Brits. They will be happy to help. That way, we keep it local, and they can make sure Mr. Declercq's car and driver are safe."

Declercq smiled and said, "See what I mean?"

Conversation continued for half an hour as they waited for the British special services to get in place. Declercq wrote the note and signed FD. He would post it from London. When the British security team was ready, Colonel Mitchell and Mel Zack prepared to escort Declercq through.

"Mr. Declercq, if we're lucky, meeting you may help bring an end to what we have been fighting for more than six months. You are sworn to protect our secret."

"Of course, Mr. President. I hope we succeed. And if I can be of assistance as you develop the Middle East, please let me know." He shook hands with all his companions and hugged General Beech. "Sorry about the suit, Jim." Fritz opened the door, and Declercq returned to London.

When the colonel and Mel returned, the president was on the phone with Tom, who would monitor Declercq's calls and as well as follow Massoud's cyber life. "Expect a lot of quick activity over the next few days," he said. "Fritz, it's time for everyone to go home."

A whirlwind visit, another mission complete, another weekend disturbed. Fritz went straight to the family room. A Phillies game was about to start, but before he changed channels, breaking news announced the death of Congresswoman Fran Davis. He went to the kitchen. "We have a problem. It looks like Fran Davis was murdered. I bet she was FD."

* * *

MORE INFORMATION came quickly. "Congresswoman Fran Davis, an eight-term representative from California and chair of the House Budget Committee, was on her way last night to a fundraiser for the fall campaign when her limousine was attacked. She and three others were killed. The limousine was found in a field." The reporter said it appeared the car had been hijacked. All the passengers had been robbed. "The local police will have a press conference at 7 pm, Pacific time."

* * *

THE PHONE CALL WAS expected. The man listened and said, "Thank you." When he hung up, he said, "I need a new congressman" and returned to his *Wall Street Journal.*

* * *

THE RUSSELL family room filled with TV viewers once again. Jane's phone rang. Anxious faces waited for her to put her phone down. She told them that FD's limo had been searched and a phone found. The car was hers, and she kept an extra phone in a charger in the glove box. "The memory card is intact. It's being sent to Tom Andrews."

* * *

FRITZ WANTED the yellow pads to expand, to break down the doors that seemed to be hiding the clues. Since the portal had first opened, nothing in his life had been normal. The president protected them as best he could, but would that be enough? They had found him once, why not again? The attacks flooded his thoughts. *This can't be about money, or even business advantage. So what is it all about?* Killing the president made no sense, he would be out of office soon. The Middle East? The summit proposal would be an economic powerhouse for the region and potentially the world. As would the social and political stability the leaders envisioned. "Lin, do you think whoever is behind all this is just playing a game?"

"Why? It's so dangerous. It's almost like chess, sacrificing pieces to get advantage. And knowing what the next move will be. But not being able to counter surprise moves."

Ashley said, "It's more like playing simultaneous matches. You know, more than one match at a time. Multiple boards. We don't know which board they're playing on."

"Maybe that's what I should do. Make yellow pads for each kind of game. Instead of trying to tie them together, split them up and maybe we can figure out the next moves."

Jane poked her head around the corner from the dining room. "Let's try it."

On fresh pads, he listed the groups of possibilities. The list began with "Caballeros." He added attacks, murders, the Middle East, and the portal. Ashley said, "The portal is us. The others are them. If it is a game, let's put portal as a move after their moves. Hang on." He left the kitchen and returned with a chess set and board. "It helps me think."

"We can add new games as we go," said Linda. "Let's start with Naria and Eledoria." Fritz wrote, Naria, portal, Eledoria, portal, Israel, portal, Pakistan, portal. Then he switched pads. "Geneva, portal, White House, portal, Camp David, portal." Another list, the Navy base attacks. On the pad titled *murders*, he wrote, "portal, Wixted, portal, school bombers, portal, Koppler."

"Counter moves," Ashley said. Fritz passed the pads for the others to review and tinker with. Then he looked at the pad for the Caballeros and said, "We have to fine tune this, but it seems the portal has thwarted most of what they've tried to do."

"It hasn't stopped anything," said Linda.

"But it's disrupted their plan, whatever it is. If we hadn't caught Wixted at Thanksgiving, the school would have been destroyed. If the North Korean had escaped Cuba, we'd never have known about his teams. But they keep going from board to board."

While Fritz was announcing each move, Ashley was moving chess pieces. The portal was black, the Caballeros played white. He lifted another black pawn. The damage to his defense had created unprotected attacking lanes. "We're playing strategic defense. They have some big plays available," he pointed at the board, "but that opens them for a rapid attack by us." He held a bishop in his fingers. "Then checkmate."

"Ash, we're losing," said Fritz.

"But all we need is to win one game."

Jane said, "Florian Declercq."

Chapter 38

IBRAHIM MASSOUD, paced his office holding a letter. The note asked him to come to London. Someone had disclosed their identities, and FD had been trapped. Subterfuge and double-talk had interfered with his dealings over the past year. Would a phone call be a problem? It was too early in California. Who had broken the silence? He knew a mistake in judgment could be fatal, and he wasn't ready to meet Allah. He liked his life just as it was. Allah wouldn't be happy with him anyway.

He looked at the beautiful city to which he had contributed so much. His efforts had increased his wealth and power in turn and increased the well-being of his associates. That had to count for something. He read the letter again. His smile was short lived. He was skeptical.

* * *

"MR. PRESIDENT, IM is on the move. He took the bait. He didn't call, but he'll arrive in London by evening. He booked a hotel and return flight for tomorrow."

"Thanks, Tom. Keep an eye on the calls. He's not done yet." The president called Jane and said they needed to be in London as soon as possible after school let out for the day. "Massoud is headed to find out what he can about FD. But we need to get him, take away his phones. So far he hasn't made any calls."

"Do you want me to call William?"

"That's probably smart, yes. Stop Massoud at Heathrow and isolate him. But it has to be discreet. No news, no suspicion. Then we can bring him here."

"Mr. President, I think it would be better to go there. If he becomes aware of the portal, we'll be in trouble. William can hold him."

"I'll get the president of the UAE. Bring him here and take him to London. Let the Sheikh see for himself. Jane, tell Fritz and Linda that I'm sorry to do this to them. But it has to be done."

* * *

FRITZ LOOKED AT the face in his window and waved Tony in.

Ted whooped, "Mr. R, are we gonna get a trip?"

"Mr. Almeida is here for a lecture and stopped by to say hello." The chorus of boos sounded like a Flyers game. "That's enough. We're done for today. You have your homework assignment. You can start now." He took Tony to the hall.

"Jane told me," said Fritz. "We need to get the hall cleared quickly." The bell rang and doors opened along the hall.

Ashley joined them, shirt sleeves rolled up and ready to go. "I'll get George. He can shuffle the kids out."

Fritz said, "Ash, get Al Kennedy. I'll get Liz Chambers and Tom Jaffrey to stick around. Everyone in your room, okay?"

"Sure. Do you need help with the generator, Tony? We don't have much time."

"I'll park right at the door once the kids are gone. The president said he wants to get this over fast."

Ashley headed for the office, and Fritz ran to get the teachers. Tony waited in Fritz's classroom. While he watched the students depart, the door opened.

"Hi, Mr. Almeida. Are we having another trip?"

"Hi. It's Eric, isn't it? No, sorry. I'm just visiting."

"I went to see Mr. Gilbert, but he wasn't in his room. I thought he might be in here." Fritz returned with George on his tail. George, ruder than usual, told Eric he had to leave. Just then, Ashley opened the door.

"Good. Hi, Mr. Gilbert. I wanted to talk to you for a minute." He glanced at the principal. "If it's okay."

"Come to my room, then, Eric. A meeting is about to begin." Ashley nodded at Fritz's quizzical look. The teachers were coming.

"Fritz, we can't keep doing this," protested George. "It's bad enough that you're here at all hours of the night and weekends. Lois worries about something going wrong."

"George, the president asked for our help. Maybe this time we'll get some answers. But we need to keep the kids away from the hallway now. We're tight on time."

Tom, Liz, and Al understood what was about to happen when they saw Tony. He asked them to guard the hall.

Jane walked in. "Ash said you were here. We need to go now. Tony, call the planes and get the generator."

"But the kids are still wandering the halls," said George.

"George, tell them it's an emergency. You don't need to say what it is. You're the principal."

"Good idea," said Fritz. "Al, go with George. Tom, cover the door. Don't let anyone in."

"I can lock the exit," George said. "That's easier."

FRITZ OPENED the door, and the president, Mel, and Colonel Mitchell came through from Washington.

"Thanks, Mr. Gilbert. I'll see you tomorrow," said Eric from Ashley's doorway. He turned to face the crowd he had spotted from the corner of his eye.

"Oh boy," Fritz said. He whispered, "Problem, Mr. President."

"No problem. We'll play it by ear." The president strode toward Eric. "Fritz, introduce me," he said in a hushed voice.

"Eric, I'd like you to meet the President of the United States." The president reached out to shake Eric's hand.

"Nice to meet you, Mr. President."

Ashley looked out from his door window, put his hand to his forehead, and pushed the door open.

"Eric, I'm here for a meeting." Eric looked around at the people gathered and directed his stare at Fritz.

"You can really do it, Mr. R, can't you? You can time travel. You can bring people with you. That's how we met General Lee. But this is the present. How does that work?"

The president said, "Eric, come inside with us." He went through much the same routine he had with David.

"I need to get the president of the United Arab Emirates now and take him to London. Would you like to watch?"

"Yes … Sir." Like a protective net, soft laughs surrounded him.

"When I'm done, perhaps we can talk more. Can you stick around?"

"Yes, sir."

"Fritz, let's go." The president checked his watch. "We're late."

Colonel Mitchell handed Fritz two sheets of paper. "Eric, come with us. Mr. President, where are you meeting him?" The president tapped the spot. "Eric, there's a connection between the desk and the door. When I put a paperclip on a map or floor plan or picture, we can go there. Okay, let's try it."

"Mr. R…"

"Later, Eric."

Fritz opened the door to a well-appointed room. The Sheikh was surprised at the sudden appearance, but not frightened. He strode straight to the hallway. "Mr. President, this looks different." He looked at the people surrounding him. "I recognize some faces."

"Mr. President, you won't be returning here," said the president. "You will fly from London with Mr. Massoud after we talk to him. We will discuss the plan further when you arrive at home. Shall we go?"

Fritz had set a new floor plan for a hotel in London and opened the door. Sitting in an armchair, reading a newspaper, Massoud was reaching for his phone when two pistols were aimed at his face.

"What is the meaning of this, Mr. President?" he said to his leader.

* * *

THE PRESIDENT, MEL and Colonel Mitchell returned to the hallway. The president's tight lips and clenched jaw suggested that things hadn't gone well. Indeed, Massoud had been silent.

"Mr. Massoud knows," said the president. "Maybe when he realizes what's in store, he'll be more loquacious. They will be home by morning, their time, and he will be tried by their courts."

The crowd in the hallway increased when Al, Liz, and Tom joined them. "Hello, Mr. President, nice to see you again," said Al, who then realized Eric was there.

"I'm not as well as I'd like, Mr. Kennedy. Thank you again, all of you. Eric and I have had a conversation, one that you and I also had. I'll be out of here in five minutes. The Sheikh agreed to hold him in confinement until we talk again. The British SAS agents are going to escort him back to Abu Dhabi. He had a phone stuffed in his sock, so now we have phone numbers to trace. Jane, here are the numbers. I'll give the phones to NSA. Maybe they'll find something." With a grin, he said, "Sorry again, Ashley. No sneakers."

"You're afraid I'll win. I get it."

"Sounds to me like a double-dare," the president answered. "The stakes are going up. It's been a pleasure to meet you, Eric. Mr. Russell has told me you're one of his best students. And he said I can be sure of your discretion."

“Thank you, Mr. President. You can. But I’d sure like to visit the White House. Could I?”

“Maybe we can work something out later in the year. And again, thank you all.” Fritz opened the door, and he was gone.

* * *

THE SHEIKH called the president. Massoud’s trial would take place by noon. The president had alerted news teams to be in Abu Dhabi by late afternoon the next day.

“Mr. President,” said the president, “this is what I would like you to do.” The president gave exact instructions and explained his next steps. “Please record anything he says and give that recording to our ambassador. I’ll speak to you when it’s done and see you shortly after. Thank you for your cooperation.”

* * *

ABU DHABI HAD PROVIDED a perfect launch pad for Ibrahim Massoud’s career. A city of massive skyscrapers and resplendent parks jutting into the Persian Gulf, its oil and natural gas resources provided a vibrant and wealthy international setting. Born to an oil fortune, Massoud expanded the family business to include banking, construction, insurance, and sundry small businesses that supported his primary investments. His sideline was brokering weapons. An entrepreneur and successful risk-taker, he was regularly invited to participate in organizations around the globe and became a close advisor to his own government.

From the top of one of the many towers in the city’s skyscape, the vast desert sparkled in hues of pink. The gulf reflected the dying light. Lower down, lights flicked on as evening shadows climbed the buildings. Earlier in the day, he had been tried and found guilty of supporting international terrorism, which he had angrily denied.

Now, at the top of his world, he faced execution. His options were explained to him by the sheikh. Either provide the names of the conspirators or face a firing squad.

"You must tell me," said the sheikh. "Are these people worth your life?"

Massoud, hands secured behind him, was turned to face the edge of the building, an eighty-story-high tower. "If I tell you, what will happen?"

"The world will be safer. These reporters will announce the names to the world. You have denied participation, and I believe you. But you will be imprisoned until such time as the fuss can be contained." The sheikh motioned, and a black sack was placed over the prisoner's head. He was turned around a number of times, and two soldiers escorted him to the edge of the building.

* * *

FRITZ AND Linda, Ashley and Jane stared at the scene, a tall building glowing in the sunset. The news anchor was saying the man was a convicted terrorist, but the cameras had only a long-distance view.

* * *

THE SHEIKH had his soldiers clear the reporters from the roof. "Massoud, you must tell me, or I can do nothing to prevent what awaits you." The clack of rifles being cocked filled the gentle desert evening.

"Your highness, I beg you. Let us sit and discuss this as the old friends we are. I will tell you all I know, which is truly very little." With his right hand, the sheikh motioned to a soldier, with a quick wave of his fingers, to push.

"Massoud, the world now thinks you are dead. A mannequin dressed like you has just been pushed off the roof. To the public, you are no more. Now tell me."

"The only name I can give you is the financial backer, who controls private banks and has investments in farming communities from Canada to Texas. His name is Atkinson, Marvin Atkinson. He lives in South Dakota."

"That is good, Massoud. The President of the United States has threatened to tie up our international trade and banking. Thank you, my friend. Now, let's get down from here." The sheikh told the guards to turn Massoud around and free his hands.

* * *

"OH MY GOD, ANOTHER one," said Linda. In the failing light, the camera followed the descent.

"He looks like he's swimming," said Ashley.

The camera angle was blocked by a high-walled courtyard where the falling man would land.

"I've seen that before," said Fritz, softly. "When we witnessed the Triangle fire, we stood across the street as the girls jumped. I'm glad the camera can't see it.

* * *

"THAT WASN'T SUPPOSED to happen," said the president. His office was full of those who needed to know. "I told him to toss the dummy so people would think he'd carried out the execution, and then we would take him. I don't believe this. I want to speak to the sheikh. I'll give him a few minutes." Pointing to the televisions, he said, "And turn those things off."

* * *

"HE JUMPED, Mr. President. I'm sorry. I know you want the recording. It has been dispatched to your embassy. He gave me a name. Would you like it?"

"I would, Mr. President. I cannot tell you how disappointing it is that we are now unable to find out more."

"Perhaps the recording will provide what you need."

"What was the name he gave you?"

"He said the man was a banker in your South Dakota, Marvin Atkinson. Again, please accept my apologies, Mr. President. As you know, so many things are beyond the control of those of us who govern." The smile on the sheikh's face did not travel through the phone. Lying to the President of the United States distressed him not an iota. "I'm sure we will speak again soon." On his desk sat the blindfold he had had removed just before Massoud was pushed.

* * *

"HELLO, MR. PRESIDENT," said Jane.

"I'm sorry you saw that. Tell the others. The first one down was a mannequin. That way we could question Massoud while everyone thought he was dead. The sheikh told me he jumped."

"Did he give you any names?" She walked to the dining room table.

"Marvin Atkinson, a banker."

"We have an MA on the lists. What are you going to do?"

"The FBI is already on the way."

"Are you bringing him to Washington, sir? I think you should."

"He'll be here by morning. Hold on, Jane." The president took another call. "Sorry, Jane. Ambassador Carnegie will return from Abu Dhabi by morning. I think you should be here. Tonight if you can use the portal."

"Sorry, but he wants me at the White House tonight." Another breaking news bulletin flashed on the TV screen. "Mr. President, check out MSNBC." A reporter from Sioux Falls, South Dakota yelled into her microphone that Marvin Atkinson, a well-known local banker was being arrested by the FBI as she was speaking. The camera zoomed to the front door of a large house in the background.

"Fritz, he's going to call back. If I'm right, someone has already been sent to kill Atkinson."

Ashley said, "Remember our chess game. When we use the portal, we screw up their plans. Blindfold him and bring him here."

* * *

"RIGHT NOW, he's at the jail in Sioux Falls," the president said. "He's a prominent citizen, so the police are being fairly lax."

Jane said, "Mr. President, we have to get him here. Remember Caitlin Morgan. Hold on, Fritz wants to talk to you."

"Mr. President, the meeting room is still set up. If you bring him here, you'll have no interference until the morning."

"I don't want to use the portal with all the people around."

"How about the FBI guys start driving him around until we can figure out what to do? It's South Dakota. I'm sure we can find some open space." Jane reached for the phone.

"Mr. President, there's an airport in Sioux Falls. We can set up the portal in twenty minutes. Tell the FBI to leave now, just drive around and meet us in half an hour. Sir, I have a feeling about this. He's too big a fish to let off the hook."

"Jane, call me when the portal is set. Tony and the colonel are already on the way."

* * *

"HOW QUICKLY CAN you get to Sioux Falls, South Dakota?" asked the man. "He's in FBI custody at the police department."

"I'll need the private jet. Probably a couple of hours. Maybe longer."

"You have the lawyer credential still?"

"Yes. What do you want me to do with him?"

"The middle of that lake in Yankton will be fine."

* * *

THE PRESIDENT was sitting at the head of the table. Mitchell removed the handcuffs and blindfold. Atkinson, an almost comical visage of bulging eyes and open mouth, stared at the president.

"You know who I am, Mr. Atkinson. It's late, and I'm a busy man."

"I want my lawyer."

The president's finger tips brushed his lips, and he took a deep breath. "I'm a lawyer. So you don't need one. Are you aware of what happened in Abu Dhabi tonight?" The man stared at the president. "Your friend Ibrahim Massoud confessed and provided names. You are implicated in the murders of Jonathan Hartmann, Georg Badenhof, Fran Davis and others. We know you provided the financing for North Korean mercenaries to attack and sink American warships, destroy American warplanes, and kill young soldiers and sailors." The president slammed his hand on the table. "AMERICAN MEN AND WOMEN!"

"I did not."

"Then why did Massoud say it was you?"

"I have no idea." The banker lifted his manacled hands to block the verbal blows.

"Mr. Atkinson, I have a recording of his statements. He said you also financed Eledorian mercenaries to attack a conference in Geneva last fall. I was there. You almost killed me. So add conspiracy to assassinate the president to the list. And I haven't begun to talk about your banking practices and your investment schemes."

Atkinson's lips moved, but no sound left his mouth. He rubbed his hands together. "I would like to use the bathroom."

"And I would like my ships back. And my soldiers and sailors. Can you trade them? Why don't you start by telling me how you found nuclear warheads. Who sold them to you?"

"Mr. President, please. I tried to stop it."

"Then who was it?" the president whispered.

"Thomas."

The president leaned back. The rest would be easy.

Chapter 39

"**YOU SHOULD** have seen him," Jane said. "He yelled, he whispered. He broke the guy down. He blamed him for everything that's happened."

"Then why did he let him go?" asked Linda.

"Breaking news in the morning will focus on his fraudulent investments. His customers will tear him apart. And he will stand trial for that."

"Do we have the names?"

"Every law enforcement agency in the world will be looking for the rest of them. What's weird is that no one's ever heard of Thomas Richter. We have some digging to do."

Fritz said, "I still don't understand the biggest question. Why?"

* * *

TWO HOURS BEFORE sunrise, an annoying buzz woke the man from troubled slumber.

"Do you know who this is?"

"I do," said Thomas Richter.

"You have about ten minutes. Atkinson talked. You have options. When you decide, let me know."

"Thank you." He had prepared. Two small attaché cases and two packed suitcases sat in a closet. He slipped on his shoes and hurried downstairs. A hidden lever in a wall panel opened a door to a staircase leading below his driveway and onto a landing. He pushed a screw head on what appeared to be a floor drain and opened an entrance into a tunnel.

Three stories above him, thirty-two men, agents of federal, state, and local authorities surrounded his home. Four men entered, scattering through the first floor. Finding no one, they climbed the wide staircase and began checking the second floor rooms. The house was empty.

One agent remarked, "He doesn't even have an alarm system. With all this stuff, you'd think he'd worry about burglars."

"Have we checked everywhere? Has anyone seen a door to an attic or basement?" another asked.

"As big as this place is, there has to be one. Turn on the lights." Thirty men scoured cabinets and closets and looked for indications of another living space.

* * *

THE TUNNEL CROSSED under the road and ended in an open field behind the house across the street, a house he owned in another name. Pushing through a turf-covered door, Thomas Richter lifted each suitcase through the opening to the ground below and climbed out. Hidden from view, he stepped through the high grass to the back of the empty house. He dug through a clay planter for the key. As he unlocked the door, an explosion rattled the panes and lit the sky. He strolled to the front window, now illuminated by a fireball, and sat down to watch his house burn. He thanked his grandfather again for teaching him to always have an escape route.

* * *

IN HIS OFFICE AWAITING the ambassador, the president watched the morning news and scanned his reports for the day. One screen flashed a burning house. Thirty men had been inside at the time of the explosion. The fire was so intense that no one could enter. "Back to you, Katie."

The president muted the TV and picked up his phone. Sam Clemmons entered the office.

"That fire. Were those our guys?"

"Yes, sir. Thomas Richter's house. The reports we have so far say no one could have survived. The blast blew out walls and windows, and the roof collapsed after first lifting off the house. Mr. President, initial reports say no one was home."

"Were all the men we sent inside?"

"No, sir. Two stayed outside just to keep watch. Both are badly injured."

"Let me know when you know something."

"Yes, Mr. President."

* * *

AT THE END OF the first period the next day, Ashley came in, his worry ruts pronounced. Fritz waited for the story. Jane had told him that Atkinson was dead, shot on his front porch by a sniper. And the man named Richter had blown up his house. "Killed thirty agents and cops."

"He's still loose?"

"They don't know. The house has been on fire, so they haven't been able to check."

"We should have expected something like this when he let Atkinson go."

* * *

THE PRESIDENT PACED the empty office, waiting for a report on the fire. He'd already been told that two men from the Caballeros lists were in custody, a third man at large. Another was found dead of an apparently self-inflicted gunshot. Yellow pads covered his desk. Even with the men identified, something was missing. He stopped at his desk and stared at the yellow. The words he read were hollow. They still didn't know why.

Sam Clemmons walked in, disturbing his distress. He told the president that the fire was out, and the search for bodies had produced most of them. Most of the bodies had been found near what had been the front door. "We'll find out later, sir, but the investigators said the fire worked down from the roof as if the walls had been filled with explosives and flammables. In some parts, it was so hot that glass melted. The front door had an electronic deadbolt."

"What about the men in the hospital?"

"Burns and lacerations, but they'll live."

"Did anyone talk to the neighbors? Does anyone know anything about Richter?"

"Mr. President, we've looked for records everywhere. Other than his name, there is no Thomas Richter."

* * *

THE DOOR OPENED. Eric Silver looked at him and said, "What's wrong, Mr. R? Are you okay?"

"I'm fine, Eric. Just tired. It's been a long year. Do you have a question?"

"Well, if I met the president and Robert E. Lee was real, I was wondering if you've been able to go into the future?"

"This is between us, Eric. Don't ever forget the oath. You saw how it works. No floor plans or maps for the future exist. It seems time moves forward, like you said last spring. What appears to happen is the past connects to the present, and sometimes it takes a little time to meet up. When we connect to the present, we create a hole or a tunnel from place to place. Travel to the future may be possible, somewhere, someday, but not with what I know now. At least that's what I think goes on."

"If it's an electrical connection, how do the maps or floor plans generate the connection? I've been wondering about that."

"That's a good question. The paperclips are what take me to the specific location, but I don't know how the maps, or books, or floor plans work."

For a moment, Eric squinted, processing the information. "The books are printed. Photographs capture images of things that contain electrical charges." Fritz wondered if Eric had found another piece of the puzzle. "But maps and floor plans have no electrical source."

"Eric, I can't explain it, and believe it or not, I haven't had time, and I don't have the science background to figure it out. It's not like I can just ask. I don't even know the right questions."

"Maybe I can help. Do you have any of the maps or floor plans you use?"

On another day, Fritz would have ended the conversation. Instead, he went to his desk drawer. He had kept everything in case he needed it again. He opened a folder and removed the documents. "We went here last night."

"South Dakota? Is that the guy who was shot?" Fritz looked up. "I have a news feed on my phone, Mr. R."

Fritz shook his head and smiled. "I guess I shouldn't be surprised. Yup. That's the guy."

"Where did this map come from?"

"The internet. We printed it before we came here."

Eric scanned the pages. "Mr. R, your printer runs on electricity." Eric continued slowly, as each step became clear to him. "Look here. These are GPS locations. The paperclip conducts the electricity back and forth, like Wi-Fi, from your doorknob and from wherever you're going. I think that's it. And the paper holds electrical charges, like static. You know, like a new ream of copy paper sticks together unless you fan it."

Fritz looked at the paper on his desk and then at Eric. "Even to a history teacher that makes sense, Eric."

"Mr. R, I wanted you to know I've been thinking about this. Remember last spring when you got hit by lightning?" Fritz chuckled and said that he did. "I think that the school was electrified, at least a little. I was in the locker room and I think I felt it. You're the link." Eric looked at his teacher. "I think this has been hard on you, Mr. R. Not being able to talk about it. I know it's hard for me. And I only just found out."

"Thanks, Eric. You're right. And believe me, it's not going to get easier."

Eric reached for a floor plan from a Geneva conference room. "Mr. R, did you save the president from the attacks in Geneva?"

In spite of himself, Fritz felt the relief of telling the story. "Yup. The day we had the lockdown. Remember?"

"Wow. What else have you done, Mr. R? You're a hero, and nobody knows it."

"Thanks Eric. And no one will. It has to be that way."

"I get it, but I also wanted to tell you. After I met the president, I decided to go to MIT. If time-travel is real, then I want to learn as much about science as I can. So much could be done."

"Congratulations. Great school. And I hear you're likely to be valedictorian."

Ashley opened the door, startling both of them. He knew immediately what they were talking about. "Pretty interesting, huh, Eric?"

"Hi, Mr. Gilbert. Yeah, it is. Maybe I can go with you somewhere?"

"Eric has an hypothesis for how the portal makes the connections. I'll tell you later. You have rehearsals, and I'm going home."

"Let's go Eric. Time to pick your brain. Fritz, I'll see you later."

* * *

THE MAN NOW KNOWN as Thomas Richter watched through the night from the house across the street as the attempt to kill the fire dragged on. Badenhof had been thorough. His house ignited and burned like the trick birthday candles that kept re-lighting.

As the darkness faded, he sat motionless, hands pressed together, considering his options and, more important, what had not worked. Thomas Richter would be hunted globally. Unimportant. As was how he would leave. But he wondered how the government had reached his circle. Had Massoud caved? What had fat Marvin told them? But first, some sleep. Before he stood, two men crossed the road and climbed the hill. When the bell rang, he remained in his chair, knowing they would check windows. One walked to the front window and tried to peer into the darkness.

"I can't see a thing," said the agent. "These windows are like mirrors."

His companion said, "That's not unusual around here. Keeps the inside cooler, cuts the bill in half."

"Let's check around back."

Richter followed their trail until a shake of the locked rear doorknob sent his visitors back down the hill, no more informed than when they had arrived. When he awakened after a restful six hours, his next plan had a starting point. He opened a suitcase and withdrew a cell phone. He gave instructions. In three days, he would arrive in Sioux Falls.

"You will tell me then what happened and why Atkinson was found on his front porch, not in Lewis and Clark Lake."

* * *

WITH NO FINAL word that Thomas Richter's body had been identified, Fritz and Linda went about their days with neither speaking of their fears. Spring moved on toward graduation, Linda's and then Riverboro High's. Jane had boxed the paperwork from the dining room table, but the boxes remained in Ashley's living room. For two weeks, Jane and Ashley were invisible. The president hadn't called. Only Mary reminded them of unfinished business. The play, now deep in rehearsal, would be performed four times. What little help Fritz had provided had not been noticed. Once again, the students had done it all. Eric had enlisted Fritz's ninth graders to provide the marketing. More than half of the tickets were already sold. Even George bragged happily about all the school activities.

But each day on his way home, Fritz used the quiet time to consider what could happen. In spite of bright flowers and the greening of his route, he failed to find cheer in his surroundings. On a Wednesday in mid-May, Jane was at the kitchen table with Linda when he walked in. Linda was biting her lips.

"Hi, honey," he started. "What's wrong? Hi, Jane."

"LW," said Jane.

"Loren Whitmore. Yeah, so?"

"He's dead, Fritz. He was hanged," said Linda. "More like someone strung him up."

"He was dead already," said Jane. "In Montana. Hanging from an overpass."

"They still haven't identified Richter," said Linda.

He squinted, thought, and then said, "So only the two in jail and Richter are left?"

"Fritz, there's something else. I'll tell you when Ash gets here."

Ashley arrived a few minutes later, but Fritz stayed at his desk. The banging in the kitchen furthered his resolve to remain in the sunroom. Jane came to get him. "They have composite pictures of Richter from the other two," she said. "Fritz, he looks a little like the missing guy at the Hay-Adams."

Pushing food around his plate, he said, "Great. The one that got away. And he's gone again. He built an exploding house, but he's not dead. Just great."

"Fritz," said Linda, "the president is sending Mary some help."

* * *

BEFORE LEAVING California, Thomas Richter ceased to be, replaced by the gentleman farmer Richard Salzmann. The escape was easy. A tan Camry, parked in the garage of his escape house, was shrouded in boredom. No one would pay attention when he drove away. He laughed at the directions—go east and turn left at Nebraska. At the busiest motel he could find in Sioux City, he met his associate, a former sniper and disaffected soldier. And also his nephew. There was no small talk.

"Atkinson was found on his front steps. Why did you leave him?"

"He had company. A man was walking to the front door when Atkinson just appeared out of thin air. I didn't wait around."

Richter/Salzmann said, "The president. That's what he meant."

"Who?"

"Massoud said the president has a secret weapon. Even the sheikh wouldn't talk about it." He rubbed his face. "You'll be traveling soon. Do you know my new number?"

"Give it to me. Where are you going?"

"For now, the farm. Drive. Take your time. You know where to leave the car. Bring your uniform."

Thomas Richter moved his base to suburban Washington, a farm in Virginia owned by a subsidiary of a company held in a trust registered in the Caymans. His plane sat in a hangar, his pilot awaiting his next trip. Thomas Richter owned nothing. Thomas Richter had never existed.

* * *

"MR. PRESIDENT, I THINK this trip is a huge mistake and not just for you," said the secretary of defense.

"Charlie, this was my plan, my idea. They accepted it. I have to go."

"Mr. President, you'll be in the open. Hundreds of workers we can't screen will surround you. Heavy equipment can be sabotaged, picks and shovels are handy weapons. Sand dunes are hiding places, and we can't provide even foreign military for protection."

"I know what the risks are, Charlie. I'll have agents with me, and they've already checked out the area."

"Then at least don't make the speech. Shovel the dirt and leave."

"By the end of the day, we will have started building two plants, and I've been told enough earth movers to trench a hundred miles will be warmed up and ready to go. We're two months into this thing, and I don't have that much time left. I'm going."

Able to use the Oval Office again, the president sat at his desk. In front of him was a speech about a new birth of possibilities. The ceremony would be near dawn, which he chose as a perfect symbol. The leaders would all arrive by helicopter and head to the Turkish border with Syria when the ceremony ended.

* * *

"HI, MR. PRESIDENT," said Fritz. "What can I do for you?"

"You know that I'm going to Palestine tomorrow."

"Yes, sir. Good luck."

"I've kept you out of this for a while, to let you finish the school year without me. First, I want to say thanks to you and Linda for tolerating all I've done to mess up your lives. I wish I could say it was over."

"You and me both. I keep waiting for the other of our mutual shoes to drop."

"I've been thinking. I have to ask another favor. At midnight tomorrow, our time, I'll break ground for the first desalination plant. With all that's happened, I don't have a good feeling about what might occur."

"I know. Jane said she has a feeling. She said she told you not to go."

"Fritz, I'm going. I have to. But, would you consider having the portal ready, just in case?"

"Mr. President, as much as I've been glad not to have been involved, you know I will. I don't want to, but I will. Will we have company?"

"I've told Colonel Mitchell to get his guys ready. I'm sending a wide screen TV to the school so you can see if we need to move quickly. We expect everyone who was at the summit."

"I think you guys call that a target-rich environment. Why not just take the colonel with you?"

The president said that all the leaders agreed not to have soldiers present. Even the Israelis would remain at the border. "So really, none of us will have protection. That was the idea."

"Has anyone at least checked for places to hide? How about setting up a perimeter to keep people away?"

"I've sent a map of the area to Jane. It's topographical. We've identified three places where an attack could originate."

"Are news cameras going to be there?"

"Only three. One for us for a pool feed. One for Europe, and one from Al-Jazeera."

"Mr. President, if the cameras scan the area until your speech, we can see anything unexpected. Frankly, watching you shovel dirt isn't very interesting."

The president chuckled. "You don't think so?"

"If nothing happens, do you want to come back through the portal?"

"No. I'll head to Turkey to break ground for the second plant. So, is it okay?"

"Yeah. I hope you don't need it."

"Thanks, Fritz. Me too."

Fritz relayed the conversation to Linda. He told her that it was a precaution and with Mitchell and his men, they could move quickly. He would be safe.

"Fritz, he has only a few more months. I really want this done. Graduation is next week. My parents will be here on Saturday. After this, I want you to tell him to wait for a while until he does anything else to save the world." Noting the sarcasm, he hugged her, but her arms remained at her side.

Chapter 40

FRITZ WENT STRAIGHT to the office. Ms. Sweeney announced him and led him to George, who was scarlet already. "Don't say a word, George. I know you're upset. We've been through this before. I want you to plan for a substitute for me tomorrow. I expect it will be late, and I'm tired enough. I'm taking a day off."

"I talked to him last night, and I've never heard him sound worried before. Do you think something will happen?"

"Like I told him, it's a perfect trap. I hope nothing happens. But I've been hoping that all year. Lot of good it did."

"I really don't want to be here. But Lois said we should. What do you think?"

"I hope we won't have much to do. But they've learned not to come up short. If all goes well, the only thing we'll need is someone to check the bathrooms and sweep the floors."

HE TRIED OUT his new lecture on his first period World History class. He compared the importance of the Middle East development project to the Panama Canal, the Hoover Dam, and development of atomic energy all in one. He told his seniors in second period they were witnessing what most likely would be a critically memorable event in their lives, like curing polio, walking on the moon, taking down the Berlin Wall, and developing the internet had been for previous generations. For his American History classes, he talked about courage in the face of great challenges such as Washington setting the precedent for two terms, and Lincoln asking for "malice toward none" and charity for all. He told them about FDR's Second Bill of Rights. "If this succeeds, the president will be among those considered greatest."

He hit his ninth graders with homework first thing. "Discuss why you think the Middle East development plan is important. You know the president and leaders from around the world will break ground for two water desalination plants tomorrow. Progress will be gradual. By the time the first steps are completed, you will have graduated. But, if it works, you will have witnessed one of the most dramatic events of your lives."

"Wow, you're cookin', Mr. R," said Ron.

Fritz looked at his giggling class. "You know I try not to get too worked up about what's going on in the world. It changes all the time. But I've been following this story, and I'm both excited about the prospect and a little worried that they won't keep working together."

Susan said, "Mr. R, everyone, I think the president's speech is live around midnight. If I'm up, I'm going to watch." Heads nodded in agreement.

"Don't stay up too late. Tomorrow is a school day. You can record it and watch at a reasonable hour. Or see replays."

"Okay, Mom," said Ron.

* * *

WHEN FRITZ TURNED into the lot that evening, the yellow buses were waiting. George stood by the doors.

"Where's Lois, George?" Linda asked.

"In Ashley's room, closing the blinds. She already did your room." Tony was already at work down the hall. Fritz asked if Ashley had arrived. George said he hadn't, but the buses were waiting when he entered the parking lot. George pointed and said they were full. George's voice was shaky, a different kind of nervousness than Fritz expected.

"This should be pretty easy, George," Fritz whispered, his hand on the principal's shoulder "It's a speech and a shovel of dirt. Then they blow a whistle, and the backhoes start digging. He'll be gone in ten minutes. We're only here in case things go wrong."

At H hour, 10:30, the buses unloaded. Through the doors came the supplies and the medical equipment, followed by two large screen televisions. One was placed in the hall next to the extension cord, ten feet down from Fritz's classroom. The other went into the converted classroom. "We're using the conference room tonight," said Colonel Mitchell. "We still have our connections in place, including the secure comms. The second TV will pick up surveillance from a couple of sources." Then he handed the room signs to a lieutenant, and pointed to the room they would use for the medics.

"Colonel, are you expecting trouble? He sounded worried to me."

"He was adamant. He said they all agreed. But there's too little protection, only a handful of agents. Our only intel is from the plane overhead.

"Have you got maps?"

"Here's an aerial of the site. We marked potential spots where someone could hide. One well-placed rocket grenade and we'll have a world war." He pointed to the photo. "That's why we erected a canopy."

"You have four spots picked out. Do you have more copies?"

"Jane has them."

Jane was talking to Captain Dolan when Fritz interrupted. She reached into her satchel.

A soldier poked his head from the conference room and called the colonel. They'd spotted activity on the monitor. Fritz hollered that the mission might have to start early, that something was happening. Jane and Dolan joined Fritz as the colonel hurried from the classroom, his jaw set. "Fritz, we need to go now. The AWACS picked up what appears to be infiltration. Come look."

Blocked from view on the ground by sand dunes, specks moved toward the leaders exiting a large helicopter. The TV cameramen set their hookups. Whatever was about to happen would be captured live.

"Can we call them?" asked Fritz.

"No reception anywhere nearby."

"Colonel, how about the Israelis?"

"Ten miles away."

Dolan said, "Colonel, they have cover until the last three hundred yards. They're within range now about one thousand yards out."

"How much time do we have?" Fritz asked again. He looked at Dolan's new pin. "Major."

Dolan smiled. "Yeah, promotion. Thanks for noticing. They're coming slowly. Maybe ten minutes until they're in the open."

The colonel told the comms team to contact the AWACS and tell them to notify the Israelis that a ground attack was possible. He asked someone to get General Beech on the phone.

Fritz ran into his classroom with the colonel and Jane. Fritz asked where to go and placed the clip and drew a pencil outline. He asked if it wouldn't be better to bring the leaders and any others through the portal instead of sending soldiers in.

"We may have to. The attackers know they're close enough," Mitchell said.

Jane said. "Colonel, my group will go first. I'll try to hold them off. Let's go."

Activity swirled around Fritz as Major Barclay's team lined up. He yanked the door open.

Fifteen feet inside the entrance, Major Barclay directed the soldiers, telling them to spread out and move forward. A series of twenty-foot tall dunes rose in front of the advancing Americans.

"Colonel Mitchell, General Beech is on the line."

* * *

A LARGE WALL of sand blocked the view of the Mediterranean. On the seaward side, a cave-like hole had been dug and the opening carefully covered by a matching tarpaulin. Adhesive had been sprayed on one side and sand thrown onto it. Perfect cover. Facing the ceremony at the other end of the hole, the rifleman had dug an opening, sighted his rifle, and waited.

* * *

WITH ALL THE soldiers in the desert, Fritz watched the TV screen. "Look," he said, and ran to the TV. "A hole, big enough to shoot from." From the camera's view, he tried to visualize where on the map the hole was. "Straight line to the president." Fritz glanced again at the TV. He watched the president check his watch and turn east to the brightening horizon.

"Set a map, Fritz." said the colonel. "I'll try to find him." He asked a lieutenant for binoculars. With the portal reset, the colonel was ready to go.

"Colonel, don't go alone," said Fritz.

"My guys know what to do. Get them in, Fritz."

* * *

AN AMERICAN ARMY OFFICER appeared out of thin air onto the European feed. A Virginia TV, one of three he had turned on, broadcast the startling sight. The camera changed direction.

"Don't shoot him," Richter/Salzmann said to the empty room. He had told the sniper to wait until the others had distracted the ceremony and to avoid the president but to go after the Arabs. They would never trust each other again. After the ceremony collapsed, he would begin to regroup.

* * *

ONCE THE SOLDIERS were in, Fritz reset group one and returned to the hall. He turned to the TV. He wanted to see where the attackers were. They were still under cover, and darkness on the ground kept them out of sight. Jane's group moved up the dunes. He returned to the hallway and stood next to Ashley in front of the television. The camera angle had changed again. Another scan picked out the colonel and focused on him. About ten feet above him, like a demonic eyeball, the hole Fritz had seen came into tighter view. The camera swung to the group of dignitaries at the canopy, milling around, waiting for sunrise.

A tap on the microphone brought everyone's attention to the canopy. The president of the newly formed State of Palestine spoke first. He welcomed the small gathering. "Salaam aleichem," he began. Before the expected response, the sound of fireworks reached the cameras and microphone. A rifle barrel poked from the dune. Fritz said, "No one is close to the colonel, and he still hasn't seen the hole in the sand."

"Fritz, reset the portal to where he went in," Ashley said. Fritz stared at him, horrified. "Now. Do it."

"You can't."

"Then you go. He's aiming at the president. Take the medics, or I will. See if you can open it where the guy can't see me. Now, Fritz."

Fritz checked the point where Colonel Mitchell had entered, adjusted the paperclip to a higher spot, and crossed his fingers. When he returned, Ashley was arguing with Linda.

"Stop him, Fritz," she said.

"Lin, we have to move fast. We have no contact with the others, and the guy has a direct shot at the president." On the TV, they watched briefly as the sniper's shots began.

"Open it, Fritz," Ashley said. Fritz twisted the knob.

"Mr. Russell," called a soldier monitoring the surveillance, "our guys are outnumbered."

"We need to get everyone back here," said Fritz. "I need to get Major Dolan. He has the most guys."

"Fritz, you can't go," said Linda. Fritz pointed to the TV.

"I need to get Jane some help, Lin. No one else here knows how this works." He ran to his desk, moved maps and paperclips. He told Linda he was sorry, and then went through.

Fritz spotted Dolan running toward the shooting. He rushed toward him, kicking sand as he came. "Bring your men back. I can get you directly to where the fighting is, but hurry." Dolan called his men, sent some to guard the president, and followed Fritz back to the hallway. Fritz switched the maps. He told Dolan they would enter at the top of the dune and everyone should take cover. As the soldiers entered, Fritz saw Jane and told the last man through to tell her to come back now. Moments later, Jane panted into the hallway. The scream of a rocket was replaced by the explosion of its target—the helicopter. The U.S. feed panned the rocket to its point of impact.

"Jane, the president is being attacked, too. Dolan sent some men."

"Set me up, Fritz. Where's Ash?"

"He's inside. There's a sniper on a dune, I think to the west." He looked at the TV. "There he is. On the hill."

"Get me to the president now, Fritz." He switched the maps again.

Fritz had picked a spot east of the canopy, hiding her entry from the sniper's view. But not from the Al-Jazeera cameraman, who almost dropped his camera.

“Mr. President,” Jane yelled, “this way. Everyone.” Surprised though they were, they reacted quickly. The cameras caught the action and followed the crowd. The president led everyone through the portal. Two soldiers carried the British prime minister.

“Mr. President, Ash is inside trying to get Colonel Mitchell out,” said Jane. “They’re looking for a sniper. I’m taking these guys back in. Fritz, get us to Ash.”

* * *

AS HIS TARGETS disappeared, the sniper retracted his rifle. He knew he’d been spotted. He removed his pistols with as little sound or movement as he could. Waiting and listening for his hunters, he heard sand sliding across the tarp. Alerted to the movement above him, he pointed.

* * *

“ASH, THE SHOTS came from lower down. Can you see anything on the other side?” Jane called.

“Nothing. Just sand. Get the colonel out of here. I’ll be down in a second. With all these hills, Fritz could have put me in the wrong place.”

“Come down. The shooting is done.” She pointed to the cloud of dust to her right. “The Israelis are coming. We need to be through the portal before they get here. I’ll tell the Israeli prime minister his troops have arrived.”

Ashley worked his way slowly down the dune, caught his foot, and flopped face-first to the bottom.

“Are you okay? What happened?” Jane asked.

“Don’t know.” He looked up, slapping sand from his shirt and pants. “I stepped in something. Felt like a hole. There.”

Jane glanced upward, in time to see a metal tube emerge from the dislocated sand. “Down,” she yelled. Spreading red blots on her legs and on Ashley's shirt and pants formed her last conscious memory.

* * *

AS THE HALLWAY filled, George took over Ashley's job. As in previous missions, wounded soldiers came through the portal. The president came into the hall with the Palestinian president, who was bloody from hand to shoulder.

"The Israeli prime minister patched him up, and he's working on the Eledorian president now."

"Mr. President," said Fritz, "the medics went through the portal. They went to get Colonel Mitchell. And Ash and Jane too."

The president called down the hall for help. Major Dolan led a dozen men to the commander-in-chief.

"Major, we still have men inside. Bring them back."

"Yes, sir."

Fritz reset the maps to where Jane had entered and told Major Dolan he would enter on a sand dune. What the major saw first were two still bodies below him. Above him, the medics were sliding down.

"Major, a shooter is hiding here somewhere. We can't find him," one medic told him.

"Go help them," said Dolan, pointing to Jane and Ashley. Then he told his men he would meet them at the bottom of the dune.

"Mr. Russell, can you put the portal opening lower? We have wounded to bring out." Fritz made the adjustment and Dolan returned to the desert, gunfire loud as he stepped through.

Fritz stood by the door, impatient. No one returned. "Mr. President, we need doctors. The medics aren't back. They should have just come through."

The president called down the hall. Another group ran to the doorway. Fritz stopped the Marine lieutenant at the doorway. "We heard gunfire when Major Dolan went in. Maybe you should crawl in and take a look first." Sliding in, the officer looked around and pulled back as sand exploded in a spot where his head had just been.

"Someone is up near the top, still shooting. No one inside is moving."

"What about Jane and Ash?"

"I can't tell, but no one was moving. I saw dust clouds in the distance. Israelis, I think."

WHEN THE ISRAELIS reached a safe distance, they began to shoot across the upper third of the dune. After ten minutes of waiting, their prime minister received a call. The shooting had ceased.

Fritz pulled the door open and walked through with a dozen soldiers. A few feet in front of him, Ashley's motionless body lay face-down with Jane prone over his legs. Above him, a hole emitted sunlight like a flashlight. He knelt next to Ashley and noticed the gentle but steady rise and fall from his back. "He's breathing," he yelled. Leaning to Jane, he couldn't see any movement.

Fritz stumbled back through the portal. George grabbed him.

"Fritz, were you shot?" George asked.

"Ash is hurt. I think Jane is dead. Colonel Mitchell is dead. A lot of men are down. They need help."

The president turned to the Israeli. Both men had heard. "My troops have arrived. Can I go through?" asked the prime minister. Fritz tested the door. The portal was closed. He reset the clip and tried again. The prime minister hurried through.

"Mr. President, we should have gurneys here. They'll be bringing a lot of people out," said Fritz. "George, will you hold the door, please? I can't hold it." He slid down the locker and sat on the floor. He shuddered as he held back tears.

Chapter 41

AS BODIES WERE carried into the school, ambulances waited at the exit. Numb, Fritz waited for Ashley and Jane, tears rolling down his cheeks.

The prime minister returned and said, "Mr. President, we've chased the attackers away. My medics have transported everyone else out of the area, and helicopters will take them to hospitals. The Eledorian is bloody, but he'll live. We should all leave now. I suggest we confiscate the camera film and any other recording devices. A helicopter for the leaders is waiting."

"Thank you, Mr. Prime Minister. I'll cancel the ceremony in Turkey when I'm back in my office."

The Israeli shook his head. "Mr. President, you should come with us now. Everyone will wonder how you got to Washington so quickly. You can stay with me, and we'll work out what we need to do."

The president looked at Fritz, who was staring at the lockers. He needed someone to end the mission. He looked for the soldier with the highest rank and called Captain Washburn. "I'll take care of everything, sir," said the captain. "We've been here before." He walked out and waved. A truck backed up to the door. He gathered some men and emptied the hospital room.

"Mr. President," said the Israeli prime minister, "we should take the prime minister with us. We will prepare his body for transport to London when we reach Tel Aviv. I've ordered helicopters to meet us on the way."

"Thank you. Would you tell the others? I need to talk to Fritz." The Israeli said he would. "Fritz, we need to go back to the canopy. Will you set it up?"

"Where's Ash?"

"They flew him and Jane to a hospital, along with the colonel and everyone else that was still alive."

"Alive?"

"He's alive, Fritz," the president told him. "I'll call you later."

Fritz started to rise, but slid back to the floor. Linda stood and held out her hands, and the president reached out also. On his feet, Fritz went into his classroom, thumbed through the maps, and found the one where Jane had rescued the leaders. He dropped the others on his chair.

"Ready," Fritz said.

Fritz held the door as the leaders crossed the hall, but none spoke to him as they stepped into the sand. Last through, the president said, "I'll talk to you later. I'll be with the Israeli prime minister. We'll work this out."

"MR. RUSSELL, I'm Hal Washburn. The president asked me to finish up. The clean-up guys are here. We're ready to move out."

"Sure. Sorry. Been a rough night. Do what you need to." Within ten minutes, the buses were headed out of the parking lot.

"Remember George. I won't be in tomorrow."

"You and Ashley."

"Go home, Fritz," said Lois. "George and I will take care of it." Fritz nodded, staring at the floor.

"I'll call you in the morning," said George. "Good night, Linda."

LINDA DROVE. Fritz stared out the window. The number of houses with lights on surprised him. It was past one in the morning.

"Something must be going on," said Fritz.

"Those people are watching the news. They saw what happened. They might even have seen you. And Ash. How could you have let him do that?" He didn't respond. Linda glanced at the silence. "You didn't have to open the door." She sounded like the bullets he had just watched. "You could have tried to stop him."

"But I had no other way to let them know. No soldiers were left at school."

She turned into the driveway. "Those cameramen picked up everything. Now everyone knows about the portal. And they know where it is."

"They may know about it, but no way that they know where. The president took the video." For the first time, Linda wasn't on his side.

* * *

"COLLATERAL DAMAGE then," said Richter/Salzmann. "The Brits won't care or do anything. They'll just have an election. If we're lucky, they'll pull their support."

"People just popped up. I was inside the dune. One man tripped over my shooting hole and opened it up. They were thirty feet away and could see me. I had to shoot."

"I don't care. The grand opening hit a snag. That's all that matters. Good job."

"When they were talking outside my burrow, I heard them mention "Fritz, the portal, Jane."

"That's good. We can find them."

* * *

MARY OPENED THE back door when she heard the car doors shut. "The TV is on. They're rerunning all the footage. Lots of questions about where you all came from and disappeared to."

"Wonderful," said Linda. "That's just perfect."

"Did they say anything about casualties?" Fritz asked.

"Nothing yet. Is the president okay?"

"He is, but they shot Ash and Jane. And Colonel Mitchell. I'm going to bed," Linda headed out of the kitchen.

"Good night," said Fritz.

Linda turned. "Fritz, it wasn't a good night. Right now, I'm tired and upset. The whole world knows, and the bad guys are still out there." She walked out.

Fritz poured a soda and dragged himself to the TV. The anchor was reporting that helicopters had transported the soldiers to a hospital. He mentioned that unknown civilians had been observed in the area. Fritz began to flip through channels. He stopped at Al-Jazeera and watched video of his race through the sand. No military were supposed to be in the area, the report said. The Israeli army was held at the border. American soldiers hidden in the sand dunes had repelled an attack, but no one knew who the attackers were. A shot of the world leaders disappearing raised the biggest question.

Fritz responded to the anchorman's question. "I hope you never get an answer."

"What happened, Fritz?" Mary asked. Fritz told her the details he re-watched in his head. Fritz continued channel surfing, until he found a live news conference from Tel Aviv. The Israeli prime minister, surrounded by most of the leaders who had been at the morning's gathering, was answering questions. The president stood behind him. The prime minister told the reporters that each leader would have a short statement, but a press conference would be delayed. The president was the last to speak.

"As devastating as this attack has been, the second groundbreaking will take place in three hours. We have discussed our options and unanimously agree that our goal of achieving an end to the violence we have just witnessed cannot be delayed. Our resolve remains strong."

Fritz jumped when Linda said, "Is he crazy?"

"I didn't hear you come down."

The president answered the unasked question. "We pray for our fallen protectors and for the British prime minister, who was an important voice in driving us toward peace. We share the grief of the United Kingdom."

Fritz changed channels again. A report from Palestine showed video of trenches being dug and workers preparing the pipelines. The report said that in spite of the attacks, fifty miles of trenches were expected by the end of the day.

"I am sorry, Lin. Who could have guessed a groundbreaking would go so badly."

"You should be. I'm sorry too, Fritz, for Ashley and Jane. I hope they'll be okay. This isn't going to be easy."

Linda's phone woke them two hours after the groundbreaking. Her father asked if it was Fritz he had seen on the news. She asked if she could call back in a few minutes.

"It was a long night, Dad."

"Wait. Was it Fritz?"

"Yes." She disconnected.

Sitting up on the side of the bed, Fritz rubbed his eyes and stretched. Turning to the clock on Linda's dresser, he said, "We missed the groundbreaking. It's almost seven o'clock. What did he want?"

"Saw you on TV. Wanted to know if it was you."

"I'll make the coffee and turn on the TV," he said.

"He's going to call back if I don't call him."

"So call him. I need to see the news."

When he reached the kitchen, the aroma told him that all he needed was a cup.

"Morning, Mary. Need more?" She shook her head. He tipped the pot, steam curled, and he said, "I'm going to the family room."

The TV showed the most recent film of the second groundbreaking. A visible international military presence successfully assured an undisrupted ceremony. The president had asked all television, worldwide, to discontinue airing the footage until it could be studied. He had requested all content carriers to do the same. The NSA was closely monitoring transmissions. A televised speech had been scheduled for the next night.

Fritz got a second cup, returned to the TV, and passed the stairs where Linda had her phone to her ear. "They'll be here tomorrow."

Fritz shrugged. He yawned as he asked, "What time is the plane?"

"He's driving. He doesn't want to go through the airport business again."

FRITZ'S DAY OFF crawled by. He spent it mostly hoping to hear about Ashley and Jane and waiting for a call from the president. He helped Linda get ready for her parents, and he vacuumed the house, though he was never far from a TV. By mid-afternoon, he returned to his desk to prepare for the next day's classes.

George called at 3:45. "Fritz, have you heard anything? It's been a madhouse here today. I've been asked all day if I'd seen you and Ashley on TV because you weren't here today. I told them I'd spoken to you earlier, and that you were taking a day off to prepare for Linda's graduation. Will you be here tomorrow?"

"I'll be in. That was quick thinking, George. I haven't heard from the president or anyone else. I think you can expect Ashley to be gone for a while."

Around five o'clock, just when the early news shows were starting, the front doorbell rang. Fritz backed out of the family room, looking for a breaking news banner. As the door opened, Jim Shaw faced him.

"Hi, Mr. R. Mary told me the story. Are you doing okay?"

Linda came to the door when she heard voices, offered Jim a soda, and asked him to stay for dinner. Fritz really wanted quiet, not more company. When the food was ready, he went to pick it up, driving slowly. Images of Ashley and Jane flashed more than once. He heard Ashley's voice say, "Hey buddy, pay attention." He parked at a busy time and almost lost his door when he pushed it open.

With the dinner order on the passenger's seat, he stared through the windshield, immobile. Pent-up emotion flowed off his cheeks. Tell-tale spatters sank into his shirt. *Linda's right. I have changed. I'm a teacher, not a soldier. So is Ash. What are we doing?* He heard Ash's voice again. "Get it together, Fritz."

Dinner conversation revolved around Linda's graduation. Linda described what she was envisioning for a local bike shop and her idea of a national brand. She even mentioned that she was considering manufacturing her own custom line. When Fritz's phone buzzed, all heads turned.

"Yes, Mr. President?" he answered. Fritz usually enjoyed hearing that voice, but things were suddenly not the same.

"Hi Fritz. Sorry I haven't called sooner. Jane just left surgery. They've done two operations. She's in bad shape."

"What about Ash?"

"Too soon to tell. He was in surgery for eight hours. He was hit four times, Fritz. Some serious internal damage. We were lucky the Israelis showed up. Their medics saved them."

"What about the rest? Colonel Mitchell?"

"The colonel will be okay, but we lost six guys. I don't think the sniper was a good shot, or he wasn't trying to kill them. Fritz, I'll fly back tomorrow. Saturday, I'll go to Dover to meet the plane bringing the coffins. I'd like to stop to see you after that."

"Linda's parents will be here." He covered the mouthpiece. "He wants to come on Saturday." Linda shrugged. "Call when you're on the way, Mr. President. Do you know when I can speak to Ash?"

"He's heavily sedated. Probably not right away." Fritz heard a deep inhale. "Fritz, you saved me again. Your quick thinking saved a lot of people. I'll tell you about it on Saturday. I gotta go now. Thanks again."

He put the phone on the table and stood. "That was the president," he said and walked to his desk. With his chin braced by his hands, he stared at the stacked yellow pads. Linda followed.

"What happened, Fritz?" she asked.

"Too soon to know if he'll make it. Jane's in bad shape." He knew she was behind him, but when he reached out, she stepped back.

"Did he say when he's coming on Saturday?"

"I don't know. He's going to Delaware first. He'll call." He reached for the baby, but TJ squealed and kicked him in the head.

Chapter 42

THE RUMOR OF his TV appearance had spread during his absence. His first class foreshadowed the rest of the day. He denied his role and directed the conversation to review for final exams. At the end of the period, he assigned homework for Monday.

"But Mr. R," said A.J. "Monday's a holiday." Fritz returned him a blank stare. "It's Memorial Day."

"Thanks, A.J. I'd completely forgotten. Memorial Day already. Tuesday, then."

When the bell rang, and the class departed, his door opened. Without looking up, he said "Hi Ash." Then he looked up … at George.

"Are you okay, Fritz? Ashley isn't here today."

"I know that."

"You just said 'Hi Ash'."

"I did? Sorry. Habit."

"Fritz, do you want me to cancel the play? It's next week."

"George, I'm not quite with it yet. Let me talk to the kids. I'll let you know later. Okay?"

WHEN HE CHECKED with the students, they told him that Ashley had been letting them work on their own. He'd said his job was to keep them out of trouble with the principal. They were set to go with scenery, music, costumes, and logistics. Ashley had said they didn't need him, that they could handle it blindfolded.

When the period ended, Eric fiddled with his books and knapsack, waiting for the room to clear. As he aimed for the door, he said, "Is Mr. Gilbert going to be okay? It looked like he was shot more than once." He looked squarely at Fritz. "Mr. R, I know it was you and Mr. Gilbert. And I know how. You saved the president again." The door opened before Fritz could respond. "I'll see you later, Mr. R."

Fritz dodged questions for the next two classes, and in the cafeteria. Rachel and Nicole waited for teachers to move away before cornering him. Nicole asked, "Is Mr. Gilbert hurt bad?" Rachel elbowed her. "Badly," she corrected.

"He is."

Rachel asked, "How many times was he shot? I saw it, Mr. Russell. I saw you too."

"Rachel, Nicole, you didn't see what you think you saw. Mr. Gilbert was in a car accident, and it wasn't me."

"See. Rachel, I told you he'd deny it. Mr. R, we know you're some kind of spy, but we won't say anything."

Fritz laughed for the first time in three days. "I'm flattered that you think that highly of me. I'll see you later." George was waiting when he returned to his classroom.

"Hi George. I still have some teachers to round up, but the kids say they're ready to do the play."

"How's Ashley? Really?"

He pulled George away from the door. "George, I don't know how bad it is, but he was shot four times and had eight hours of surgery. We only have three more weeks of classes. If he survives, he won't be ready to come back."

The mere mention of final exams kept his classes subdued. On his way out after seventh period, Eric said he'd be back to talk about the play after school.

Todd said, "Doesn't look like the president's plan worked out too well, Mr. R."

"No, Todd, not an auspicious start. But over a hundred miles of trenches have already been dug. The desalination plants have begun construction. A series of water storage farms will start going up in a couple of weeks. So only a little setback."

John Boardman asked, "How did you get back so fast, Mr. R?"

"That was easy, John. I didn't go anywhere."

Fritz was half-annoyed and half-proud of the prodders. The day ended with a barrage of variations on the theme. The final question quieted the class and caught Fritz by surprise. Jay Bennett asked, "Did you time-travel there, Mr. R?"

* * *

FRITZ WENT IN the backdoor. Mary was sitting alone at the table with her laptop. "They're in the family room, Fritz. Just to warn you, Linda's been arguing with her father."

"Thanks, Mary. Keep your gun handy. I may need it." Mary was reading from the screen. "Any news?"

"Sorry, Fritz. Nothing. A lid has been tightened on everything."

"If anything happens, feel free to interrupt. Please."

"Hi, honey, I'm home," he called.

Fritz bent and kissed Emily and then Linda. He took a deep breath and reached to shake Tim's hand, but was greeted with a scowl. "Glad you could make it. How was the trip?"

"Linda told us you're using that portal and that was you on television."

"So much for small talk. Yeah it was. So?"

"We pay taxes to have a military to take care of those things. Not a teacher."

Fritz bit his lip and crossed his arms. "They were in trouble, Tim. A sniper was hidden in the dunes that they couldn't see. No other way to warn them volunteered."

"It was reckless. What would happen to your family if something happened to you? Did you think about that?"

"Every day."

"That doesn't seem to matter much."

"Well, Linda's the beneficiary on my life insurance." His snideness raised Tim's voice.

"Don't get smart with me, Fritz." Tim was on his feet.

"You're in my house. Don't tell me what to do."

"Daddy, Fritz. Sit down"

"Look what you've done now. You've got her crying," said Tim.

"Of course, she's crying. You're embarrassing her by being an ass. So sit down and drink your drink."

"Stop it, Fritz," said Linda.

"I'm not doing this for the next five days. Ash and Jane are almost dead, the bad guys are still loose, and I'm the one who's wrong? I don't think so."

"Fritz," Linda shouted.

Ignoring her, Fritz turned to her father. "Tim, you're welcome to visit Linda, but stay the hell away from me." Fritz rumbled back through the kitchen and slammed the door. He slid into the driver's seat of his SUV and banged the steering wheel.

A few minutes later, Linda walked to him, a glass of soda in hand. She opened the door.

"Fritz, come back in. He apologized."

"Not to me, he didn't."

"Fritz, damn it, it's my graduation. I don't see them very often. Please don't do this now. For me."

"I'm not putting up with his crap, not for another minute. I've done it for you since we got married. I've never been good enough."

"Fritz you know how he is."

"Only too well. But he's the problem, not me."

"He thinks he knows what's best for me."

"Yeah, and I'm not it. Sorry Lin, but I'm not giving in this time. You'd think he'd cut me a little slack. And you should be pissed as hell that he has never respected your judgement or choices."

"He doesn't understand what you've been doing, and I don't have an answer anymore."

"Stop defending him. He's been through the portal, he's met the president, he's been to the White House. He's not stupid, and I sure as hell wish he'd stop acting like it. My ninth graders are better behaved."

"For my sake, come back in, apologize for being rude, and let's put this behind us."

"Apologize, are you kidding? For what? Oh. I've got it. You think I'm wrong."

"Fritz, only you can end this. If you apologize, maybe he will—to you as well as to me. I'm not going to beg. Fritz, someone out there isn't afraid to kill people. Now he knows about the portal. That's not Daddy's fault. Come inside." She stopped for a second. "Please."

Mary turned quickly to the computer when they came inside. She rolled her eyes when he glanced at her.

"Linda, did you tell him who Mary is?"

"I thought it would be best not to say. I told them she's an au pair.

Tim put his drink down when Fritz entered the family room. "Tim, Emily, I'm sorry I lost my temper. A lot's going on right now."

"Linda told us. I just don't understand why you're still involved. The United States doesn't need magic to control terrorists." Fritz turned to Linda.

"The portal isn't magic." Fritz felt the knot in his stomach tighten. "Without it, a peace treaty in the Middle East was impossible."

"That's working out really well. I'm sure the British can see the benefits." Fritz turned to leave.

Linda said, "People are getting killed, and we're trying to stop it."

"That's my point. Why should you be doing anything? It's not up to you. Your boy has the greatest military force in the world at his fingertips."

"That's enough," stormed Fritz. "Our *boy*, not a good touch, Tim, happens to be the President of the United States of America. He's your president, too, whether you like it or not. He most certainly isn't a boy, and I have to think you meant that like an old-time segregationist. He thinks we're doing something valuable. That's why we're under constant protection."

"Don't be ridiculous," said Tim.

Fritz called Mary. He glared at Tim. Linda scowled at him. When Mary stepped around the corner, Fritz asked her to tell Tim who she really was. Mary gulped and looked at the Millers. "It's okay, Mary. He swore an oath … to the president." Fritz emphasized *president* with a snarl.

Mary looked at Linda, who nodded. "I am a secret service agent, assigned by the White House to protect the Russells and the portal."

"You're making that up."

"And you're arguing for the sake of hearing your own voice," barked Fritz. "Mary, would you turn your back to him and lift your sweatshirt?" Her holstered pistol dropped Tim Miller's jaw.

Linda said, "Mary has been here since New Year's, Daddy. After Thanksgiving and the accident and the bombings of the naval bases, the president has been worried about our safety. You both swore an oath, so I'm going to tell you this. The summit meeting, when the White House was attacked, was taking place in the room across the hall from Fritz's classroom. The agent you rode with on Thanksgiving was wounded that night and died. So did the president's personal secretary. They were our friends."

Still angry, Fritz said, "This isn't a game. It's not a TV thriller. We live with this every day. I've stopped asking why. It just is."

Emily Miller sat and listened. In a soft, almost reluctant voice, she said, "And you saved the president again."

"Tim, I called you about Jonathan Hartmann."

"You always think rich people are the problem."

Linda said, "We know this isn't Arab terrorists. It's an international conspiracy to take down the government. You knew Jonathan Hartmann, and I'm sure you know about Georg Badenhof."

"You never told me he knows Hartmann." Fritz wondered what else she hadn't told him.

"Badenhof's companies made the acid that caused our car accident. The banker in South Dakota, the California congresswoman. All a part of that group. We can't find the one man who's left."

Tim looked at his wife, then back and forth from Linda to Fritz. "Can I have another drink?"

"Help yourself," said Fritz. "Ice is in the freezer."

"I'll get it."

"Stay there, Lin. He can get it himself." She went to take her father's glass. "Linda, leave it, I said." The room crackled, her hands on her hips, until Tim stood and left the room with his glass.

"Why are you doing this? I've never seen you like this," Linda said. "He's my father. And you have no more right to order me around than he does."

"When you defend him, he thinks I can be bullied, but I've never been afraid of him. I'm certainly not now. I have wanted your support for years. But you are afraid to cross him even though your home is with me."

Chapter 43

TIM LEANED FORWARD toward his son-in-law. Fritz had balled his fists in anticipation of another round, but Tim's tone was quiet and thoughtful. Fritz sat back. "Hartmann was lucky. His programmers wrote brilliant cyber-security software. I don't know how it works. That's how he explained it to me. Until then, he had a successful computer consulting company. The new program was explosive. He priced it as high as he could, with residuals. The contracts were worth billions. And cost next to nothing." Tim described the effect of massive wealth. "Hartmann went on a personal spending spree and reached an orbit of wealth most people don't know exists."

"Why would he be involved with a conspiracy to kill the president? To overthrow the government? How would that help him? Or any of them?"

"You don't know he was."

"Yeah, we do. He knew all those people, and they were responsible for almost killing you. They killed plenty of others. They attacked the naval bases and the summit. What I want to know is why?"

"Knowing them is not proof of involvement. That's why we have the police, FBI, and intelligence agencies. Not teachers. Not you."

"That doesn't tell me why? What do they gain, because that's all you people understand."

"Always the same with you. Blame those who make the world work."

"Work for you, you mean. What more could they want or ever need? What do they have in common that makes wrecking the government make sense?"

"Well, Badenhof made parts for weapons and chemicals for explosives, and he sold to anyone who could pay cash, even if sanctions had been imposed. I've heard his products are excellent."

"Daddy, do you know any of these other names? Marvin Atkinson, Loren Whitmore, Massoud, Max Ingram, a guy named Trellingham?"

"I'll have to think about it. Some of them sound familiar."

Fritz wasn't done. "Why would a group of wealthy businessmen want to kill the president—or kill me?"

"You? You don't matter. Either you're rich, or you don't matter."

"Don't, Fritz," Linda snapped.

"Look. Disrupting government guarantees that nothing changes. You got in the way with your toy. Those guys make money just by breathing. They're competitive and ruthless. They know how to manipulate and how to create chaos. If someone gets killed, oh well. People are pawns."

"So this whole thing is chaos for its own sake? No matter who gets hurt?" asked Fritz.

"Maybe a little extreme, and maybe something personal, but when you consider who gains from it, that's the answer. Problem is that a lot of people fit the profile. People you never hear about."

"Like the man we're looking for," said Linda. She glanced at Fritz.

"Fritz, you're in over your head. You can't solve this," said Tim.

"I have to try. Ash and Jane being shot hasn't helped. We still don't know if they'll make it."

"Ash and Jane?"

"You met them, Daddy. Ashley is the English teacher, and Jane works for the president."

"The tall guy and the pretty girl? They were shot?"

SATURDAY MORNING, Fritz and Tim watched the president's address from Delaware. Afterwards, Fritz got a call. "See you then." Tim stared. "He'll be here in an hour. Lin, I'll go to the store and get some snacks or something. Any ideas?"

"Fritz, he probably ate on the plane."

"He took Marine One, so I doubt it. I'll just get some stuff."

"Do what you want," she answered. Fritz rubbed his face as if she'd smacked him.

* * *

FRITZ WAS AT the curb as the black SUV stopped in front of the house. Parked across the street, Jim Shaw waved. At the front door, the president kissed Linda's cheek, and spotting her parents, said, "Emily, Tim, good to see you again."

Although Tim was silent, Emily said, "We're glad you're okay, Mr. President. Please come in." She led him to the dining room, where the table was filled with cold cuts, bread, and salads. Mary carried in two pitchers of iced tea.

"Hello, Mary. How are you?"

"I'm fine, thank you, Mr. President. How are the girls?"

"Making me feel old. They said to say hello."

"Please give them my best."

"Jim's across the street, Mary," Fritz said. "Why don't you bring him a sandwich and a drink." He asked the president, "How's Ash?"

"Fritz, he's still critical. They had to sew him together. A lot of internal damage." Fritz sucked in his lips. "And they still don't know if Jane will make it. The sniper hit spots where she wasn't wearing armor. The Israeli prime minister said the flak jacket stopped ten bullets. One shot hit under her arm."

"What about the attackers? Could they be identified?"

"That's what I wanted to tell you. No one knows who they were."

"And you believe them?" asked Tim.

"I do. Someone would have talked because they were all blaming each other. But the sniper was after them, not me, I think."

"Was it the Caballeros?" asked Linda.

"I think so. The sniper didn't start until the broader attack began. If he was serious, he'd have killed me. It looked more like random shots coordinated with the other confrontation. I don't know what we would have done if we'd been alone. So once again, Fritz, I owe you."

"Did anything happen in Turkey?" Fritz asked.

"Not a thing. It was a unanimous decision to go on to the next stop. Even the Palestinian president went with his arm in a sling."

"Mr. President, you could have told us all this on the phone. You didn't need to come here. There's something more. What?" Linda asked.

"You won't buy that I like it here?" The president laughed at Linda's raised brow.

"What happened to the colonel?" asked Fritz.

"He's fine. Took a few shots in the vest, but he played dead trying to find where the shooter was."

"You seem to think that Ash will survive."

"They said he'll be in bed for a week, maybe more. He'll have a problem walking for a while."

"Mr. President, you wanted to know about our play. It's next weekend. It was Ashley's baby, but I'm taking over for him. Eric Silver is really running it."

"He'll be getting a little surprise this week. I've spoken to George. He sent me Eric's transcript. Looks like he'll be valedictorian. George said it's almost impossible for him to slip in the class rankings."

"Let's eat," said Linda.

"I forgot something." He started to rise, but Mel said she would get it. When she returned the president gave Linda a gift-wrapped package. "Happy graduation." Linda slid the wrapping from the weighty package and lifted the top. Beneath the tissue paper was a brass elephant with hand-painted adornments. "The raised trunk symbolizes happiness and good fortune, Linda. We know you collect elephants. The First Lady found this one on her last Asian trip."

"It's beautiful, Mr. President. Thank you both so much." Linda's words were shaky.

"We hope it will bring your bike store success even beyond that stemming from your own cleverness."

"I hope you'll all come to the grand opening, whenever that is." Linda was saying the right things, but with no pleasure in her voice.

While Emily examined the elephant, Tim examined the president and Fritz, their relationship still strange to him. "Excuse me for asking, Mr. President," Fritz shot a quick look at Linda, "but can't the government find a way to get things done without Fritz's portal."

Fritz inhaled and began to speak, but the president jumped in. "Tim, you might call the portal a public sector/private sector joint venture."

"That's a glib answer. I was hoping for substance."

Placing his hand on Fritz's arm, the president said, "Not glib at all. We have a private sector resource," he tapped Fritz, "which has been very useful and very valuable. We've saved a great deal of money, and incidentally, a great many lives. You could say it's been a good return on investment."

"Investment? What investment? A school door?" Tim's argumentative tone elevated Fritz's temper.

"You're talking to the President of the United States, Tim. You might consider being a bit more polite."

"Don't talk to me about polite," Tim snapped.

"Whoa. Tim, let me answer your question before we get too far afield. The most valuable aspect the portal provides us is speed. The second is surprise. Twice in the past few months, it's let us thwart the theft of nuclear weapons."

"You should have better control of them," said Tim.

"I agree. One was in Russia and the other in Pakistan. The portal allowed us to reach them, stop the thieves, and recover the material. Once they were located, the portal gave us a pinpoint arrival with enough time for surprise. Neither the Russians nor the Pakistanis were capable of stopping what could have been a future international incident. And the weapons ended up in our hands."

"I never heard any of that," said Tim.

"Of course you didn't." Fritz glowered. "The portal is secret. Did you expect us to tell the world about loose nukes? How much sense would that make?"

"More sense than you playing hero."

"He is a hero, Tim," the president said, speaking softly. He glanced at his wrist. "We have to be going. Congratulations again, Linda. Fritz, walk me to the car."

Side by side at the waiting doors, the two men chatted briefly. "I don't know what that was about, and I don't mean to be rude, but it's been a long few days, and I'm not in the mood."

"It started yesterday. I thought we were done. He's like that, and I've had enough. I exploded. They'll be here until Wednesday. Oh, I forgot. Are you coming to the play?"

"No, Fritz. Sorry. My schedule is jamming up, especially with the election and the convention coming. And I think you're right. We should divert attention from the school."

"Between us. How are Ash and Jane?"

The president took Fritz's arm at the elbow. "Ashley is going to need physical therapy before he can come home. The muscles in his right leg were torn pretty badly. It'll take the internal injuries a while to heal."

"What about Jane?"

"Jane took some serious hits. It's still touch and go." The president didn't look at him. "The doctors don't know, Fritz." He reached into his pocket. "This is for you," handing Fritz an envelope. "A small thank you." Taking a step to the car, they shook hands. "I'll be talking to you." Nodding to the house, he said, "Good luck."

"Thank you, Mr. President."

Fritz waved as the car drove away and to Jim as he went in. He sat down at the dining room table, vacant except for the trays of food. He slit the envelope with a clean knife and then made a sandwich. The quiet hum of conversation from the family room gave him a moment to think. He pulled out a letter from the president and a check. A short, hand-written note of thanks said that a presidential scholarship would await Timothy John Russell. The president wrote that a formal letter would follow. Taking another bite, he turned over the check.

"Lin." He hurried to swallow. "You need to come here."

When she was in view, her grimace and clenched jaw startled him. "What?"

"What's the matter now?"

"What do you think?"

"Lin, I have no idea."

"You can't let things go, no matter what."

Placing the check on the table, he said, "Let's go outside, and you can explain what you're talking about."

“I don’t need to go anywhere. You are obviously determined to wreck my graduation. My parents are going to a hotel until then. I’m having dinner with them tonight. Take care of TJ.” She headed to the family room.

“Linda.” She ignored him. He folded the check, took his sandwich, grabbed a beer from the refrigerator, and went to the backyard. Mary watched as the door closed. Confused and dispirited, Fritz sat on the back steps.

Chapter 44

WHEN LINDA LEFT, she said she'd probably be late. Fritz wandered around the backyard. They'd never had a fight they couldn't resolve. This time he was in another galaxy. Having Tim in the mix wasn't helpful. "To either of us," he said aloud. The vegetables were planted and growing, but they needed water. When he finally went inside, Mary was feeding TJ. "Sorry, Mary. Do you want me to do that?"

"I'm okay, Fritz. Are you?"

He rubbed behind his left ear. She laughed. "What?"

"You know the president does that too."

"Does what?"

"When he's thinking, he rubs his head, always on the left. You just did it. You're more alike than you think. Want dinner?"

"I'm not hungry."

The sun's final rays drew lines of pink across the room, reminding him of the sunrise in the desert. He flipped a page on a yellow pad and lifted a pen. Another list, he thought, glancing at the stack to his left. The top line said "Linda." His cheek in his left hand, he stared at her name.

Fritz climbed from an empty bed. The door to their guest room was closed.

The Sunday talk shows featured guests who argued about the president's failures with the development plan. Everyone's favorite choice for critic, the senator from Texas reminded the president that he wasn't redecorating the White House but changing the course of history in the Middle East, redecorating someone else's house. While Fritz was feeding TJ, Linda came down and poured a cup of coffee.

"Hi Lin," said Fritz. "How was dinner?"

"Fine." She turned to leave.

"We should talk. We've always worked things out."

"Talk's cheap, and times are changing, Fritz. I'm having breakfast with my parents."

He took a walk. Later he worked in the garden, watching for Linda's return. He mowed his lawn, and went to cut Ashley's. As the afternoon turned to evening, he watched TV. With TJ on his lap, he said, "This is the quietest you've ever seen around here, buddy. We'll have a new president soon. Hopefully, by then, this mess will be over."

After he put the baby to bed, he took a yellow pad to the kitchen. The equations had changed. The only remaining mysteries were Thomas Richter and why people were trying to destroy the government. He started to make notes but the pad was covered. While he was thinking, he had doodled. The word *Linda* covered the page.

He set up the coffee maker and wondered who would have a cup in the morning. All the lights were out, except the one in the family room, where he was sitting. In the dimness, visions of their visitors flashed. The president, Tom Andrews, and James. Jane on her first visit, and how Ashley had responded. Robert E. Lee. After midnight, car lights passed across the windows.

Linda came in the back, the kitchen already dark, and walked to turn off the family room lamp. When Fritz asked if she'd had a nice day, she jumped. "You scared me. I didn't see you. Why are you sitting in the dark?"

"Can we talk, Lin?"

"I'm going to bed. I'm taking my parents to New York tomorrow."

"Then we should talk now. Lin, I'm sorry."

"You should be." She went upstairs.

LINDA WAS GONE by the time he poured his first cup. Fritz went outside. The black clouds matched his mood. He wished he could talk to Ashley. *What's all this been for? We're still in danger, but from whom? Does this guy know about me? What does Linda expect me to do, just forget everything that's happened?* Sitting down, he opened the book he had brought out and read the same paragraph over and over. Even though he expected rain, he watered the vegetables. He dropped a pebble in the puddled water and stared at the ripples. *Is this the portal too?*

Mary stepped out on the back steps. "Fritz, do you want company?"

"Who?" he asked, walking toward the door.

"Me."

He took a moment. "Sure."

With a mug in her hand, and TJ in her other arm, Mary said that he needed to talk about what was going on.

"I can't figure it out. Capturing the Caballeros didn't stop it? They can't find the last one."

Mary looked up at the roiling sky. "Fritz, none of it makes sense. But someone has to know where the guy is."

"He had to know they were coming. There haven't been the usual leaks. Nothing is tying this together."

"I know. The sniper just disappeared into the desert. And no one claimed credit for any of it."

"What are you thinking, Mary?"

"No one claimed anything for the naval bases or the White House either. But they seemed to know, like the Camp David thing." Fritz listened to her careful choice of words. "When I first heard the story, a mystery man, concealed in the background, knew the workings of the secret service, the military, and the people who were involved. Koppler was giving orders, but he had another guy feeding information."

"Wixted."

"High enough up, but not visible. A bureaucrat. There may be others. And like terrorist cells, no one knowing what the others know or who the others are."

Fritz scratched his chin, processing her thinking. "So who could have known about Camp David? It can't have been many. The president only decided that afternoon. And none of the Caballeros could have known."

At the first rumble of thunder, they headed inside. Avoiding another bout with lightning seemed like a good idea.

"Mary, do you have any suggestions? I'm at my wits' end."

"This is very uncomfortable for me. I won't get in the middle. I can see both sides. It's the portal. She's afraid that they'll find it and come after you. And now she's even more afraid than ever that you might end up like Jane and Ashley."

Fritz gritted his teeth. "Thanks, Mary." He picked up a spoon and rolled the handle in his fingers. "That doesn't give me much room. The portal exists. I can't do anything about that." He tapped a fist against the wall. "She tried to stop me from letting Ash go through the portal. The president was being shot at, and Jane was outnumbered. Nothing I could say could have stopped him." Taking a deep breath, he said, "Her father picks a fight with the president, and she's mad at me. God, he'll never learn. He's one of the most tactless men I've ever met. It's amazing he actually has clients."

Mary said, "Once, when Natalie was here, she reminded Linda about a party in New York, when Tim got into an argument with another guest. 'The man loves to argue,' she said. "He's such a dinosaur, but Linda adores him, and she's the only one who can control him. Her brother won't even talk to him."'

"I never thought about Joe. We rarely see him. Come to think of it, Linda doesn't talk to him very often."

"That goes way back, Fritz. Nat said it was father–son stuff. Linda took sides. Looks like she's doing it again."

"Thanks, Mary. It's good to know."

MARY CHECKED the beep on her phone, ran to the family room, and turned on the TV. The breaking news banner headlined the president's speech being interrupted. "What happened, Mary?" Fritz asked.

"Two of the soldiers moving the wreath at the Memorial Day ceremony had some kind of reaction. They're both in the hospital. Some kind of nerve agent was put on the flowers or the frame. The president gave an abbreviated speech and laid a bouquet instead."

Fritz said, "That was stupid. And sloppy."

"Or intentional. A warning."

* * *

"DO YOU KNOW who this is?"

"Of course."

"Where are you?"

"Kennedy Airport."

"Good. Can you see the news?"

"I've been watching. But my plane is boarding now."

"Are you coming here?"

"No."

"I'll keep you informed." He wrapped his phone in his lunch trash and dropped it as he passed the waste can.

* * *

AFTER SCHOOL the next day, Fritz considered the sky. When lightning flashed, Fritz pulled down a book about the Declaration of Independence and examined the pictures. Intrigued by John Trumbull's painting of the draft's presentation and many of those who would later sign, he placed a paperclip. In the hallway, he touched the doorknob, but no buzz. *Because it's not a photo or floorplan or map.* He tried a book about Thomas Jefferson, placed a clip on a sketch of Monticello, and returned to the hall. Lightning flashed, but again, no shock. He clipped together both the Trumbull painting and a photo of Independence Hall. After the next flash of lightning, he tried again and stepped into the Assembly Room of the Pennsylvania State House. Men in powdered wigs and heavy jackets milled around.

"Pardon me, sir. May I ask why you are here?" Fritz turned to face the man who would become the country's first postmaster.

"I'm here to see you, Dr. Franklin. Your work has inspired me, and I would like to show you something. My name is Fritz Russell. I am a teacher."

"At the moment, Mr. Russell, I'm afraid we are a bit busy. Perhaps you might join me at my rooms later?"

"That will not be possible, sir. But if you will indulge me, I have a most interesting discovery. This will only take a moment, sir. Would you follow me?"

Franklin glanced at the glowing rectangle, reached out, and touched it with an index finger. He pulled back from the soft buzz, but curiosity won, and he joined Fritz.

A startled look on his guest's face, looking up and down the hallway lined with lockers, Fritz wondered if he might have some magical power that convinced so many historical figures to believe him with so little fuss.

"Where am I, sir?"

"Come in here." Fritz welcomed him by opening his classroom door and walked to his desk. "Dr. Franklin, you are in a school classroom in New Jersey. But you have just traveled to the twenty-first century. It was your experiment with electricity that made this possible."

Franklin was inching toward the door but looked around the room. "You are quite a collector, Mr. Russell. So many books."

"We don't have much time right now, but let me show you." Taking Franklin's elbow, he pulled the reluctant scientist to his desk. Opening a book titled, 'The Declaration', he showed Franklin the title page and the date. "This was printed in 2010." Fritz reached into his briefcase and removed the day's newspaper. "This is today's edition."

A short beep from the school driveway lifted Franklin's head. Puzzled, he pointed, no words available.

"It's called an automobile. When first invented, people called it a horseless carriage." Franklin removed his glasses but kept staring as more cars drove past.

"Have I fallen asleep?"

"Doctor, please look here." Fritz motioned to the painting clipped to Independence Hall. When Franklin reached for the illustration, Fritz grabbed his hand. "That's how we connect, how I will get you back home."

"This is most strange, Mr. Russell," leaning on the desk. Looking at his hands, he asked, "What is this material?" Franklin tapped the desktop.

"It's steel, with some kind of top for the desk surface."

"I am familiar with steel. But not with such a use. A very durable product."

Fritz took a textbook from his shelf. Flipping to the section on the War for Independence, he showed Franklin pictures of Washington, Jefferson, and himself. "Dr. Franklin, you invited me to visit you. If the invitation still stands, at a future date, I may be able to reconnect us, and perhaps we will have more time to speak."

"Mr. Russell, a future conversation would be in order. I would offer a caution, however. Meddling with the past can change the future. But I do have a question now."

"Of course."

"If this is real, then our efforts toward independence are successful?" A broad grin spread on Fritz's face.

Chapter 45

FRITZ DIDN'T NOTICE the rain tapping on the windshield or the rhythm of the wipers as he drove home. Linda, Mary, and Mel were at the kitchen table when he walked in.

"Hi honey, I'm home. I have a story to tell you." Whatever the conversation had been, they dropped into silence. "Hi Mary, Mel." He glanced at the table, but as he leaned to kiss Linda, she pulled away. He took a step back and asked if anyone wanted a drink.

"So what's your story?" asked Linda.

He poured his soda, and said, "It's not important. Sorry to interrupt."

"LINDA, I don't know what's eating you, but the silent treatment is making me nuts."

"So what's your story?"

"Do you care?"

"Not really."

"Is this about your father?" Fritz was afraid to push. He knew a line had been drawn, somewhere, and that once crossed meant no return.

"No, Fritz, it's about you. The fact that you would even ask that tells me how clueless you've become."

"So tell me."

"Not tonight. Are you coming to graduation? I have to be there early."

"Of course I'll be there. Why wouldn't I be?"

"I don't know. My parents are going on their own. Maybe I'll see you after. We're going to lunch, and then they're leaving."

His frustration had raised his voice. He could feel his shoulders knot. "Good. Tell them it was good to see them." She scowled. "I'll drive you over."

"I'm going with Mel. She'll be sitting with me, president's orders." She went to bed.

Again, Linda left with few words. He had never felt so alone.

LINDA'S GRADUATION was hard on him. He found an open seat at the rear of the ceremony, but also distant from his wife, physically and emotionally. The high spirit of the graduates and their guests bounced off and floated by him. He shared none of their joy and excitement. When the exercises ended, he worked his way through the milling crowd, trying to reach her first and avoid her parents, but when he found them, her father's arm was draped around her shoulder.

"Congratulations, Lin. Well done." When he stepped to kiss her, she offered a cheek as her father pulled her close. "Have a safe trip, Tim, Emily." His father-in-law ignored Fritz when he offered his hand.

Having parked far away made his escape easier. A long walk and a quick drive up I-95 gave him time to distance himself from the emotions of the morning. He turned into the parking lot at school just in time to run to the cafeteria and buy a sandwich. He was grateful his classes all revolved around reviewing for finals. At the end of seventh period, Eric Silver told him that they were ready for a full dress rehearsal. Susan Leslie stopped at the end of eighth period and asked if something was wrong.

"Mr. R, you look terrible. You should get some sleep or something. You just reviewed the same stuff as you did yesterday. Did you know?"

"I guess I am tired, Susan. You guys should have said something."

"I just thought you were emphasizing it, like it would be important for the exam. See you tomorrow, Mr. R."

He sat in the middle of the first row for the rehearsal. The background screen projected scenes from each decade to broaden the context. For the 1920s, the kids did the Charleston.

Standing with Jean after rehearsal, Eric said, "We'll do the second half tomorrow, Mr. R. Pretty good, don't you think?"

"You've done a great job."

"I haven't told you. Yesterday, I got a letter from the president." He beamed. "I got a presidential scholarship. If I keep a B average in college, it's for $15,000 a year." Eric leaned and whispered, "Thanks, Mr. R."

"Eric, I didn't do anything. You did it. But you should tell Mr. McAllister."

"I will. Anyway, see you tomorrow."

HE WAS GREETED by an empty table when he walked into the house. The TV was on. Mary was watching the news, and TJ was napping. "Hi Mary. Anything important?"

"Hi Fritz. Not really. How was graduation?"

"Like they always are. Where's Linda?"

"She said she was taking her folks to lunch with a couple of professors."

"Right." Fritz felt the room press in. "I'll be out back." He grabbed his copy of Franklin's *Autobiography* and went to the yard. Not an easy read, he thought, and flipped through, reading random pages. He was distracted by birds pecking for their dinners. Tomatoes were forming, and the peppers had flowers.

Beans had begun to sprout. Looking at the book cover, he envisioned Ben Franklin standing in his classroom. Clouds blocked the sun, and the temperature dropped, so he went in. Linda sat at the kitchen table.

"I didn't know you were home."

"I know. No problem."

"Who'd you have lunch with?"

"One of my professors wanted to meet my father. And I asked my advisor."

"The one who didn't like your business plan?"

"Not him. My advisor liked the idea." She turned back to her laptop.

"Do you want to go out for dinner to celebrate?"

"I'm going out with some of my classmates later."

"The play is coming together really well," he said.

"I'm glad. Ash should be happy. Too bad he won't see it." Fritz started to respond, but walked out of the kitchen.

THE SCHOOL YEAR ended in a blur. The students put on the play with minor glitches unknown to the audience. Linda skipped all the shows.

"I'm glad that's over," Fritz said when he arrived home after the Sunday matinee. "I think the kids are, too."

Linda said, "That's nice."

"Would you like to go out for dinner? We haven't been out in a while."

"Not really. But you can if you want."

"I meant us, together."

"I know what you meant. I don't want to go."

"Lin, I was thinking about calling Tony and going to see Ash. What do you think? Wanna come?"

She erupted. "You just don't get it, do you? My father was right. Fritz, the hero. Go see your friend, use the portal. Is that all you think of now? What about me? How many times do I have to remind you that it terrifies me? You can't do anything for Ashley now. You could have prevented it. And you didn't."

"I didn't shoot him. And we were saving the president."

"And now you've jeopardized your family. People know about the portal. I talked with Daddy about how dangerous it is. Now the world knows. How long do you think it will be before they know exactly where to go? And come after us again."

"Linda, we, you and me, have spent hours, months, trying to end this. The portal has worked for us, too. I can't make it go away. Neither of us knew how important it would be."

"So important you choose the portal, every time, over your family?"

"But you know what's been at stake."

"And I also know that you've used it for fun, and I also know the president takes advantage of us, and I also know that you've never said no to him."

"But you agreed. And what we do for the world is also for us."

"But now a ruthless, crazy killer who is obviously very smart is probably already looking for the portal."

"You don't know that. We don't even know who he is."

"But he probably knows who we are. Will you use the portal to save us?"

"Linda, you sound like your father. What are you going on about? I do all I can to protect us. You know that. I'm not a hero, but I'm also not an idiot."

"You think my father is an idiot. He's right, Fritz. Why does the president need you? Because it's easier."

"It's easy for your father to criticize. He does it so well. And so often. He's managed to turn you. Your brother won't even talk to him."

"Fritz, my father merely pointed out what I've been ignoring. You choose the portal. Okay, I understand. We all have priorities. Now, I have to choose." Before he could answer, she left the table and went upstairs.

* * *

His moment of quiet was interrupted by the Israeli Prime Minister's call. He asked how Jane was.

"Hold a second." The president could hear the rustling in the background.

"Hi, Mr. President." Her voice was soft and raspy.

"Good to hear your voice, Jane. But we can talk more later. You need to recover. But I need to ask you if you're willing to keep working. We need to end the Caballeros."

"How's Ashley?"

"He didn't make it. I'm so sorry, Jane."

Chapter 46

THE HIGH SCHOOL'S graduation was somber for Fritz. He felt apart from the crowd. George had awarded him a special award in addition to Teacher of the Year. But none of that mattered. He was alone. Ashley wasn't sitting next to him. Linda and TJ had gone to Ohio, and he didn't know when they'd be back. Mary had moved to a room at the airport, and now shared Fritz's protection with a revolving group of agents. Jim had told him he was leaving at the end of June to begin his agent-training program.

Fritz met Ashley at the airport. Charles Dougherty had personally escorted him to the gate. When Ashley appeared, Fritz gasped. Bearded and unkempt, fifteen hours traveling, Ashley sat in a wheelchair, a security guard pushing him. Fritz's only greeting was a blank stare. In Ashley's lap sat a small bag with some toiletries and his medications.

"Welcome back, buddy," said Fritz.

"Yeah."

"How was the flight?"

"Long."

They headed for a quick exit. The president and Dougherty had arranged to bypass customs, and Ashley had no luggage. But his baggage weighed far more than a suitcase.

At the car, Fritz offered his hand. Ashley said, "I can walk." Fritz's hand slipped to his side. When Ashley had his seat-belt fastened, Fritz thanked the guard and Mr. Dougherty and climbed in. The morning sun had just poked above the horizon.

"Do you want to talk about it?"

"No."

"How do you feel?"

"Fine."

Leaving the airport, Fritz wondered how to help his friend. Even light conversation had little response. He told Ashley the play was a hit, and they had made a video for him. "I have cards for you from all of them, Ash."

"Good."

Fritz told him that Eric was the valedictorian, and he got a scholarship to MIT.

"Yeah. No surprise there."

"No one's home, Ash. Linda's with her parents. Do you want to stay at my place?"

"No."

"Do you want me to stay with you?"

"No."

"You're not making this easy. How can I help?"

"Turn back time."

Fritz pulled to the curb in front of Ashley's house. The red convertible sitting in the driveway should have been a welcome sight. Ashley unhooked the seat belt and opened the door.

"Hang on. I'll help you."

"I'm fine." He stepped out and catching his foot, hit the recently mown grass strip, barely missing the sidewalk. Fritz ran to him as he tried to reach his knees.

"Ash, go slow. Let me help you." Ashley batted away Fritz's hand.

"Leave me alone."

"I'll leave when you get inside," Fritz barked back. "You shouldn't be alone at all. I'm going shopping for you when I get your sorry ass in the door. So stop fighting me."

Ashley took a deep breath and pushed up to one knee with a long, slow moan. Fritz lifted him under one arm. They gingerly crept up to the house.

"Fritz, I can do this. I'm not a cripple, and I'm not dead." As if on cue, the word hammered them both. Tears filled and overflowed. Tracks on his cheeks, Ashley looked away, the keys dangling from his fingers.

Fritz opened the door and hoisted Ashley across the threshold. Untouched for almost a month, the coffee table still held piles of folders and a purse. Ashley's usual vibrant energy was gone. His slumped shoulders told more about his ordeal than his healing wounds. Fritz parked him in his favorite recliner and went to the refrigerator for drinks.

With two sodas in hand, Fritz said that he would go shopping later, but that now they needed to talk. "I have to talk to you, too."

"There's nothing to talk about. She's dead. The doctors wouldn't even let me see her. I could have saved her, I know it."

"That's a lot of guilt to carry."

Ashley gave him a menacing look Fritz had never seen. "She needed me. If she just knew I was with her, she'd be okay. Damn the doctors. All they did was make excuses. And then she was gone. They always leave."

"Ash."

"Get out of here. I want to be alone."

* * *

WHEN HE STOPPED outside the store, he took out his phone and looked at his speed dial list. He wanted to talk to Linda, shook his head, and called the White House.

"Mr. President, do you have a minute?"

"Not now, Fritz. Can I call you back?"

"Yeah, sure. I guess." The despondent voice alerted the president.

"I'm in a meeting, but I'll call you as soon as it's done. Ashley's home, isn't he?"

"Yeah." He felt abandoned. How could so much go so wrong so fast? *Let's get this done. Just get enough for a couple of days. Next week, we'll go together.* A few quick items, through the checkout, and back to the car, he reached for the door handle when his phone buzzed.

"Thanks for calling back."

"You have your hands full, Fritz. I'm really sorry. Mary told me about Linda, and Ashley is beyond your scope. He may not like it, but I'm sending Mel and Dr. Dutton. She'll be in Riverboro this afternoon. I'll give her your phone number, and she'll call you so you can meet her. She said it's probably best for you to be with him when she arrives. And you should talk to her, too."

"I'm fine, Mr. President. Linda just needs to cool down."

"Talk to Dr. Dutton anyway. She may have some suggestions. I'll talk to you later. Fritz, we're trying to coordinate with Interpol and the airlines. We're using the Hay-Adams video and the composites from Ingram and Trellingham to see if we can find Richter. Talk to you later."

Fritz turned into Ashley's street and eased to a stop. Ashley's car was gone.

Chapter 47

IN FRONT of his house, a black Suburban idled. He walked in the back door and called.

"I'm up here, Fritz." Mary said she had stopped back to pick up the last of her things and drop off the key. She had been reassigned back to Washington. "Other agents will be watching and checking in with you from time to time. The president wants you covered, but not too obviously, so you may not know when they're around."

"Thanks for all you've done, Mary. Good luck. Come back and visit." She kissed his cheek, said goodbye, and walked to the waiting car. He watched the car until it turned at the end of the street and closed the door. The click of the latch rattled in his head.

At his desk, his yellow pads were a reminder of what had become of his life. Linda and TJ were gone, and Linda hadn't returned any of his calls. Ashley had vanished to somewhere unknown. Now Mary had left.

Thomas Richter was at large.

Chapter 48

"**AH. WELCOME BACK**, Monsieur Richemartel," said the maître d'. "Would you like your usual table?"

"I would prefer a quiet corner, perhaps in the rear today."

Pointing in the doorway, the tuxedoed guide said, "How about one of those?"

"That would be fine, Paul. Thank you. A dry martini will do nicely. Then, no further disturbance, s'il vous plait."

His patrician arrogance posed no difficulty for the equally haughty defender of the best that money could buy. "Of course, monsieur." A fifty dollar bill went in his pocket. He enjoyed this guest who always appreciated service. Paul escorted his patron to the dim rear. Pictures adorned the walls, writers and artists reputed to have been regulars in the years after the First World War. No one could prove otherwise. The Nazis had ended the fun.

Telesphore Richemartel removed a small pad from his satchel and withdrew a gilded pen from his jacket. The perfect fit of his father's Montblanc added to his aura. He shrugged at the strange thought that a pen could be so impressive.

On the pad, he listed initials. From the inside left pocket of his suit coat, he pulled out his plane ticket. He would arrive at Washington-Dulles at eight that night.

A Last Request

If you've read this far, I hope you enjoyed the journey. My relationship with Fritz and Linda, Ashley and Jane, the president and all the rest has become a family event for me, and I hope for you too. I would ask a favor. Reviews are important to the success of a story. By giving your opinion, you inform other potential readers what good and bad you've experienced. Please let me know, and let the world know what you think on Amazon, Goodreads, or any literary site where people can visit.

If you would like to contact me, or if you have questions about the story, about writing or about me, please check the sites below:

Email – sternmike52@gmail.com
Facebook – https://www.facebook.com/michael.r.stern.5
Twitter – https://twitter.com/sternmike52
Amazon –
https://www.amazon.com/Michael-R.-Stern/e/B008OP4DVU

Sneak Peek

Storm Surge,

Book Five of the Quantum Touch series.

Chapter 1

After Midnight, *Thursday, August 25*

"Jim? Florian Declercq here. Sorry to call so late. Have you a moment?"

"No problem, Florian. Just sitting and reading." The general clicked mute on the TV. "What can I do for you?"

"Jim, I've received an invitation to join a group of businessmen. You were my first thought. A man came to my office in Antwerp, saying he represented someone whose interest was stirred by my company's participation in the president's development plan." General Beech listened with a pen in his hand, a yellow pad on his lap. "When I asked about the group's purpose, he referred to them as 'the Caballeros.' "

The pad flew from his lap and smacked the floor. "Florian, may I call you from my office? In say, an hour?"

* * *

THE PHONE BUZZED in the residence. The White House operator told the president that General Beech was holding. Sitting up and turning on the bedside lamp, he said, "What's happened, Jim?" The general reported his conversation with the Belgian shipping magnate. When he heard "the Caballeros," he stood up. "General, where are you now?"

"At my office, Mr. President. I wanted the call recorded and secure."

"Give me a half hour."

Chapter 2

After A Long and lonely summer, Fritz Russell had spent another day preparing for the new school year, only a couple of weeks away. As he reached for the front porch light switch, the doorbell chimed. The outside light threw shadows in its forty-watt beam. Shoulder length hair and a full, unkempt beard stared in at him.

"Good to see you, Ash." He held the screen door open. Not sure what to expect after two months, Fritz reserved his joy.

"I saw the light on. Then I saw the family room light go off." Ashley remained motionless on the porch. "I know it's late."

"Not like I have anywhere to go. Come on in."

Ashley downed a first glass of soda and poured another. Across the kitchen table, Fritz waited to hear a story, of where Ashley had been, what he had done. But mostly, he wanted to know what had happened that day in Palestine, two months earlier. Ashley hadn't answered his calls or returned his messages.

"Ash, first thing. You need to call your folks. They're worried. Your mother calls me every few days to see if I've heard from you."

"I guess you want to know where I've been."

"I want to know whatever you want to tell me. It's been a long summer, and I have a few things to tell you too." He studied his disheveled friend. So prominent only an eye-blink ago, the joyful gleam in his eyes was gone. Before he could say another word, his phone rang. "Who can that be at this hour?" Fritz ran to the family room, switched on the light he had just turned off, hurried to the sunroom, and grabbed the phone just before it switched to voicemail.

"Hello?" he panted.

"Sorry Fritz. Hope I didn't wake you."

"Hi Mr. President. You didn't, but I had to find my phone. Things are a little less orderly since Linda left. What's up?"

The president said he needed the portal. Tony Almeida was on the way. When he said that there might be a break on the Caballeros, Fritz said, "I'll be there in twenty minutes." Returning to the kitchen, he told Ashley what the president had said.

Setting his glass on the table, Ashley asked, "Can I stay here? I'm not sure I want to see him yet."

"Ash, it wasn't his fault. It was mine. You should see him and then you'll know how you really feel."

"I know what you're saying and you're probably right, but not now. Not yet."

ON HIS WAY to Riverboro High School, following the same route he had driven for the past decade, Fritz reflected on the portal. Since he had discovered that he could time travel, his entire life had changed. The Naria mission had created a pattern. Quiet, then action, then quiet again. It couldn't have been quieter, then Ashley shows up and the president calls. He tried not to hope that the next thing would be Linda coming home.

Also by the Author

Book One of the Quantum Touch Series

Storm Portal

Time travel is real, of that, Fritz Russell was certain. He'd just done it. Meeting Robert E. Lee was fascinating, but witnessing the Triangle Fire with his class was scary. His job was to teach, not participate in, events long past. His classroom door had become a portal to the past and a tunnel through the present. How did it happen? Can he control it? Is he changing history? When he walked into the Oval Office, he had no idea how his life would change.

With his wife and his friends, Fritz investigates the mysteries of time travel and the power of the portal, while the nation's security apparatus gears up.

Can they find the answers in time?

Book Two of the Quantum Touch Series

Sand Storm

How do you say no to the President of the United States when he's asked you to stop a nuclear war?

After Fritz Russell discovered his classroom door was a portal through space and time, he helped the United States resolve a foreign policy emergency. Now the president wants him to use the portal to avert the threat coming from a Middle Eastern nation that is on the verge of developing nuclear weapons.

For a history teacher, travel to the past is entertaining, enlightening, and a great way to engage students. But Fritz hasn't learned all the portal's secrets. Could others put the world in danger by forcing him to use what he doesn't even understand? If he uses it to help the president, there might be a war. But if he says no, he will be permitting his family, friends, and the world to remain in great danger.

Should Fritz agree to be the heart of the U.S. operation? And if he does, is there enough time for him to learn all he needs to know about the mysteries of the portal?

Book Three of the Quantum Touch Series

Shadow Storm

Will evil prevail? Can the portal "Give Peace a Chance?"

What will Fritz Russell have to confront next? And where? After he opened the portal into the Oval Office and became friends with the man who works there, Fritz reluctantly agreed to help the president make the world a safer place. He saved hostages, helped prevent a nuclear war, and began a life of excitement and danger he never saw coming.

Now an ominous shadow has been cast by a hidden enemy prepared to use violence to upend world affairs. The president has only a year left in office, and every disruption fuels his concern. As violence escalates and Fritz himself becomes a target, the portal may be the only way he and the president can end the growing danger and bring peace to the globe.

But the voice in the shadows believes they cannot thwart his plan. "Uncertainty breeds fear," he says. "Fear wins elections. Scared people don't want more of what makes them afraid."

SHADOW STORM plunges Fritz into the portal's mysteries and dangers.

Reflections on a Generous Generation

Reflections on a Generous Generation tells the story of a generation of Americans who created the richest, most powerful and most successful nation in world history, as seen through the life of a remarkable man. A soldier, businessman, student, teacher, inventor, world traveler, volunteer, Murray Stern was truly a participant in the world in which he lived.

If you appreciate history or teach history, if you know someone who lived through the Depression and World War II, this remarkable story shares the life and times of those who lived the journey.

Lightning Source UK Ltd.
Milton Keynes UK
UKHW022322220221
379219UK00012B/1282/J